T0246044

MR. GOOD-EVENING

ALSO IN THE RAINCOAST NOIR SERIES BY JOHN MACLACHLAN GRAY

The White Angel

Vile Spirits

MR. GOOD-EVENING

A Mystery

JOHN MACLACHLAN GRAY

Douglas & McIntyre

Douglas and McIntyre (2013) Ltd.
P.O. Box 219, Madeira Park, BC, V0N 2H0
www.douglas-mcintyre.com

Edited by Pam Robertson
Dust jacket design by Anna Comfort O'Keeffe
Text design by Libris Simas Ferraz / Onça Publishing
Printed and bound in Canada
Printed on 100% recycled paper

Douglas and McIntyre acknowledges the support of the Canada Council for the Arts, the Government of Canada, and the Province of British Columbia through the BC Arts Council.

Library and Archives Canada Cataloguing in Publication

Title: Mr. Good-Evening : a mystery / John MacLachlan Gray.
Other titles: Mister Good-Evening
Names: Gray, John, 1946- author.
Description: Series statement: Raincoast noir ; 3
Identifiers: Canadiana (print) 20240293118 | Canadiana (ebook) 20240293150 | ISBN 9781771623957 (hardcover) | ISBN 9781771623964 (EPUB)
Subjects: LCGFT: Historical fiction. | LCGFT: Detective and mystery fiction. | LCGFT: Novels.
Classification: LCC PS8563.R411 M7 2024 | DDC C813/.54—dc23

For Beverlee, the love of my life

When [people] say "The Radio" they don't mean a cabinet, an electrical phenomenon, or a man in a studio, they refer to a pervading and somewhat godlike presence.

—E.B. White

Capitalism is the legitimate racket of the ruling class.

—Al Capone

AUTHOR'S NOTE

IN MY TELLING of the well-known tale of Brother XII, I have taken huge liberties, shamelessly using facts for my own fictional ends. For a thorough account of the true Brother XII story, I recommend *Brother XII: The Strange Odyssey of a 20th Century Prophet* by John Oliphant.

My approximation of African American Vernacular English is indebted to Zora Neale Hurston, Dizzy Gillespie, Smitty Smith of Eric Mercury and the Soul Searchers, and to friends I remember in Truro, Nova Scotia.

Although deeply offensive by today's standards, racial terms in the book are authentic to the era and should be taken as an indication that some progress has been achieved.

Some Al Capone quotes have been edited, for concision only.

PROLOGUE

POLICE ARREST ACCUSED MURDERESS
Max Trotter
Staff Writer
The Vancouver World
May 30, 1929

From her outward appearance, few would imagine that the attractive young woman on the veranda steps could be capable of murder.

Yet shocked onlookers could only gape in awe as Miss Dora Decker was ushered out of Miss Mildred Wickstram's Residence for Professional Women by two policemen, charged with having brutally stabbed her employer, Ralph M. Tucker, to death.

According to police reports, the murder occurred in the downtown offices of Tucker, Palmer and Pine, a Howe Street brokerage and securities firm affiliated with Addison and Partners in New York City.

Pressed for comment, Mr. Tucker's partner Edgar Palmer replied, "I am presently on my way to see to Mrs. Tucker, who is under a doctor's care. We are all devastated. Please respect our privacy at this tragic time."

Alvin Pine, the third partner, was unavailable for comment at the time of writing, as he was in New York on company business.

SHOCKING MURDER IN VANCOUVER!
From Our Own Correspondent
The News of the World
June 2, 1929

A ghastly scene confronted police in Vancouver, Canada, upon entering the plush offices of Tucker, Palmer and Pine, where Ralph M. Tucker sprawled lifeless on a blood-soaked rug, having been stabbed twenty-five times in the face, neck and head.

Officers could barely recognize the successful stockbroker, a well-known figure in that port city on the Pacific coast.

A charwoman, Mrs. Louise Duffy, was first to witness the dreadful scene. "It was a frightful mess," she told the *News of the World*, "and I am not the one to be cleaning it up, thank you very much. I've had more shock than is good for me as it is."

What proved yet more shocking to that colonial metropolis of a quarter million was the subsequent arrest of Miss Dora Decker, a stenographer barely out of her teens.

When asked for comment, Miss Decker's landlady, Miss Mildred Wickstram, with a lit cigarette in hand, replied, "I am too shocked for words."

Shocked by the crime itself, or shocked to have harboured an accused murderess under her roof? Miss Wickstram refused to comment further.

The *News of the World* has ascertained that the murder weapon was a suede T-strap spike-heeled shoe—strikingly sophisticated for the colonies. Yet the tufts of hair and layers of caked blood that marred the four-inch heel gave away its murderous purpose.

Its companion, stain-free, lay innocently several feet away, as though to distance itself from its grisly mate.

The sheer horror of the scene stunned even experienced policemen.

Constable Frank Sproule described the spectacle: "It was the goriest thing you ever seen."

Added Sproule's partner, Constable Vaughn Poskett: "Blood? You'd need a hose to put that kind of spatter on the wainscotting, plus the condition of the body—cuts, bruises, pocks all over the scalp, arms, hands, horrible, seeping wounds, the eyes were just sockets of blood, oh it was a real mess."

Interjected Sproule: "You'd have thought Tucker took a blast of birdshot in the face. An officer had to leave the premises to avoid contaminating the scene."

Asked for comment, Inspector Calvin Hook, the officer in charge of the case, remarked, "Anyone who served in the war has seen worse."

WORLD SHOCKED BY VANCOUVER MURDER
Cecil Harmsworth
Staff Writer
The Beacon
June 3, 1929

The murder of stockbroker Ralph M. Tucker and the arrest of his secretary, Doris Decker, has drawn shocked attention throughout the British Commonwealth.

Regrettably, a lurid *Vancouver World* photograph of the accused, in an abbreviated slip dress and with a stout policeman on each arm, has engendered a spate of unsavoury comments in the gutter presses of London concerning the accused—and the city of Vancouver as well.

Likewise the figure and comportment of Miss Mildred Wickstram, who wore a frock more appropriate to a Regent Street lady of leisure than to the landlady of a colonial rooming house.

England's most prominent tabloid, the *Daily Mirror*, dubbed Miss Decker "the Fatal Flapper" and Miss Wickstram "the Mysterious Madam," and virtually every news bureau in the Empire followed suit.

Reached in his office by telephone, Mayor William Malkin described his dismay at such coverage: "It deals a blow to our city's reputation as a decent, Christian, safe city to do business and raise a family."

Others see a worrisome trend—a not-distant future in which yellow journalism comes to dominate public discourse.

According to Reverend Angus McPherson of St. Columba Presbyterian, "Christians are increasingly alarmed by a sensational press that has so lost its way as to make a celebrity of an accused murderess."

The officer in charge of the investigation, Detective Inspector Calvin Hook, cautions against premature judgment: "We urge the public to remember that the investigation is far from complete."

Likewise, Vancouver Police Chief Morris Blatchford warns against jumping to conclusions: "The presumption of innocence is fundamental to British justice, even when common sense and the evidence suggest otherwise."

PART I

I don't even know what street Canada is on.

—Al Capone

CHAPTER 1

INSPECTOR CALVIN HOOK perches on the corner of Ralph Tucker's mahogany desk and stares glumly at the bloodstains on the cream Bigelow rug, for the removal of the corpse had left a clearly defined splatter outline, one that could be seen two ways—the unstained part as Mr. Tucker's shadow in a film negative, and the stain about the head as a map of Europe.

To DI Hook's eye, Europe seems to be changing colour from Bolshevik red to Brownshirt brown, but that could be just him—a product of chronic sleeplessness where the brain, supposedly awake, enters a sort of dream state.

Perhaps this is true of Jeanie as well, she gets no more sleep than he does.

In the twenty-four hours since the supposed murder, the smell hasn't changed a bit. Hook well knows the smell of rusted iron and rot. He knows that the sweet, metallic pong of death will remain in the room forever, like Mr. Tucker's ghost. The future occupant of Mr. Tucker's office can only hope that years of smoke and perfume will manage to shroud that unnerving smell...

He jolts to attention. But what to do? What is the procedure here? To investigate a murder that has already been solved?

Coppers want an arrest. Their superiors want an arrest—for the VPD, an open case is like an open wound; the force's credibility seeps out, drop by drop. Meanwhile, the press wants a story and a story needs a beginning, middle and end. With an open case, readership drops off by the day.

These days, an accused can be convicted in the public mouth a day after the crime itself; in this case, the mental picture of a girl murdering a gentleman with a spike-heeled shoe will never entirely disappear from the public memory.

Bloodstains on the page become bloodstains in the mind: Hook finds it oddly troubling that he should have gained that insight from a newspaperman who didn't serve.

Some things in life bring out Hook's Scottishness, though he has never been to Scotland, and one of them is a foregone conclusion—which your Scot sees as unearned, and therefore not to be trusted. (The man who looked a gift horse in the mouth had to have been Scottish.)

A foregone conclusion such as the one at hand can also bring out a less becoming aspect to Hook's character—the contrarian accountant, who won't rest until he has at least triple-checked the figures. Around the VPD he has a reputation for persistence; to his superiors he is an annoyance, like a dog who won't lie down when you tell him to lie down, or stay when you tell him to stay.

But what really gets him going is a series of anomalies—starting with the departmental cables to New York.

CANADIAN PACIFIC RAILWAY COMPANY'S TELEGRAPH
TELEGRAM

MAY 30 1929

ALVIN PINE
ADDISON SUITE
HOTEL ASTOR
1515 BROADWAY
NEW YORK
USA

RE TUCKER MURDER PLEASE CONTACT VANCOUVER POLICE SOONEST DEPOSITION REQUIRED

INSP CALVIN HOOK
VANCOUVER POLICE DEPARTMENT
200 CORDOVA ST
VANCOUVER
CANADA

Within the hour, Hook received this terse reply:

WESTERN UNION TELEGRAPH
TELEGRAM

MAY 30 1929

INSP CALVIN HOOK
VANCOUVER POLICE DEPARTMENT
200 CORDOVA ST
VANCOUVER
CANADA

REGRET PINE TRAVELLING AND OUT OF REACH

BEE CALDWELL
SECRETARY

Hook finds it odd that the supposed secretary (Pine's? Addison's?), who calls herself Bee Caldwell, expressed no surprise or shock at the word *murder*, if only as a courtesy.

Is this the New York attitude? Is a murder too commonplace to be worthy of mention? Or is Bee Caldwell's apparent bloodlessness a matter of frugality at ten cents a word? Or is it possible that Bee Caldwell is not a human being at all, but some class of robot—an automatically generated response to any Tom, Dick or Harry who inquires about Alvin Pine?

Has Bee Caldwell *met* Pine? Does Bee Caldwell exist?

When the telegraph became a tool for international communication, it was assumed that it would aid the police in obtaining information on a case; however, here it seems to produce more questions than answers.

CANADIAN PACIFIC RAILWAY COMPANY'S TELEGRAPH
TELEGRAM

JUNE 3 1929

BEE CALDWELL
ADDISON SUITE
HOTEL ASTOR
1515 BROADWAY

NEW YORK
USA

PLEASE FORWARD PINE LOCATION SOONEST OR WILL
ASK FBI ASSISTANCE

INSP CALVIN HOOK
VANCOUVER POLICE DEPARTMENT
200 CORDOVA ST
VANCOUVER
CANADA

WESTERN UNION TELEGRAPH
TELEGRAM

JUNE 3 1929

INSP CALVIN HOOK
VANCOUVER POLICE DEPARTMENT
200 CORDOVA ST
VANCOUVER
CANADA

PINE CURRENTLY AT RONEY PLAZA MIAMI BEACH

BEE CALDWELL
SECRETARY

CHAPTER 2

MCCURDY FOLDS THE newspaper so that the front-page photo is uppermost: in which two VPD cops usher a stylish young woman out of Miss Mildred Wickstram's Residence for Professional Women while Miss Wickstram herself watches from the veranda, smoking a cigarette, in public.

He warned her against the venture more than once—for more reasons than one.

For someone with her background to run a rooming house is about as fitting as a nun in a pool hall—especially when Mildred's previous rooming experience involved a landlady who painted pictures of Indian totem poles and kept a monkey.

He never doubted that Mildred would eventually leave the telephone exchange at the Hotel Vancouver, even if it produced a lucrative sideline in overheard information. As an upper-class Badminton girl, she was never motivated by money, or anything else, really.

But a *rooming house*?

Given that her posh accent got her the hotel job, why not pose behind the sales counter at Birks, selling Cartier baubles? Or open a shop stuffed with curios from Peru, funded by Daddy?

But no. Mildred chose to buy a rooming house on Venables Street and rent out rooms, pointing to the lack of secure accommodation for single working women. Miss Proletariat, fighting for the lower classes—given her pedigree, it's like a well-fed cat supporting the rights of mice...

He rereads the *News of the World* report, which couldn't have broken at a worse time.

As God or bad luck would have it, the arrest coincided with a slow news day—meaning that there is, really, no news to deliver—meaning there's no relevant information to fill the narrow but vital strips between ads for cigarettes. Throughout the English-speaking world, the jackals were sniffing about for violence and lechery.

For the English-language press, the Fatal Flapper arrived as an angel from heaven; a story about a murder in a colonial city at the edge of the Empire that would normally merit a page-two sidebar in the *Daily Mail* appeared on front pages everywhere (above the fold as well), stamped on the public brain, photo and all, and in permanent ink.

Unless and until Miss Mildred Wickstram's Residence for Professional Women burns to the ground, it will forever be known as the home of the Fatal Flapper.

Hence, he expects that Mildred will be even more thin-skinned than usual, eyes peeled for signs of gloating at her misfortune— which is the logical position for McCurdy to assume, given that her resignation from the switchboard crippled a weekly newspaper column that had come to depend on her operator's ear for a useful conversational slip—quotes that might lend rigour to what had come to be a hodgepodge of snide remarks and underhanded piss-taking.

Although those days are well behind him now, their strained association has continued, their conversation pocked with testy pauses and acid cracks.

It occurs to him, given his own changed circumstances, that she might request a loan to bridge the inevitable pause before Daddy turns on the tap. The mere thought of it warms the cockles of his heart.

Sipping a second Gibson in the Stranger's Lounge of the Quadra Club, to pass the time he opens the Little Leather Library copy of *As a Man Thinketh* (it came with a box of Lowney's Chocolate Creams): *Self-control is strength. Right thought is mastery. Calmness is power...*

MARCH 1927, TWO YEARS EARLIER

IF YOU IGNORED labour riots, race and immigrant vigilantism, the booming business of organized crime, a resurgence of Spanish flu and fighting in China and Mexico, the world was, relatively speaking, at peace.

Having reconciled himself to life as an ink-stained muckraker and not a literary lion, and having become proficient at annoying men he didn't like, life for Ed McCurdy of the *Evening Star* had become somewhat less fraught, in keeping with the general atmosphere.

Even so, from experience and general pessimism, he couldn't avoid a sense that this was the hush before the hurricane—which turned out to be the case, thanks to the Board of Trade luncheon at the Vancouver Club.

Of course, McCurdy wasn't present (muckrakers are seldom invited anywhere), but his employer, General Victor Newson, CB, CMG, DSO, owner and publisher of the *Evening Star*, attended—and came out of it a changed man.

The event in question featured Sir Henry Thornton of Canadian National Railway, who delivered a speech entitled "The Future of Radio Broadcasting" to a crowd that included big names such as MacMillan, Spencer and Rogers, with Mayor Malkin demonstrating how many arses he could kiss at the same time.

A master pitchman, Thornton leapt onto the dais and proceeded to unleash a barrage of facts concerning the CNR's latest triumph in communications technology—radio.

Having added four thousand miles of wire along its telegraph lines, the CNR could now transmit not just dots and dashes but actual radio programs aboard its transcontinental trains, coast to coast. These broadcasts were then relayed as airwaves in all directions, so that anyone with a receiver could listen to drama, music and—most significantly—advertising.

"Advertising, gentlemen. The lifeblood of every man in this room. For any business hoping to sell goods and services to the public, radio is a golden opportunity—and a life-or-death challenge.

"Your ability to compete in the marketplace will depend upon your capacity to adapt to the new medium. Sadly, I predict that in a very few years we will witness the death, not just of companies, but of entire industries—some of which are represented in this room.

"And the first to die will be your daily newspaper."

The general, who up until now had been mentally wandering around some battlefield in northern France, snapped to attention.

What followed was, as far as Newson was concerned, a salvo aimed directly at him.

"Within a very few years, by the time a broadsheet hits the streets it will no longer be news—it will be history.

"And where does yesterday's news belong? At the fish-and-chips shop!"

The quip drew a laugh from the audience, and a wintry silence from the owner of the *Evening Star*.

"Throughout the Commonwealth and in America, newspaper presses will stand idle and the industry will wither, as it loses its raison d'être—its advertising revenue.

"Gentlemen, answer me this: What business will want to see its up-to-the-minute product displayed to a modern audience—over a medium that is *itself* years behind the times?"

The president of the CNR took a sip of water to let that sink in.

Newson eyed the faces around him. His gaze penetrated their thick skulls, revealing the gears of their cuckoo-clock minds grinding, reassessing their public relations plans with regard to the printed word. Mercenaries. Were he in command, these men would be dispatched to the front lines so their comrades would know what spineless pulp they're made of.

Without the printed word, what was the point of teaching the masses to read in the first place? What was the point of *civilization*?

Imagine the lower classes—those who can afford to buy radios—floundering in a swamp of propaganda, signs, slogans and the titles of photoplays.

Not to mention what it would mean for Newson himself, for whom the *Evening Star* functions as a pulpit for stating his moral, social and political views, and a stage for his quadrennial campaign for re-election as a provincial minister.

He envisages a life in retirement, shuffling from one boardroom table to the next, paid a walloping stipend to attend a few meetings per year. Having denounced "scarecrow generals in the halls of power" in one editorial after another, to become one himself would invite an unacceptable amount of humour at Newson's expense.

Retirement at fifty is a fate to be hoped for, some would say, a reward for years of loyal service to the land.

Perhaps. If one is a horse or cow.

Never one to flinch in a crisis, in the days following that pivotal luncheon General Newson began to feel a resurgence of the old piss and vinegar that coursed through his veins when sending men over the top, to be blown to pieces by mortar fire.

Within a week, he laid the groundwork for the campaign to follow —in a combat zone known as electric communication.

Forward!

See me at once. —VN

Whenever McCurdy received that summons he felt the proboscis descend from three floors above his head to enter the back of his neck and Hoover the life out of him.

What would it be this time? What bee was buzzing in his employer's bottled brain?

Was it the Asian invasion again? Bolsheviks in labour unions? Or, with the July 12 Orangemen's Walk coming up, an exposé about hordes of dogans pouring across the border, breeding like possums and answering to the pope and not the king?

Or maybe the Italians (who are Catholic as well)—an exposé about Joe Celona's hoodlums, crime in the streets and so on and so forth, bark, bark, quack, quack.

For McCurdy, the latter worried him most—he would prefer not to undertake another series probing the activities of men with pistols in their pockets.

In his six years of employment, after similar meetings with his employer, McCurdy had been shot at, kidnapped, attacked by a madman and beaten to a pulp.

And yet, for want of an acceptable alternative, he continued under Newson's command, writing articles of questionable value and taste at two and a half cents per word.

Mr. Freud might have attributed McCurdy's devotion to an Oedipal rebellion against his father, Newson's polar opposite—a cautious man in the insurance business whose most radical decision was to switch from the Presbyterian to the United Church. On the other hand, it might just be a nervous urge to make a living, a reluctance to find himself under the Georgia Viaduct, nestled in a newspaper sleeping bag.

Standing in the reception room, he faced the twin portraits of General Newson and General Haig, glaring at him from the opposite wall.

Below the painted generals, clacking away at her tank-like typewriter, Miss Webster peered over her carbon-paper sandwich... and smiled—at least it was something like a smile, or a glimpse of her dentures, an unnerving sight in itself.

"General Newson is expecting you, Mr. McCurdy. You may enter."

Highly unusual. Normally, the general let him cool his heels on the couch, in order to build up an appropriate sense of doom before entering the gates of hell.

All in all, McCurdy felt reasonably certain that he was about to be sacked. Axed. Given the old heave-ho from the only real job he'd ever held. It was bound to happen sooner or later.

In the business of writing a regular news/op column, there comes a point when the well—of adjectives, metaphors, trenchant observations and laugh lines—has run dry. The clapped-out columnist then contents himself with the mythic French family stew—a familiar brew containing the carrots of past generations, with morsels added as acquired.

Briefly, it would actually come as a relief—very briefly, for savings he had next to none.

Once inside, he turned to the general's desk (a customized version of a field table), tensed and ready for the hangman—then paused at the sight of another visitor, a plumpish gentleman in a plaid mohair suit with clean-shaven jowls the colour of slate, and a rooster-like wattle of fat joining chin to neck.

Choosing not to interrupt the apparently close communication between the two, he moved across the carpet to the window, took out his handkerchief, wiped his glasses and gazed down at the blurred autos lurching back and forth in the intersection below, beneath a grid of intersecting tramway wires.

And what fresh hell is this?

Perhaps it was his silhouette against the window that finally caught Newson's attention, for the general abruptly stood up, leaned forward (arms splayed out in the field gun position) and bellowed, "Well, here he is, the man of the hour!"

The guest in the chair chuckled appreciatively.

Man of the hour? Sarcastic bastard.

"Come, lad! Be seated, and introduce yourself to Mr. Wilson Larke!"

If only McCurdy had taken a little something to calm his nerves, or increase his confidence, or render him numb from head to toe, or to do all three at once...

Newson continued: "Mr. Larke serves as director of programming with CNR Radio. I have called the three of us together on a matter that has to do with your future. That said, I'll give Mr. Larke the floor."

Wilson Larke peered at McCurdy with eyes the colour of shotgun pellets. "Mr. McCurdy, do you have any idea how many radio sets are installed in Canadian homes at the present time?"

Though braced for all manner of unpleasantness, the question caught McCurdy off guard. "I haven't the slightest idea, Mr. Larke. A good many, I should think."

Larke smiled indulgently, with an alarming number of small teeth, and leaned forward as though to share a confidence. "No fewer than sixty thousand, Ed!"

McCurdy sensed that he was expected to gasp at the number. Instead, he settled for an impressed nod.

"And do you know what they're listening to, Ed?"

McCurdy was becoming annoyed by this pretentious knob and his rhetorical questions. "Music and talk, I suppose. What else—bird calls?"

The general tapped a horny finger on the table surface. "None of your lip, son." Then, to his guest: "Mr. Larke, our friend here is given to flippant, juvenile humour. He's made a goddamned career of it—so far."

Wilson Larke emits another agreeable chuckle. "Something of a wag, yes, I can sense that."

"Son, there's a time and a place for everything, and this is the time to stand down."

"Beg your pardon, sir. A momentary lapse."

"The terrible irony," Wilson Larke continues, "is that, for all our investment of money and ingenuity to develop the technology, Canadians from coast to coast are listening to *American* stations. Even as we speak, American programs are pouring over the border in waves: *Amos 'n' Andy*, the *Grand Ole Opry*, the *Ipana Troubadours*—"

"Think of it!" The general's fist strikes the table with sufficient force to topple two miniature flags. "It's a goddamned invasion! It's the War of 1812, fought over the blasted radio!" Then, rising once more to the field gun position: "Believe you me, gentlemen, I didn't fight a war to witness our unconditional surrender to the goddamned Yankees!"

Wilson Larke's wattle quivered in agreement. "Sixty thousand Canadian households are already hearing American voices on a daily basis—the *Palmolive Hour*, the *Eveready Hour*. Given the average family of five, more than three hundred thousand Canadians are, literally, becoming more American and less British with every passing day."

Newson returns his miniature flags to their proper place. "Our British heritage is about to be swamped by a bloody tide of American muck."

"A bit like the Yellow Peril, would you say, sir?"

"Worse, son. Far more insidious. You can recognize a Chinese or an Indian by the colour of his skin—but sound is invisible, don't you see? It creeps into the ears and up the tubes into the command centre of the brain, and before you know it you're thinking like the enemy."

He points his little Red Ensign at McCurdy's nose. "Believe you me, lad, we're facing a new war. A war that will be won or lost over the airwaves. And I'll be goddamned if the *Evening Star* will be a casualty on the ground!"

A dispiriting wave of déjà vu came over McCurdy. General Newson was known for his daring campaigns and their stunning casualty rates—night raids and mass charges in which men waddled over the top fully loaded into the line of fire, with their commander in his officer's tent, surveying an area map and receiving second-hand reports on how things were going.

Wilson Larke went on to explain how a partnership had been struck between the *Evening Star* and the CNR Radio network to provide an evening news broadcast every day (Sundays excepted), to compete with WBZA in Boston, KDKA in Philadelphia and KOMO in Seattle. The program would be delivered over transcontinental trains and to homes within receiving distance of relays.

McCurdy's mind wandered as the two associates flaunted their knowledge of relays and affiliates like boys with cigarette cards. All wonderfully technological, but like the *Evening Star* itself, its primary purpose would be as a pipeline for toothpaste promotions, sensational tidbits and the personal opinions of men like the general.

McCurdy wondered how long it would take them to get around to the only question that mattered to him: *What's in this for me?*

Wilson Larke extended an enamel cigarette case. "May I offer you a cigarette, Ed?"

"Thank you, Wilson, but I don't smoke."

"Good for you. We must take care of that voice."

What the devil is that supposed to mean?

With a minuscule smile, Wilson Larke produced an American Marlboro—oddly, a *women's* cigarette ("Mild as May"). He lit a match, sucked the smoke down and blew it into the air, enveloping McCurdy (who is asthmatic) in a miasma of burning tar.

"Ed, over the past few weeks, do you recall receiving any telephone calls? Anonymous telephone calls?"

McCurdy couldn't deny that—in fact it happened all the time. For any newspaper columnist, fielding complaints from cranks was part of the task.

At the same time, it had to be said that over the past few weeks, he had received a remarkable number of suspiciously innocuous inquiries on general topics—current events and Canadian politics, spoken in tones remarkably lacking in vitriol...

"Ed, that voice over the telephone was our consultant from BBC Radio." Wilson Larke awaited the appropriately slack-jawed reaction, which McCurdy refused to supply.

"Brought from London at considerable expense," added General Newson, selecting a cigar from the humidor on his desk and closing the lid with a snap.

Holding his Marlboro in thumb and forefinger like a European intellectual, Larke continued: "The challenge of supplying talent for a brand new medium involves an entirely new approach to hiring practice. In the case of radio, rather than conduct face-to-face interviews, our expert prefers to speak to prospects over the telephone—so that the interviewer can focus on the speaker's voice alone, with no visual cues to distort the message.

"*Why*, you ask? Because it's the closest thing to what the radio audience will experience—a disembodied voice from the heavens, if you will." Wilson Larke allowed himself another chuckle.

"In this case, our man rang up every male in the employ of the *Evening Star*. Mr. Newson prefers to keep the position in-house."

"The last goddamn thing this paper needs is a fucking show-off swanning about the place and demanding more and more goddamn money!"

Wilson Larke stared at the lit end of his cigarette as though it contained a message. "To make a long story short, Ed, of the fourteen male employees of the *Evening Star*, you alone are the possessor of what our expert calls a *radio voice*."

A pause follows. McCurdy does not respond.

"You see, Ed, just as the camera gave birth to the photogenic face and the cinema gave birth to star quality, radio demands a radio voice. Announcers must accord with the public's perception of what the voice should sound like. Research indicates the voice the audience wants presenting the news is"—he makes an attempt at oratorical depth and resonance—"the voice of God."

"For Britons, the voice of God is Arthur Burrows. When he says 'London calling,' Britons trust Burrows, as they would trust the word of the Almighty, if He were to... er, speak.

"For Canadians, the voice of God will be yours, Ed."

Like nearly everyone else on earth, McCurdy had never truly heard his own voice—for what he did hear of himself through layers of bone, muscle and fat was surely not the voice heard by others.

It was like being told he had a particularly valuable mole on the back of his neck.

And then came the offer, which went as follows: In addition to writing occasional columns, McCurdy was to put his precious radio voice in the service of the *Evening Star*, as news reader for CNR station CNRV. His job would be to read aloud into a microphone pages of print, fed by a wire service; this was to occur at precisely nine o'clock each evening, for fifteen minutes, seven days a week.

At twice his current salary.

What would he *not* do for a raise like that? To his ear, it seemed like the next best thing to a pension.

He thought back to his mother, reading to him at bedtime, and imagined it would be like that.

Unfortunately, the task of reading a script aloud over the radio proved trickier, by several orders of magnitude.

Mom wasn't called upon to read ninety items at the rate of a tickertape (for dynamic urgency), from wars to murders to cats up a tree, in a neutral but concerned tone, with an implied smile for the "lighter side" of the news.

Nor did Mom read *The Wind in the Willows* standing up in evening clothes (a requirement inherited from the BBC), into an alien-looking gadget suspended from the ceiling, watched from behind a window by the electrical engineer—a vole-faced chap named Elwood Mertle, who manipulated rows of control knobs set in a wooden cabinet.

To add to the challenge, not everyone celebrated when McCurdy's appointment was announced—including Mrs. Dixon, his telegraphist-editor, whose husband, a proofreader, had been briefly considered for the position. Mrs. Dixon seemed to go out of her way to create tongue twisters, consecutive alliterations and consonants that caused the news reader to spit and drool. As well, he suspected Mrs. Dixon of arranging the order of events to achieve a surreal effect, undermining his tone of reasonable *gravitas*.

For some reason he can't remember, he began ending each broadcast with "Have a restful good evening." The word *restful* came out on its own—restful as in "rest in peace," for he wished he were dead.

But the greatest hurdle turned out to be of his own making—a growing awareness that untold thousands of listeners were noting every stutter, mispronunciation, sneeze, burp and tremor.

To view one's performance from the audience's perspective is a mental death trap, like an acrobat looking down while walking the wire.

And almost immediately, the letters arrived.

You pronounce words wrong.

Your tone says you are biased politically.

The way you pronounce S—you sound like a poof.

I don't like you, nor does anyone else.

Over ensuing broadcasts, a paralyzing self-consciousness set in, eventually giving rise to a stammer. Mrs. Dixon was kind enough to point this out, her face a parody of concern.

He confided his dilemma to Mrs. Somerset of CNRV *Players*, with whom he had been conducting a desultory affair for some time, who pointed out that Arthur Burrows, dubbed by listeners as Uncle Arthur, was in fact a character, and that Burrows was *acting*.

An experienced theatre director, Mrs. Somerset guided him to developing a Canadian version of Uncle Arthur, who spoke in an accent precisely halfway between Toronto and London, in tones a benign Sunday school teacher might well describe as the voice of God.

Broadcast by broadcast, his panic diminished, and his nascent stutter disappeared.

"My boarders would object to sharing the bathroom facilities with a man. They know what a man does to a commode."

Innocently, he takes a sip of his Gibson. "I see you're using the present tense. Have your boarders stuck by their Mysterious Madam, despite recent events?"

Her eyes throw little needles from beneath her black fringe of hair. "Try not to be cute, darling. As you well know, my boarders evaporated like steam—except for Miss Aspen, who is too blind to read the papers."

"I suppose that's the price you pay when half the world thinks you run a whorehouse."

"A whorehouse that harboured an accused murderess, let us not forget. In fact, that is the subject I wish to bring up."

"You don't say." On alert now, McCurdy removes his horn-and-gold spectacles, cleans the lenses with his handkerchief and forms a blank face with a knowing smile in front.

Mildred knows this trick—his gaze piercing, as though he were looking into one's essence, when in fact the man is as blind as Miss Aspen. She casts a gimlet eye over his bespoke suit, silk tie, gold collar bar, trimmed chevron moustache and dilated pupils. She imagines a svelte mannequin in a Savile Row window with an owl for a head.

A strained pause is broken by a resonant basso above their shoulders. "A good afternoon to you, madam. Welcome to the Stranger's Lounge."

A tuxedoed waiter has materialized above them, with a silver tray balanced on a palm the size of a dinner plate.

McCurdy orders another Gibson; Mildred requests a sidecar, the most expensive drink on the menu—a classy dame—at the gentleman's expense.

"Will there be anything further, Mr. McCurdy? Pretzels? Some roasted nuts, perhaps?"

"Not at the moment, Paris, but thank you."

"You're most welcome, sir." With a look of benevolent neutrality, their waiter glides away to a small bar situated in the far corner, panelled to blend with the wainscotting—and, as it happens, its occupant.

"Goodness, Eddie. Our waiter is a Negro."

"Very perceptive of you, Millie. His name is George Paris. He's the concierge, and the Quadra's lucky to have him. An ex-boxer who plays drums around town. Apparently, he backed Jelly Roll Morton at the Patricia."

"Goodness me—a ladies' side entrance, a Stranger's Lounge to coop them in, and an African drummer for a concierge. Isn't this all a bit *primitive* for 1929?"

"A tad atavistic, yes. Think of it as a fortress against a gentleman's enemies—male and female."

"Tell me: How does one make enemies by reading the news over the radio?"

"Oh, you'd be shocked. I receive absolutely poisonous mail—much of it in women's handwriting. One woman followed me to the Quadra every night for weeks, haranguing me over the night's newscast.

"You see, Millie, some listeners think the reader *causes* the news. Others think we make it all up—that it's a hoax. Or that the news is government propaganda. Others think that news is code for a coming alien invasion..."

McCurdy decides to leave it at that. No need to bring up the episode involving his acting coach, Mrs. Somerset—and her husband, Wesley, who didn't share Darla's bohemian disdain for outmoded institutions such as marriage. It will take many whiskies to wash away the bitterness of that altercation at the Peter Pan, when Wesley Somerset emptied a tureen of hot bisque onto his lap.

A pause follows. Mildred lifts her hand for another beverage.

Looking more closely, McCurdy can see how being a landlady has taken its toll. Her impish features are more hard-edged now, and she has a nascent frown between the precise arc of her eyebrows. The stem of her cigarette holder is riddled with tooth marks.

"Thank you, Paris," McCurdy says on Mildred's behalf.

"Always a pleasure, Mr. McCurdy."

At length, fortified by alcohol and nicotine (the fuel that won the war), she eases into the subject on her mind.

"Eddie, let us suppose you were capable of stooping to your former profession—by which I mean *writing* something."

"Yes, it's true. My contract does allow for occasional pipe-smokers under my byline."

"And?"

"I haven't been able to spare the time."

"With a fifteen-minute workday?"

"Less than that. It's Mr. Good-Evening who does the dirty work. He speaks the words while I think about something else."

"Have you seen *The Great Gabbo*? It's about a ventriloquist and his creepy dummy who reverses the relationship."

She has a point, he has to admit. Thanks to his plummy job, the area between his ears has become an empty playing field covered with weeds.

"Millie, the conversation is getting chippy—why not return to the subject of our meeting? I assume it's about your famous Fatal Flapper."

"Brilliant. Put simply, I'd like you to devote what is left of your mind to the possibility that Dora Decker didn't murder anyone."

"Oh? You gave up feeding me factual nuggets—or don't you remember?"

"Still bitter, Eddie? Feeling jilted?"

"Don't flatter yourself, Millie. In any case, the VPD seems to think otherwise. So does everyone in the Western world who can read."

"So you've buckled under. You didn't always take the police at their word, or adopt the general view. You were a rather interesting bloke, once."

Behind his glasses the eyes roll upward. He knows she will twist the existential thumbscrews until he surrenders.

"Very well, Millie. If you can produce an iota of evidence in her favour, I shall endeavour to present it to the public by means of the printed word."

"Fair enough. Here is your evidence: no woman on earth would murder somebody with an I. Miller shoe."

"Excuse me?"

"Those shoes had to be specially ordered from New York. They cost eighteen dollars a pair. Dora earns thirty-eight dollars a week."

"Millie, I doubt that the price of women's shoes will swing a lot of weight in court."

"Perhaps not, but take this on anyway and I shall waive my fee."

"Your fee for *what*?"

"I mean it would even the ledger."

"What ledger?"

"I'll cancel some resentments."

Paris has materialized above her with another sidecar.

"Mr. Paris?"

"Yes, ma'am?"

"May I ask if you read minds?"

"No, ma'am. I read the room."

With a shadow of a bow, he retrieves their empty glasses and glides away. She watches him pensively, then lapses into a darker funk.

"And there's something else. It's about..." She stops mid-sentence; her eyes moisten as she digs out a handkerchief.

A pause follows. McCurdy re-cleans his spectacles and focuses on his drink, then his watch, then the crease in his trousers.

Finally, she opens her compact, adjusts her mascara in the mirror, reaches into her purse and extracts a telegram, which she extends between finger and thumb as though it were a dead mouse.

"Righto, Eddie. You might as well see this."

CHAPTER 4

*True discipleship is diametrically opposed to the
preferences of the self. Therefore, the first requirement is
the surrender of personal possessions, a surrender that
must be actual, not theoretical. If there is a worldly object
you value or hope to attain, then the Path is not for you.*

—*The Aquarian Gospel*

FIFTY MILES NORTH of Vancouver, well beyond the professional universe of either McCurdy or Hook, sits a small island, not far from Nanaimo, occupied by one of a dozen isolated religious colonies scattered over a sparsely populated region twice the size of France.

The Aquarians of De Courcy Island have settled here to await the end of civilization.

Based in California, the Aquarian Foundation, through its monthly magazine, the *Chalice* ("The Herald of the New Age"), has acquired a paid membership of eight thousand from all over North America, owing to the writings of its leader, one Edward Peter Collins, known by readers and disciples as Brother Osiris.

For the Aquarians, the end times are on their way.

According to *The Aquarian Gospel*—a compendium of beliefs, sayings and instructions purportedly from the dark, unwritten pages of human history—at some point in the prehistoric past, a group called the Brothers of the Shadow seized control of the spiritual progress of humanity.

In the words of *The Aquarian Gospel*, "Their whole world lieth in wickedness, and their God of that world is Satan."

In this interpretation of twentieth-century history, the Great War and the Spanish flu, which together destroyed half a billion human beings, heralded the Last Time—when the Creator launched the planet Aquarius, the eleventh sign of the zodiac, to collide with the world and decimate the human species.

To prepare mankind for this epochal event, the Great White Lodge called on the Brothers of the Light to form Arks of Refuge, secure from outside interference, and safe from global chaos.

THERE ARE SEVERAL arks on the planet. One of them is on De Courcy Island.

Thanks to the karma of past lives, the disciples on De Courcy Island (called "the Chosen") have several common traits, or signs.

First, all survived both the war and the Spanish flu (the Great Winnowing)—though it is true that *non*-survivors would be hard to recruit. Another sign is that all have achieved financial success ("worldly value").

A third distinguishing mark is the simple fact that these success-ful, intelligent people found the courage and conviction to surrender their possessions and uproot their lives—a sign in itself that they have been recognized and acknowledged as seekers, dedicated to the service of humanity.

As final proof of their commitment, each disciple, with his or her own blood, has signed the Commitment: to serve the Work for a thousand years of lifetimes on this earth.

CHAPTER 5

POST OFFICE TELEGRAPHS
RECEIVED TELEGRAM

MAY 27 1929

MILDRED WICKSTRAM
MISS WICKSTRAM'S RESIDENCE
1695 VENABLES ST
VANCOUVER
CANADA

COMING FOR YOU DEAREST STOP ALL IS FORGIVEN STOP

ANDREW IN LONDON

MILDRED PEERS ACROSS the table as McCurdy uncrumples the small sheet of yellowish notepaper, smooths it on the table and absorbs the words taped to its surface. Her hands are shaking; if she picks up her drink now she'll send cognac and orange flying everywhere.

As he absorbs the telegram's contents, absurdly, she feels as if he is taking up some of their weight.

For his part, McCurdy is surprised by the unease in the pit of his stomach at reading the word *dearest*.

"*Coming for you dearest*? What the devil is that supposed to mean?"

"Romantic, isn't it? Andrew liked to think of himself as Sir Lancelot."

"How did you get mixed up with this bird?"

"*Mixed up* is an excellent way to put it. I was certainly confused when I married him."

38

"So Miss Wickstram has a husband. Frankly, that is one of the few things about you that never occurred to me."

"A lot of people married during the Great War. It was a time for grand gestures."

"I'm starting to picture it: bridesmaids, rose petals, four-in-hand coach—all paid for by Daddy, of course."

"Oh fuck off, Eddie—with a war on? Andrew was in France. I was in Whitehall. But of course you didn't serve, did you?"

A sore point. "Are you going to continue your story or hand me a white feather?"

"My point is, our furloughs seldom matched."

McCurdy waits for elaboration. An uneasy pause follows. She puts out her cigarette, and sees that her hand is no longer trembling. Raising her glass by the stem, she removes the lemon garnish, licks a spot on the sugared rim, then lifts the drink to her lips. She takes a small sip, then another, then carefully sets her glass down and stares at it as though it contains nitroglycerin.

When she looks up, he meets her gaze readily, thanks to a pair of glass lenses thick enough to be bulletproof. If it's a staring contest she's after, she has met her match.

"Righto, Eddie. Where shall I start?"

He adjusts his spectacles, returns them to the bridge of his nose and clears his throat. "I assume that Consort Andrew has a last name."

"He does. Andrew Rhys-Mogg."

"The name sounds familiar—or maybe it's the hyphen. Hyphens all look alike to me."

"His gov'nor is lord mayor of Nottingham. But with Andrew there's a DSO, a DFC and MC attached."

"The devil, you say!" McCurdy nearly drops his drink. "You were married to that Andrew Rhys-Mogg?"

"Very sorry to butt in, sir." Paris clears the spill in one swipe and withdraws.

"Cripes, Millie, I wrote a piece about him in the *Varsity War Supplement*."

"Oh, Eddie, please don't tell me it's a small world."

"The article won an award, I forget what. It was called 'Daredevil Dogfight: Rhys-Mogg Wounded in Epic Air Battle Triumph.' Do you know, I even remember some of it? In a descending battle against fifteen or more enemy machines, bullets ripped through the cockpit of his Sopwith Snipe, shattering his legs and arms. With only his right arm spared, Rhys-Mogg headed for home...

"And so on and so forth. Real boy's book stuff, it was."

"Yes, that was the general approach to air battles then. But this is about what happens after the hero comes home draped in glory."

"Do you mean a sequel, like *Zorro: The Family Man*?"

"Not quite, Eddie, and stop being cute. In episode two, I'm afraid the tale becomes somewhat Gothic. As the reality of peacetime set in, it became clear to me that the hero had split into two people—not unlike you and Mr. Good-Evening."

"A Jekyll-and-Hyde type. Doctors treat these chaps at Essondale. The lobotomies do them a world of good."

"Except that Andrew was a national hero. Heroes don't have flaws, darling—certainly not *British* heroes. Andrew received a hero's welcome everywhere he went. Never paid for a drink, ever. His entire wardrobe was 'compliments of.' He held court all day at his club, then sat up all night nursing a bottle. And in between he could become rather... violent." Her eyes take on a certain glaze. Her pupils are ball bearings. She has a habit of scratching her elbow when agitated.

"How British of you, Millie. He was a wife beater, is the long and the short of it."

"There were scenes of that nature, yes. Dr. Fox-Pitt would patch me up from with the reassurance that Andrew's behaviour was out of character, that it did not run in the family, that he would shake it off once he got into the swing of civilian life.

"Instead, Andrew became violent about everything. He *ate* violently, like a wolf—always with the correct fork, of course. And it was suicidal to be in an auto with him at the wheel."

"Pilots call it *flying low*, I believe. They prang their autos rather a lot."

"But of course Andrew wasn't responsible for anything he did or said. Fucking war heroes, they can get away with anything."

"Watch your language, Millie, our waiter can hear you."

They glance at the man in the corner, who appears to be reading an issue of the *Ring*.

"In any case, there are limits to everything. After a year of this I decided that I would rather be a surplus woman than a civilian casualty. A bit wet of me, I admit."

"I don't see how anyone would blame you."

"That is emphatically not true. I was a deserter, almost a traitor. I received threatening letters, bundles of them—and sometimes I recognized the handwriting. Since served at Whitehall, it was rumoured that I had passed secrets to the Boche.

"Then the tabloids began to speculate about other members of my family, including that Father had paid for his knighthood."

"Ah, the honours scandal. A fellow could become a knight for ten thousand quid, a baron for forty."

"Consequently, I did what errant Brits have been doing for a century: I booked a ticket for Canada. Third class; the press is forever scouring the first-class boarding lists for infamous people fleeing the country."

"Extraordinary. Mildred Wickstram is a remittance man."

"Piss off, Eddie."

McCurdy rereads the telegram.

COMING FOR YOU DEAREST STOP ALL IS FORGIVEN STOP

"On the positive side, I should think one might find this talk of forgiveness reassuring."

"So it might seem. But you see, Eddie, I know his war stories by heart—and he knows I know. 'Coming for you dearest' was what he would say to himself, aloud, just before he blew up the gas tank of an Albatross, or shot the pilot in the back. It's one of those magic rituals fighter pilots acquire..."

As she fires up another cigarette, it occurs to McCurdy that, for the first time since he has known her, Miss Wickstram is afraid.

CHAPTER 6

AT THE CENTRE of De Courcy Island is a semicircular grassy hollow like a Greek theatre, around a platform containing the Ever-Burning Flame. Towering over all is the Tree of Knowledge, a bigleaf maple perhaps two hundred years old, said to contain the spirit of a Cowichan shaman.

Here, as always, the disciples have gathered for the Prophecy.

Among the men and women shivering on the hill are barristers, professors, businessmen, a publisher from Ohio and a millionaire organ manufacturer. Yet to look at them now, they could be mistaken for hardscrabble farmers, with their calloused hands, haggard faces and hat lines of pale skin along their foreheads.

Each day, of their own free will, they arise at dawn, eat a sparse breakfast, then clear and till the land with axes, picks, shovels, hoes and mattocks, breaking rocks and hauling them to the sea in sacks— knowing all the while that the purpose of their exhaustion is to render them receptive to insights that were unattainable in their pampered former lives.

It is now well past nine. They have been waiting since seven.

All day, while the disciples laboured, their leader secluded himself in the House of Mystery, a tree house incorporating the trunk of a century-old Sitka spruce, reached by a series of wooden steps and landings. There, he communes with the other eleven Brothers, collectively known as the Brothers of the Light.

Since the founding of the colony, nobody but the Brother has climbed those stairs. The tree house's cleared surroundings are off limits to everyone, including Alma, his wife. It is a known fact that anyone who approaches the perimeter will be heard and seen, and a black mark will be made against them.

A cold mist has descended. The disciples huddle under blankets against the chill, smoking cigarettes for the illusion of warmth.

Grouped as near as possible to the Ever-Burning Flame, some are in conversation with Robert Nettles—lanky and awkward, with a neat moustache and goatee on a face with far too many creases for a man still in his thirties.

Nettles is the foundation's secretary-treasurer and the Brother's closest advisor. Formerly an agent with the US Treasury in Santa Rosa, and with a remarkable head for figures, Nettles runs the colony's entire physical operation. If the Brother is the mind, Nettles is the hands.

As he surveys the audience, Nettles notes three disciples disappearing behind the trees.

Attendance is compulsory; Nettles knows it is his duty to inform the Brother—but he knows he will do nothing of the kind, as he is not yet ready to turn his back on the man who saved his life.

At long last, a figure in a yellow Buddhist robe with black markings emerges from the forest and steps onto the platform beneath the Tree of Knowledge, by the Ever-Burning Flame. A man with a compact body, a small pointed beard, a long nose, penetrating eyes and a conspicuously large Adam's apple.

Lit by the flame, he lifts his arms to the heavens and, in a language his followers understand to be Ancient Egyptian, invokes the four elements. As a master of space and time, the Brother uses his astral body to shield his disciples from Dark Adepts who lurk in the stratosphere, waiting to penetrate the auric egg and engulf Aquarians in a welter of confusion.

The Brother surveys his people, his eyes casting from one face to the next, lit by the Ever-Burning Flame. His eyes grow so pale that the irises seem to fade into the whites.

Their weariness forgotten, the disciples lean forward as the Prophecy begins.

My people, today I sat with the Brothers on the rim of the universal void. At the bottom of the void we could see the stars, and below them the earth and its puny solar system, as we listened to the spiteful chatter of the masses.

They are saying: He is a madman.

Fellow Aquarians, the same was said of Moses, Gideon, John the Baptist and even Jesus. They were not madmen. Indeed, they were not entirely men.

Each of these individuals was born, not just as an earthly being, but

*as an Entity in human form. As a Brother, in touch with the Anima
Mundi, in touch with the Soul of the World.*

They have heard this speech many times, but listen carefully,
for each day's prophecy is peppered with specific references to
current events.

Though confined to the island and ignorant of the outside world,
a few disciples regularly solicit news from Nanaimo suppliers, only
to find that several of Brother Osiris's predictions have come to pass.

Armageddon approaches at a relentless pace.

*Europe, together with its offshoots and colonies, has entered a per-
iod of rapid decline, rooted in moral and spiritual degeneracy. The
spectre of Teutonic hegemony continues to rise: Germany is re-arming,
preparing to rain destruction upon Europe...*

IT HAS NOT escaped the Brother's attention that devotion among his
flock is beginning to falter.

It began last year when he took up an extramarital affair with a
disciple named Muriel Riffle, who had arrived with Roger Flagler, a
wealthy businessman known as the Poultry King of Florida. Though
unmarried, they were welcomed as a couple after Flagler donated
ninety thousand dollars to the Work.

A fetching woman with a knack for making herself indispensable,
Miss Riffle demonstrated valuable office skills—typing, sorting, fil-
ing—that qualified her to carry out minor administrative duties in
place of the secretary-treasurer, who is in a perpetual state of nervous exhaustion.

Within a few months she became the Brother's de facto secretary-
assistant, and very soon after that the Brother became aware of her
spiritual power. While sorting the mail, she could predict what was
inside a sealed envelope and brush away vestiges of negative vibra-
tions hovering over the document. On occasion, she would even
throw an envelope into the stove unopened, knowing of the danger
that lurked inside.

After a period of spiritual growth, Miss Riffle announced that
her mystical identity had been revealed to her in a dream: her name
was Madame Zura. From that point she would not answer to any
other name.

Though the reborn Madame Zura became heartily disliked by the
disciples, the Brother came to trust her completely. "She is my eyes,

she is my ears, she is my mouth," he once said during a prophecy.

Meanwhile, Alma, the Brother's wife, doggedly tended to her chores, a silent reminder that the union was a flagrant violation of *The Aquarian Gospel*, as written by the Brothers of the Light.

For his part, the Poultry King kept a dignified if resentful silence, for the sake of the Work in which he had invested ninety thousand dollars.

When confronted with the discrepancy between his words and deeds, the Brother explained that their wedding had in fact occurred thousands of years ago, in the court of the pharaoh. As the reincarnation of the Egyptian god Osiris (Judge of the Dead, Potentate of the Kingdom of Ghosts), the Brother reunited with Muriel Riffle (the reincarnation of Isis, Osiris's sister-wife) in order to produce a son, Horus, who would lead humanity into a new age of enlightenment.

Fellow Aquarians, do not taint your minds with unworthy thoughts. The marriage of two initiates is marriage on a higher level. In such a marriage, physical union is undertaken solely to provide a vehicle for a specific Incoming Soul. Its purpose is not sexual gratification. Its purpose is to fulfill the plan of the Great White Lodge, which supersedes the primitive urge aroused by the lower chakras...

While most disciples accepted his explanation, seeds of doubt took root and began to sprout among even the most devout, to be expressed in various ways.

A rumour developed, seemingly on its own, that a Dark Adept had taken possession of the Brother. Then Celia, Sydney Backstone's wife, claimed to have actually seen the Dark Adept, which she described as "a helmeted and evil-faced monk, with a face like leather that had been smoked for a month."

Though a trifle Gothic, Mrs. Backstone's vision proved sufficiently graphic to play a role in the public imagination on De Courcy Island, providing a face and a costume for what had previously been a metaphor; to become a fleshed-out character in the community's spiritual universe, a presence that can only grow more vivid with each reported nightmare, and produce strange results.

However, at this point the most disgruntled disciple on the island was Elliot Linden.

As a lawyer with Feetham, Campbell and Linden, he had led a deeply cynical existence as defence counsel for a variety of unsavoury types, almost all of whom would be in stir were it not for Linden's ability to convince a jury and his eye for a legal loophole.

That is, he was until the evening his wife dragged him to hear Brother Osiris speak at the Ayar Lodge of the Theosophical Society in Victoria. By the end of the Brother's talk, it was utterly clear to him that, unless he put his life on a more spiritual path, he would go to his grave with nothing but a legacy of happy shysters.

Linden donated two thousand dollars to the Aquarian Foundation, took an indefinite sabbatical from the firm, built a small house on De Courcy Island, and became a disciple.

But although he had foresworn his profession, it didn't follow that he had gone soft in the head. The Brother's flouting of his own law prompted Linden to question his handling of the fortune the disciples had entrusted to his care.

Linden had defended many shysters in his career. To think he had fallen for one himself was a hard pill to swallow.

A fortnight ago he had appealed to Nettles for reassurance. Curiously, the secretary-treasurer insisted that their meeting take place in a partially constructed two-storey blockhouse on Pirate's Cove. Later, Linden wondered if the location was chosen for the thickness of the walls, to provide a measure of protection from the Brother's mental powers.

Inside the structure he found the awkward, angular secretary-treasurer pacing the cement floor (barely dry, by the smell) from one wall to its opposite, like a prisoner awaiting his sentence.

"Elliot, I hope I can count on your discretion."

"I'm a lawyer, Bob. Keeping secrets is my profession."

"Of course. Pardon me. I'm at my wit's end. If things continue as they are, I'm not sure I can carry on." Indeed, the man appeared as though he might shatter at any moment.

"Bob, can I offer you a drink?"

"What?"

"A drink."

"Of alcohol?"

"What else?"

"Alcohol is forbidden on the island, Elliot, you know that."

"I thought you were charge of weekly supplies."

"Actually, Madame Zura has taken that role."

"Ah. Well, Arvid Pedersen, the ferryman, told me French brandy and wine were among the stores—in fact he sold me a bottle. Breakage, he called it."

After two generous swigs, Nettles's nerves settled somewhat, though he continued to pace; for Linden, it was like watching a very slow tennis match,

"Elliot, I must tell you that the Brother's, er, domestic situation has been a serious test of faith. Then I was ordered to authorize funds for something in the US called the Protestant Protection League. He called it the *crusade*."

"Crusade to what end?"

"Supposedly to counter the pope's influence on presidential elections. The money went to a Senator Helfin, a spokesman for the Ku Klux Klan—now, I ask you, Elliot, what does that have to do with the Work?"

"Beats me, Bob." Linden extended his cigarette case to the secretary-treasurer, but Nettles was too preoccupied to notice.

"And there's more, Elliot. A few weeks ago, another *Chalice* subscriber arrived—Mrs. Ida Arrowsmith from Asheville, North Carolina—with a donation of twenty-five thousand dollars. I was directed to place Mrs. Arrowsmith's money in an account for the Brother's personal projects.

"That was unusual in itself, but what raised my hackles was that he told her to bring the money personally—which, as you probably know, is a common way for a swindler to avoid mail fraud. A felony punishable by twenty years in prison."

"I wouldn't know, I'm Canadian. Jim Barley told me you were in the secret service in California."

"I was an accountant in counterfeit and white-collar crime. The 'secret' part was so that criminals wouldn't be knocking on my door."

"And so what did you do with Mrs. Arrowsmith's money?"

"What do you think? As the Brother requested, I placed it in a separate account with our Vancouver brokers: Tucker, Palmer and Pine."

...THE FOUR HORSEMEN again stalk the land, driven by Mara the Destroyer.

The Prairies, the breadbasket of the Commonwealth, face the prospect of famine. Explosions will rock the nation's capital. Alberta is about to suffer an outbreak of diphtheria...

While Brother Osiris has settled into his dismal survey of disastrous events in the outside world and the hard times to come, his exhausted audience huddled at his feet, Roger Flagler, Sydney Backstone and Elliot Linden have been thrashing their way through the dense underbrush to avoid being seen on the beaten path, until eventually, burrs clinging to their clothing and exposed skin scratched by thorns, they come to the cleared area surrounding the House of Mystery.

Pausing a step away from the edge, already Sydney Backstone regrets having become involved. It's said that the Brother can dispatch his astral body at will, and can kill a man by severing his ethereal body from his physical body. Roger Flagler, the Poultry King, has already lost sleep over the prospect; even Elliot Linden, the confirmed skeptic, is beginning to doubt the wisdom of what they are about to undertake.

Flagler, however, is not about to appear a coward in front of the others; his cuckolding was embarrassing enough. He steps boldly into the clearing—and immediately has difficulty breathing and staggers back to the bushes, then collapses on the ground, struggling to catch his breath.

"It's my asthma acting up," Flagler says in a hoarse whisper. "It's the cottonwood. Just carry on."

Though shaken, Linden and Backstone step forward into the forbidden zone—and within three paces, Linden is starting to lose feeling in his legs. The affliction worsens with every step, until by the time the two men reach the wooden staircase, both his feet have gone numb. Like Flagler, he drops to the ground.

"I'll be fine in a minute, Sydney, start up ahead of me."

Backstone reaches for the labret he put in his pocket as an afterthought—a lip ornament he obtained on the Queen Charlotte Islands, sanctified by a Haida shaman. And thank heaven he did, for it seems to be protecting him from whatever forces are about.

Taking a deep breath, he ascends the steps—gingerly, keeping well away from the edge, testing the strength of each step, until he reaches the top landing.

He isn't surprised to find the door to the House of Mystery unlocked, given the powers at work.

Clutching his labret while intoning a protective mantra, he steps inside—into a small, dim room with the exposed tree trunk forming part of one wall, furnished with a couch, an oak armchair, a side table and a framed quotation he recognizes as the Invocation to Light.

On the side table sits a small, arched wooden box with curious openings, like cathedral windows covered with fabric. On the front of the box, three knobs form a triangle below a small window, and the name *Philco*.

Trembling almost beyond control, he reaches out and turns the top knob with a click. Behind an overlay of crackle and hiss he hears a deep, rich voice, speaking as though from far away.

Backstone recognizes that voice, feels the grip of its psychic power holding him frozen to the spot; only with the greatest effort, and the labret in his pocket, does he manage to disengage from the terrible magnetic pull emanating from behind the speaker cloth, and to let out something like a scream.

CHAPTER 7

WERE THE PANTAGES Theatre situated in the West End of London and not Hastings Street in Vancouver, the section they chose for their periodic in-camera meetings would be called the royal circle—above the commoners in the loges, with private boxes at both sides for those who wish to avoid the company of strangers.

The royal circle is less regal these days.

As part of the Pantages Theatre's ungainly metamorphosis from a stage for live performance to a screen for photoplays, the theatre provided for the sensitivities of the white audience by confining Orientals to the upper section, so that spectators in the loges need not flinch at the prospect of an Asian in the next seat. Naturally, the royal circle became generally known as Chinese Heaven.

For their part, Asian spectators prefer the central section of the royal circle, there to form a compact group, to interpret the sequence of pictures and argue over their meaning while sharing salted plums. (The pits rattle like moist pebbles underfoot.)

Meanwhile, to their left and right, the once-prestigious side boxes have been left to moulder, patronized by moviegoers for whom the movie itself is of no significance; for whom these enclosures, beyond the spill of the house lights, provide a nest for private rendezvous, such as the one taking place between Ed McCurdy and Detective Inspector Calvin Hook.

Few policemen want to expose their informant; fewer reporters want to expose a source; no police captain is likely to promote a leaker.

These tête-à-têtes have been going on for years, with mixed outcomes.

Below the royal circle, a gaunt piano player in the orchestra pit has undertaken a medley of "Makin' Whoopee," "Tiptoe Through the Tulips" and "Ain't Misbehavin'," joined by a female cornetist and a drummer on snare drum and cymbal. The matinee presentation is *Bulldog Drummond*, a talkie. Hence, the loges are packed with female spectators eager to hear Ronald Colman's preternaturally resonant baritone for the very first time.

In the royal circle, however, attendance is sparse this afternoon. Asians prefer silents; there is less to translate, and no accent to decipher.

Hook and McCurdy have taken their usual box, with its peculiar odour of perfume, tobacco, excretions and mould. Hook produces a pony of whisky, the largest bottle that will fit into a plainclothes jacket without a telltale bulge.

Like many encounters between male associates after a prolonged separation, the conversation follows a template where the subject isn't broached until a familiar rhythm is established, a sign that not too much has changed.

"Howdy, Ed. It's been a good while."

"*Howdy*? Calvin, what kind of talk is that?"

"It slipped out. I've been reading Zane Grey."

"I didn't know you were a fan of westerns."

"I can't stand cowboys. They mistreat their horses."

"Zane Grey is a *dentist*, Calvin, for Pete's sake. What does he know?"

"I inherited him, that's all. The previous owner left his collection in our root cellar."

The pony of middling rye is opened and shared.

"Ed, I'll level with you: it's not Zane Grey, it's the infant."

"Ah. I heard Jeanie gave birth to—a son, was it?"

"A daughter. Name of Lucille."

"Congratulations."

"Thanks, Ed, four months late. Four months since I've slept more than two hours at a time."

Ruefully, Hook reaches for his packet of Ogden's. "I read Zane Grey while Jeanie nurses. Then I read Zane Grey while shouldering Lucille at dawn while Lucille hollers in my ear and spits down my neck. It's no life, Ed."

"Actually, you do look like something that's been dug up by the roots."

"And Jeanie looks no better, bless her heart, stuck in the house at the mercy of a creature from space."

Most of all, Hook resents Lucille for her ability, at the first indication of affection between Mommy and Daddy, to lurch out of a dead sleep with a wail like a klaxon horn.

"Maybe I'm not cut out to be a father, Ed."

"Believe me, Calvin, nobody is. Bringing up children is an anachronism. In future they'll emerge from a vat as educated adults."

Below the royal circle, the three-man orchestra undertakes the finale—an inadequate rendition of *Rhapsody in Blue* with the cornetist attempting the clarinet part while the piano player sweats his way through the rest.

Hook sips from the bottle. Something has indeed changed, for both of them. Looking at McCurdy, in a bespoke suit and with no dependants, Hook experiences pangs of existential doubt—*Look at him, leaning over the railing sleek as a seal, as though posing for a magazine ad for menswear*—the difference being that in *Vanity Fair* the models don't peer through glasses as thick as ice cubes.

Hook slips an Ogden's between his lips and fires it up with a grateful sigh: at least one of life's great pleasures is still available, on demand.

Lost sleep isn't the only tiresome consequence of new parenthood. At some point, Jeanie joined a program for new mothers at St. Giles Church, where the women from Lancaster and Yorkshire have formed a sort of coffee klatch. Hook has heard them in the parlour, discussing who knows what topic. Once they get going, the accent becomes indecipherable.

And they're giving Jeanie all manner of tiresome health advice. Last week she brought home a pamphlet entitled *Plain Facts for Old and Young*. Now he can't extract a gasper from the pack without Mr. Kellogg carping in his ear: *The child who smokes at seven will drink whisky at fourteen, and take morphine at twenty!*

The man who coined the term *coffin nails* did great harm to men who just want to enjoy a good ciggie, undisturbed by morbid reflections.

And now another toe in his ribs. Jeanie has taken note of the financial burden Hook's habit places on the household budget: *Oh now would ye look, ducky, at fifteen cents a pack, a year's ciggies is a month's groceries!*

Ashamed, Hook drags on his cigarette so deeply that the smoke penetrates down to his shoes.

Ah. That's better.

He unbuttons his suit jacket. (It binds in the armpits, a discomfort he never felt in uniform.)

These gloomy feelings will surely dissipate, when and if he can ever get a decent night's sleep.

A cone of light slides through the smoke haze and the Movietone News logo appears onscreen (*IT SPEAKS FOR ITSELF*), while unseen speakers blare a triumphant if somewhat tinny fanfare, and a dapper announcer with an air force moustache appears beside a microphone, in front of a stark, blank wall.

This is Lowell Thomas, flashing to you the news of the world, pictured by Fox Movietone!

The camera fades in on the Oval Office in Washington. President Coolidge puts aside his fountain pen and looks up from his desk, as though the audience has just stepped through the door.

The camera closes in while the president delivers his message.

Never has there been a more pleasing prospect for our nation. In the domestic field we look forward to decades of improvement in our standard of living. In the foreign field there is peace, mutual understanding and goodwill...

The audience in the loges gapes at the screen, agog—not at the speaker, but because they can actually hear him speak.

The film cuts to the Statue of Liberty, focuses on the torch held high, then cuts to a leading economist, also at his desk, who looks up as though surprised to see a camera in the room.

I can assure the public that, despite recent volatility, Wall Street is fundamentally sound. There will be no interruption in our current prosperity, and good stocks are a bargain at these prices...

Hook wipes the mouth of the bottle with the palm of his hand, pours a soothing dose over his sore tooth, then passes the whisky to McCurdy. "To what do I owe this visit, Ed? You can't have gone back to reporting, surely. You haven't decided to do actual *work*."

"No, Calvin, we're still renting out the larynx seven evenings a week."

"And I understand you've transformed into Mr. Good-Evening. You've reincarnated, like a Hindu."

"No, I am not Mr. Good-Evening, nor do I want to be. For one thing, you should see the mail. For every marriage proposal there's a promise to punch Mr. Good-Evening in the jaw—which is my jaw as well."

Hook savours the pleasantly bitter liquid as it slides down his throat. "Blame on the messenger is an occupational hazard, I suppose. People have to blame someone for the news. Why is the news always bad, Ed?"

"Because the good news is in the ads."

Onscreen, three prosperous-looking men in tailored suits walk along a boardwalk past the Harvard Inn—a compact accountant type, a matinee idol type and a man with pockmarked cheeks. All three wave at the camera like dignitaries, while shaking hands with eager passersby.

In Atlantic City, New Jersey, gangsters from eight US states formally became a national crime syndicate! Here, during a break in negotiations, Lucky Luciano, Meyer Lansky and Bugsy Siegel take a stroll along the boardwalk!

Now the film cuts to an airstrip, where a number of women pose seated on the lower wing of a biplane, in jodhpurs, neckties and white mechanics' overalls, followed by a woman in a cockpit receiving a bouquet from a well-wisher, then a number of airplanes take off from a field, blowing clouds of dust in all directions.

In Santa Monica, California, it was Powder Puff Derby, in which twenty spunky ladies competed to be the first to reach Cleveland! Twenty-eight hundred miles of dead reckoning through dust, boiling temperatures, threats of sabotage and machines as temperamental as the girl at the controls!

"Calvin, I'm having doubts about the Fatal Flapper case."

Hook lights up another Ogden's and hauls the precious smoke down to the depths of his lungs.

"I know what you mean, Ed. The whole thing smells *off*, somehow. I can't get hold of Tucker's partner, which is suspicious in itself. But Chief Blatchford has decided it's open-and-shut and has no time to listen to arguments. As for the public, I see no 'Free the Flapper' movement. So what do you expect a poor, lonely policeman to do about it?"

"You're the officer in charge of the investigation, Calvin. Does this mean that, in effect, there *is* no investigation?"

"The case is still officially open, but we're told not to waste man-hours on it. I understand that defence counsel is pushing an insanity plea."

"That is why we're gathered here today. I possess information relevant to your so-called open case. Get out your notebook, Inspector Hook, I wish to make a statement."

With a show of professional patience, DI Hook extracts a notebook and pencil from his side pocket, wets the point with his tongue and prepares to write. "You are to be commended, sir. The police are always pleased to receive information from the man on the street."

"To be filed in the wastebasket."

"To be given due consideration."

"By the janitor."

"Ed, let's put aside for the moment your vendetta against the police. Do you have something to report or don't you?"

"It has to do with the murder weapon—which is assumed to be a women's shoe."

"Correct. I saw the thing myself. That spike heel would make a dent in a hardwood floor."

"Inspector, I have it on good authority that those shoes are haute couture."

"How do you spell that?"

"Never mind."

"And the point is?"

"The point is that they're *very* expensive."

"All the more evidence that it was a crime of passion."

"Calvin, those shoes retail at eighteen dollars!"

"My God, you're joking! My entire wardrobe costs less than that!"

They exchange pulls on the bottle.

"I put it to you that an office worker making forty dollars a week, even one who *loathes* her employer, is unlikely to take her revenge with a pair of eighteen-dollar shoes. Especially when the murderer had a letter opener close at hand, and a crystal ashtray heavy enough to fracture a man's skull."

DI Hook holds the bottle up against the flashing image onscreen: three-quarters empty. "To be frank, Ed, I doubt that the price of shoes will constitute reasonable doubt."

"Are there any female police officers around who could weigh in on this?"

"There's Bessie Say at the jail. She can club a man to death with her ankle boot, but she can't tell a T-strap from a T-bone."

Onscreen, H.G. Wells, a man with eyebrows as thick as his moustache, glares at the camera.

People lull themselves into a false sense of security by following easy paths that seem to lead away from war but do nothing of the kind. They humbug themselves by peace demonstrations that demonstrate nothing. For my own part I think the world is drifting very fast toward another Great War.

"All I ask is that you give it serious thought."

"And so I shall. But what does Mr. Good-Evening think?"

"Oh please, not that one again."

For McCurdy, it has become a standard wisecrack. He finds it mildly depressing that the public is more intrigued by Mr. Good-Evening than they ever were by Ed McCurdy.

In fact, the reality of Mr. Good-Evening as a separate entity has spread well beyond his daily fifteen minutes. It is Mr. Good-Evening who receives respectful service at restaurants (even at the Peter Pan), and while it was Ed McCurdy who signed the application for Quadra Club membership, it was Mr. Good-Evening who merited acceptance.

It all feels a bit peculiar—but is it really? When Dr. Tolmie, inspector of livestock, became Premier Tolmie, was he the same man whose days were spent reaching into the rectums of cattle?

Onscreen, the newsreel cuts to a series of news photographs of men in expensively tailored suits, lying spread-eagled on a concrete floor, with liquid antler shapes sprouting from their heads. The same plummy baritone that proclaimed peace on earth identifies these individuals as members of the Bugs Moran gang, having been mowed down with Tommy guns by the North Side Mob led by Al Capone.

Then, with dizzying abruptness, the audience finds itself looking at the lawn of a mansion in Miami Beach, where Al Capone himself, wearing a striped beach robe and smoking a cigar, denies everything: *Every time a boy falls off a tricycle, every time a black cat has grey kittens, every time someone stubs a toe, every time there's a murder or a fire, the newspapers holler, "Get Capone!"*

"For Christ's sake, Ed, it's not as if DI Hook can shoot off his mouth and the course of the prosecution will change. Policing today is like the Catholic Church. Nobody below chief has say-so in anything—and even the chief has to crawl upstairs on a regular basis and explain himself."

"Blatchford is an arse-kisser and a pen-pusher who slid up the ranks like a rat up a drainpipe."

McCurdy finishes the bottle and they prepare to leave separately, as always. "So, Calvin, in this situation, what is an inspector expected to *inspect?*"

"Ed, I inspect what I'm told to inspect. Then I file a report to Superintendent Mosely, who forwards to the deputy chief, who drops it onto the chief's desk. Then I inspect something else. That's the job."

"Calvin, you've become a butterfly in reverse: remove the uniform and out flies a bureaucrat."

GOOD EVENING. HERE is the CNR news service, brought to you by the Vancouver Evening Star.

In British Columbia, fishing licences have been cut by forty per cent other than for white British subjects and Indians, while at New York City's Easter Parade, a large group of women openly smoked cigarettes as they marched down Fifth Avenue, and at Princeton University, researchers successfully turned a live cat into a functioning telephone...

In Germany, Albert Einstein has received the Max Planck medal for his theory of relativity, which continues to baffle the public. In the United States, Justice Oliver Wendell Holmes Jr. has rejected the argument that the Fifth Amendment protects criminals from reporting illegal income, thus placing prohibition profiteers under the purview of the Internal Revenue Service...

You have been listening to the radio voice of the Vancouver Evening Star. As we end our broadcast, special greetings go to Mr. and Mrs. Ilia Krysaka of Gravelbourg, Saskatchewan, who just celebrated their diamond anniversary.

And of course we wish all our listeners, on the trains, in the woods, in the mines and the lighthouses, a restful good evening.

CHAPTER 8

SITUATED IN THE basement of the Cordova Street station, the women's holding cells make for a depressing visit—a cave, really, lined with vomit-coloured linoleum, war-surplus paint, and with its own distinctive smell: a medley of sour breath, stale sweat, Lysol and fear. After this visit, the pong of the holding cells will skunk Mildred's clothes for weeks.

As Dora Decker's landlady, she applied for and received permission to conduct a private meeting, ostensibly to discuss the settling of unpaid rent. (Although personal visits are carefully screened, the cell doors remain wide open to creditors.)

The matron, Miss Say, opens the cell door, a middle-aged woman of about six feet in a man's khaki-green uniform and thick-soled workboots.

"A visitor, Dora," she says in a terse but not unkind tone.

Despite their having lived in the same house for over a year, Mildred doesn't immediately recognize the figure seated inside, who bears little resemblance to the flapper she saw each morning and evening—and the difference is not just the lack of lipstick, mascara and rouge.

She casts a curious glance at Miss Say, her escort, as though to ask, "Are you sure?"

The matron heaves a seen-it-before sigh. "Poor dear, it's the shock, don't you see. Guilty or not, the place changes a person. And folks wonder why we seize their suspenders and shoelaces!"

"So do you think she might be innocent?"

"It's not my place to say, miss."

Seated stiffly upright on the edge of a wooden army cot, wearing the sort of frock cleaning ladies wear, Dora Decker has skin as waxen as a cathedral saint. She doesn't seem to hear their conversation, or the harsh clang of iron as the door slams shut; nor does she seem aware that another human being has joined her in this tiny, hard, melancholy room. She stares steadily into the distance, as though waiting for a ship to come over the horizon.

"Hello, Dora."

Receiving no response, Mildred takes the only available seat, a wooden stool beside the metal commode. She opens her purse and extracts a Gauloise cigarette, then a packet of Swan rolling tobacco and Roll-O papers. (From the contents of the wastebasket in Dora's room, Mildred knows her tenant's rural taste in smoking materials.) She places the tobacco and papers next to the inflatable rubber pillow (made flaccid by a slow leak), near a tin ashtray containing moist butts badly rolled with newspaper.

Mildred leans her elbow on the cell's tiny cast-iron sink, thinks about what on earth to say, and decides to say nothing.

Minutes pass. Mildred smokes, Dora stares. When she made the appointment, Mildred expected Dora to be in rough shape, but not altered beyond recognition and in a catatonic state.

"Hello, Dora."

Silence. She might as well be talking to the sink.

"It's me. Miss Wickstram. Mildred. Your landlady. Surely you remember me."

From a nearby cell Mildred hears another prisoner quietly sniffling. People who await trial and sentencing may not yet be condemned, but it's almost worse to be waiting in limbo, like a suicide, or an unbaptized infant.

Mildred opens her mouth to speak, then shuts it again, feeling like an idiot even before the words form sentences. What does one say to a young woman who faces the possibility of hanging by the neck until dead? Cheer up, it could be worse?

The girl she remembers may have been a bit clueless, but she seemed sensible enough, and her personality seemed not at all flapper-like, otherwise Mildred wouldn't have rented her a room in the first place. Having a flapper in the house means having a queue of male visitors scuttling about. Like rats, suitors get into the house no matter what you do, followed by inevitable complaints from other boarders about unpleasant squeaks leaking through the walls.

But Dora was more like a Sunday school teacher in flapper costume; in fact, she once mentioned that she came from a devout sect in Rosthern, Saskatchewan—which was fine with Mildred, as long as her new tenant didn't try and convert the others.

Dora may not have been a convincing flapper, but it is dispiriting to think of the clueless girl with the bob cut and the eyes painstakingly mascaraed and plucked shrivelled into this sad husk.

At Badminton School Debating Society, when one cannot think of what to say, one learns to simply open one's mouth and speak, and make sense of whatever comes out as one goes along.

"Darling, first of all I need you to understand something. You must understand that despite the press, I for one do not believe that you murdered Ralph Tucker with your spike-heeled shoe."

Dora responds with a blink, if at all.

Mildred knows about men with shell shock retreating so far into themselves that they must be warehoused in hospitals and fed with tubes. If that's the case here, she thinks, this is a waste of time.

Let's put it to the test.

Heaving a sigh that says she has reached the utmost limit of her patience, Mildred butts her cigarette in the tin ashtray, rises briskly to her feet and makes like she is about to call Miss Say.

"You really think so?"

It was barely audible, and the girl on the cot hasn't moved a muscle, but still...

Mildred returns to her stool. "I most certainly do think so."

She waits for the words to sink in, then continues: "Unfortunately, darling, the price of women's shoes amounts to the sum total of evidence in your defence. Cops and judges will require more than that to dislodge their smug certainty that they already have the answer. Men don't understand women's shoes and never will, anything beyond a clog is an extravagance..."

Dora's lips, cracked almost to bleeding, begin to move.

Take your time.

"The shoes were part of what we had to wear."

"In the office?"

"Yes.

"Oh. I see. Do you mean you wore costumes, like dancers in the *Follies*?"

"Sort of. The girls called it 'the uniform.'"

"Dora, do you know anyone who might want to murder Mr. Tucker?"

After a long pause: "Everyone."

"Can you be a bit more specific, darling?"

"We all wanted to murder him. All three of them."

"Do you mean the partners?"

"They're a pack of weasels with wandering hands."

"Oh dear. How awfully familiar. You remind me of the War Office."

"The what?"

"The War Office. I was on General Callwell's staff. Our skirts were much lower, but that didn't discourage them. We put up with it because our pests outranked us."

"We did too—because our bosses knew people."

"What sort of people?"

"Celona and Valenti and Chung Young Lee. Vera said she heard of girls kidnapped and hooked on drugs and used as white slaves at the Maple Hotel."

"I've heard of that sort of thing happening—but not on Howe Street."

Dora rolls herself a cigarette, wistfully. "I shouldn't have stayed on. My parents will disown me when they find out. But I sure liked those shoes."

CHAPTER 9

I got nothing against the honest cop on the beat.
You just have them transferred someplace where
they can't do you harm. But don't ever talk to me
about the honor of police captains or judges. If they
couldn't be bought, they wouldn't have the job.

—Al Capone

HOOK WILL NEVER fully understand why he was promoted to the rank of inspector, but it had something to do with the death five years earlier of Peter Verigin—called "Lordly" by his followers, a group of Eastern Orthodox heretics from Russia.

Lordly was blown to kingdom come on a CPR train out of Castlegar.

The resulting investigation lurched forward in fits and starts for months as the RCMP, the provincial police and the CPR police squabbled over jurisdiction, tripping each other up and destroying each other's evidence, until the whole thing became a public embarrassment.

Who killed Lordly? At first, the prime suspects were disgruntled fellow Doukhobors appalled by his taste for pubescent girls. However, the Doukhobors declined to participate in such an investigation, so that line of inquiry petered out.

As the file gathered cobwebs, theories bloomed in the Kootenay imagination, until opinion converged on the suspicion that there had been some sort of government cover-up.

The uproar grew loud enough to rattle the chain of the provincial government, which would face a by-election in a few months.

With orders from above and few men to spare, it was somehow

MOST URGENT DEPOSITION RE TUCKER MURDER STOP
SECRETARY CHARGED TRIAL UPCOMING

INSP CALVIN HOOK
VANCOUVER POLICE DEPARTMENT
200 CORDOVA ST
VANCOUVER
CANADA

WESTERN UNION TELEGRAPH
TELEGRAM

JUNE 9 1929

INSP CALVIN HOOK
VANCOUVER POLICE DEPARTMENT
200 CORDOVA ST
VANCOUVER
CANADA

ALVIN PINE CHECKED OUT TUESDAY ALL CORRESPOND-
ENCE FORWARDED TO ARLINGTON RESORT HOT SPRINGS
NATIONAL PARK ARKANSAS

ELIAS KOTNER
MANAGER
RONEY PLAZA

BABY LUCILLE SEEMED relatively content until just past one, when
her gentle gurgling sound quickly expands to a full-throated roar—
an impressive sound, coming from a person slightly bigger than a
loaf of bread.

Hook tosses aside *The Rainbow Trail*, gropes blindly for his
dressing gown and stumbles to the nearby crib, a rectangular zoo
enclosure containing blankets, stuffed toys and a spitting, stinking
demon with tiny red claws... a gargoyle come to life.

An inexplicable tenderness comes over him as he carefully lifts
the creature over the barred fence and onto the changing table, coo-
ing like a pigeon.

Once upon a time, the changing table was a games table for checkers and cribbage; now it's for the unpinning of diapers that smell like diluted cow shit, to be thrown into a putrid-smelling wicker bin, followed by successive applications of washrags and Vaseline, then folding and re-pinning, then the shoulder carry and back slap, humming whatever stupid tune comes to mind at this time of night.

Tonight's melody fails to appease Lucille.

"She's hungry," mumbles a weary voice beneath a pillow.

Jeanie rolls over and takes a seated position with her back against the headboard. Hook transfers the creature to her waiting breast, and experiences a pang of jealousy as Lucille clamps onto a nipple and makes slurping sounds.

"Pet, what do you pay for shoes?"

Jeanie's eyes haven't opened yet. "You mean *my* shoes, like?"

"Yes. Say, at Ingledew's."

"Ducky, it's after one in the bleedin' morning and you ask a question like that?"

"It's just something at work that stuck in my mind. About a pair of women's shoes that cost eighteen dollars."

Jeanie laughs. "Ducky, if I was to own a pair of eighteen-dollar shoes, I should nae take them out of the box I'd be so feared of scuffin'."

Hook takes a moment, then continues. "Pet, could you answer me this: In a... an emergency, would you consider using such a shoe as a... a weapon?"

"Not on yer life! In Manchester we carried grannies' hatpins. They were *this* long, stick it right in 'im!"

He doesn't know what to say to this.

CHAPTER 10

Graft is a byword in American life.

—Al Capone

UNSURPRISINGLY, AT MIDMORNING snack time Hook locates Quam in Leonard's Café, where the sergeant has become a regular; in fact he reserves a booth for that time—a rear booth, so that he can concentrate on his food.

There he is as expected, hunched over a slice of custard meringue pie. His upper lip has a white, fluffy moustache; the face itself could have been sculpted out of cookie dough.

DI Hook pauses beside the counter where a man with red suspenders, who may or may not be a fireman, is wielding his soup spoon as though it were a wrench. He seats himself two stools away, sufficient distance to avoid being elbowed in the jaw.

The young woman at the cash, whose name is Carmella, hasn't yet glanced up from her copy of *Photoplay*, and the waitress is nowhere to be seen, but eventually he orders coffee from a sullen twenty-year-old with bitten nails and lipstick on her teeth. As ever, the steaming coffee cup features the profile of a setter with a dead bird in its mouth. (The emblem lost its meaning when George Leonard sold the place, but the bulletproof crockery endures.)

"What d'ye want in it?"

"Just white, please."

The waitress, whose name he has forgotten, sighs disdainfully and produces a small pitcher, also with bird dog attached. He takes a sip and wishes he'd ordered it black, then swivels around on his stool to watch his former partner devour pie as though each forkful might be his last.

Finally, the sergeant sighs, dabs at his meringue moustache with his napkin, folds it carefully and lays it atop his meticulously clean plate. Only now does he become aware of being watched.

"Inspector Hook, sir! I didn't see you there."

"Didn't want to break your concentration, Mr. Quam. There are times when a man should be left in peace."

Quam's brow furrows slightly. "Are there, sir? Or are you being sarcastic?" Throughout their partnership, the use of sarcasm was a recurring bone of contention.

"Not in the least. I envy any man so attuned to the here and now that he can sit down and enjoy a piece of pie the way you do."

"Now that *was* sarcasm, surely—" Quam stops mid-sentence, noting the pouches hanging from the inspector's eyes like sacks of sand. "Oh. I remember now, sir. You have a little one. Up at all hours sort of thing?"

"Well observed, Sergeant." Hook extracts three Aspirin from his jacket pocket and washes them down with sour coffee. "Now I know how it feels to be an urchin."

"Hungry and dressed in rags, sir?"

"Not that class of urchin, Mr. Quam. A *sea* urchin. They never sleep and they're prickly. A small joke."

Quam pretends to chuckle. "Ha-ha. But surely you sleep in separate rooms. You are, after all, the breadwinner, the man of the house."

"Irrelevant in this case, Sergeant. Married couples keep a ledger. If I don't watch out I'll be drowning in red ink."

"Ha! An accounting joke! Sir, do you mind if I share it at the office?"

"Not at all."

"*Marriage is unmathematical*—oh, that's a good one!"

"No, it isn't. But I suppose there aren't many jokes in the fraud department."

"Jokes are thin on the ground, sir, it's true." Quam's expression returns to its normal resting expression of hound-like melancholy.

"It's not a barrel of laughs, spending the day adding and subtracting."

"I tell you, sir, the tedium is beyond all. My colleagues are even more boring than I am." Quam glances over his shoulder for imaginary eavesdroppers. "I do hope our conversation won't go beyond these walls, sir."

"It's in the vault, Mr. Quam, you can count on it. In any event, your department is doing valuable work. The stock exchange has to be held to account."

"No, it doesn't. The new mayor isn't in favour, any more than the old mayor was. Our orders are to give the institution maximum leeway—time to find its feet."

"It looks like they've learned some fancy footwork."

"Oh very good, sir. Another good one!"

Quam takes out his notebook and pencil and makes a note, while Hook sips his now-cold coffee.

When it opened in 1907, the purpose of the Vancouver Stock Exchange was to weed out an outgrowth of frontier fraud— fly-by-night exchanges that popped up after the gold rush. Success has been mixed, at best. As an institution, its main achievement has been to gather the same shifty operators under one roof, and to provide them with an aura of respectability, enabling swindlers to become not only wealthy but politically influential as well.

For their part, city fathers have adopted an unofficial hands-off policy similar to the blind eye granted to Joe Celona (born Giuseppe Fiorenza in Tuscany, Italy), who operates a range of local bawdy houses and bootlegging activities, as well as a cigar store near City Hall with plenty of the mayor's favourite brand.

As the mayor once put it, "Face it, Vancouver will never be a Sunday school town!"

If investigating the VSE is a largely symbolic gesture, it occurs to Hook that Quam was put in charge of the VSE probe in the hope that it would produce as little result as the Verigin investigation.

But still, Sergeant Quam has access to files...

Bringing his coffee with him, Hook seats himself across from the sergeant. "Mr. Quam, the murder took place at the VSE; surely you can see how the Fatal Flapper case might have something to do with your fraud investigation."

"Murder, sir? Oh, that's for you people in homicide."

Hook's tooth is acting up again; he washes more Aspirin down the neck with the last of his coffee as Quam continues.

"The chief has made it clear we're not to horn in on another department's investigation. Besides, isn't the perpetrator in custody?"

"Innocent 'til proven guilty, Sergeant."

"Or perhaps not, sir."

"What do you mean?"

"There is no denying the unknown."

"I hadn't thought of that."

"But why would someone's personal secretary do such a thing?"

"We at homicide are asking ourselves the same question. It can't have happened in a vacuum—would you not agree?"

"Not a vacuum, sir. My understanding is that it happened in the victim's office."

"That's not my point, Mr. Quam. In your current investigation, I wonder if you might have had dealings with the late Ralph Tucker?"

Quam's eyes glisten. "Of Tucker, Palmer and Pine? What has that got to do with... *Late*? Oh dear! Are you saying that the victim was *Ralph Tucker*? Ralph Tucker is *dead*?"

While he waits for Quam to absorb this morsel, Hook fires up an Ogden's and orders another coffee (black this time). "Mr. Quam, I'm sorry to be the bearer of bad news, but the murder took place over a week ago. You didn't actually *read* about the Fatal Flapper case, did you?"

"Not in detail, sir. I overheard some members discussing it over lunch."

As often happens, Quam has, in his own fashion, provided an unexpected insight: not every policeman follows the news—in fact, coppers are every bit as ignorant as the general public.

"Sergeant, at VPD headquarters these days, would you agree there's a certain lack of, shall I say, *exchange* between different branches of the force?"

"Oh no, sir. I would say that there is none at all. As I just told you, interdepartmental meddling is expressly forbidden. Certain to get a reprimand, if not worse."

DI Hook reaches into his inside pocket, produces and unplugs a pony of rye, and lashes it into his coffee, which has been on the burner too long and tastes of ashes and tar. "May I take it that your department had dealings with Mr. Tucker?"

"Oh certainly, sir. Tucker, Palmer and Pine are as crooked as fish hooks. But they're a hard nut to crack, compared to the penny stock traders, the pump-and-dump artists pushing salted mines, and the non-existent Mexican railways. Mr. Tucker's files are well concealed in numbered accounts, traced to some suspect religious organizations and what's left of the Ku Klux Klan. It's not nearly enough to fetch a warrant."

"I was just wondering: Do you think Mr. Tucker's murder might have had something to do with his activities as a broker?"

"That's not for us to say, sir. As I said, Chief Blatchford specifically warned us not to intrude on other departments, and not to muddy cases with unnecessary detail. And in this instance, is it not obvious who the perpetrator was? The man was killed with a high-heeled shoe!"

CHAPTER 11

SITUATED UP ON the fourth floor and down the hall from the morgue, F.C.V. Condon's door has a reinforced window with the legend *Forensic Analysis*—in letters partially obscured by a small, round hole and a lacework of tiny cracks.

Hook steps inside, closes the door behind him, and pauses—to allow his sense of smell to adjust to the alien aroma of sour pickles and a butcher's cabinet. An overlay of pipe tobacco alerts him to Condon's presence—which comes as no surprise, for the fellow is rarely spotted anywhere else.

Condon is known about the precinct as a loner who keeps to himself—which is just as well, for other members regard him as odd and sinister, with his machines and scales and test tubes. They are thankful he doesn't frequent the lunchroom; nobody wants to look across one's meat loaf at a pair of hands sawing away at a slice of brisket, knowing that same pair of hands dissected someone a half-hour before.

Hook is at the foot of a long steel table, whose slightly concave surface is angled to allow body fluids to drain in one direction. A curved notch has been bolted to the far end to support the neck of the corpse; nearby is a butcher's scale with an overhead dial the size of a railway clock. Along the wall to the right is a school blackboard displaying chalked scribbles about weights and characteristics, while in the far corner beside the window is an enclosed incinerator, currently not in use.

The room is chilly of course, but that doesn't account for the shiver up Hook's spine and the rise of his sphincter as the atmosphere sinks in.

This isn't a place where people die. It's where their bodies are taken apart, analyzed, recorded, then disposed of, leaving nothing behind but an overwhelming question.

He lights an Ogden's in the hope that the smoke will help over-come the smell he now identifies as formaldehyde, congealed blood and chicken gone slightly bad—a remarkably long-lasting scent; once taken in it will stick to the nostrils for hours.

The coroner is standing at the blackboard, seemingly transfixed. Hook is not at all sure whether Condon is aware of his presence or in a trance.

Hook turns his gaze to the row of glass cabinets containing sam-ples of pistol types, tyre treads, poisons, soils, glass, foliage, wools and bones.

Various contraptions in various stages of construction occupy the countertop in front of the cabinet. Two of them are Condon's own inventions and are well-known: an ultraviolet lamp to detect the presence of body fluids on fabrics, and an assembly of hardwood and brass for mounting and measuring a pistol and examining the barrel.

Condon reaches up with a piece of chalk and adjusts a series of calculations, mutters to himself and stares at the blackboard some more. Hook is beginning to feel like a ghost.

When word first drifted through the precinct that a room adja-cent to the morgue was to be given over to what was then called the city sanitary inspector, it was not well-received.

A sanitary inspector is an official who checks grocery stores for spoiled milk and counts the rats in restaurants; he is not someone to be provided with a laboratory and conferred with the medieval title "coroner."

The job and its title suggest a manufactured sinecure for an alder-man's relative, yet another example of bureaucratic empire-building.

Then Condon proceeded to make fools of his detractors. Again and again, the city analyst produced key evidence that proved guilt or innocence with the certainty of arithmetic—lawyers can argue over police methodology, but you can't argue with a spectro-scope—to the point where Condon has become a quasi-legendary public figure.

After several sniffs of unfamiliar smoke, the coroner turns to face the intruder. "May I ask who you are, sir?"

F.C.V. Condon (as he prefers to be called in press reports) wears a tweed suit a size too large, and has a pronounced stoop for a man in his forties (the tall individual's natural response to repeated headers against door frames).

Condon's long neck cranes forward at such a precarious angle that one might think it puts too much leverage on such a large head, with its high, wide forehead and an occiput shaped like a trunk for spare brains. His hair has been trimmed in a precise line like a hedge; Hook notes the dark circles under the eyes—meaning that, like him, F.C.V. Condon has poor sleep habits. The city analyst is smoking the bulldog pipe that inspired reporters to name him "Canada's Sherlock Holmes."

"Good day, Mr. Condon, sir. I'm Detective Inspector Hook."

"Who?"

"The officer from homicide who called yesterday afternoon. Inspector Hook. From homicide."

Condon frowns, still as a photograph, until the mists clear, then the face brightens and becomes almost boyish. "Oh. Oh. Oh yes! Yes, of course! It all comes to me now. Welcome, Inspector Snook."

"It's *Hook*, actually."

"Inspector Hook. Indeed, indeed. Pardon me." Condon looks at the palm of his hand as though wondering what to do with it, then extends it for a handshake.

Hook shakes the hand, avoiding thoughts as to where it's been.

"And what may I do for you, Inspector Hook?"

"As I mentioned to you on the telephone, sir, it's about the Fatal Flapper case."

"The what?"

"The Fatal Flapper case. The victim was murdered with a spike-heeled shoe."

"*Fatal Flapper*? Is that what they call it? Gosh bless my soul, what will they think of next?"

"Newspapers need headlines to catch the reader's eye, sir."

Condon makes *tsk* sounds. "No respect for facts, that's their problem. Well, you'd better come into the lab."

They enter a space whose first impression is of a high-ceilinged master bedroom that has been put to use storing odds and ends from a laboratory, a workshop and a restaurant kitchen. A continuous counter lines the perimeter, while a long table in the middle takes up so much space that it's necessary to twist sideways to cross the room. Industrial pendant lamps made of green enamel hang from the ceiling, lending the space an air of concentration not unlike a pool parlour.

The central table contains a bewildering array of scientific glassware—flasks, beakers, phials, test tubes, adapters, desiccators, pipettes, retorts and a bell jar, with a separate space for a brass microscope and two racks of slides.

In one corner of the room is an army cot next to a rolltop desk; above the desk is a window. Seated at the window is a huge mound of fur, with a foot-long tail that wags back and forth like a metronome.

"Mr. Condon, sir, what is that?"

"What?"

"That animal over there."

"That's Lewis, my cat. A marvellous ratter, Lewis. Rats are a problem here, as you can imagine."

Lewis lifts his head to glare at the intruder.

Hook has no experience with house cats; the only cats in Waldo, his hometown, were of the semi-feral variety that would tear a man's legs to shreds. He has encountered many cats since, but is still unsure whether he likes them. They lack the innocence of dogs. They refuse to obey commands. They have a sneaky look, as if they're planning something you're not going to like.

Lewis blinks twice, as though aware that his name has entered the conversation, and glares at the inspector with undisguised malice. His face consists of a white patch shaped like the skull on a poison label, with a single fang that droops over his bottom lip like a walrus tusk.

"Lewis is a Maine coon. Sailors used them as ship's cats. They claimed Maine coons could stop or start storms through magic stored in their tails..."

Ignoring Condon's tedious homage to a cat, Hook examines the room and its contents, pausing in front of a particularly baffling contraption made of brass, glass, hardwood and electricity.

"I'm curious, Mr. Condon. To me this looks a bit like a crystal radio—I remember building one in Boy Scouts when I was a boy."

"Indeed! Indeed! Very good, Inspector. Do you know, I used a number of parts from the Marconi version—for an entirely different purpose of course, still in development don't you see, but the concept shows promise. Allow me to—" He grows suddenly silent, as though a thought just occurred to him, then hurries to the desk, takes a pencil from behind his ear, scribbles a note on some foolscap.

Shoving his pencil back behind his ear, Condon returns to the table, taps the ashes of his pipe into a Quaker flour tin, reaches into his coat pocket and produces a leather tobacco pouch, then refills his pipe, tamping it down with a nicotine-stained forefinger.

Hook fires up another Ogden's. He's well over the day's limit, but under certain circumstances smoking is part of the job.

His tooth throbs softly, like an extension of his pulse.

"By the way, Inspector, what looks to you like a jumble of spare parts is in fact my latest project. You see, tests have led to the conclusion that each individual possesses a distinctive chemical aura born of a particular substance, some of which clings to every object he touches. Think of it as the substance a fugitive leaves behind for bloodhounds to follow." Condon waggles his pipe as though it were sniffing down an imaginary trail.

"With this machine, investigators will have the capacity to pick up this aura, measure it and classify it. I tell you, Mr. Snook, the day is near when an officer can cast the machine over a suspect area, and produce evidence as certain as a fingerprint."

In his notebook Hook writes *Robot bloodhound.*

"And what do you intend to call this remarkable machine?"

"I'm glad you asked. I was thinking of calling it the Muzzle, but as a verb it can mean the wrong thing entirely—so there could be confusion there, don't you see. And the Snout is far too undignified, and Odour Calibrator is too hard to remember, whereas Smell-O-Meter smacks of hucksterism—"

"Perhaps it might simply be called the Bloodhound. As though it were a sort of robotic dog."

"Oh! Very good! Indeed! Well done!" Condon dashes to the rolltop desk, pulls the pencil from behind his ear and makes a note.

"Sir, I wonder if we might perhaps move on to the business at hand?"

Condon re-lights his pipe. "What business?"

"The Fatal Flapper case, sir."

"Oh. Yes. Of course, that. Stupid name—and completely inaccurate."

"Inaccurate in what way, sir?"

"You don't drink, I hope?"

"I'm afraid I do, sir."

"Fancy a drop?"

"Certainly."

"By the way, you may call me John."

"Thank you for that, sir. Do you collect initials?"

"Haw! Indeed! Indeed!" Condon produces an Erlenmeyer flask containing amber liquid, pulls the cork and pours a generous measure into two glasses stolen from the cafeteria downstairs.

"Cheers."

"Cheers."

A pause for an appreciative swallow, though the taste of peat may have come from the lab and not Scotland.

"Sir, you mentioned something being inaccurate about the Fatal Flapper case."

"Of course. Stupid name, that. I think it was the so-called spiked heel that seemed somehow *off*. So I decided on an experiment—now I warn you that this might seem a bit unorthodox, but if you'll just come along with me—"

The coroner takes Hook by the arm and ushers him into the loo, a former storage closet refitted to contain a toilet, a sink and an army-surplus metal shower. "Just take a peek at this."

Condon sweeps the shower curtain aside to reveal what looks to be a side of pinkish-grey meat hanging from the shower head, pocked with apparently random indentations.

Hook drops his cigarette butt into the toilet and suppresses the urge to gag, while Condon puffs his pipe at the dimpled corpse.

"Interesting, isn't it?" he says, poking his finger (not, thank heaven, his pipe stem) into a particularly deep indentation. Hook can only stare in wonder at the man's sense of detachment.

"Excuse me sir, but, er, is this Ralph Tucker in the shower?"

A pause, then Condon expels a long, horse-like, gasping sound that must surely be laughter. "Haw! Haw!" He strikes the wall of the shower, which makes a sound like thunder.

"Oh dear! Oh good heavens no! It's a side of pork I purchased from James Inglis Reid! As a matter of fact, I'm hoping to take it home for supper... Please excuse me while I fetch something."

Condon abruptly leaves the room and almost immediately returns with a women's shoe—a suede T-strap with a long, narrow heel. "This, Inspector, is a shoe identical to the one that was found at the scene of the crime, supposedly the murder weapon."

"I recognize it. It does look rather deadly."

"Let us see about that, shall we?" Condon steps into the shower, grips the shoe in both hands, clamps his pipe between his teeth, and administers a series of blows to the carcass with considerable force, using both arms as though the shoe were a pickaxe. After several swings, he takes a moment to catch his breath, then points at the carcass with the stem of his pipe.

"There. Do you see?"

Hook looks at the imprints, trying not to touch the thing.

"Actually, I'd have to say no."

"Indeed. So now let's take a closer look at this heel. It may be slender, but the bottom is *flat*, don't you see, it's not a spike by any means. It will bruise, certainly, but in order to pierce human flesh it would have to taper to a point—a dull point maybe, but a point nonetheless. Try as I might, I could barely break the skin with this."

"Even so, sir, it does look as though it could do considerable damage."

"Yes and no, Mr. Hook, yes and no. A blow to muscle or bone or torso would certainly be painful—but death? I tell you, were this a human body—not unlike a pig in most ways—it might possibly have produced bruising, even a slight concussion—but hardly death."

"People in a blind fury have been known to perform extraordinary feats of strength, sir. Perhaps she severed a major vein."

"Blind fury? I grant you that there was a cluster of indentations about the neck and ears, and blood vessels in the head will bleed like the very devil, but nothing that penetrated his skin—would you like to see the photographs?"

"No sir, I'll take your word for it."

"And I'll grant you that the marks about the jugular vein were deeper than the others, and deliberate. But none effected anything remotely like a killing wound."

In his notebook Hook writes *Deliberate blows to the neck.* "But, sir, you must admit that the office was a terrible mess. The amount of blood—"

"Actually, the office wasn't as much of a mess as it appeared to be. There's something about pools and splashes of blood that has an exaggerated visual effect. Believe me, Officer, had the jugular been pierced, with each heartbeat it would have been like a firehose sprayed red paint about the room."

"And what is your conclusion, sir?"

"Only tentative, pure conjecture and a long way from admissible evidence, and it certainly won't save the accused from the hangman, but I have a sense that the blows were planted for spectacle. That the victim was already dying or dead."

Hook writes *Wounds as disguise*, and closes his notebook, eager to leave the room before the coroner decides to explain another contraption involving bodily functions. "Mr. Condon, sir, you have provided the investigation with a new angle, and I commend you for it."

"Not necessary, Inspector. All in a day's work."

As the coroner walks Inspector Hook to the door, Lewis follows, then jumps onto the steel table and hunches there, displaying his single fang and making odd clicking sounds.

The two men shake hands. Hook plans to wash the moment he finds a loo.

"Only one last question, sir, if I may."

"Of course."

"I happened to notice the bullet hole in your window."

"Indeed, yes. A suspect took umbrage at evidence I produced on a charge of aggravated assault and wanted revenge—kill the messenger type of thing.

"Criminals think I'm the grim reaper, when I might just as easily prove them innocent."

WESTERN UNION TELEGRAPH

TELEGRAM

JUNE 10 1929

INSP CALVIN HOOK

VANCOUVER POLICE DEPARTMENT

200 CORDOVA ST

VANCOUVER

CANADA

REGRET ALVIN PINE CHECKED OUT STOP HAVE FOR-
WARDED TELEGRAM TO HOTEL SEVILLA BILTMORE
HAVANA CUBA

IRVING MOUNCE
MANAGER
ARLINGTON RESORT
HOT SPRINGS NATIONAL PARK
USA

CHAPTER 12

THE THREE DISSENTING Aquarians, having more or less recovered from their unsettling adventure at the House of Mystery, have arranged to meet in the partially constructed two-storey block-house on Pirate's Cove, at the south end—where, according to Bob Nettles, there exists some protection against the invisible forces at work on De Courcy Island.

Only Sydney Backstone continues to suffer. The radio in the House of Mystery appears in dreams as an evil apparatus with tentacles. Celia reported having received another spectral visitor—whose voice, they are both certain, exactly matched the Dark Adept.

Only the first floor, about ten foot squared, is complete. The walls are of squared timbers, with one tiny window per wall. The floor is made of cement, with a trap door in one corner. Above, joists and boards have been laid for the second floor, which is to overhang the first by two feet.

Construction is slow. Tradesmen from the mainland are no longer permitted to stay on the property overnight.

"Where is Nettles?"

"He should be here."

"And why *here*?"

"He insisted on it."

"Most annoying."

Backstone's pipe flares rhythmically in the semi-dark, like a warning signal.

They are growing nervous. It is almost time for the Prophecy, and their absence will be noticed—if not by Brother Osiris, then by his Isis, Madame Zura. It is said she functions as his spiritual antennae, detecting pockets of negativity like unpleasant smells.

"Roger, I warned you Bob might not appear. This is a very sensitive situation for him. I tell you, he was shaking when I last spoke to him."

"Bob is pretty high-strung," Backstone agrees. "Celia heard that his wife died in an auto crash and he hasn't been the same since."

"I expect he was high-strung to begin with," Flagler adds. "Jim Barley says he spent some time in the cuckoo's nest."

"Actually, he's been locked in his quarters all day," Linden says.

Backstone lifts a pair of bushy eyebrows like tufts of cat fur. "Locked in? There are no locked doors here. It's part of the Gospel."

"Not if you're sick. Could be contagious."

"It's the damp," Backstone says.

"Up here someone *always* has a cold," Flagler adds.

"Actually, I think he's afraid of the Brother," Linden says.

"Poppycock. Surely he doesn't think a locked door will protect him."

"That's only your opinion, Sydney."

"There must be some other explanation," Backstone says. "With the Dark Adept standing behind him, the Brother has no need for protection from human beings."

"Unless the Dark Adept is a figment of the imagination," Linden says, thinking about his legs—one step toward the House of Mystery and they went numb, yet returned to normal when he left the clearing. "Or it could have been a product of hypnosis—are we being hypnotized, Sydney?"

"My wife saw the Dark Adept, Elliot. I heard his voice. It wasn't all in our minds, and we weren't hypnotized."

"You switched on a radio, and you heard *someone's* voice. Which doesn't pass as solid evidence. As for your wife, everyone has nightmares."

"We have the evidence of our eyes and ears!"

"Sydney, if you want a Dark Adept, look no further than our Madame Zura. The hag does nothing but shriek at people—isn't that so, Roger?"

"Yep, that's my Muriel," Flagler says. "But in other ways she was a peach—with gifts that I miss... very much."

An embarrassed silence follows, broken by Flagler himself.

"To change the subject, what is this hole we're in?"

"It's a blockhouse, obviously. Did you not serve, Roger?" Linden harbours a veteran's scorn for shirkers.

"Poultry is an essential service, Elliot. In Florida we used blockhouses to protect plantations, only ours were made of stone."

"Bob said two more of these things are to be built. They're to fend off attacks by savages, following the collapse of civilization."

"Well, I say that makes good sense, Roger," Backstone says, tapping his pipe on a timber with a shower of sparks, then refilling the bowl from a leather pouch.

"Except," Linden says, "that the blockhouses are designed with firing positions on all *four* walls—facing seaward and facing *inland* as well, don't you see. Gentlemen, I am of the growing opinion that the Brother is not a prophet but a would-be tyrant."

Backstone re-lights his pipe, producing an odour like burning rope. "If that's the case, Elliot, then what earthly power crippled you on the way to the House of Mystery?"

Linden lights another cigarette. "I'm not ready to accept a hocus-pocus explanation. It could have been cramps in my feet."

Backstone's pipe puffs like a locomotive. "That seems like a bit of a stretch, Elliot—but then, a doubting Thomas will grasp at anything. And what's your opinion, Roger?"

Flagler, the non-smoker, speaks while coughing: "There is a third possibility. Could a Dark Adept be speaking to the Brother—*over the radio?*"

Another pause. Flagler himself doesn't know quite what he meant by that.

Backstone removes his pipe from his mouth. "By heaven, you may have hit on it."

Linden heaves an audible sigh but says nothing.

"Radio waves," Backstone observes, "are invisible. Their reach goes beyond the five senses. By Jove, surely it's not a stretch to think that powerful thoughts can do the same."

"Electrical waves passing through the air..." Flagler flutters his hands hopelessly, for the subject has gone beyond him.

"Or through *bodies*," Backstone says. "I recall Dr. Wickland, who treated patients with electrical shocks to dislodge spirits of the dead."

"I heard that violet rays will cure anything," Flagler says.

Having run out of hypotheses, they reach a preliminary conclusion: that the most plausible explanation is that a Dark Adept is guiding the Brother over the radio, using the voice of the announcer—who is himself possessed—as a medium.

Linden finds this utterly preposterous and would say so, if only he could explain his numb feet.

WOMEN WILL MURDER *their husbands. Armies will rebel against their commanders. Allies will fire upon one another—as the spiral spins ever faster, criminals grow richer, and honest people bow down to the swastika and the red star.*

The hour has struck for the world to be plowed under. The soil is to be prepared, and the seeds sown for the coming New Age.

I am the farmer, who must drive the plow.

The disciples have become fully absorbed in the day's prophecy, so that Linden, Flagler and Backstone manage to settle onto the grass without being noticed—or so they think.

GOOD EVENING. THIS *is the nightly news service of the Canadian National Railway, brought to you by the Vancouver* Evening Star.

In China, a rogue regiment of the National Revolutionary Army has thrown the city of Peking into chaos, while Australian coal miners have been locked out by their employers for refusing to accept a wage cut. In Nagyrév, Hungary, over forty men were poisoned by their wives, using arsenic extracted from flypaper and mixed into duck soup...

The US Coast Guard sank the Canadian schooner and alleged rum-runner I'm Alone *off the coast of Belize, while in British Columbia, Premier Tolmie voiced his support for the use of the lash and the deportation of Asians convicted of crimes involving drugs...*

In Chicago, gangster Al Capone has offered to pay tax on proceeds of crime, admitting to a large taxable income, and in Vancouver work has begun on the Marine Building, set to become, at eighteen storeys, the tallest in the Commonwealth, described by Mayor William Malkin as, quote, an emblem of Vancouver's growing stature on the world stage, unquote. In sports, Henry Segrave set a new land speed record of 230 miles per hour, while in women's hockey the Vancouver Amazons defeated the Edmonton Monarchs two to one, and Hapoel Allenby of Tel Aviv shut out Maccabi Hasmonean of Jerusalem four to nothing, winning the Palestine Cup...

You have been listening to the nightly news service, courtesy of the Vancouver Evening Star. *As we end our broadcast we wish all our listeners—in the air, in the woods, in the mines and lighthouses, and especially our shut-ins—a restful good evening.*

THE WEST INDIA AND PANAMA TELEGRAPH COMPANY
TELÉGRAFO

JUNE 11 1929

INSP CALVIN HOOK
VANCOUVER POLICE DEPARTMENT
200 CORDOVA ST
VANCOUVER
CANADA

SORRY ALVIN PINE LEFT CUBA SEND MESSAGES TO
COPLEY PLAZA BOSTON

MANUEL YEPE
MANAGER
HOTEL SEVILLA BILTMORE

CHAPTER 13

MCCURDY LEAVES THE studio in a sour mood.

Before the broadcast, as always, he skimmed over the day's mail; it consisted of a pronunciation critique, an objection to something coarse in the news, a proposal of marriage—and one message that drew his full attention.

> *You have put yourself in the service of demons. You hate-inspired misanthrope, you prevaricator, you cowardly traducer, you pusillanimous purveyor of empty words, you will die, choked by the lies you spread, your mind dead to truth, loathsome maggots infesting your brain.*
> *—A Friend*

He stops by Mrs. Dixon's desk on his way out and stands there until she stops pretending he's invisible.

Turning her wheeled office chair in his direction, Mrs. Dixon lights a Sportsman (though well aware of his allergies). "Yes, Mr. McCurdy, what can I do for you?" she asks, like the woman in the complaints booth at Hudson's Bay.

"Nothing, Mrs. Dixon. Nothing whatsoever. You have done quite enough today, in fact you've outdone yourself. You've turned the news—tragic news, comic news and human interest news—into a hallucination on par with the work of René Magritte."

"Mr. McCurdy, I don't have the least idea who this person is you're talking about, but I have said it before and I will say it again—the copy sequence is *sequenced*. Your copy is in the order it came on the wires."

"Oh but you're not just the telegraphist, are you, Mrs. Dixon? You're the telegraphist-*editor*. You remove items that in your estimation aren't of public interest, am I right?"

"And what is your point?"

"One might refer to your work as a sort of collage, like a Picasso or Braque."

Mrs. Dixon narrows her eyes and extends a short, sharp forefinger. "Mr. McCurdy, I have no idea what you are insinuating, but understand me when I tell you, there is no meaning to the sequence. No. Meaning. Do you understand me? There never was a meaning, there never is going to be a meaning. Any meaning derived from the order of the news is the product of your sick imagination. You are making spurious allegations against myself and I am on the verge of lodging a complaint of harassment."

"Ah, dear Mrs. Dixon, now I get the picture."

"And what picture might that be, Mr. McCurdy?"

"While you are driving me to a nervous breakdown, your husband is on deck, winding up, getting ready to step up to the plate—mind, he'll have to do something about that lisp."

Before Mrs. Dixon loses her dentures, he turns tail and heads down the hall and out of the building, repeating to himself the phrase from *As a Man Thinketh*: *Self-control is strength. Right thought is mastery. Calmness is power.*

To that he might add, *And Mrs. Dixon will be a corpse one day.* Smiling with imagined satisfaction, he pushes open the plate glass door and descends the wet stone steps to Hastings Street.

"Mr. Gowd-Evening!"

As McCurdy steps into the drizzle he is startled by the man's tone of sardonic mockery, spoken in a hard Manchester accent. He turns to behold a horse-faced fellow with protruding ears, dressed in a sharp three-piece suit, a long, heavy overcoat and a·tweed flat-top cap.

The situation itself is a familiar one. Every so often he comes out the door and is greeted by someone who wants to see what Mr. Good-Evening looks like, or to take issue with something Mr. Good-Evening said. He reminds himself not to be drawn into conversation, or he'll be here all night.

"Actually, sir, the name is McCurdy. Mr. Good-Evening exists only on the airwaves. So if you don't mind, I'll bid you—"

"They said yow'd say that. Yer a cute hoor, ain't ye? A real high-hat yer be..."

Feigning deafness, McCurdy turns away and heads briskly west, past the Strand Hotel and the Bank of Nova Scotia.

"Just a quiet word, Mr. Gowd-Evening, if yor nawt mindin'..."

Blast! The bugger is following him. Without glancing back, McCurdy pulls the collar of his coat up against the rain and presses on.

"They knows—yer get me? *They knows* 'bout yer Dork Adept!"

Oh, excellent. A lunatic as well.

Jaywalking briskly across Granville Street, McCurdy continues west at a speed walker's pace, past the enormous hole in the ground that will one day become the tallest structure in the Commonwealth, to the Quadra Club. The six-floor building covered with ivy was originally built to house the Veterans' Association, then repurposed as an alternative to the swankier Vancouver Club down the street. A facility for construction engineers, plant managers and that sort.

As he approaches the Quadra Club he quickens his pace, because he can sense his pursuer catching up—which inspires unpleasant memories involving schoolyard bullies, being pushed to the ground and having his glasses broken...

No. This line of thinking must stop. *Self-control is strength. Right thought is mastery.* He halts abruptly and wheels around to confront his pursuer.

Nobody.

He looks up and down the street, which is empty all the way to Granville.

Relaxing a bit, he turns back toward his destination—and there he is again! Now blocking the sidewalk ahead of him—a dandy with a cosh in one pocket and a razor in the other, leaning on a root knob walking stick.

How did he do that?

A bogeyman from childhood pops into his mind, based on the dime novel *Spring-Heeled Jack: The Terror of London*, about a demon with claws for hands and eyes like red balls of fire. Fear of Spring-Heeled Jack compelled him to lock his bedroom window throughout one scorching Toronto summer.

The chill trickling down the nape of his neck has nothing to do with the weather.

IF BROADCASTERS ARE more susceptible, even credulous, than other performers when it comes to bizarre and mystical events, it may be because, as an invisible presence coming from the sky, radio is easily the most ephemeral and mysterious.

Oliver Lodge, who first detected radio waves through a wave detector called a coherer, was convinced that his receiving apparatus enabled spirits to communicate with the living.

And since the war, if one is to go by the news, mystical events have been common as house fires.

No news broadcaster fails, once a week at least, to report on a strange occurrence: the family photograph with the dead soldier reflected on the china teapot. The farmer's wife who watched the sinking of the *Lusitania* through her kitchen window.

Such events have been steady news fodder since the Angel of Mons.

Only last night, with a straight face, Mr. Good-Evening read a spirit message from murdered Czar Nicholas II, delivered by Sir Arthur Conan Doyle. Listeners hearkened to the words of a murdered Romanov, as received by a writer of mystery novels and reported by the redoubtable Mr. Good-Evening—followed by stock market reports and a political scandal.

And now he is faced with a man who can be in two places at once.

Self-control is strength. Right thought is mastery. Calmness is power...

McCurdy takes a deep breath and prepares to brass it out against this menacing creature in an Ulster overcoat by attempting a Lon Chaney impression.

"Listen, buster, I'm tired and wet, I don't make or write the news, so buzz off outta here before I call a copper."

With a grin that is anything but friendly, his pursuer takes a step toward him. "Oh blarmey, ain't the Dark Adept talkin' toof?"

"What did you say?"

"Ar, they said yow might pretend yow donna what 'tis."

"Is a Dark Adept like the Phantom of the Opera?"

"Oo yor a cool one in yer monkey suit." He moves another step closer with that sideways grin, one hand buried in his coat pocket, the other with a tight grip on that nasty-looking walking stick.

"Booter nay melts in thy big fat gob..."

McCurdy's left leg has begun to quiver, which may be a sign he is about to piss himself.

"Is this gentleman pestering you, sir?"

The concierge.

Dressed for the evening in a checked suit, boater hat and precisely clipped Duke Ellington moustache, Paris stands in the vapour under the street lamp as though in a spotlight.

"I will repeat my question. Mr. McCurdy, sir, is this gentleman bothering you?"

McCurdy's leg begins to relax. As a matter of fact, Paris, yes, yes, I'm afraid he is."

Paris nods, then turns his focus on the attacker. "Sir, Mr. McCurdy is a member of the Quadra Club, of which I am the concierge. I would ask you to please continue on your way."

"A conchee aire, are ye?" Exposing some long, brown teeth, the hoodlum opens his coat to display a heavy belt buckle with sharpened edges. "Mind thy business, darkie, an' get yorself back to the zoo."

The concierge makes a *tsk-tsk* sound. "Sir, I am afraid you are seriously out of order."

"Yer gettin' uppity are ye, moss-head? Well, take this for a start—"

In a smooth, well-practised motion, the man pulls his belt free of its loops and doubles it so that the buckle becomes a weapon, while his other hand holds his stick by the end, so that the root serves as a head basher, and strides purposefully toward the concierge, lifting the stick overhead and wielding the belt like a whip—and finds himself seated on the sidewalk with an exploded nose in the middle of his face and blood cascading onto his waistcoat.

Neither he nor McCurdy saw the blow. The concierge seems not to have budged, except that his hands are knotted into fists the size of bowling balls.

Staunching the blood with a wadded handkerchief pressed against the middle of his face, the hoodlum picks up his cap with his free hand, struggles onto his feet with the help of his stick, stuffs his belt into his coat pocket, then turns to McCurdy and speaks in a voice distorted by the blood-soaked handkerchief and his broken nose. "I got a message fer ye. Get thysel' off the radio or yor in fer a shock."

"What in the blazes are you on about, sir?"

"Oi give you yor warning."

As Paris steps between them his voice takes on a different tone: "Let me give you a warning, you low-down honky ofay!"

The hoodlum backs away until safely out of reach. "Stick it up yor arse, Mr. Gowd-Evenin', an yors too, ye coon."

For a long moment McCurdy and the concierge watch the man's receding back as he slouches under street lamps as far as Granville, then turns the corner and disappears.

"May I ask, sir, what that was about?"

"I don't have the faintest idea, Paris. If I didn't see blood on the sidewalk, I'd think he was some sort of spook."

"Man oh man. Whoever he is, that Cletus is baked."

"Whatever it was you just said, I completely agree."

"Will there be anything further? I have a gig at nine thirty."

"You've exceeded all expectations, Paris. Expect a handsome gratuity in the morning."

McCurdy enters the Quadra Club lobby, beset by the mental image of Spring-Heeled Jack.

CHAPTER 14

THE FRONT DOOR jangles as DI Hook enters Leonard's Café and nods to the cashier, who sits slumped on a stool behind the cash register, preoccupied with an issue of *Photoplay*.

Halfway down the counter sits a bull-necked man in a railway cap, its stripes obscured by oil and grease, and a worn locoman's jacket with patched cuffs and elbows. He is currently digging his fork and knife into a slab of meat loaf, using his fork as a shovel and his knife a saw.

The waitress is, as usual, nowhere to be seen.

Standing beside Quam's booth, Hook watches Quam as he digs into a steamed apple dumpling slathered with syrup of some sort, with a large tumbler of milk on the side. (There was a time when he and Jeanie could sit down and eat an entire meal without strident interruption from a third party.)

The man's concentration is such that only when Hook clears his throat does Quam sense a presence and glance upward, forkful in mid-air.

"Inspector Hook, sir. Hello." He puts his fork down, licks the syrup from his lips and gazes at the piece of dumpling he's saving for last: *Adieu my love, for now.*

"Please, Mr. Quam, keep going. A man must eat."

"Do I hear sarcasm in your voice, sir?"

"Not sarcasm, Sergeant. Envy."

Taking the bench opposite, Hook waves to Carmella at the cash register until the unfamiliar back-and-forth motion in her peripheral vision inspires her to look up from a glossy photo of Anita Page: *How Stars Suffer to Be Beautiful.*

"Coffee please, Carmella. High and dry."

With a put-upon sigh, Carmella rises from her stool, retrieves a mug, crosses to the urn and twists open a spigot allowing black, steaming liquid to pour into the mug. Hook envies her poise, her ability to serve and sulk at the same time as she performs this menial chore, which is not in her job description.

At this point in his life it seems as though he envies just about everyone.

His molar throbs agreement.

He takes a sip of less-than-terrible coffee, ponders the dog and dead bird on the cup, then looks up—only to find Quam looking back at him with an expression of concern.

"Yes, Sergeant Quam, what is it?"

"Excuse me, sir, but... you don't look quite up to snuff."

"What?"

"Peaky. Poorly. Under the weather."

"Well observed, Mr. Quam. Lucille has colic. Do you know what that word means?"

"Never heard it, sir. Words mean nothing until they do." Quam scratches his chin thoughtfully, as though he has just said something interesting.

Hook takes a sip of hot coffee, careful to avoid his bad tooth. "Mr. Quam, can we move on to the purpose of our meeting? Do you or don't you have anything to report?"

The sergeant opens his notebook—reluctantly, as though it contains a small poisonous snake. "Yes, sir," he says, nodding fatalistically. "I'm afraid we do."

Hook counts the remaining cigarettes in his pack; he must postpone lighting another if he is ever going to get down to ten a day...

"As you suggested, sir, I took a good look at Tucker, Palmer and Pine's client list. Mr. Tucker's accounts were chiefly via New York— no doubt deposited in numbered accounts as well—and it struck me that Mr. Pine is in New York as we speak."

"I took it that far myself, actually. Sent any number of wires. People on the other end have been coy—as has Mr. Pine himself."

"I'd hate to suggest you use the telephone, sir."

"A long-distance call to New York is eight seventy for the first three minutes, and the clock doesn't stop there. Do the math, Sergeant, it's your specialty."

"I give you that, sir, the cost is theoretically limitless. But it is a murder investigation, after all."

"Not really. The chief's mind is made up, as is everyone else's."

"A made-up mind is a thing of the past."

"What is that supposed to mean?"

"It can never be altered."

"Oh. I see. Quite."

Hook remains unconvinced that Quam understands a word of what he just said; maybe there's a ventriloquist in the next booth.

"Mr. Quam, the chief isn't fond of having his judgment questioned, and the chief isn't fond of me. If I were to request extra paper clips he'd laugh in my face. You, on the other hand, might have questions to pursue in your capacity—as part of a *fraud* investigation." Hook sits back and lets the suggestion hang.

Quam blanches at the idea. "Oh dear."

"Think about it, Sergeant: Why would New Yorkers collaborate with a Howe Street brokerage? Don't they have chisellers of their own?"

Quam returns to his notes. "It seems that, for the New York Stock Exchange, Vancouver might as well be Timbuktu. But that's precisely the attraction, don't you see. The VSE is, to American investors, an invisible place to put one's money—and no brokerage on Howe Street is as discreet as Tucker, Palmer and Pine. They have many more than their share of untraceable accounts, and their name appears on an unusual number of subpoenas involving tax audits.

"As for New York, funds to Tucker, Palmer and Pine flow from Logan and Bryan, through a Canadian whose name is J. Walter Addison. Addison has been doing business in New York ever since parliament denounced him as a war profiteer."

"Rugeley Camp was a gold mine for black marketers. Fortunes made in off-ration tobacco and sausages."

"Oh, Addison was bigger than that, sir. As an advisor to General Hughes, he sublet contracts to companies that had little money and no facilities, in return for a whopping commission. It was a major scandal—but I expect you didn't follow Canadian news when you were overseas."

"Every man in the army knew about the cardboard boots. And I remember a trenching shovel that weighed a ton and had a hole in the blade."

"That was the MacAdam Shield Shovel, sir. Designed by a young lady who happened to be General Hughes's personal secretary."

Hook's tooth has begun to throb in earnest. He notes, with alarm, the lit cigarette that seems to have jammed itself between his fingers.

"Mr. Quam, you realize I'm going to have to speak to the chief about this."

"Do your duty as you see it, sir. But for heaven's sake, please don't mention my name!"

FOUR FIFTEEN IN the morning after a miserable day at work, and for a blessed half-hour Lucille has been sleeping soundly. Jeanie has dozed off as well, her head in the crook of his shoulder, pinning his left side to the mattress. Splayed across his chest is his open copy of *The Rainbow Trail.*

His tooth thuds softly, like the bass drum at a funeral parade.

His meeting with Chief Blatchford didn't go well.

Staring at the ceiling, picking at that fresh scab of a memory, he tries to piece together at what point the interaction went so desperately awry.

Hook's plan was to advance the suggestion that, given the reputation of the VSE, investigating the business affairs of Tucker's firm was nothing more than due diligence. That the sheer violence of the murder might, for example, be the rage of a fleeced investor.

Not to mention Tucker, Palmer and Pine's connection to J. Walter Addison, whose past dealings were denounced by Ottawa.

Quam's findings determine that the firm's bills were routed through Mr. Addison's suite at the Hotel Astor in New York City.

Hook's conclusion—that the scene of the crime was relevant to both investigations—seemed obvious.

After making his case, DI Hook looked up from his notes, fully expecting at least a tentative nod.

Not so.

To Blatchford, the linking of a murder investigation and a fraud investigation amounted to "blaming the victim for the crime." This absurd conclusion was followed by yet another sermon on interdepartmental meddling, bureaucratic empire building and the slippery slope to a breakdown of the chain of command.

A union agitator could not have received a colder reception from Chief Blatchford, who informed DI Hook, in no uncertain terms, that, despite their past association, he and Sergeant Quam are to conduct their respective investigations as though they live on separate planets.

This was followed by a verbal kick in the teeth and the bum's rush out the door.

The inspector is now stuck with a direct order—disobedience a fireable offence. And he with a mortgage and two other mouths to feed.

It's simple: Blatchford will not agree to any idea that comes out of his beak.

Snookered again.

His tooth is a small fist pounding the wall.

He attempts to focus on *The Rainbow Trail*, which has something to do with cowboys and Mormons. Soon the creature at the foot of the bed will emit a sound like a Tasmanian devil, and another round will begin.

CHAPTER 15

SERGEANT QUAM DOFFS his hat, which has a small rip between the brim and the crown.

"Miss, my name is Detective Sergeant Quam, Vancouver police, and I wish to speak with Mr. Palmer."

"Do you have an appointment, sir?"

"No. As I said, I'm with the police." Quam adopts a placid expression, a face people can neither read nor remember.

A small wrinkle appears between the receptionist's sculpted eyebrows, which Quam takes to be a frown. Around her pale neck is what appears to be an expensive dog collar, made of silver and studded with large, red stones shaped like Chiclets.

The receptionist emits a resigned sigh (*Some people!*), lifts one eyebrow, and with a shrug of her silk blouse (top two buttons open, swelling of soft cleavage) casts a pitying glance at the copper's tattered straw fedora. She then rises slowly and heads for the frosted-glass door leading to the inner office.

Behind the door, Quam can hear a male voice hollering at someone.

He takes note of the receptionist's gams (pleasingly muscled), and below them an expensive-looking pair of spike-heeled shoes, not unlike the shoes that...

No. Rather than allow his mind to intrude on the business of homicide, he looks at his own shoes, which are too narrow for his feet and give him blisters.

A direct order, according to Hook. No interdepartmental meddling. Disobedience a fireable offence.

Police work wasn't always like wearing a harness and blinkers. Top brass didn't always follow a policy of industrial specialization, with specific limits to what avenues a member is permitted to pursue—as though a criminal can't be guilty of two separate crimes, and the victim can't be a criminal as well.

This is not what Quam had in mind when he applied to the force.

As a boy in Moose Jaw, he regularly spent his entire week's allowance in order to view all fifteen episodes of the *Master Mystery* at the Rex. As much as anything, his choice of career was inspired by Quentin Locke; he aspired to be Locke, whose fast thinking combats an organized crime syndicate, directed and protected by an evil automaton.

Sometimes he wonders if he has become not Quentin Locke but the automaton—a bug-eyed robot.

No. A voice within distinguishes man from machine—his conscience. As a small child, his conscience was his mother, applying a strap to his rear; then his conscience was the Lord, as described by Reverend Savage of the Church of God, who spoke such words of wisdom as "There can be no good in society if there is none in the people. You cannot make a good omelet with bad eggs."

It was Reverend Savage who put Quam in touch with his inner policeman, on the lookout for bad people in a world where everyone who isn't a policeman is a person of interest, if not a suspect.

And the result? After ten years' service, are there fewer bad people now than there were before?

Quam checks his pocket watch (nickel plated, brass peeking through); he has been cooling his heels for nearly fifteen minutes in this overheated cigar box.

When he joined the VPD a decade ago, Quam was one of the last to experience the crusader-like certainty of purpose invested in a policeman under the War Measures Act, to investigate a crime as he saw fit, in a hands-on quest for a solution. (These days, if you tap a man on the shoulder it's a police assault.)

Gloomily, he examines Palmer's tickertape machine perched on a table in the far corner, making a constant metallic chatter like a barber on pep pills. He runs his palm over the bullet-shaped glass bubble while the machine vomits a tapeworm of numbers into a metal basket.

The frosted-glass door opens and the receptionist emerges with the same air of strained patience. "Mr. Palmer is very, very busy, sir, but he will see you now, for just a few minutes."

"Thank you, miss. You've been most co-operative."

The receptionist watches the copper disappear behind the glass door and frowns. Something about his attitude makes her nervous. Polite bozos in cheap suits are the creeps a girl needs to worry about.

ALTHOUGH THE SMELL in Palmer's office still retains a faint whiff of paint and lumber, it already reeks with the pong of stale smoke—thanks to the cigar box on Palmer's desk, the rack of pipes on top of the rosewood liquor cabinet and the cigarette protruding from Palmer's mouth.

Quam loathes the smell of tobacco. (He didn't dare mention that to Hook during their Nelson confinement.) Yesterday at Leonard's Café, even before he lit one, the inspector reeked of smoke—mixed with, for some reason, oil of clove.

Seated in a tufted leather office chair behind a massive mahogany desk, Edgar Palmer waggles his cigarette up and down as he speaks on one of his two telephones—unnaturally loud, with exaggerated consonants and with frequent repetition; obviously he's on a long-distance call.

"What? What's that? Did you say *contract* or *contact*? Oh. Yeah, that is a factor. No, not an actor, a factor. That's right... Pardon, didn't catch that..."

Alcohol-infused smoke wafts through the room with each syllable the man utters.

Quam knows when he is being deliberately ignored. Palmer wants him at a disadvantage straight off, to stand here cooling his heels, waiting politely to be noticed. The sergeant maintains a calm demeanour. It may or may not be true that he dislikes this man, but personal feelings have no place on the front lines of justice.

"What? What was that? Jesus, is that a fact? Sharpe and Dohme is doing market's what? Okay, okay, then that's a buy. I said, a buy! Buy—as in 'buy and sell'! Right, yeah..."

Roaming about the room, Quam surveys the mahogany mantel above the fireplace insert, the silver trophy cups and the little statues of a man swinging a golf club grouped around a photo of Palmer, looking raffish. (Quam can't get his hair to lie down like that, no matter how much brilliantine he slathers on.)

"What? No, no, don't... Miss, we haven't finished! Don't cut us off! Goddammit! Miss, the girl was trying to cut us off!"

In a framed photo at one end of the mantelpiece, the subject, in a tailor-made tuxedo (Quam's armpits are chafed raw), poses beside a number of women who look like or wish to look like Fay Wray, and who seem to be demonstrating the number of ways it's possible to wrap one's head in silk.

A bounder and a cad. Quam has known the type since Mother read him *Hurlbut's Story of the Bible* at age ten—Absalom, the traitor who laid with his father's concubines...

At last, the conversation behind the desk, or the pretense of a conversation, winds down.

"Can tell it's a *what*? What was that? Yeah, things are, er, stable for the moment. Stable, I said. Stable. Rhymes with *table*!"

Standing near the window, Quam pretends to examine two team photographs—rugby and hockey—evidently from high school and college. Further along the wall, he pauses before the mounted trophy of a deer who looks as though he stuck his head through a window and is startled to see someone in there.

"Yes, in fact there's one of them here now. Christ, not now, later! Right. Okay. I'll keep you abreast. Abreast! Oh, never mind..."

The subject disconnects without saying goodbye, suggesting familiarity, if not collusion, with the person on the other end of the line.

After butting his cigarette in a triangular silver ashtray, Tucker turns to acknowledge the pathetic copper in the cheap suit, standing beside the buck's head and looking just as stunned.

"Yes, Officer, what do you people want from me now?"

A cheeky fellow. Though the sergeant maintains his placid half smile, his eyes have begun to water.

"Mr. Palmer, sir, my name is Detective Sergeant Quam. I'm with the Vancouver Police Department, and I've come to ask you a few questions, if you don't mind."

The subject heaves a theatrical sigh. "*Mind?* Sergeant, I've been questioned by half a dozen officers already. I've given you people hours of my time. I've already told you everything I know. Ralph was like a brother to me. I had hoped you'd have the decency to allow myself and Ralph's widow to mourn in peace."

A smooth customer.

"Mourn in *peace*, Mr. Palmer? Do the recent, er, unfortunate events, seem *peaceful* to you, sir?"

A pause, while Tucker extracts a cork-tipped Player's from a silver box without offering one to his visitor. "And what's that supposed to mean, Officer?"

Quam forms his expression of wide-eyed simplicity. "Sir, as his close friend and colleague, surely you're eager to get to the bottom of this. And by the way, how close *were* you and Mr. Tucker, in reality? Is it possible you weren't quite as close as all that?"

Palmer taps the desk surface with his cigarette, several times as he gives this copper the once-over. Without breaking contact with the copper's watery gaze, he fiddles with his gas lighter so that the stink of petrol fumes merges with the current pong—in effect, a gas attack.

"Are you accusing me of murder, Officer? Should I call my lawyer?" Palmer pretends to reach for the telephone.

"Oh no, sir. Not a bit of it. Homicide isn't my department, you see. I'm with the *fraud* department."

While framing an appropriate response, Tucker contemplates the lit end of his cigarette. His face is soft for an athlete, pale for a golfer, and his skin has acquired a slippery, frog-belly look.

At the same time, the sergeant has to admire Palmer's suiting and haberdashery—the five-button waistcoat, the striped shirt with starched white collar, the maroon bow tie with pointed ends. Once again Quam misses his uniform; it may have been scratchy, but it commanded more respect than a fourteen-dollar business suit.

"Did you say the *fraud* department, Officer?" Palmer's eyes turn flinty.

"That's correct, sir. This visit is part of an ongoing inquiry into illegal practices at the Vancouver Stock Exchange."

Palmer lifts his eyebrows in a mock display of alarm. "*Practices*, Officer? What sort of practices are you talking about?"

"Regretfully, sir, it's quite a list. There is false underwriting—as with Verity and Sims—and we found bucketing and wash trading everywhere. And in your case, there is the question of—oh dear, what's the word?"

"This is all Greek to me, Officer. I don't understand a word you are—"

"Jitney! Of course! That's the word I was looking for."

"Is that a farm implement, or a new dance?"

"Ha, sir, a witty riposte indeed! It involves stock needlessly passing from one broker to another—in order to disguise the identity of the buyer, don't you see."

Palmer makes a point of looking at his wristwatch, a rectangular Gruen that cost at least seventy-five dollars. "Sergeant, I don't know what you're insinuating, but I think it's time—"

"The department also took a look at Tucker, Palmer and Pine's client list, sir. We noticed that almost all of your files are numbered companies—owned by other numbered companies. And when the client's name did appear, we couldn't source the holdings. For example, there is a Mr. Addison of New York, whose investments seem to be itemized in some sort of code. Such secrecy rings alarm bells, as you can well imagine."

As Quam expected, the subject promptly climbs onto his high horse. "I see, Officer. That's what you do for a living—sniffing around company files for technical infractions." He takes a deep drag of his cigarette and leans back in his chair, a display of patience before a pest.

"Anonymous numbered bank accounts are a Swiss practice, sir, not British at all."

"Sergeant Quam, it will surely come as no surprise to you that privacy and security are fundamental here in Canada, as in Europe. In some cases, yes, our clients invest through intermediaries, whose names appear on a separate file."

"Such as our Mr. Addison?"

"Mr. Addison may or may not be one example. In other cases, the client prefers to invest through the registration number of the company involved."

"Registered with what, sir?"

"Well, it depends on the jurisdiction, of course," Palmer says, as though reminding the officer that grass is usually green.

"I understand you, sir, but surely you also have files in your possession containing names to go with the numbers."

"Certainly—but it would not necessarily be *my* files. Ralph, Alvin and I sometimes blend accounts, but there are others we hold separately. And of course everyone has access to the general files. But if the files were in another partner's account, the names behind them would be a complete mystery to me."

"But surely you do know the names behind *your* files—am I not right in that, sir?"

"Yes."

"When may I see them, sir?"

"Not before you obtain a judicial warrant."

"Mr. Palmer, it is unusual for an individual who is not under suspicion to demand such a step." Quam dabs a tear from at his right eye, as though a sadness has come over him.

"Sergeant, I know my rights, and I know the rights of my clients. I doubt that any judge will provide a warrant on the basis of your whimsical fishing expedition."

With a reluctant sigh and in a surprisingly adroit move for a husky man, Quam circles the desk to Palmer's plush chair and clutches a fistful of the subject's shirt and tie, with sufficient force that both collar stays spring to the floor with a musical *ping*, hoisting the broker out of his chair by the neck. Momentarily, Quam checks Palmer's ankles and sees that—yes indeed, he is wearing a pair of dove-grey spats. (From seeing Lew Cody in *Souls for Sale*, he knows that shady characters have a fondness for spats.)

Holding the subject by his shirtfront so that he dangles inches over the chair, Sergeant Quam explains the situation: "Mr. Palmer, since Mr. Ponzi—"

The subject croaks, "Oh shit, that again."

"It caused six banks to fail in Boston, sir. The fraud department has orders to examine the Vancouver Stock Exchange. Due diligence, don't you see. Do you see, Mr. Palmer? Do you?"

Palmer, whose face has turned a cranberry colour, makes a vague hissing sound with the back of his throat.

For one shining moment, in his mind Quam is Quentin Locke in "The Challenge," shorting the enemy's circuits with an audacious move.

"The fraud department takes a dim view of firms that are less than transparent in their dealings. You can understand that, can't you, sir? It indicates a devious nature. For example, say a man has an affair with the wife of his dead partner..."

DS Quam sees the gelid glaze of terror cover Palmer's eyes, and knows he has hit the mark—though he was thinking of a Lew Cody movie at the time.

For emphasis, he takes hold of the subject's brilliantined hair with his free hand to hoist him just a bit farther above his chair. "Do you hear me, Mr. Palmer, sir? Do you understand what I'm saying? *Do you?*"

The subject's head twitches forward and back while his mouth opens and closes like a landed fish. DS Quam lets go of Palmer's hair and shirtfront so that he drops onto his chair, where he doubles over, with soft gurgling sounds coming from the back of his throat.

Using his handkerchief, Quam wipes the orange-scented brilliantine from the fingers of his left hand. "We would appreciate your co-operation, sir. I wonder if we could have the names behind those numbered companies by, say, this afternoon?"

Palmer nods and makes more guttural sounds.

"Otherwise, by heaven, I shall come back and kick your guts around the room. Thank you, Mr. Palmer. No need to see me to the door, I'll let myself out."

As he exits Palmer's office, DS Quam nods to the receptionist in a friendly way.

He once discussed the justifiable use of force at Bible study with Reverend Savage, including the acceptable actions of a policeman in a Christian context. They concluded that, while the Old Testament proscribes killing and stealing from thy neighbour, and bedding his wife, it holds nothing against *intimidating* thy neighbour. And did Jesus not drive out the money changers with a whip, smash the furniture, and denounce the temple as a den of thieves?

Could not the same thing be said of the Vancouver Stock Exchange?

On balance, the interview went well.

After years working at a desk job, one becomes rusty. It's a tonic to get back to old-fashioned police work, once in a while.

ASSUMPTIONS QUESTIONED IN FLAPPER CASE
What of the Deadly T-Strap?
Edward McCurdy
Special To
The Evening Star

There is nothing like a female murder suspect to bring out the banality of the male imagination.

In the Dora Decker case, the ink was hardly dry on the arrest warrant before the young lady was dubbed the Fatal Flapper (headline writers are apes for alliteration)—who, it is claimed, gored Ralph Tucker to death with the heel of her I. Miller shoe, for no apparent reason.

Based on what can scarcely be called an investigation, Vancouver police have chosen the road that leads to Hollywood, with a titillating title to complete the package. Surely by now a movie producer—perhaps Louis B. Mayer?—has approached Louise Brooks to play the role.

Publishers are understandably reluctant to abandon a profitable storyline just because holes have begun to appear in what was assumed to be an open-and-shut case.

By general agreement, an attitude of "let things be" prevails, starting with the VPD, who are understandably reluctant to face the prospect of looking like dolts.

To see how this entire cock-up began, let us begin with the shoes themselves.

The fact that the stiletto shoes in question retail at eighteen dollars made no impression on the men running the case, who could hardly be expected to get their wives to check the price of shoes at Eaton's. Nor was anyone moved to ask Miss Decker herself how a secretary manages to budget for shoes that cost half a week's wages.

While the price of women's shoes alone would scarcely sway a man with three-dollar oxfords on his feet, investigators might have opened one eye to the fact that the shoes were purchased, not by the accused, but by the *victim*.

Asked about this, the receptionist at Tucker, Palmer and Pine (who asked that her name be withheld) confirmed that the purpose of her employer's generosity was to present the client with an attractive, stylish female staff: "We were told it would speak to the success of the brokerage and allow for business to be conducted in a conducive atmosphere."

Put another way, the girls wore costumes in a stage show, for the benefit of an extremely small audience.

Asked who of the remaining partners is paying her salary, she replied, "Oh, it arrives every two weeks, same as usual."

Asked whose signature appears on the cheque, she replied, "Why Mr. Pine, of course. Mr. Pine has always signed the cheques."

Speaking over long-distance telephone from New York, a woman claiming to be his secretary informed this reporter that Mr. Pine was "out for the day," followed by something indecipherable, at which point we were disconnected. Leaving one to wonder if Mr. Alvin Pine, in fact, exists.

But to return to the shoes: Had investigators taken more than a glance at Miss Decker's suede T-straps, they might have noted the total lack of scuffing from everyday wear—which means that they cannot have been worn on a Vancouver street, even once.

Indeed, another employee confirmed the existence of a standing order that, outside working hours, shoes must remain in the office; when on their own time, staff were to slog through the mud in their own footwear.

Conclusion: For Mr. Tucker to have been beaten to death with Miss Decker's shoe, Miss Decker herself *need not have been in the room.*

Adding to this rather large sliver of doubt, the eminent city analyst F.C.V. Condon, unable to identify the death-dealing blow, now doubts whether the Fatal Flapper's shoe was the murder weapon at all.

Thanks to one scurrilous headline, an innocent girl could be the victim of a grotesque injustice.

Meanwhile, sources within the VPD revealed to this reporter that Tucker, Palmer and Pine are currently under investigation by the fraud department, particularly with regard to their arrangements with J. Walter Addison, a Canadian investment broker, based in New York, who stands accused of war profiteering.

And yet, sources say VPD chief Blatchford has specifically forbidden officers with either the fraud department or the homicide squad from investigating a possible connection between Tucker's business dealings and his murder.

Like naive racetrack gamblers, investigators have bet the farm on one horse—the premise that a slender young woman beat a burly man to death with her shoe, with a crystal ashtray, a letter opener and bronze rugby trophies well within reach.

It would seem that, with reputations and promotions on the line, the VPD has become a train of one-track minds.

Toot, toot, Chief Blatchford.

PART II

Don't test the depth of the river with both feet.

—Al Capone

CHAPTER 16

STANDING IN FRONT of the microphone with his earphones on, waiting for Elwood to give him his cue, McCurdy skims through the day's mail: a pronunciation critique, an objection to something, a proposal of marriage—and another poison-pen letter, this one written in either blood or brownish ink.

> *Mr. Good-Evening, we know the beast inside you spewing evil. For the sake of all you must be gotten rid of, and you will. We know where you live. This is not a joke.*
> *—A Friend*

At this point, Elwood's voice intrudes over the headphones: *Mr. McCurdy, can you hear me?*

"Yes, Elwood, I can hear you."

Transmitting.

A raised hand appears behind the glass for the five-second countdown, followed by a forefinger thrust in his direction, his cue.

GOOD EVENING. HERE *is the* CNR *news service, brought to you by the* Vancouver Evening Star.

In the Italian general election, where opposition parties have been banned, the Fascist Party won in a landslide, receiving ninety-eight per cent of votes cast, while in British Columbia, opposition leader Patullo has presented to Premier Tolmie a dozen accusations of corrupt patronage practices, and in Saskatchewan the Conservative government unseated the Liberals over the Catholic schools issue, with the support of the Ku Klux Klan...

In the United States, the Internal Revenue Service and the treasury department have begun a full investigation into the activities of Chicago

gangster Al Capone. And in sports, the Boston Bruins have won the
Stanley Cup, beating the New York Rangers in a two-nothing sweep...

You have been listening to the nightly news service of the Vancouver
Evening Star. As we end our broadcast, we wish all our listeners, in the
air, in the woods, in the mines, in lighthouses, a restful good...

Something happened.

An enormous hissing neon sign tells him that he has somehow
been transported to Happyland, the amusement park at the edge of
town, teeming with visitors on a Sunday afternoon.

How did he get here? Did he fall asleep mid-broadcast?

To his right, accompanied by the strutting strains of *Entry of the*
Gladiators, thrill rides dip and whirl—the shoot the chute, carousel,
Ferris wheel and, towering above all, the Giant Dipper.

To his left stretches the midway, a temporary street of canvas
shelters where pedestrians gather in jostling clumps, eager to play
the six cat game, the test-your-strength challenge and the wheel of
fortune. At the far end, beyond the sounds of winning and losing,
stretches an extended line of platforms where, beneath lurid canvas backdrops, tuxedo-clad speakers with walking sticks invite the
passing tide of humanity into tents, to behold the Pincushion Man,
Martha the Armless Wonder, Ray the Pony Boy, Jolly Pot and the
Dancing Fat Girl.

From the far end of the street a strangely familiar voice stands
out above the others: *Step right up! See the world's greatest daredevil*
perform a death-defying feat! A dizzying spectacle of speed! See it now!
Looky looky looky! Your mind will fail to believe what you see before
your eyes! Hurry, hurry, hurry! Go now! There's the cashier, why wait?
Step right up!

He slides a quarter under the window to the cashier in the booth,
whom he recognizes as Carmella from Leonard's Café, masticating
a mouthful of Chiclets.

Ticket in hand, he is swept through the tent door by a rush of
humanity into a dimly lit amphitheatre whose tiered seating over-
looks a circus ring; and at that moment, a powerful spotlight creates
a blazing disc centre stage, in the middle of which stands General
Victor Newson, in full dress uniform with medals dripping from his
tunic, top to bottom. He lifts a megaphone to his mouth and points
his swagger stick at the enormous piece of machinery hulking

above—a Big Bertha howitzer, the dreaded German siege gun, with a firing range of thirty thousand feet.

Ladies and gentlemen! Boys and girls! You fortunate folks who are about to witness the sensation of the century! A living person is about to be shot through space with violent velocity from the mouth of this howitzer cannon! And with no safety net! I repeat: no safety net!

And who, you ask, is this paladin who would undertake to become a death-defying human projectile? That man is none other than the hero who has thrilled millions across the globe—the amazing, the fearless, the peerless, the man they call the Bullet—

Ed McCurdy!

To McCurdy's horror, the general's stick is pointing in his direction, and the spotlight is on him.

He looks down to discover that his suit has become a leotard with a cape, as he is picked up by strongmen, carried to the mouth of Big Bertha, and shoved into the barrel, feet first. Now he is in utter darkness, except for a small, bright hole sixteen feet away.

The audience roars with excitement.

The howitzer swings around so that it aims upstage, away from the audience and toward a field beyond the livestock barns of Happyland.

With a deafening report, he is blasted into the universe, an expanding mass of smithereens, each fragment a minuscule Ed McCurdy, whizzing upward above the earth's atmosphere into the blackness of space, then arching downward toward the Pacific coast, then British Columbia—down to the peak of Grouse Mountain and a structure he knows to be Solomon's Temple, which he recognizes from *Hurlbut's Story of the Bible*.

In that temple, the ultimate mystery of his existence and purpose is to be revealed.

He is standing before a throne, before the one who knows.

The figure slowly lifts its head, revealing the face of... Wilson Larke, with his slate jowls and the wattle joining chin and neck.

Larke tilts his head sideways, to reveal an enormous ear, spinning like a swirling eddy, with a black hole in the middle.

McCurdy is sucked, Hoover-like, into the ear canal, another long, dark tunnel with another bright, circular mouth in the distance, in which he can barely make out the bat face of—

Mrs. Dixon. Now he hears Elwood's voice: *Cripes, Mother! If he's dead, I'm going back to Rossland.*

Mother?

He opens his eyes and sees Mrs. Dixon's face peering down at him, her expression a blend of alarm and speculation. Behind her shoulder is Elwood, with a worried expression on his mug.

"Mr. McCurdy? Can you speak? Can you hear me? Don't try to move, we've called an ambulance."

"What are you talking about, Mrs. Dixon?"

"You received an electric shock. A bright blue flash and you sailed straight across the room."

"Bounced off the wall, you did," adds Elwood. "You touched the microphone, you see. You must have had wet shoes on your feet."

"Have you been out? Who *doesn't* have wet shoes?"

"That's as may be. It looks like some jackass pulled the ground wire."

"What's a ground wire? For that matter, what's electricity?"

"I think he's confused," Elwood says.

"Where are my glasses?"

"I've never seen such an alarming sight in my life," Mrs. Dixon says, with a noticeable lack of alarm. "Mr. McCurdy, we wondered if you'd been killed."

Elwood hands McCurdy's glasses to Mrs. Dixon. "He does look confused. I had a mate who took a jolt installing an electric stove— gave him a stutter for life."

Planting his glasses on the ridge of his nose, McCurdy sees a glint of anticipation in Mrs. Dixon's tiny, speckled eyes.

"Tell me, Mr. McCurdy: How many fingers am I holding up?"

"Several," he replies, feeling obdurate.

"Aha. I see. Now can you tell me what day it is?"

"A good day for your husband, I expect."

"There you go, Elwood. Mr. Good-Evening is speaking gibberish. It could be an injury to the brain."

CHAPTER 17

NEXT WEEK'S FEATURE at the Pantages is to be *The Love Parade*. Jeanie announced that she and the girls would like to see this photoplay, for it stars Maurice Chevalier in a fancy European uniform, and Jeanette MacDonald as Queen of Sylvania.

Hook is all for it. His wife deserves to go to the movie with her friends—Mrs. Fletcher and Mrs. Jump, and a woman whose name he forgets—and to have a grand time. A movie is the closest thing to foreign travel Jeanie will ever experience. For her husband, the war supplied quite enough foreign travel for one lifetime.

The catch is that, while his wife is enjoying her well-earned entertainment, Hook will be spending several hours at home, alone, with Lucille.

Certain tasks require a female touch, when male hands are like baseball mitts. It's the same with the soothing murmur; Lucille is put off by Hook's voice at any pitch.

He suspects that Lucille doesn't like him any more than Chief Blatchford does.

Thinking about his domestic circumstances prods his molar, which has begun to inflict sharp pangs whenever he bites down. Sooner or later he'll have to bite the bullet and have the damned thing pulled out—but not yet, not as long as his supply of Aspirin, clove oil and Jiffy drops holds up.

McCurdy hasn't arrived. He's probably with his tailor, being fitted for a new tuxedo.

The theatre grows dark, and down a chute of dusty light tumbles the news, in a dizzying array of short moving pictures whose rapidity is meant to convey urgency, thereby distracting from the fact that this "news" could in fact be weeks old.

As a standard fixture of moving picture presentation, newsreels don't deliver information so much as they commemorate news itself.

Current events appear as a parade of spectacle, death, hilarity and famous faces, narrated with feverish excitement, accompanied by violins sawing away at a pastiche of the *William Tell Overture*.

On the screen, backed by Corinthian pillars, a plain woman in a sensible suit descends the steps of the US Supreme Court in front of an entourage of men in cheap suits.

If Al Capone meets his downfall it will be thanks to this woman! Her name is Mabel Willebrandt, and she's the gal who heads the treasury department!

Mrs. Willebrandt has won her case before the Supreme Court! From now on, illegal income will be subject to tax, just like any other!

Cut to gangsters in expensive suits, climbing in and out of expensive autos, either smiling or covering their faces with their fedoras.

For the first time in history, high-living gangsters like Bugs Moran and Al Capone can be charged with tax evasion!

In an unidentified city, determined-looking men in cheap suits emerge from a nondescript brick building: *These are Mrs. Willebrandt's agents from treasury, known as T-men, who are ready to follow the money, and to gather evidence on gangsters who have made millions on income that was never taxed! At last, organized criminals will be required to account for their ill-gotten gains!*

With a swelling fanfare and hardly a pause for breath, the baritone goes on to describe the landing of the *Hindenburg*: *The gargantuan flying wonder piloted by Hugo Eckener, a modern day Columbus of the air, completes its second transatlantic crossing!*

At some point during the *Hindenburg* item, McCurdy slips into the seat next to Hook and produces a pony of rye.

Firing up an Ogden's, Hook bends down to fetch an empty bottle from their previous meeting, for use as an ashtray.

"Ed, before we start, I have a grievance."

"A union man, are you?"

"What?"

"Never mind. What's the problem?"

"Your piece in the paper was less than a boost to my standing downtown. Thank you for making me look like a right wally when I'm in deep enough shit already."

"Jesus Christ, Calvin, I only referred to investors and police, can you think of anything less specific? What do I call them—*humans?*"

"Ed, you know how the chain of command works. How my superiors would see it. As far they are concerned, bad press means failure on the ground—and right now I'm nearly under it. Chief Blatchford was never my friend. He just can't stand me."

"Don't be such a poof. Nobody likes me, and you don't hear me complaining."

"You weren't at the last meeting. To call it a disaster would be like..."

Unable to accomplish such an understatement, Hook takes another lash of whisky.

Onscreen, the audience is taken to a chic Mayfair neighbourhood, as a procession of London bobbies carries a series of flat, rectangular objects into a waiting van.

British police seized twelve paintings of nudes by D.H. Lawrence from a London gallery after viewers swamped the show! While issuing a fifteen-guinea fine the judge was heard to remark that the author of Lady Chatterley's Lover *should be destroyed like a dangerous wild animal!*

"Calvin, I apologize. In future pieces about policemen, I'll stick to the passive voice."

"What's that going to do?"

"Nobody will be held responsible for anything."

"Well, I wouldn't go that far."

"Okay, I promise that in future I'll single out Inspector Hook for a favourable adjective, maybe even a phrase."

"But don't go overboard. Coming from you, it could be seen as sarcasm."

Hook fires up an Ogden's and takes a closer look at his companion, who looks somewhat worse for wear, and it can't be the pressures of the job. Now he feels more pangs of envy to go with the throb of his tooth. What would tire a bachelor? Sex. Shagging some bint with a passion for the voice.

"Can we move on to the reason I called?"

"Please do."

"I was accosted by a yob with teeth like a horse and an accent like your wife."

"You mean from the North Country?"

"I wouldn't know, Calvin, I've not been overseas." McCurdy points at his glasses. "Unsuitable for service, remember?"

"What did the yob say to you?"

"He said I was in for a shock. Then, wouldn't you know, two days later my microphone electrocuted me. The engineer said something about a missing ground—whatever that means. Do you think it could be a coincidence?"

"Probably. What was the fellow's point?"

"He said something about a Dark Adept, whatever that is."

"He sounds like another nutter who blames you for the news. The country is full of that sort of nonsense. In the Prairies they blame the *Farmers' Almanac* for the weather."

"But they don't go down to the publisher's and *electrocute* the editor."

"It is worrying, I admit. As a police officer I recommend caution. Keep an eye out for suspicious-looking characters."

McCurdy hands back the bottle. "You're not much help, Calvin."

"What can I do, Ed? You have no evidence." Hook lifts the bottle. "A toast to police procedure!" He holds the whisky in the left side of his mouth to temporarily numb his molar, then swallows. "By the way, I have a spot of tooth trouble. Having your finger on the pulse of the city, can you recommend a dentist?"

"I had a tooth pulled once, at a Painless Parker concession. To prepare, I took a pint of Scotch and enough powder up the nose to pierce my septum. By the time I got in the chair I was anybody's baby."

"How did the dentist go about it?"

"I don't remember. Thinking back, I'm not even sure it was a dentist. For all I knew, it could have been the janitor."

CHAPTER 18

IT IS PAST ten o'clock, and while the other disciples hearken to the day's prophecy, hunkered on the hill against a fine but penetrating shower, the three mutineers have gathered once more in the shelter of the blockhouse.

Thanks to his age and knowledge of theosophy, and as a former editor of the *Quest*, Sydney Backstone has been accepted as the de facto leader of the group, at least for the time being.

For which he has paid a heavy price.

All this week, the man has suffered through dreadful nights crying out, horrible dreams of spectres in black cowls, waking up paralyzed and with a death grip on his magical labret.

"Well, Elliot, do you have something to report?"

Linden lights a Sweet Cap and takes a deep drag to relax, so as not to reveal his certainty that their undertaking has taken a wrong, even absurd, turn.

"Yes, Sydney. I managed to contact my former office and they have hired operatives to assist us. Individuals who will make necessary inquiries. Frankly, they think I've gone completely cuckoo."

Backstone lights his pipe. "Inquiries, did you say?"

"A certain amount of intimidation might be involved, but they get results."

"It sounds unsavoury. Are they criminals?"

"They face no charges under Canadian law."

"And what is the result of their inquiries?"

"Indeterminate at present. It's all quite embarrassing."

"And Mr. Good-Evening?"

"He seems to be carrying on as though nothing happened."

Flagler heaves a sigh. "I think the Dark Adept is laughing at us."

"There's nothing amusing about it, Roger," Backstone says.

"I didn't say it's funny, Sydney. I had a dream where demons were dancing around the Tree of Knowledge. I couldn't sleep for the rest of the night."

"I sympathize with you. That voice I heard in the House of Mystery froze my blood. Elliot, I'm not certain even an exorcism will expel such a powerful Adept once he has settled into a body."

"And what is to be done, Sydney? Are you suggesting we silence the voice on the radio by separating his ethereal body from the physical?"

"Elliot, one thing is certain: we must stop these broadcasts."

Linden treads on his cigarette and makes for the door. "This has gone far enough. Gentlemen, we can't just kill people over what might be a simple case of fraud. I shall speak to Bob Nettles—maybe he still has a head on his shoulders."

Without waiting for a reply, Linden heads out the door and through the woods to the clearing, skirting the seated devotees, until he reaches Nettles's usual station near the Ever-Burning Flame.

Nettles isn't there.

Alarmed, Linden turns to Melvin and Hannah Durnford, who are warming their hands beside the Ever-Burning Flame. "Have you seen Bob Nettles?"

"No," Hannah says. "He didn't come for the Prophecy."

"He always stands here," Melvin says.

"Has from the very beginning," adds Hannah.

"It's very strange."

Today I sat with the Brothers beneath the Eye of the Cosmos, on the rim of the Void. At the bottom of the Void were the stars and below them the earth and its puny solar system. Strange aeolian music floated as the Brothers of the Light gathered to consider the state of the world.

And so did I, your Brother Osiris.

The Brothers affirmed that the process of destruction has accelerated: Europe has become a dictatorship of brutes. In North America, "business principles" have concentrated power so that a few individuals seek to control the fate of the planet.

Violence is everywhere, and dissolution, and the loneliness of loss— as the ties that bind fray and break, and hope sinks beneath the oceans and drowns in a sea of whisky, while ghostly creatures burn churches, and wild beasts devour their hunters...

CHAPTER 19

*At every critical period in world history, certain
individuals are born into the world with a distinct
mission, who come fully equipped with the knowledge
and power needed to accomplish an important mission.
The mission is never easy, and it's not always kind.*

—The Aquarian Gospel

THIS MORNING, WHEN Nettles arrived in his office, his diary—in
which he had recorded his doubts and concerns—was missing from
his desk drawer.

He is in no doubt as to who has taken it.

He might have known that Brother Osiris would suspect that his
closest ally has turned against him.

It is a given that the Brother can read minds—at least to the
extent that he senses negative thoughts, in the way that a sea captain can call a change of wind before crewmen notice.

Stories abound of one-on-one moments in which his uncanny
insight went well beyond the five senses. In fact, Nettles himself
is here because he had just such a life-altering experience with the
Brother, in front of the Blue Star Memorial Temple.

Though highly valued at the treasury department, Robert Nettles
was the type of agent who never managed to leave the job at the
office, and after an unusually long and demanding assignment, his
superiors sensed that he was beginning to crack under pressure.

So when his wife died and he lost his mind, the department had
a severance package and a treatment program on hand.

Nettles was turned over to the head doctor at the psychiatric
clinic in Napa State Hospital, who rendered a diagnosis of "nervous

disorder" and recommended the Halcyon Sanatorium in Oceano, California, a nationally respected institution run by a spiritual community—not the Catholic Church but the Temple of the People, under Mrs. Francia La Due and Dr. William Dower.

The two founders took on separate leadership roles in the institution. Mrs. La Due presided over the temple, where, as "Blue Star," she channelled messages from the Master Hilarion, a third-century anchorite.

Meanwhile, at Halcyon Sanatorium, Dr. Dower, as "Red Star," specialized in the treatment of such maladies as alcoholism, drug addiction, nervous disorders, schizophrenia and epilepsy.

Dr. Dower based his work on the theory that electricity, radioactivity and subatomic particles provide the key to the cosmic energy forces that lie beyond the physical world, and that certain disorders require specialized electric machines to detect and correct mental imbalances on a molecular level. Under his care, Nettles underwent analysis, with the aid of an Oscilloclast, a Radioclast and a Dynomizer—the last of which looked something like a radio, and could diagnose any known disease from a single drop of blood.

None of Dr. Dower's treatments did Nettles a particle of good— in fact they did the opposite, by alerting him to the presence in his body of malaria, diabetes and cancer.

With no hope of relief, Nettles was seriously contemplating suicide—until the evening he ventured into the Blue Star Memorial Temple to hear a talk by the Canadian theosophist Edward Peter Collins, known as Brother Osiris.

On listening to the words of this dapper little gentleman with piercing eyes, Nettles found the torment he had endured gradually began to make sense. When the audience at last filed out of the temple, he was finally beginning to understand how all of it served as preparation for the Work that would fulfill his Life's Purpose.

He hesitantly approached Brother Osiris, simply to shake hands, but the Brother initiated a conversation that continued until long after attendants had closed the temple for the night.

Following that pivotal meeting, Nettles settled his affairs in Los Angeles to join Brother Osiris's settlement in British Columbia, where he became so indispensable to the financial management of the colony that the Brother appointed him a governor of the foundation as well.

And now, after all that has happened, how is it possible that the man who saved his life is a fraud?

As a former investigator into financial malfeasance, Nettles can now see the purpose behind the *Aquarian Gospel* requirement that new disciples liquidate their securities at home and reinvest in Canada.

Given that their money would migrate to the foundation anyway, it's clear that the purpose was to avoid scrutiny from the disciples' former brokers.

And given Howe Street's reputation for unsavoury transactions, any underhanded dealings by the Brother would be in safe hands with Tucker, Palmer and Pine.

Nettles feels as though every vein in his body is about to explode.

He must know the truth; this is why he is not at the Prophecy as he should be, but outside the Brother's office, about to commit an illegal entry.

He has chosen the one time when the Brother's mind and spirit are fully engaged, when the meadow hums with spiritual forces from near and far, and the Brother is half in this world and half in another.

Fraught with misgiving, Nettles lets himself into the office using a duplicate key the Brother entrusted to him as his friend and advisor.

As he rifles through the Brother's private files, a part of him feels like the meanest wretch who ever lived—until, in the bottom desk drawer, he finds his missing diary, and a Colt .32 revolver.

MY BROTHERS AND sisters, do you not hear the bell? It has rung out the triumph of might, and sounded the call of intolerance. It has heralded conquering armies and rung the assembly for execution by fire and stake. It is the last sound in the ears of the dying; it has silenced the anguished cries of humanity.

The bell was made by human hands, my friends, fashioned in the minds and hearts of men. Chemists, brewing death in new and horrible forms, have heard it. The boots of millions march to it.

Now comes the hour when the bell tolls for thee, and me—sounding the death of the old order and the birth of the new.

Now is not the time to abandon the Work. The Work is guided from beyond us. None of us is an agent. Each in our own way, we are all conduits for a higher wisdom. That is what we are here for. If we would only listen.

I, your Brother Osiris, am the messenger of the fire, the messenger of the whirlwind.

As we pass through our time of trial, remember: the personality of the messenger is nothing. The message is everything. On it we stand—or fall.

CHAPTER 20

All I do is supply a demand.

—Al Capone

A STUBBY FIGURE emerges from the arched Art Deco entrance of the Vancouver Stock Exchange and descends the steps to Howe Street, hunched beneath an umbrella. He has a peculiar walk, as though intermittently trying to kick off his shoes.

He carries a salesman's sample case made of wood, leather and brass. It seems much heavier than it was in San Francisco. He wonders if his left arm has become longer than his right.

Avoiding the commotion on Pender Street, he makes his way to Hastings, uncomfortably, for the rain lashes the back of his neck and seeps beneath his collar.

Since he boarded the train in San Francisco, he has not seen the sun once. White flecks spatter the felt of his sagging fedora, which has the musty, pungent pong of mildew. His shoes and spats are ruined. His socks are perpetually damp and his feet have cracked and peeled, and fester between the toes.

His father once told him that soldiers sometimes lost their legs due to foot rot. He plans to consult a podiatrist as soon as he gets home.

At the Louisa Hotel in Seattle, a Fuller Brush salesman from Kansas warned him that Howe Street was known on the circuit as Rainy Hollow. He thought it was a joke.

It wasn't a joke.

Do these people know how to build a sidewalk? Do the men who designed and constructed these tall buildings on Howe Street know how to put up an awning?

Not that Granville Street is any kinder to the pedestrian, where the intermittent shop awnings are riddled with leaks, and if you don't watch out, a stream of water goes straight down the nape of your neck.

Like Newtown Creek in Queens, the closer you get to the water the worse the stink; the difference being the stench of creosote instead of crude oil, and of rotten fish instead of sewage.

He pauses at Hastings Street where, a half block to his left, an end-of-shift workman is headed his way. He turns right and heads east, quickening his erratic pace toward Granville.

He feels sluggish—water in the air means less oxygen for the lungs.

It's a good ten blocks to his hotel. In New York he would be sitting warm and dry in a taxi, but it is standard practice when leaving an assignment to hoof it a few blocks and then take a trolley—except they're not running yet.

With another call to make, it will be at least another week in this dismal Podunk before he returns to civilization.

Once he is on the train heading east, they can hand the place back to the Indians.

SECOND DEATH AT TUCKER, PALMER AND PINE
Office Staff Live in Fear
Max Trotter
Staff Writer
The Vancouver World

Just a week before its formal opening, the palatial Vancouver Stock Exchange Building has experienced a second frightful tragedy, as police investigate the apparent suicide of Mr. Edgar Palmer, who fell from his office on the ninth floor after business hours on June 12.

Still reeling from the murder of Ralph Tucker a fortnight ago, in what is known as the Fatal Flapper case, one stockbroker remarked, "Folks are wondering whether the new building has caught the Warden Curse"—a reference to Duncan Warden, who shot himself on the trading floor of the Hornby exchange after his broker, Alvin Pine, invested his life savings on the Muir Creek oil venture, a fifteen-hundred-foot hole into which investors poured over three hundred thousand dollars.

Eerily, the two dead men and Mr. Pine constituted the brokerage firm Tucker, Palmer and Pine. (Alvin Pine is currently away on business and unavailable for comment.)

"I will never get over that sound as long as I live," said Eamonn Dunphy, a night watchman on his way home who had just passed the building when he heard "a loud, wet thud, like a sack of melons dropped from the roof."

Added Owen Mumford, an ambulance attendant on the scene, "The cadaver looked just sort of compressed, but getting it onto the gurney was a mess. There were so many bones broke, you could sit him up facing backward."

Given no apparent sign of a struggle in the office from which the victim fell, police have tentatively ruled the death a suicide.

Observers note that, should foul play be suspected, it could become a major factor in the Dora Decker trial now in progress, as Miss Decker has been under lock and key since the end of May.

According to Miss Rosalind Tryder, a secretary with Tucker, Palmer and Pine, "Mr. Palmer had a visit from the police just a few days ago. He seemed nervous and upset after that."

"It's like *The Terror*," added Miss Tryder, referring to the photoplay starring May McAvoy. "We come to the office each morning, wondering who will be next for the chopper."

On the night in question, a man was seen leaving the Stock Exchange by passerby Laird McMeekan, a streetcar driver on his way to work, who described the man as "short and stocky. I couldn't see his face, but he had a funny walk, like he was trying to kick off his shoes."

Inspector Calvin Hook of the Vancouver police, currently in charge of the so-called Fatal Flapper case, remarked: "We have called for the gentleman in question to come forward."

CHAPTER 21

STELLA ASPEN IS less than pleased with her landlady at present.

Something is going on. For over a week the hall has been silent, with no chirping girls, no shrill laughter, only the kind of echo you find in an empty closet.

Stella's bed is unmade, her ashtray hasn't been emptied, and she is beginning to sneeze. For all she knows, the joint has been condemned as a fire hazard, and is about to be knocked down by a steam shovel.

Blindness can be such a bother.

Settled in an upholstered side chair at a drop-leaf table by the window, she hums a tune from *No, No, Nanette* and gazes blankly at the pale light coming from the window, while her manicured fingers automatically withdraw a Chesterfield from the cigarette case by the telephone. She taps both ends, then lights up with her Ronson De-Light.

The case and lighter, along with the ashtray, were a gift from Ann Murdock after *The Beautiful Adventure* wrapped. At the time, they were bright silver; she expects the ashtray is tarnished green by now, so that the engraving is no longer legible.

The windowsill is cool and clammy. When she leans closer to the pane, she sees blurred, moving abstractions, with a big black disc in the centre.

The air outside smells of mist turning to rain, which is what passes for a clear day in this part of the world.

Compared to California, she might as well be at the bottom of the sea.

In Vancouver, June is always like this. After the promise of May, June casts you straight back to February, as though the calendar is a Snakes and Ladders game.

Senile retinitis, the doctor called it. (*Senile!* She'd never been so insulted in her life.)

She should have moved back while the disc was a small black spot in the centre of the universe, only California doesn't suit her anymore. Now that the spot has become a smudge, and the universe can be seen only as shapes and colours moving about, she could be anywhere.

As she remembers it, her window provides a view of power lines and a muddy stretch of Union Street. She hears voices on the sidewalk speaking Chinese, Italian, incomprehensible Limey dialects, and of course Japanese, with Little Tokyo just a few blocks away.

Downstairs she hears the bell jangle and the front door slam, followed by Mildred's footsteps down the hall to the kitchen—and again, that empty-house echo in the hall.

In the morning there has been no queue beside the door to the water closet. No steam in the bathroom, no lingering smell of recently applied toiletry products.

Where has everyone gone?

This inability to get info has got to stop. Sooner rather than later, she'll have to settle down and learn Braille.

The last time she learned a language, it was the fashion lingo a seamstress needed to master if she was to pass herself off as a designer—*croquis, bias, swim form...*

Now it's Braille. A language of little lumps.

Mildred's footsteps approach, the door swings open and Miss Aspen's landlady enters the room—and about time. It's been days. Stella hears ice clinking in a highball glass.

Two glasses, in fact—Mildred sets them on opposite sides of the table, then leans over and opens the window a few inches wider. Stella can smell her perfume (Yardley London, wouldn't you know), as she takes the second side chair.

For the two of them, this is a well-established ritual inaugurated by Miss Aspen, who has a way of extracting admissions and putting one at her beck and call. This she accomplishes by sharing personal details about herself and her marriage that most women would find hideously embarrassing. After two years, relations between Stella and Mildred have become chummier than is usual between a landlady and her tenant. As far as Mildred is concerned, she might as well have rented the room to a rather profligate aunt.

One of the first confidences they shared was that both had husbands who served in the war and were never the same afterward.

Mildred straightens out the bedclothes and empties the ashtray into the wastebasket, haven fallen badly behind in her custodial duties. She takes the empty chair and sets fire to a Gauloise, while Miss Aspen lights another Chesterfield.

Miss Aspen sips her pink gin. Mildred wonders how she manages to draw her plum lipstick in such a precise Cupid's bow.

"You might have put in more ice, darling. This is as warm as spit."

"Oh, you Americans and your ice. Perhaps I should store your drinks in the icebox."

"Don't high-hat me, doll. Where have you been? And why is the joint empty? Why do I hear no girlie shrieks and smell no My Sin? Spill, sister. What the hell happened?"

Mildred sighs—she wasn't looking forward to explaining to Miss Aspen why she is her only tenant.

"Dora has been charged with murdering her boss. Everyone moved out but you. They don't want to be associated with what the papers have chosen to call 'the case of the Fatal Flapper.'"

"Hell's teeth! When I heard a siren, I thought, 'Where's the fire?' You're saying it was the coppers?"

"And photographers, of course."

"So your dizzy dames spend hours trying to look like movie stars, now suddenly they're camera-shy?"

"When the ship is sinking, it is no good blaming the rats."

"Generous of you, darling. A murder, did you say?"

"Dora is charged with beating her boss to death with her spike-heeled shoe."

"Dora wouldn't slap a masher's face, let alone murder him."

"She's a farm girl from Saskatchewan. It was the flapper outfits that did it. According to Dora, her boss made employees wear them in order to attract clients."

"Ah. Another sort of working girl. Call them *ladies of the business hours*." Miss Aspen cackles softly, displaying a good set of teeth for her age.

"It's all rather sordid, frankly."

Miss Aspen snorts in response. "Honey, have you been to Hollywood?"

"Stella, I didn't know Hollywood was a real place until you arrived. I thought it was a state of mind."

"I dressed the stars, dear. You don't want to know what Mabel Normand had to do for Mack Sennett. Small wonder she was such a cokehead."

"Spare me the details, darling. I don't need the mental imagery."

"So has Dora got a mouthpiece?"

"Court-appointed."

"Public defenders are palookas where I come from."

"In this case he's a prehistoric fossil with a drinking problem."

"But of course you know a good lawyer—in the Biblical sense, I mean."

"Tristan's firm does occasional pro bono work—but not of that sort."

"So pay him. You can always get it back in jewellery."

"I'm afraid the business has a cash-flow problem. To make ends meet, I'm filling in for a sick girl at the Seymour exchange."

"Hire him, darling. My treat."

"Are you sure, Stella?"

"Then we might see some housekeeping around here. Be a dear and get me another drink, would you? And put some ice in it this time."

AS A JEWISH seamstress from Brooklyn, Sarah Cherindoff's threadbare prospects took flight thanks to *Our Mutual Girl*, and crash-landed thanks to Jimmy Paxton. Along the way, she became Stella Aspen, and made a good deal of money.

Our Mutual Girl, starring Norma Phillips, was a weekly series of two-reelers by Mutual Film, featuring current women's fashions, as well as cameo appearances by notable figures from the worlds of politics, sports, entertainment and business. It was the first time a studio aimed a series directly at the female audience.

Miss Phillips will wear gowns at one hundred fifty to four hundred dollars, hats at seventy-five dollars and six pairs of gloves per picture at four dollars a pair. A dresser has been employed at seventy-five dollars per week to keep her "duds" in order and "hook up the back," or tell her if her hat is on straight—very important trifles to a well-dressed woman...

The dresser mentioned in the promotion was Sarah Cherindoff. Mutual paid her half the amount publicized, and only when she was needed.

To supplement her income, Sarah fashioned sewing patterns for Miss Phillips's gowns, and peddled them to shops as the dresses they saw in *Our Mutual Girl*. To throw Mutual off the scent, she called herself Stella Aspen, the classiest goyish name she could think of.

By the time Stella Aspen Patterns had its own little cubby on the second floor at Macy's, Mutual Films had threatened legal action, but suing their own enterprising dresser would alienate the female audience, so they settled.

As the punks on Thirty-Eighth Street would say, it was a clean sneak.

Meanwhile, the *Our Mutual Girl* serial continued. Episodes featured cameo performances by politicians seeking election and actors promoting their next movie—including one Jimmy Paxton, who played all-American boys in growing-up movies. (He was hardly a boy when she married him.)

When you measure a man's inseam, you never know what will come up next.

MILDRED RETURNS FROM the kitchen with two fresh pink gins and a newspaper, having relaxed somewhat.

Her tenant clinks the glass and nods her approval of the amount of ice. "There are chocolates in the dressing table, darling. Fetch them for me, would you?"

The Whitman's Sampler has been well picked over; Miss Aspen seems to be able to distinguish milk from dark and to avoid the chewy centres by touch alone.

Mildred chooses a Pickaninny Peppermint, which she holds in her mouth to turn the pink gin into a sort of stinger.

"Stella, I'm afraid I have another bone to pick. My plate of bones is rather full at the moment."

"Another bone? Darling, you're turning into a crypt."

"It's about Andrew."

"Ah, our war hero." Miss Aspen lights another Chesterfield. "That's one thing I can say for Jimmy—he was a drunk, but he didn't hit."

"Bully for you darling. It seems that Andy is coming to Vancouver on Churchill's speaking tour. Let me read this to you."

CHURCHILL TO VISIT VANCOUVER
"Private Citizen" Seeks Investment Opportunities
Max Trotter
Staff Writer
The Vancouver World

Premier Tolmie announced yesterday that Winston Churchill's upcoming three-month tour of North America is to include this province, where he plans to deliver a public address at the opening of the Provincial Exhibition in New Westminster and at the Vancouver Opera House, where he will speak on the restoration of order in Palestine.

As part of his tour, the former chancellor of the exchequer and minister of war intends to inspect the BC logging and mining industry for investment purposes, having taken a substantial position in the Alberta oil fields.

Winnie will be accompanied by his son Randolph, his brother Jack, and Jack's nephew, Andrew Rhys-Mogg MC, DFC, the celebrated air ace.

In Vancouver the group will be joined by Mr. Walter Addison, who will provide investment advice. Mr. Addison served as honorary colonel with the Canadian Militia, and as advisor to war minister Sir Sam Hughes.

"Who is this bird Churchill?"

"He's the ex-chancellor of the exchequer."

"He sounds like a board game."

"He's British. What you Americans would call a big shot—Andrew's second cousin or something."

"You Brits are all related. No wonder you've got bleeders in the attic."

"Andrew sent me a telegram. 'Coming for you, Dearest,' is what it said."

"How touching."

"Not in this case." Mildred knocks back her pink gin and burrows into her purse for another Gauloise.

"You're frightened, aren't you?"

"How can you tell?"

"Your hand is shaking. I could hear the drink sloshing in your glass." Stella feels across the table for Mildred's hand and gives it a pat.

"That's the problem with having a heel for a husband, darling. He just keeps showing up."

CHAPTER 22

SERGEANT QUAM STEPS inside, scratches his armpit and looks about with distaste.

Surely, Hook could have picked a better venue. One glance at the Lumberman's Club and he can see multiple violations—provincial laws broken, municipal codes ignored, card games with liquor, money in plain sight—all in all, an unsavoury environment for a servant of the law.

Masses of grey-blue cloud envelope each table, an indication of insufficient ventilation, as is the smell produced by the pores of eighteen workmen in hats and wet wool coats. Taken together, it all adds up to a pong that would knock you sideways.

"Would you care for a beverage, Officer?"

The bartender, who says his name is Truman, gives Quam the stink eye while wiping the bar's surface with a rag that could belong to an auto mechanic.

Quam sizes up the fellow: a tough customer whose face has greeted many fists. "Pardon me, Mr. Truman?"

"A little something to wet your whistle, sir?"

"Oh. Um, just a glass of water, thank you."

DI Hook intervenes: "Are you certain, Mr. Quam? Whisky would be less conspicuous. And safer as well."

Quam eyes the glasses lined up behind the bar, grease shimmering in the light. "Whisky it is, sir."

They carry their glasses—another code violation—to a corner table.

"Sir, are you certain this is an appropriate place for a meeting between two officers?"

"Mr. Quam, long ago, a contact introduced me to the Lumberman's Club as the place to go if you don't want to be seen by anyone who matters."

"I certainly wouldn't want to be seen on the premises, sir. Every man here is a lawbreaker."

"True for you there, Sergeant. And among this deplorable group we must include two policemen in the act of violating a direct order."

A frown ruffles the placid surface of Quam's forehead. His eyes grow misty. "I wish you hadn't brought that up, sir."

Hook reminds himself to keep a close eye on Quam. A number of changes have occurred in his former partner since their separation. He no longer smells of fermenting fruit, for one thing. For another, the fellow has become cagier, somewhat less bovine, and can be downright chippy at times.

Hook raises a toast. "Here's to street-level police work."

Quam wipes the rim of his glass with his handkerchief. "To our health, sir." He puts his lips to the rim, gently pours a small portion of whisky into his mouth, then lets out a horizontal geyser of a cough that goes on long enough to inspire men to lift their eyes above their cards.

Hook shakes his head and extracts an Ogden's from the pack—in this room, the distinction between smoking and breathing is practically non-existent.

"Mr. Quam, when you've recovered, shall we get down to the Flapper case?"

Quam speaks with an effort. "No, sir. For me it's the Tucker, Palmer and Pine case. Please remember that. I'm with the fraud squad. My recent interview with Mr. Palmer had absolutely nothing to do with Mr. Tucker's murder—if indeed it was a murder—and neither does our meeting today."

"Good grief Mr. Quam, you're talking as though there's a microphone under the table."

"Well, you never know, sir."

"In actual fact, Sergeant, we do know. If it's not a raid, not a man here gives a shit. Gadzooks, man, I told you, that's the reason we're here."

"You're right, sir. We're here because it's here, and"—nodding toward Hastings Street—"not there."

We're here because it's here and not there.

Hook wonders if he should give this some thought, and decides not to.

"Be that as it may, sir, I'm pleased to report that the interview with Mr. Palmer was a success. The individual was most co-operative. He added considerably to our understanding of the brokerage business, and committed to providing information in future."

"Not so, Mr. Quam. Palmer is dead."

"He didn't look well."

From experience, Inspector Hook chooses not to pry into Quam's methods for extracting information from a subject.

"Sir, are you familiar with the practice of cleaning dirty money?"

"Is that a laundry joke, Sergeant?"

"What's a laundry joke, sir?"

"That was a joke."

"I never tell jokes, sir. We in the fraud department deal in facts, not humour—though in this case it does have to do with laundries in New York, which might be a sort of pun."

Something to go on? The back of Hook's neck tingles with anticipation. His molar throbs almost pleasurably.

Quam takes a modest sip of his whisky, dilutes it in his mouth, swishes it about, forces it down the neck, wipes his lips carefully, burps and opens his notebook.

Hook signals to Truman for another round and sticks an Ogden's between his lips—only to find that there is already one there.

"It has to do with Al Capone, sir. The gangster in the news."

"'In the news,' Quam? Jesus, these days I wonder if there's a crime that doesn't involve Capone."

"But this has more to do with Mr. Capone's accountant, one Edward O'Hare, also known as Easy Eddie Money. It seems that, to balance Mr. Capone's official records, Mr. O'Hare bought a chain of cash-only laundries, which made unrealistic profits in nickels and dimes. The racket expanded to include other anonymous cash businesses—restaurants, theatres, peep shows—as well as, it seems, the stock market. Once money is exchanged for stock certificates, it's almost impossible to trace. And Tucker, Palmer and Pine have an unusual number of apparently anonymous accounts—"

Abruptly, Quam's head swivels toward the wall to his left. "What's that, sir? A small cat?"

Hook follows his line of sight. "Not a cat, Mr. Quam, no."

"Surely it's not a..." Quam's face takes on an expression of dread as his eyes film over.

"A rat. Yes, Sergeant. That's indeed what it is."

In Quam's mind, the dreadful thing is about to streak through the air straight toward his face, and sink its teeth into his eye.

He takes a more generous sip of whisky. He has begun to understand why men drink the stuff—it's to alleviate fear. No wonder the Legions are packed.

"Sir, I didn't know rats came in that size."

"Around the wharves, you could mistake them for alley cats. That little fellow over there has been around so long, the boys call him Mickey Rat and buy him drinks."

Mickey remains frozen by the wainscotting, one glittering eye looking straight at Quam, who remains transfixed by the animal—two feet long if you count its repulsive tail...

"Sergeant, you were talking about unusual accounts."

The sergeant looks as though he might chunder. His face is the texture and colour of pastry dough.

"Sir, I may have to leave the building."

"Oh come on, man. We have rats in our basement, so do you. So does every homeowner in the area. They say that for every rat you see, ten more are lurking behind the scenes—and if you get a good look, well..."

"There may well be rats, sir, but not one rat."

"Please parse that for me, would you?"

"When I was fourteen I was sitting in the outdoor privy early in the morning, and, and... Well, the long and the short of it is, I looked down between my legs and there was... a rat. Between my legs. A rat. Staring up at me, its sharp teeth inches from my—my—my privates. I still suffer from constipation."

"And the 'roids that follow."

"The 'roids too, sir, yes."

"My sympathies. You need to start smoking, Mr. Quam. It loosens things up down the way." DI Hook extends his pack of Ogden's. "Try one, it can't hurt you."

"No thank you, sir. I have an enema kit at home."

"Anyway, no need to worry about rats here. Truman keeps Mickey fed, and Mickey keeps the others out. It's like protection money."

With an effort, Quam takes another glance at the creature by the wall. It has disappeared.

He decides to pretend it was never there.

"Mr. Quam, perhaps we could return to the subject at hand?"

"What subject, sir?"

"Unusual accounts at Tucker, Palmer and Pine. You said Palmer was forthcoming."

"He was, sir. Most co-operative. We learned about a major account administered by something called the Aquarian Foundation. It appeared suspicious."

"Suspicious in what way?"

"I have a sixth sense, sir."

"A sixth sense for what?"

Quam taps his temple with a forefinger. "Suspicion, sir. Suspicion itself."

"Sergeant, what the fuck is that supposed to mean?"

"No need for profanity, sir. In this case, it's the Aquarian Foundation account. It's owned by a cult on De Courcy Island, and its earnings are far, far beyond what you would expect from a nest of kooks."

CHAPTER 23

"DORA, YOU HAVE a visitor."

Mildred notes that, considering her size and her boot-faced demeanour, the matron's voice is almost motherly.

And she is nonplussed but relieved to see Dora propped up on pillows with a copy of *Photoplay*—and that she hasn't withered to a sallow wraith; on the contrary, mascara, lipstick and a hairbrush have been applied to good effect, and she is wearing a cheerful gingham dress.

"Thank you very much, Miss Say." Dora says this like a schoolgirl upon receiving a compliment from the teacher.

Mildred is especially pleased to see the alert expression—or at least the lack of despair—on the girl's face.

"Miss Wickstram! I was hoping I would see you before long, because I'm ever so grateful."

"And why would that be, Dora?" Mildred fishes a pack of Gauloises from her purse.

"Mr. Sweet said it was you who talked him into representing me, instead of that pickled old souse. You are so kind, thank you."

"It just took a telephone call, darling. Mr. Sweet is rather sweet on me."

Even that feeble pun draws a smile; that's what a glimmer of hope can do for a girl.

Dora has evidently had visitors, to go by the feather quilt on the cot in place of the scouring cloth that called itself a blanket.

"Prison standards have improved, I see."

"Oh, this. The girls at work made it. Vera made the blocks and they sewed the quilt sandwich during lunch hour. To cheer me up."

"I would never have imagined that you office girls know how to quilt. I certainly don't know how to quilt."

"You don't, Miss Wickstram? Really?"

"Where I came from, patchwork was for spinsters and grannies."

"Oh, all the girls in the office can quilt. Mind, their stitching isn't perfect. Back home, ours always had to be perfect, or mother would make us rip them out and start over."

Mildred finds it odd to think that, unlike in London, there are flappers in this part of the world who grew up pitching hay and making quilts.

"I do hope you take further comfort in knowing that Mr. Palmer is no longer with us."

"Eleanor told me he fell out of a window. She said there's a rumour he was pushed. Something about a man with a funny walk."

"In either case, I must say it couldn't have happened to a nicer fellow."

"Oh Miss Wickstram, it's a sin to joke like that!"

"Darling, a heel is still a heel, dead or alive."

Dora puts tobacco in a cigarette paper, rolls and licks the paper, pinches off the shreds sticking out of both ends. "I hadn't thought of it that way."

"In any case, according to Mr. Sweet, Mr. Palmer's suspicious demise, combined with the coroner's opinion of Mr. Tucker's wounds, suggests a clear case of reasonable doubt."

Dora heaves a long sigh and becomes quiet, as though making up her mind about something. "Miss Wickstram, there's something I haven't told anyone. I was afraid to."

Mildred lights their cigarettes, leans uncomfortably against the iron bars, and waits.

"You see, I did have a motive for... murdering Mr. Tucker. He did things that made me want to beat him to death."

"Though not with an I. Miller shoe, surely."

"No, but once I tried to smash his head with his crystal ashtray. I made a terrible scene. All the girls saw and heard."

"Did he... take advantage of you?"

"What?"

"Interfere with you? Rape you?"

She shudders at the word. "No. Not quite. He was afraid to make a girl pregnant. But he did things... kissing and... with his hands, and he... made a mess."

"Frankly, darling, what you describe is not an entirely uncommon situation. It's why hatpins were invented. But still, I imagine it came as a shock for someone from... from your prairie upbringing."

"It did. I thought I left that sort of thing behind when I left Saskatchewan."

Mildred chooses not to follow up on that.

"So then tell me, Dora, why didn't at least one of you girls speak up earlier?"

"Because, as I told you, Mr. Palmer has—had—connections. With unsavoury people. You don't—rather, you didn't want to get on his bad side."

"You also said he dealt with gangsters."

"Oh dear Miss Wickstram, I have another confession to make." She takes a deep breath. "I sometimes listened in on the telephone."

"Oh dear. A girl can get sacked for that."

"Yes, she can—and left without a reference. Please promise not to tell."

"You're in good company, darling. Your secret is safe with me."

CHAPTER 24

AT THE ANNUAL Rummage Sale at Knights of Columbus Hall in support of the Catholic Children's Aid, one can count on finding the most excellent bargains, thanks to a network of affluent supporters who can discard unwanted possessions and feel generous as a result.

For the budget-conscious homemaker, it's an event that must be planned and saved for well in advance.

By attending the sale as a group, Jeanie, Bonnie and Tilly can, if necessary, pool their money for a big purchase—which was exactly what happened when Jeanie came upon the wicker pram, every bit as good as new, and with the optional convertible hood as well.

Thanks to their pre-arrangement, she was able to meet the two-dollar price tag by borrowing fifty cents from Tilly, who has no bairns to feed. (Earl says she's barren, though the doctor doesn't think so.) The girls were all pleased as punch, because by the end of the day they had enough money left over for pastries at Notte's.

This is what has enabled the Hook family to stroll the promenade around Douglas Park on a Sunday, like members of high society.

At this hour, a low, watery light plays across the mown, moist playing fields, so that the grass seems to glow from underneath. In a very British way, the park is sufficiently idyllic that even Lucille, gurgling in the open carriage, seems to find the atmosphere agreeable.

Hook's mind is on his toothache, which is getting worse, to the degree that it has joined Lucille in keeping him awake at night.

He's going to have to see a dentist. The very thought causes his sphincter to contract. Memories intrude like uninvited guests, of the dental tent at Rugeley, which teemed with shirkers—recruits who, desperate to avoid the muddy fields of Flanders, would bribe dentists to pull out all their teeth, intending to throw away their army-issue dentures at the front, then be sent back to base.

Rumour had it that dentists had received orders to make the process as miserable as possible to discourage shirking.

Hook can still hear their glottal screams—sounds that might come out of a triage tent during an amputation. And in his mind he can still see the after-effects of treatment: men with jaws that would no longer shut tight or open wide, or whose faces became permanently numb on one side, or with infections worse than trench mouth. It would take a man of steel not to come home with a dread of dentistry.

Civilian dentists in peacetime recognized this tendency as a barrier to business, so now every dentist on the street attaches the words *painless dentistry* to their nameplate.

When the molar first began acting up, Hook was tempted by the spectacular success of Painless Parker, an avatar of modern methods who legally changed his name to avoid the ban on medical advertising, freeing Parker to drum up business any way he pleased by means of stage productions, in which he performed extractions accompanied by a brass band and interspersed with contortionists and dancing girls. The show regularly takes place at the Rex, where it inevitably sells out.

Thinking it might ease his mind on the subject, Hook took in the presentation, in which Parker, in a lab coat, top hat and a fat necklace of human teeth, performed extractions at fifty cents a tooth, telling jokes between patients.

Suspecting these patients to be plants, following intermission, Hook moved to the front row, close enough to see Dr. Parker operate a pedal on the floor, which seemed to signal the band to swell in volume just when a patient opened his mouth to scream...

"You're fair glumpy, ducky. Ye've something on your mind."

"Oh, nothing really, pet, I was just thinking."

"I'm a copper's wife, dinna forget. Ye'd better tell me or I'll widdle myself sick."

He could set her mind at rest immediately, but is not prepared to complain about a sore tooth to a woman who has given birth. "Actually, it's about work, love. We're on a search for a suspect, and no luck so far."

"Who's the crim this time, ducky?"

"That's the problem. All we have to go by is that he's short and has a funny walk."

"He sounds like Charlie Chaplin."

"It's more likely a limp, I expect. As a description—cripes, pet, can you imagine? With all these vets hobbling about, if we brought in every short man with a limp, the lineup would stretch to Chilliwack."

"'Tis true, ducky. Sometimes I walk up Hastings Street past Victory Square and 'tis a rare bloke who has both legs working proper."

"It's a needle in a haystack, pet, for sure."

"In fact, Bonnie mentioned one bloke on our out. Bonnie works for the Cohens, of the Army and Navy Store. Jewish, but she says they're ever so nice. She overheard Mr. Cohen tell Mrs. Cohen about an odd little bugger who came in hawkin' yard goods—which ain't the Army and Navy's business."

"Odd in what way, pet?

"Well, speakin' of limps, she said he did have a funny walk, like was trying to kick either one shoe off or both shoes off—I forget which."

CHAPTER 25

ONSCREEN, AN AUTO climbs a cedar-lined driveway to a mansion on a steep hill, followed by uniformed police inspecting a corpse lying in a dimly lit hallway, then more police and then another corpse lying prone by a bed, like a throw rug.

Los Angeles, California! In the guest bedroom at Greystone, his palatial mansion in Beverly Hills, Ned Doheny, thirty-five-year-old heir to an oil fortune, lies dead, shot through the head, while his secretary and friend Hugh Plunkett lies in the hall, also dead of a bullet wound! With no witnesses, whether it is a murder-suicide, or made to look that way, may never be known!

"Calvin, in a word, someone is after me."

"Is this the same goon you think electrocuted you?"

"This one is more educated, but just as bonkers."

From an inside pocket McCurdy retrieves and unfolds a piece of letter paper. Turning sideways in the flickering cone of light, he reads aloud, "*Vetus quomodo sanies significatur Tacita deficta.*"

"I didn't get a particle of that."

"So you didn't get Latin in school."

"I was deemed unsuitable for academic study."

"Pity."

"Not at all. The teacher showed me how to fix a motorcycle."

"Well, whoever wrote this took Latin. In a Catholic school, I'll bet."

"Read it to me again, will you?"

"*Vetus quomodo sanies significatur Tacita deficta.*"

"It sounds like 'tactical defect.'"

"No, from the little I remember it's something about putrid gore. Another one in Latin said, simply, 'McCurdy accursed.' Then came a really dreadful one about limbs dissolving, along with words for warts, tumours and vermin."

"The Romans were vicious animals who killed Jesus. We learned that in church."

"Point taken." McCurdy folds the note and produces another. "Now listen to this recent one. It's in English and it goes like this: 'You hateful misanthrope, you are a willing stooge of the Dark Entities, a mouthpiece for forces beyond your control that have already begun to separate your ethereal body from your physical body, already loathsome maggots are infesting your brain...'"

"Jesus, Ed, he talks like Lon Chaney."

"I know. I can't get it out of my mind. What does it mean to separate the physical body from the ethereal body?"

"Beats me, but it doesn't sound good."

"I get this sort of mail all the time, but the words are smaller; and look at this—it's on Quadra Club stationery. Not only do they know where I live, they got into the building!"

By holding the paper close to his face, Hook can just barely make out the crest with its crowned helmet. "Well, I'd question the maid service, for certain."

"The maids are Chinese, Calvin. Most of them don't speak English *or* Latin."

"Let me look at that thing." By leaning over the railing into the spill of the light, Hook can just make it out. "I hate to say this, Ed, but it doesn't read like a threat. More like a prediction."

"Prediction of what?"

"Well, there again, it doesn't look good. When they get Biblical you know for certain they're off their noodle."

"Barking mad, yet lucid enough to find my rooms. Thank you, Calvin, for putting my mind at ease."

"I'll show this around the office and see if the lingo rings a bell. In the meantime, watch yourself."

"Not difficult to do, Calvin. I've hardly slept a wink in three days."

"Something we have in common, Ed."

GOOD EVENING. THIS is the nightly news service of Canadian National Railway, brought to you by the Vancouver Evening Star.

In today's news, Stanley Baldwin has resigned as prime minister of the United Kingdom. In Chicago, the bodies of gangsters Giovanni Scalise, Albert Anselmi and Joseph Giunta, named by police as suspects in the Saint Valentine's Day Massacre, were discovered on a roadside near Hammond, Indiana, beaten and shot dead. Reached at his head-quarters at the Lexington Hotel, Al Capone declared, quote, I have always been opposed to violence, unquote.

Yesterday, the Graf Zeppelin completed its transatlantic fight in Lakehurst, New Jersey. Canada penned a protest to the United States over the sinking of the rum-running ship I'm Alone, claiming a viola-tion of international law. In London, twenty-five years after the sinking of the Titanic, eighteen nations have produced a pact requiring pas-senger ships to proffer lifeboats for all passengers, while in Ottawa a series of sewer explosions has claimed the life of one man due to a fly-ing manhole cover, and in Italy the Fascist government has banned the use of foreign words.

You have been listening to the radio voice of the Vancouver Evening Star. As we end our broadcast, we wish our listeners on the farms, in the towns and on the trains in between, a restful good evening.

CHAPTER 26

"MRS. DIXON, YOUR SCRIPT had enough Ps and Ss to soak the microphone, while your inane connections between completely unrelated items—"

"Mr. McCurdy, as usual I haven't the slightest idea what you're talking about."

"Are you going to sit there and tell me the wire service is responsible for *passenger ships to proffer?*"

"As I've told you before, I simply type the sentences as they arrive. It is you who are paid—*well* paid—to pronounce them properly."

How he would like to lunge horizontally over Mrs. Dixon's desk and wring her neck—one of several unworthy urges that bedevil him while in her presence. He flees down the hall and through the front entrance, pausing only to collect a discarded *Evening Star* by the door. Using the newspaper to protect his hat from the rain, he crosses the sidewalk and ducks into a MacLure's cab waiting at the curb, its engine idling and its wiper blade waggling back and forth. (After that unpleasant experience with Spring-Heeled Jack, he made up his mind to avoid further risk of stage-door Johnnies waiting by the entry to hound him all the way home.)

"The Quadra as usual, Dennis." He removes his tie and unbuttons the top button of his shirt—a ritual gesture proclaiming that his neck is now his own.

As the Plymouth rattles its way up Pender Street, he carries on the usual conversation with the back of the cabbie's head, on one of the two topics they are certain to agree on—weather and sports.

"So cripes, Mr. McCurdy, I hear Myasaki is leaving."

"Yes, Herb, you have to wonder what will become of the Tigers now. Myasaki is the brains of the team."

"Plus they're in the A league now, and look at the Firemen, especially the way Duff is swattin' 'em."

"I completely agree."

He recalls watching a Tigers game a few years ago, but base-ball tends to make him tense and bored at the same time. Still, he keeps reports about the Tigers in mind, as a subject to bring up with people he doesn't want to talk to in the first place.

Passing through the Quadra Club foyer, he drops his damp news-paper into the umbrella stand (the last thing he wants is to *read* the thing), and heads briskly down the entrance hall to the main stair-case, pausing to wave a greeting to Paris, who is currently serving a couple in the Stranger's Lounge.

He climbs the stairs to the third-floor bar, pausing before a bank of wooden lockers in the cloakroom, each locker just large enough to hold a half-dozen bottles for safekeeping—a lifesaver during Prohibition, now used by members to store objects that might cause trouble if the wrong parties saw them.

He opens the latch with a small brass key, reaches inside the box, extracts a vial of white powder, closes the locker and makes for the lavatory.

Standing before the marble urinal (sufficiently large to hide in), he stares at the ADAMANT label, with the griffin poised atop the Twyfords crest, above the gentle waterfall skimming down.

Before buttoning his fly he turns his head in both directions in order to make certain that nearby booths are unoccupied (he has nightmares featuring the headline "Mr. Good-Evening a Dope Fiend!"), then carefully opens the vial, shakes out two lines of pow-der onto the porcelain shelf next to the cistern pipe, and uses a rolled-up dollar bill to inhale one line per nostril. After taking a pause for the powder to settle, in a single motion he pockets the bill, buttons his fly, turns, exits the loo and heads for the bar.

The third-floor bar is a slightly less atavistic version of the Stranger's Lounge, with windows replacing worthies on the walls. At this hour—post-cocktails, pre-nightcaps—it is sparsely populated by two men on stools at opposite ends of the bar, morosely nursing tumblers of brandy and soda.

The bartender, who bears a slight resemblance to Wallace Beery, has McCurdy's usual ready for him by the time he reaches his preferred seat—a wing chair by a window with a view of the court-house. After an exploratory sip, he takes out a pocket notebook and the twenty-year-old Parker Duofold pen he won in a high school poetry contest.

He stares at the street lamps below, watching the lights of autos shimmer through a lens of pelting rain while scribbling lines, automatically, not in hopes of writing a poem (a prospect growing fainter by the day), but for the purpose of ridding his mind of flying manhole covers and sinking ships and bullet-riddled gangsters, away from the world of Mr. Good-Evening and back into his skull where it belongs.

His pen hovers over the open notebook. So far, the writing is garbage.

MCCURDY'S ROOMS (BEDROOM, sitting room and bath) on the fourth floor feature a view of the railway, with forest and mountains in the distance, as though in retreat from the mess men have made of the landscape.

From the railway in the foreground comes the near-constant metallic non-rhythm of shunting boxcars clanking into each other, from dawn to dusk.

The moment he steps through the door, McCurdy is aware that someone has been in the room, and not just the cleaning staff. Partly it's the smell. Plagued with asthma, McCurdy is one of the few men in BC whose nose is not inured to the pong of cigarette-soaked wool. This sense of an intrusion is confirmed the moment he switches on the ceiling light and sees that the bedclothes have been roughly pulled back, with a message, in India ink, crudely printed on the pillowcase.

> *Mr. Good-Evening your voice will wither your body decay*
> *and burn may dark Satanic Beings bear your soul to Hell*

Sleep is out of the question now.

He reaches into his coat pocket and retrieves his scuffed copy of *As a Man Thinketh: A man only begins to be a man when he ceases to whine and revile, and commences to search for the hidden justice which regulates his life...*

There is nothing more exasperating than wisdom tainted by smugness. He chucks *As a Man Thinketh* across the room hard enough that it bounces off the opposite wall. Then he heads straight downstairs to the Stranger's Lounge for a stiff one under the care of its capable concierge. At this moment, it might well be the only safe room in the building.

The Stranger's Lounge is empty of guests (women aren't permitted entrance after ten), and the concierge is about to close up shop; he has already changed out of his regulation tuxedo in favour of a loose, double-breasted yellow suit with pegged trousers, cinched at the waist. Worn by Paris, it confers an easygoing, muscular grace; on McCurdy it would be a clown costume.

As with Ivy League cardigans and motorcycle club insignia, only a jazz musician can put on a suit like that and not look ridiculous—and sure enough, in his right hand Paris carries a set of drumsticks and brushes.

"I know you have a gig, Paris, but could you spare a moment?"

Paris inclines his head, English butler–style. "Certainly, Mr. McCurdy. I shall re-open the bar. Please take a seat."

"A whisky please, and one for yourself." McCurdy checks his wristwatch. "You are off duty as of, I think, three minutes ago."

Paris checks a pocket watch at the end of an enormous chain. "Not gonna say no to that."

He returns with two half-full tumblers, then sits back to size McCurdy up with a street-experienced eye. McCurdy notes how his manner, his affect, has changed with his outfit.

"Mr. McCurdy, man, you look under the weather."

"*Ed* would be preferable in the off-hours."

"Ed, you look like shit."

"Yes, I am out of sorts. Someone has been in my room, and it wasn't to change the sheets. They left a message on my pillowcase."

"Ain't no love note, I surmise."

"Correct. Something between a death threat and a hex."

"Jack Johnson got those every time the other fighter was Mr. Charlie."

"Who's Mr. Charlie?"

Paris throws McCurdy a *Where were you born?* look, then returns to his whisky with a frown on his mug: "Tell you, man, 'round this joint I'm plucked if half the staff don't have pass keys—plumbers, electrical cats, I got a key myself, hanged if I know what it's for, I's not s'posed to go up there."

"What the message said caused me to think about of that Brit yob you called a Cletus, remember? The one who said I was in for a shock."

"Think the Limey gorilla can read and write?"

"That was my thought as well, until I was nearly electrocuted in the studio. The technician said it was a short-circuit, whatever that means."

"You mean you got fried like Old Sparky?"

"To a lesser degree, yes. Now I find someone can get into my room and leave what you call love notes. What should I do, Paris, complain to the club president?"

Paris is amused by the suggestion. "The prez has some side hustles. He likes things quiet. He don't cotton to having buttons casing the building."

"I see. So as far as management is concerned, I'm on my own."

"Except for your concierge, man, here to see to the members' comfort and safety. You want to borrow my bean-shooter?"

"Your what?"

"A .32, stop just about anyone. You wanna keep it in your bedside table with the safety off?"

"I'm touched, Paris, but do you see these things?" McCurdy leans forward to indicate his glasses with two fingers of his right hand. "Without these I'd need a Tommy gun."

Paris nods, looks at his watch, finishes his whisky and picks up his drumsticks and brushes. "I'll ask around, maybe Gatemouth knows something, some sort of protection game happening. Sorry, Ed, but I got a show to do."

"What should I say—break a leg?"

"This is a class joint, Ed. Broken legs happen *outside.*"

CHAPTER 27

TO BROTHER OSIRIS:

There has for some considerable time past been a growing sense of dissatisfaction and bewilderment at the conditions of life on De Courcy Island, and at the methods of administration pursued by the two responsible individuals. This is now growing to a climax. The possibility exists that one or all of us, when some action proves to be the last straw, loses all restraint and takes action to be later regretted. We therefore ask that a meeting be called at which all shall be present, and an explanation given which will render existing conditions tolerable or, alternatively, an assurance that the state of things which we find unendurable will come to an end.

> *Mr. and Mrs. Sydney M. Backstone*
> *Mr. and Mrs. Elliot Linden*
> *Mr. Roger Flagler*
> *Mr. and Mrs. Bruce Crawford*
> *Mr. and Mrs. Alex Painter*

ROBERT NETTLES GOES to bed knowing he will hand in his resignation to Brother Osiris tomorrow morning. It means going back on a thousand-year commitment, signed in blood.

For Nettles, to uncover conclusive evidence of embezzlement and outright fraud was the most wrenching thing to happen to him since he discovered his dead wife in the bedroom.

He settles his head onto his sweat-damp pillow, closes his eyes—and immediately revisits that dreadful moment at the bedside when he realized that Phyllis was not asleep, and a brown haze encircled his vision, and he dropped to his knees and cried out...

For the next hour, that moment repeats itself over and over, with Nettles thrashing about until eventually he gives up the struggle, opens his eyes and lights the bedside lamp.

He spends the next few hours hunched over his writing desk, laying down his conclusions in point form in order to clear his mind and to prepare for the morning's ordeal. He worries that, in his state of disillusion and rage, he will open his mouth and sputter inarticulate nonsense—or worse, rash accusations that will make a mortal enemy of the Brother, for the man's personal power is not to be gainsaid.

> *Time has come... seek opportunities... further serve welfare of humanity... determined to carry the Work forward... critical time in history...*

At last, somewhat satisfied, he snuffs the lamp and goes back to bed and pulls the covers up to his neck; his eyes close—only to snap open an uncertain length of time later, as he is awakened by a low hissing sound. As his eyes adjust to the dark, he finds his room filled with a faintly luminous grey mist, through which a figure approaches the foot of his bed—a gaunt, leather-faced creature in a monk's cowl, with a satanic grin that opens to reveal a black hole that emits the ghastly stench of a decomposing corpse in an open grave...

He sits bolt upright, gasping for air. He is by no means certain it was a dream.

CHAPTER 28

I am a spook, born of a million minds.

—Al Capone

IN THE SHADOW of the Georgia Viaduct is an orphan neighbour-hood situated in an area of failed hotels, used clothing stores and pawnshops.

The Avenue Theatre is now a shoe repair service.

Next door is the one seemingly thriving business in this com-mercial black hole: the Lincoln, a jazz club frequented by coloured citizens from the immediate neighbourhood and by railway porters on the San Francisco to Seattle to Vancouver run, as well as by mem-bers of the European fast set, for whom the area around Hogan's Alley is an amusement park for making whoopee on the razzle.

At around nine, the house band is inside preparing to play its first set. The players are in no hurry, for the Lincoln Club won't start fill-ing up until ten.

Outside, the street lamps haven't yet been switched on, the sky is a slab of slate and the rain is so sparse one can almost count the drops. Through the distortion and gloom, a pedestrian can barely make out the outlines of hobos beneath the viaduct, in the ruddy gleam from coals in an oil barrel, in sooted business suits and scraps of old army uniforms.

The street is empty except for a short man with an odd walk hunched under an umbrella, scuttling down the sidewalk to the Lincoln; the sole of one shoe slaps the wet pavement with each step.

Tonight's headliner is Charlie See, a tenor sax player of some note. He once heard See at the Blue Rose in Seattle while doing business in the northwest.

For the professional, travel is not a pleasure—if only because you don't get to choose your destination; somebody chooses it for you. Every hotel is a barracks, every bed is an army cot, and your time is never your own—it's worse than being drafted.

When he finds himself on the road again from city to city, his only pleasure is in visiting the local clubs. He openly admits to being a jazz buff; the race issue can go fuck itself—he has nothing against the *schvartzers*.

A few years ago while working for the Shapiro Brothers he paid a visit to Connie's Inn for the purpose of collecting protection money from one of the Immermans. Connie's, like the larger Cotton Club, was a thriving whites-only venue for Black music, featuring some of the biggest names in jazz—Louis Armstrong, Sidney Bechet, Bricktop Smith.

On the night he attended, Fletcher Henderson's band featured Coleman Hawkins on the saxophone, with that barking horn stuck out in front like the biggest schlong that ever there was, producing what could only be the rich, rough melodies of the devil, and speaking to a man's soul.

His mother and father deplored the music, as did everyone else in the neighbourhood. To them, jazz was what accompanied the voodoo dance. It stimulated half-crazed barbarians to vile acts and did the same thing in Negro clubs. Newspaper reports said that the music could be dangerous to fetuses: *Music of the Savage Harms Nervous System, Says Doctor.*

But as far as he was concerned, jazz was the music of angels who broke God's rules, then flew into a basement club in East Harlem and played as angels of the night.

From that point on, he haunted jazz joints in New York and sometimes in Chicago's South Side, including Jack Johnson's mixed-race clubs along the Black Belt, before the buttons shut them down. Once, he attended Capone's birthday party in the Grand Ballroom of the Lexington Hotel; Fats Waller was featured, albeit at the point of a gun.

All in good fun, but Capone's parties could turn serious very quickly. Like the time he threw a party supposedly to honour Anselmi, Scalise and Giunta, associates for many years. Over cognac and coffee, Capone denounced them as being traitors, beat them with a baseball bat and shot them dead.

Back then, he was an ambitious independent contractor, operating out of the backroom at Midnight Rose's candy store. A hand-to-mouth business, but he was somebody worthy of respect—*self*-respect.

Now he's about three-quarters down the corporate ladder—another member of the staff, the army of bootleggers, dope dealers, bank robbers, car thieves, hit men, hold-up men, pimps and muscle heads that is the working class of the Combination.

All the old-school colleagues, the Moustache Petes, have been systematically chilled off; Egan's Rats, the White Hand Gang, he remembers whacking Little Augie Orgen himself with a .45 to the back of the head. It went well. Augie himself would have approved.

In the old days, the job involved personalities who had respect for one another. You knew the enemy as a rat or deadbeat who had to go, and usually he knew why. Today, he sometimes finds himself consulting the *New York Times* after a job, or picking up an out-of-town paper, just to learn who his victim or victims might have been.

On entering the Lincoln Club he checks the band lineup, then looks over a poster from the Patricia Cabaret featuring Jelly Roll Morton, then sidles his way to a front table—for the best view, and to ensure that fellow audience members see the back of his head and not his face.

He takes his seat just in time to hear Oscar Holden play the opening bars of "Alley Cat Strut," with a muscular stride equal to Fats; then Charlie See breaks into the opening chorus with a tone and agility comparable to the Hawk, and he has to admit that, in at least this one respect, Vancouver may not be such a shithole after all.

CHAPTER 29

To expel a Dark Adept, visualize the disintegrating power as it surges from your third eye and down your extended arm to the tip of your finger. Shoot it into the Adept with all the spiritual fire you can muster as you cry out "By the power of the One I repel you!"

—*The Aquarian Gospel*

STILL SHAKING FROM last night's vision, his sweat-dampened letter of resignation in his fist, Nettles opens the door to the Brother's office.

He stands in the doorway, unable to put his foot across the threshold. He tries to take a single step, then staggers, holding on to the knob for support. He doesn't know what to do.

"Come in, Bob, come in!"

Nettles steps into the room, and can tell by the way Brother Osiris is looking at him, he is expected; not only that, the Brother knows perfectly well what this meeting is about.

"You're shaking, Bob! Why are you shaking? There is no reason to be afraid."

Seated comfortably behind his desk, Brother Osiris gazes at him with those remarkable eyes, so pale one can barely discern the cornea.

After closing the door, Nettles stands fascinated as the Brother lights his pipe without breaking eye contact, holding the match at an angle that allows the flame to be reflected in his eyes so clearly that his eyes could themselves be the source of the light...

Brother Osiris is looking into his soul.

The Brother gently blows a puff of smoke in Nettles's direction.

"Good morning, Bob. I knew you were coming. And I know what you're here for. But why are you shaking?"

"I can't say... I cannot say... I can't say!"

"Do you truly wish to leave the island?"

At last, he manages to open his resignation letter, waits for his eyes to focus, clears his throat, and begins to read the text aloud—but the words that pour from his mouth aren't the words on the page. It's as though another version of himself had burst through the door, a mad twin brother, to blurt out the family secrets at the table, with company present.

"I have come to tell you it is finished! I no longer believe or trust you, Mr. Collins! The game is up and I will have nothing to do with you and your shabby, despicable racket!

"Since our first meeting in California, I trusted you with my life, so it was natural for me to trust the logic behind everything you said and did, and to give it the best interpretation.

"When you instructed me to convert cheques and cash into gold sovereigns on behalf of the foundation, I did so without question. I believed you when you predicted that, within two years, currency would be worthless, and gold the sole means of acquiring what we can't make for ourselves. From there, it naturally followed that we would need a cement vault, and would require armed protection from the desperate hordes of refugees driven to poverty and madness by the Great Collapse.

"It explained why you turned he Aquarian Foundation into a fortress, with a blockhouse and rifles and grenades. Because I believed in you, I didn't ask why the firing positions in the blockhouse faced inland as well as seaward. Nor did it occur to me that the barbedwire fencing around the property might be intended not to keep invaders out but to keep disciples in.

"But then I saw the 'Pay to the Order of' line on Mrs. Arrowsmith's cheque, and the whole structure—the tower of lies you so carefully built from that core of belief—came tumbling down. As your treasurer, I know that, since her original donation, Mrs. Arrowsmith has given the foundation nearly a half a million dollars, and it is now clear to me that your intention is to keep the money for yourself.

"Nor do I believe that there is a Great White Lodge working in or through Edward Peter Collins. I don't believe that the Great White Lodge exists at all, or that *The Aquarian Gospel* is anything more than a blueprint for making you and your Madame Zura rich, and reducing your followers to penniless slaves.

"As for Madame Zura, I don't believe Muriel Riffle is the incarnation of Isis, and I shudder at your treatment of your wife. Alma has given you fifteen years of faithful service. She nursed you back to health when you nearly died of rheumatic fever. Sir, it grieves me to say that your so-called Work is that of a scoundrel with no honour whatsoever.

"And for that reason I announce my resignation, and my intention to leave the island as soon as I possibly can."

An extended silence follows. In the face of this onslaught of invective, Brother Osiris remains eerily serene. Nettles holds his breath, sweating from every pore, appalled by what he has just said, but unable to contradict it or apologize.

At last, setting his pipe carefully on a brass ashtray shaped like a ship's wheel, the Brother leans forward, places his elbows on the desk and, to Nettles's consternation, he smiles—sadly, like a parent whose child has brought home a disappointing report card.

Nettles knows he will never forget that smile as long as he lives.

"The fault is mine, Bob. Out of fondness for you and a belief in your potential, I thought you were ready to undergo your first ascension, and I initiated your first test. Sadly, it was a mistake. You are not ready. This is why your subconscious mind has lashed out at me, has constructed this fable out of scraps of facts, near facts and outright lies.

"It's to justify your own failure, Bob. Your vicious attack is a cover for your mental fragility.

"I understand, Bob. I understand.

"And I mean it when I say that the fault is not with you, it is with me. I understand why you must make a clean break—at least until your true strength re-emerges. It is in that spirit of understanding that I release you from your commitment.

"Go your way, Bob, with my blessing. Peace be with you."

And again, he smiles—but not with his eyes; they are the eyes of a serpent.

THE BROTHER GAVE him leave to return to the mainland, but a voice within him tells him that he is not going to leave British Columbia alive.

Nettles is terrified.

He can't bring himself to return to his cabin with last night's horrible vision fresh in his mind, the spectre with the wide-open mouth and the rotten emptiness inside—what demons will visit him next?

He knows that the Brother, fraudulent though he may be in his finances, can strike without being physically present—as the three dissidents experienced while approaching the House of Mystery.

Other disciples gave similar testimony to the Brother's strange powers. Barney Sullivan saw him walking with a man he didn't recognize, whom he later knew as Henney Krause, one of the Brother's henchmen. Suspecting the figure to be a Dark Adept, he began to follow the pair.

"One step and I was suddenly stricken," Sullivan told Nettles. "It was as if I'd been hit on the head. I couldn't move or think. My head felt the size of a balloon."

As described in *The Aquarian Gospel*, Dark Adepts can go everywhere; they can taint food and drink, and even enter the human body, causing mental illness, epilepsy, plagues, stillbirths and the giving over of a human to the Brothers of the Dark, the guardians of the Abyss.

Then his mind goes back to the hard-bitten lawyer, the Canadian from Vancouver, the most skeptical of the three dissidents; the one who isn't buying any of it and seems not to give a tinker's damn about Dark Adepts.

Nettles heads for Elliot Linden's house at once.

WESTERN UNION TELEGRAPH
TELEGRAM

JUNE 13 1929

INSP CALVIN HOOK
VANCOUVER POLICE DEPARTMENT
200 CORDOVA ST
VANCOUVER
CANADA

   SPIDER LAKE FISHING LODGE WISCONSIN

BEE CALDWELL
SECRETARY

WESTERN UNION TELEGRAPH
TELEGRAPH

JUNE 14 1929

INSP CALVIN HOOK
VANCOUVER POLICE DEPARTMENT
200 CORDOVA ST
VANCOUVER
CANADA

ALVIN PINE MADE RESERVATION DID NOT ARRIVE
DEPOSIT FORFEITED WHEREABOUTS UNKNOWN

TED MOODY
OWNER
SPIDER LAKE FISHING LODGE

HERE IS TUCKER, Palmer and Pine. Are you there?
Operator speaking, Seymour exchange. Vancouver Police calling Alvin Pine's office.
I will put you through.
SWITCH
Alvin Pine's office, are you there?
Operator speaking, I have police Inspector Hook on the line.
Please make the connection.
SWITCH
Here is Inspector Hook, VPD, calling Alvin Pine.
Here is Bee Caldwell, Mr. Pine's secretary. Mr. Pine is in New York.
We are aware of that, Miss Caldwell. I'm calling about Mr. Pine, concerning a fishing trip.
A what, sir?
You mentioned a fishing trip. I take it Mr. Pine is an avid fisherman.
I don't know where you got that information, sir. Mr. Pine will have nothing to do with fish.
Can you explain what you mean by that, Miss Caldwell?
Mr. Pine has a severe allergy. Just the smell of fish gives him hives.

OPERATOR SPEAKING, FRAUD department, are you there?
Inspector Hook here for Sergeant Quam.

I will connect you now.

SWITCH

Sergeant Quam here.

Quam, I'm calling about Alvin Pine.

Have you got in touch with him, sir?

Actually, Sergeant, I suspect Mr. Pine might be at the bottom of Spider Lake.

CHAPTER 30

"LAND OF GOSHEN, ducky, ye look bloody ghastly. Ye poor soul, I asked the girls about dentists, and Sarah Ashley said she went to Dr. Trott. She said it didn't hurt a bit."

"Mrs. Ashley gave birth to, I think, seven children, did she not, pet? Women have a different standard when it comes to pain."

"But surely it can't be worse than the war, luv. The dentists there were butchers, plain and simple."

It can't have been worse than the war.

Like most civilians, Jeanie is always asking about the war and, like most veterans, Hook prefers not to talk about it. At first it was just that words failed him; but now there is a feeling of distaste, as if the laudable desire to understand or share the suffering has become a morbid fascination with blood and bones, a form of Grand Guignol.

Rather than try and describe the front, Hook settled for tales of Rugeley Camp, and the inevitable result when eighteen-year-old recruits mishandle trench mortars. Once, he referred to the dentist shortage in 1915, when, rather than face an exhausted and often drunk dentist, men preferred informal extractions courtesy of a rugby player with a strong headlock and a pair of pliers.

"No, it wasn't worse than the war, pet. Nothing is worse than the war. But I'm afraid Dr. Trott will have to wait. I have other things on my mind right now."

"Police work, d'ye mean?"

"A troubling case, yes."

"Oh, tell me about it, luv. The baby's asleep for once an' I've heard no decent crack today."

"You need a radio at home, Jeanie. It would be sixty dollars well spent."

"Aye, ducky, but add to that the cost of the loudspeaker—ye can't do housework in headphones. And there's the antenna kit."

"I could make a loop antenna with some wire."

"No need when I can take Lucille over to Tilly Wallwork's anytime for a listen. Her brother-in-law works in the electrical department at Spencer's. So dinna fesh yerself about a radio. Sit down with me and tell me about yer latest case."

Hook fetches a bottle of beer he's been saving in the icebox, and returns to the couch. "It has to do with Mr. McCurdy—you know, my contact with the *Evening Star*—"

"Oh, but it's Mr. Good-Evening now, don't you know? A star he is, on the pig's back."

"Not far as he's concerned, pet. Mr. Good-Evening has got into a spot of trouble, and he's taken Ed McCurdy along with him."

"I s'pose it's the fans crawlin' all over 'im."

"You're close, except this fan is the opposite of a fan—threats, curses, bloody messages on his pillow, for Pete's sake—which means his enemy has the run of his posh club.

"It's driving Ed round the twist. Do you know, he thinks it's the same Limey gorilla who chased him down the street, and listen to this, pet—the bugger can vanish and reappear a city block away, have you ever heard the like of it?"

Unexpectedly, Jeanie frowns. "Makes me think of some yobbos in the old country."

"He does sound like a rough customer. Ed says he was a tall galoot with long teeth. Carried a stick, like an upside-down golf club. And trousers with a belt buckle the size of a bread plate."

"With sharpened edges?"

"Beg your pardon, pet?"

"Did the belt 'ave sharpened edges? To use as a weapon?"

"Why do you ask that?"

"Yer upside-down golf club were no golf club, it was a shillelagh. Ye know, ducky, he sounds to me like a Norton—except they were twins."

Hook nearly spurts beer from his nose. "*Twins?*"

"They looked so alike—even dressed alike. Ye never knew which Norton ye were looking at. See, they liked to confuse people, for a joke—like makin' 'em think they were two places at once."

CHAPTER 31

LINDEN'S TINY BUNGALOW has plenty of room for a guest now that his wife has departed for Vancouver. Their story was that she needed to access family funds for the Work, when in fact Rose is every bit as disillusioned as he is. For Rose, the issue is the Brother's treatment of Alma.

Elliot has remained because he'll be damned if he'll abandon the island until he gets his money back. For a lawyer who has defended loan sharks and swindlers, it's a matter of professional pride.

When it comes to the matter at hand, Nettles and Linden are on the same team, at least for the time being; so when Nettles arrives at Linden's door, ashen-faced and trembling, he is welcomed immediately and, moments later, finds himself on a kitchen chair in front of the stove, with a tumbler of heated Old Forester in hand. (In this part of the world, June soaks one's very bones with a dank wetness that never quite goes away.)

"Elliot, I'm here because I can't go anywhere near my cabin."

"Dark Adepts about, are there?" Linden produces two Sweet Caps, hands one to Nettles and lights them both with a kitchen match.

"It's not funny, Elliot. I gave him my resignation and he literally drew my thoughts out of my mouth—thoughts I would not have uttered for the life of me. Then when the ranting finally stopped on its own, mid-sentence, he gave me a look that stopped my breath. It was as though beams of evil shot out of his pupils, like a rush of thick, black light..."

Overcome for the moment, Nettles covers his eyes. Linden examines his bourbon, holding off a response until his guest has dried his face with his handkerchief and put a good, stiff slug down the neck.

"See here, Bob: I sunk two thousand bucks into this rascal. Rose fell for him too, and we're not chumps. Now, I've defended fakes my whole career—frauds, quacks, con men—and here's something I can

169

tell you: just because a man is bent, it doesn't follow that everything about him is bent, or that he was *always* bent. More times than not, your fake clairvoyant is some guy who saw his grandfather's ghost as a kid, then tried to make money out of it—only it was something he couldn't control, see? So in order to pull in an income, he becomes a fake. But that doesn't mean he was *always* a fake.

"Now, in the case of the Brother, I still don't know why I took one step into that clearing and my feet suddenly stopped functioning.

"But even so, I have broken with the disciples who want to lay hands on a radio announcer and expel the Dark Adept that Sydney Backstone says he heard—whose voice supposedly corrupted our incorruptible Brother Osiris. And they're serious, Bob! There's talk of separating the radio announcer's ethereal body from his earthly body—can you believe that?"

Nettles sags in his chair. "Gosh bless my soul. If that's so, heaven help the broadcaster."

MY BROTHERS AND Sisters, as we enter the Last Days, consider that seismic jolt to human understanding that comes from a single event: the discovery of radio waves.

Radio waves. The outer spheres made audible, through a receiver.

A medium.

What does this mean? It means that, for the first time in human history, the spirit world can communicate with the living. Suddenly, everyone has access to a medium, with the purchase of a household receiver.

This may seem jolly democratic and good—but when the ground is moving under one's feet, that is no time to jump for joy.

For the Brothers who cast for the future of the human race, the new medium is a source of hope—but also of evil. Because when the untrained, unenlightened person turns that knob, he opens a door— and he has no means of controlling who, or what, comes into the room.

Open the door to the Light, and you also open the door to the Dark. And only a High Adept can tell the one from the other.

That is why in our community there is only one radio, and why it is kept in a safe place, available only to me and to the Brothers of the Light—so that the auric egg is not pierced and entered by the Brothers of the Shadow.

CHAPTER 32

DI HOOK TAKES the Hastings streetcar to the Army and Navy Store ("The Plain Store for Plain People"), a discount emporium featuring liquidated stock and war-surplus goods, where one can buy cheap clothing for the whole family, as well as fishing gear, a tin hat, a gas mask and a .303 Lee-Enfield with scope and ammunition.

His purpose is to put to rest Jeanie's friend's mention of a man with a limp.

As Sergeant Quam once put it, "Rumour among servants is always unreliable." How he might know that is uncertain, but it rings true.

In any case, Hook must leave no stone unturned—especially when there is only one stone.

He shows his warrant card to a preposterously overburdened clerk at the cash register, ministering as best she can to a queue of impatient shoppers, all of whom look like rag-and-bone women with their enormous mounds of miscellaneous goods, some with price tickets attached, and some not—meaning that the cashier has to chase it down. Peering over the top of the cash register, Hook tries to introduce himself, waving his warrant card.

Not so much as a glance in his direction, no pause in the clicking of the keys. In a uniform he would have her attention; in this getup he might as well speak to the cash register.

Having no alternative, for the next twenty minutes he sets out on his own, a solitary man in a maze populated by busy women— moving sideways and apologizing, up and down corridors, with hangers on each side holding items of clothing from house dress to battle dress, from business suit to boiler suit, followed by racks of hats and shoes, military and civilian. Threading his way delicately between shoppers' buttocks, at last he catches sight of the owner, a natty bird in his mid-thirties, in a double-breasted suit that didn't come from one of his racks, with slicked-back hair, rimless glasses, an unlit cigar between his teeth and an air of watchful contentment, like a jungle beast presiding over his territory.

Hook flashes his warrant card. "Mr. Cohen, sir, I'm Inspector Hook of the VPD. Might we have a word?"

Cohen grins indulgently. He is used to policemen turning up without notice to inquire about one or another of his suppliers. The last time, it was about the truckload of Frigidaires from an appliance store in Calgary that sustained fire damage while the owner was vacationing in Florida. How could he have known about that?

"Sure thing, Officer, how's tricks?" Cohen lights what's left of his morning cigar.

"Tricks could be easier, sir, but thank you. I'm looking for a bloke with a funny walk who was here selling fabrics."

Cohen laughs. "The American? I looked at his *ungapatsket* samples, crazy his prices were, and we don't sell yard goods anyway. So I sicced him on the Saba Brothers, those Lebanese *machers* on Granville—you should try them, why don't you?"

"Can you describe the individual who tried to sell you yard goods?"

Cohen watches his smoke ring hover in the air as though it contained a memory. "He told me his name was Feldman and he was from some shmatte outfit in the garment district, claimed he supplied Siegel-Cooper in Chicago. Another schlemiel, was my thought.

"He wore a raincoat and a Sears Roebuck suit—I'd say he was about as tall as Betty Boop, maybe five two, size forty. Could be any age—face like a *lobbus* and a walk like an *alte kaker*, like his foot went asleep and he was shaking it out."

Hook makes a note, sighing inwardly. That's police work for you; as if the investigation weren't complicated enough, now he has Yiddish to deal with. Just how many languages do people *speak* in this city?

Cohen studies the soggy cigar stump between his fingers. "Oh yeah, spats. He wore spats. Definitely out. We bought a gross last year, it's like they're glued to the shelves. Timing, Officer. Timing is everything, believe me."

"You've been most helpful, Mr. Cohen. Thank you."

"Don't mention it. Come in sometime, bring the wife—talk to me, I can get you such a bargain..."

DI Hook plows through the throng and out the door onto Hastings, then ankles it uptown to the Saba Brothers on Granville.

(A year ago he would ride on his motorcycle. That was before he became a family man. Now the motorcycle is under a tarp on the back porch, collecting rust.)

Mike Saba corroborates Cohen's observation that the unsuccessful salesman was short in height, of indeterminate age, had an unusual walk and wore spats. Like Cohen, he firmly informed the peddler that they wanted nothing to do with his tatty silk swatches and gave him the bum's rush.

Another trail to nowhere—unless he tracks his quarry to one of the salesman's hotels.

After all, a man has to sleep somewhere.

CHAPTER 33

GOOD EVENING. THIS *is the nightly news service of the Canadian National Railway, brought to you by the Vancouver Evening Star. China and the Soviet Union have agreed to meet for peace talks, while in Switzerland the Geneva Convention was signed, covering the treatment of prisoners of war. Meanwhile, London city fathers have announced that in future all buses should be red.*

Turning to the US, in order to strengthen enforcement of Prohibition, Congress has passed the Increased Penalties Act, and on Flag Day, President Herbert Hoover predicted an era of economic growth unmatched in human history. Gangster Al Capone is in Holmesburg Prison, Philadelphia, following his arrest for carrying concealed weapons, and Mickey Mouse has become the first cartoon character to speak. His first words were, quote, Hot dogs! unquote.

Turning to Canada, Charlotte Whitton of the Canadian Council on Child Welfare warned that a family allowance would reduce wives to economic slavery, and in sports, the Portland Buckaroos defeated the Vancouver Lions three to one; and in women's hockey, the Vancouver Amazons outscored the Calgary Hollies four to two...

You have been listening to the nightly news service of the Canadian National Railway, brought to you by the Vancouver Evening Star. As we end our broadcast, we wish all our listeners—the nurses, clerks, teachers and especially the shut-ins—a restful good evening.

WELL, THERE'S ANOTHER one over. Over past months, McCurdy's schedule has taken on an eerie regularity, a sense that he is living the same day of the week over and over, so that the only way he knows Monday from Wednesday is from his broadcast.

He throws on his hat and coat, exits the studio and heads down the hall—and is stopped cold by Mrs. Dixon, leaning in the door frame of her office in a plume of cigarette smoke, with the expression of faux concern on her mug that precedes a personal attack.

"Mr. McCurdy, what on earth has happened to your diction?"

He looks at the ceiling for strength. "What is it about my diction, Mrs. Dixon?"

"It's your consonants. Are you drunk?"

"Certainly not."

"Well, it's worrying, is all I can say. It's certainly noticeable to the listeners. Do you suppose that dreadful electric shock you suffered has affected your mind?"

"A touch of aphasia do you think, Mrs. Dixon?"

"A touch of what?"

"Surely you studied Latin in school."

"As a matter of fact, I won the Latin prize at St. Ann's Academy. Mr. McCurdy, just what are you insinuating?"

CHAPTER 34

AFTER A LONG night discussing what's to be done, Elliot Linden bribes a boatman to ferry him and Nettles across the channel with an empty tweed suitcase, and once they reach Nanaimo Harbour they walk straight to the Canadian Bank of Commerce.

Pausing briefly amid the semicircle of enormous Corinthian pillars before the entrance, Nettles thinks of Samson, who pulled down the Temple of Dagon, killing thousands of Philistines—as well as himself.

He wonders briefly if the men who designed the bank were aware that pillars aren't necessarily a sign of civilization, that philistines own the world.

"Try to appear calm," Linden says. "You look like you're about to pull a robbery."

Nettles wipes his forehead with his handkerchief. "I'm expecting to be struck dumb at any moment. Or dead."

"It won't make for any good, if you give yourself a heart attack."

"I suppose not. Well..." He takes a deep breath, straightens his tie and enters the building

Nettles's shoes squeak on the marble floor as he approaches one of the tellers' wickets; meanwhile, Linden waits in what seems like an enormous mausoleum, feeling like the getaway man.

The teller's perpetually pursed lips turn upward. "Good morning, Mr. Nettles, sir. And how may I serve you today?"

"Good morning, Alfred. I wish to withdraw two thousand dollars from the general fund." (This is the accrued amount Nettles has earned on De Courcy Island. Upon his arrival, the Brother insisted on paying him fifty dollars per month, to separate the business and the spiritual sides of their relationship.)

Though Nettles is a familiar face in the bank on Aquarian business, Alfred's eyes widen at such a large withdrawal taking place at one time.

"Gee. Wow, Mr. Nettles, are you planning to buy an auto?"

"It's a business matter, Alfred. The money is to settle a real estate deal."

"I see. Of course. Certified cheque or bank draft?"

"Neither. In cash. Twenties, preferably." Nettles dabs at his neck to stop a trickle of sweat.

At the word *cash*, the teller's eyes take on a trapped, wary look. "Oh. Oh. Yes. That is a, a, an unusual request, Mr. Nettles, I really must talk to Mr. Briggs."

He scurries off and fetches Mr. Briggs, the bank manager, whose teeth appear too big for his mouth, causing some to wonder if his lips ever touch. (Tellers and other staff like to imitate him when he's not looking.)

"Cheerio, Bob. How's tricks?"

"Just dandy, Terry, and yourself?"

"Absolutely top-drawer, old chap, now what can I do for you?"

"A matter of some cash, Terry. Two thousand on the general account."

"And the denominations?

"Twenties, if you have them."

"Sounds perfectly in order, but goodness, Bob, I don't know that we have that many twenties. Alfred will do his level best, won't you, Alfred?"

"Assuredly, sir."

"Sorry for the trouble, Terry."

"Not at all, Bob, that's what we're here for." Smiling with those teeth of his, Mr. Briggs returns to his office.

Linden approaches the wicket while Alfred piles the currency in stacks, which the two men quickly stuff into the empty suitcase.

From the steps of the Bank of Commerce, they walk directly to the Nanaimo detachment of the RCMP, where Nettles lays a charge of fraud against Edward Collins. It goes remarkably smoothly with Linden by his side, really just a matter of paperwork—in fact, when the name of the accused comes up, the desk sergeant seems unsurprised, even pleased.

By the time they make their way back to De Courcy Island, it's already mid-afternoon. They go straight to Nettles's cabin, where he packs a second suitcase, the plan being for Linden to drive him to Victoria in time to catch the *Princess Elaine* to Vancouver.

Waiting for them outside on Linden's veranda is an officer with the provincial police, in an army uniform with dark green epaulets and a Sam Browne belt.

"Gentlemen, I'm looking for a Robert Nettles. Can you direct me to him?"

"I'm Robert Nettles, Officer. I take it you're here about my charges against Edward Peter Collins."

"That's correct in a way of saying, sir, but it's the other way around. You have been charged with the crime of embezzlement, and I have a warrant for your arrest."

CHAPTER 35

DI HOOK'S RENEWED search for his person of interest begins with the Travellers Hotel on Abbott, which produces no record of a Feldman, nor does anyone remember a short man with an odd walk.

From there, one after the other, he stops in at the Manitoba, the Crown, the Rob Roy, the Ranier, the Atlantic, the New Fountain, the Stanley, the Bodega and the Alhambra, all with the same result.

With the sense that he is in another blind alley, he crosses Maple Tree Square to the Hotel Europe—a flatiron building at the intersection where Powell meets Alexander. By now it's mid-afternoon, and his arches pain him along with his head and his molar. He stops to retrieve four Aspirin from his coat pocket, pops them into his mouth and chews. The bitterness matches his mood.

Is this what a police inspector does? Trudge from door to door like a Fuller Brush salesman?

Whether it's the taste of the Aspirin, his collection of aches and pains or some sort of policeman's instinct, something about the Hotel Europe's desk clerk puts him off—a bird-faced young fellow with a sniffy expression like a vendor of expensive soap. Hook notes the speculative glint in his eye, indicating an employee with a sideline in condoms, drugs, alcohol and working girls. (There's one in every hotel, even—especially—the Hotel Vancouver.)

Hook holds up his warrant card. "Sir, I'm Inspector Hook with the VPD, and I wish to see your guest book, if you don't mind."

The desk clerk frowns as though Hook just asked him for his wallet, takes the warrant card and examines it like a suspected counterfeit, then hands it back with a put-upon sigh.

"Very well, Officer. Our guest book. Certainly."

Lifting one eyebrow, he reaches beneath the counter and produces an oblong accounting ledger, leather-bound, with *Hotel Europe* in a poncey gold script several classes above the joint itself.

"And the name of the guest, sir?"

"Feldman."

He runs a bitten fingernail down the guest list with exaggerated care. "No. No, I see nobody named Feldman registered at the hotel."

"He may be going under another name."

The desk clerk lifts the other eyebrow. "Then how would I know which guest is the real Feldman, sir? I'm not a mind reader."

Hook's tooth is starting to throb again. "He's a short guy with a funny walk. Wears spats and a checkered suit. Maybe talks with a lisp."

"Oh. Oh—yes, I remember the spats. So quaint. But I don't remember a lisp."

Hook notes that the desk clerk has a slight lisp himself.

The desk clerk reopens the guest book, runs his finger up and down one column after another, maddeningly slow, until finally the forefinger stops.

Hook would like to kill him. Maybe it's the tooth.

"Ah. Yes. Here he is. The guest you're looking for could well be Mr. Buchman."

"Is Mr. Buchman in at present?"

The desk clerk glances behind him at an open cabinet of small cubbies containing room keys. "I don't see his key, Officer. Let me just double-check."

He picks up the telephone receiver, dials a three-digit number, waits, then hangs up. "No, I'm afraid... Wait. Now that I think of it, Mr. Buchman did slip out, it was about an hour ago. To make a few calls, I believe was what he said."

"Did Mr. Buchman say when he'd be back?"

"He said in an hour or two. Feel free to wait here in the lobby, if you like."

Rather than sit here staring at the desk clerk's supercilious puss, he heads down the hall and into the inevitable beer parlour, plops onto a bentwood chair and exhales a sigh of relief, then lights an Ogden's (his fifth so far today—one over quota), and scans the room. The windows are half-covered by curtains, so that passersby can't see the shameful activity going on within; at the same time, the curtains deprive drinkers of a view of the street, which might distract them from their beer.

With its white tiled surfaces, the room could be an enormous triangular loo, were it not for the bentwood chairs and oval tables, each with a salt shaker to liven stale beer.

He overtips the sinewy waiter with the navy tattoos, swigs back a mouthful, wipes his upper lip with the back of his hand, nods approval and flashes his warrant card. "I'm looking for a short guy with a funny walk. Seen anyone answering to that description?"

The waiter pauses and scratches his armpit. "Sure. Been a regular for the past week. From New York, by the accent. One of those guys who looks like he could be anyone, except for that walk."

Abruptly, he turns to peer over the window curtain and into the street. "Well, ain't that a funny thing! The bloke just walked by!"

Hook stubs out his barely smoked Ogden's, abandons his nearly full glass of beer, rushes out the side entrance—and stops, torn between right and left, until he looks eastward: down Alexander Street, next to the City Hotel, where he catches sight of a small man with what could possibly be an odd walk, a sort of abbreviated skip.

He breaks into a run, his arches howling in pain, shouting at the fellow like a London bobby without his whistle: "Stop! Police!"

Our man stops, and turns to face the officer. Hook sees his expression of innocent alarm, and experiences a depressing wave of doubt.

"Sir, I'm Inspector Hook of the VPD. Who are you and what is your business?"

"My name is Wayne Clark. I sell hardware at Boyd and Burns down the street, and at present I'm trying to scrape dog shit off my shoe."

Mr. Clark lifts one foot to present the stinking brown clod stuck to the sole.

"Please carry on, sir. As for me, I generally use the curb for such a purpose."

"You're right, Officer, but I was in a bit of a hurry."

With a brisk nod, Hook turns and heads back to the Hotel Europe—then stops, as a thought flashes through his brain, like a signal relay warning of an enemy presence.

His tooth drumming a military tattoo, Hook marches into the Hotel Europe and pounds the bell repeatedly. The desk clerk emerges, the same desk clerk, the one whose nose he would dearly like to smash flat. "Were you ever with the signal corps, by any chance?"

"I don't know what you're talking about."

"Ah, so you didn't serve. I might have known. Show me to Mr. Buchman's room at once."

Again the theatrical flinch, the hissed intake of breath. "Oh, I can't do that, sir. I'd have to get permission from the manager."

"And where is the manager?"

"He went out for lunch."

"At three thirty in the afternoon?"

"Mr. Savory takes long lunches. In any case, for a policeman to enter a guest's room will require a warrant."

Hook reaches out, grasps the desk clerk's tie in his fist and pulls firmly until the face is within six inches of his.

"Listen, punk. This is a murder investigation. If I don't see you opening the door to that room in five minutes, twenty minutes after that the joint will be swarming with coppers. What will Mr. Savory say when you tell him the guests all checked out early?"

With a sullen expression, the desk clerk fetches a room key. "Follow me, then. I could be fired for doing this, you know."

"More likely you'd be fired for *not* doing it."

Hook follows the desk clerk's serge-covered arse (worn shiny) up to the fourth floor, down the hall, and as soon as the door to Room 401 is open he shoulders the fellow aside and steps into a room with one converging wall, containing a brass bed, a rosewood dresser and side table, window curtains with ball fringes and an argyle rug. Prints on three walls depict a horse and rider, a Dutch windmill and a ship in a storm.

Hook crosses to the bed, noting the feather pillow bunched against the brass bars at the head.

"When was this bed last made?"

"Let me see, on this floor..." The desk clerk pretends to scour his memory. "Now, that would have been around eleven thirty this morning."

"Someone's head has been on the pillow since then, and someone's shoes left dirt on the coverlet."

The desk clerk joins him by the bed and brushes off a sprinkle of road dirt. "You'd think they'd at least take the trouble to put down a newspaper, but they never do."

"That's because he was reading one." Hook picks up today's *Province* from the side table, folded to City News.

All the drawers are empty, all the hangers bare. Other than that newspaper, the occupant has left no vestige of his presence. Hook pictures himself cooling his heels in the lobby at the desk clerk's invitation all afternoon, waiting for someone who had no intention of returning.

A sharp pain in the molar tells him he is grinding his teeth. He puts that energy to better use by slamming the desk clerk hard against the wall and pinning him to the wallpaper with his shoes in the air.

"I take it your guest is a generous tipper."

"What do you mean?"

"When you called up, Buchman answered—didn't he?"

"Please put me down."

"Your call warned him off—didn't it? By prior arrangement."

"I don't have a clue what you're talking about. Please put me down!"

Hook grasps the desk clerk by the front of his button tunic, using enough force that the fabric tears, then pitches him against the opposite wall, hard enough that the framed windmill crashes to the floor.

"You asshole, you just helped a suspected murderer escape custody. Aiding and abetting will get you five years."

"What!?"

The desk clerk is now truly frightened—by the prospect of jail more than the manhandling.

"I asked if you were a signalman, remember?"

"You're crazy! What the blazes are you talking about?"

"A signalman delivers a message—in code. Like a given number of rings on the goddamned telephone when you called the room! Am I wrong? Am I wrong?" The desk clerk is slammed against the wall with each repetition until the ship in a storm meets the same fate as the windmill.

"Yes! No! Sweet Jesus, you're not wrong, now for the love of God please stop!"

Hook releases his grip, then tries to calm down, while the desk clerk recovers his breath. He has a vicious headache. His tooth throbs. Tomorrow he will ask Blatchford once again for a support team, but right now he just wants to go home.

The desk clerk sinks to the floor next to the wardrobe.

"Jesus Christ, it was just a service! Like a fucking wake-up call!"

WEIRD OCCULTISM ON DE COURCY ISLAND
Cult Leader Charged
Dallas MacElwee
The Victoria Colonist

Telephone lines throughout the province have been humming with reports of bizarre activities concerning a theosophy cult in which free love is celebrated and marriage is abolished.

New charges of financial skulduggery on the part of its leader suggest that, while the majority of his followers undoubtedly adhere to his peculiar brand of mystical exotica, a few disciples have been moved to rebel, albeit on more down-to-earth grounds.

The defendant is a self-styled "incarnation" named Edward Peter Collins, a former express clerk at Wells Fargo who went to sea for several years, experienced "mystical visions" and returned to Canada as Brother Osiris, purportedly a reincarnation of the Egyptian deity Osiris.

His teachings are a jumble of arcane doctrines from Zoroaster to Madame Blavatsky, with incomprehensible additions from Collins himself, having received, or so he claims, "personal instructions from the Masters."

However tenuous his creed, Brother Osiris has attracted thousands of supporters in the United States, thanks to its widely circulated monthly magazine, the *Chalice*, billed as "the Herald of the New Age" and featuring regular appeals for funds under the name of the Aquarian Foundation.

Since its founding, about one hundred and fifty of the society's wealthiest adherents, nearly all of them Americans, have formed the nucleus of a substantial settlement on De Courcy Island, where these "seekers" or "disciples" serve as volunteer labourers awaiting the New Age, working a property that is encircled by barbed-wire fencing to ward off refugees from the coming apocalypse.

Thanks to overwhelming public interest in the Aquarian Foundation and the antics of its adherents, this reporter has been assigned to cover the trial at Nanaimo Provincial Court.

At issue is a donation made by a disciple, Mrs. Ida Arrowsmith. Mrs. Arrowsmith has accused Brother Osiris of using over twenty-five thousand dollars for creating a separate settlement on nearby Valdes Island, devoted to another Egyptian deity and led by a woman named Muriel Riffle, who goes by the name Madame Zura and is the wife of another disciple, Roger Flagler, who made his fortune in America as "the Poultry King of Florida."

The charge against Brother Osiris is supported by Robert Nettles, who was the Aquarian Foundation's secretary-treasurer as well as the colony's paid accountant, and who claims to have proof that Brother Osiris falsified documents to obtain Mrs. Arrowsmith's funds for his own use.

Seemingly in retribution, Nettles has himself been charged with embezzlement by Brother Osiris over the former accountant's withdrawal of back wages.

Elliot Linden, a Vancouver barrister on leave whose devotion to the cult leader has likewise soured, has agreed to act as surety for the accused with a pledge of one thousand dollars.

"We were glad to serve the Brother," Linden said, "until we realized we had been deceived—that we weren't serving the movement, we were enriching Edward Peter Collins."

What will come of the trial remains to be seen. At stake in the coming days is, in effect, Brother Osiris's entire organization, and by association, theosophy itself.

FATAL FLAPPER CHARGE WEAKENS
Undermined by Recent Events
Max Trotter
Staff Writer
The Vancouver World

The preliminary inquiry into a charge of murder against Miss Dora Decker resumed as scheduled, though shaken by the death of the victim's business partner, Edgar Palmer, who fell to his death from an office window.

In what has become known internationally as the Fatal Flapper case, Miss Decker stands accused of murdering her employer, Ralph M. Tucker of Tucker, Palmer and Pine, with a spike-heeled shoe.

In his opening statement, prosecutor Conrad Lynch presented a powerful, if somewhat theatrical, demonstration in order to establish the brutality of the crime and the rage that must have accompanied it, and thereby prepare a basis for establishing a motive.

However, the sudden death of Edgar Palmer last Tuesday has complicated the prosecution's case—and will further complicate it if commonalities are found between the two, and police attention turns to the business dealings of the firm as a whole.

Adding to a general sense that the whole story remains to be told, Alvin Pine, the surviving partner in the firm, is vacationing in the United States and cannot be contacted.

According to a source within the VPD, in their effort to obtain a statement from Pine, police have traced the securities trader to hotels in New York, Miami, Arkansas, Boston and Havana, Cuba. At this time he is reported to be somewhere in the wilds of Wisconsin and, once again, out of reach.

Some observers question whether Pine has gone on the lam, or whether he is a murder victim himself.

In the packed courtroom, the excitement was palpable. Indeed, when Miss Decker was escorted through the door, spectators jostled one another for a look at her shoes, which turned out to be a modest pair of Mary Janes.

Duty Counsel Phillip Dagg having withdrawn due to health concerns, Miss Decker was represented by Tristan Sweet of Bird, Rabinowitz, Farris and Sweet, a firm known for its defence of Orientals, Indians and Socialists.

In his introductory statement, Mr. Sweet focused on his client's age, physical size and religious upbringing, then turned to the evidence itself.

"My learned friend," said Mr. Sweet, "has seen fit to occupy an entire day in presenting the alarming state of the corpse and of the office as prima facie evidence of rage on the part of the murderer.

"If that is so, then the question arises: Why a *shoe*?

"I intend to recall as a witness Inspector Calvin Hook— who, during the investigation, catalogued a number of other potential murder weapons in the office within reach of an enraged assailant."

At this point, Sweet opened a small suitcase on the counsel table and produced a heavy crystal ashtray: "My Lord, I present as evidence this crystal ashtray, found on Mr. Tucker's desk and weighing exactly three and a half pounds. Note its angular shape, the sharp edges, and think what it could do to a man's skull.

"Then we have Mr. Tucker's silver letter opener, also on the desk. Shaped like a dagger and just as sharp. Just next to it stood a black marble pen stand, also of a substantial weight, holding two long fountain pens with sharp points at both ends. Were it thrust in the eye of an enemy, one of these pens would indeed be as mighty as a sword.

"And yet my friend here would have it that, rather than bludgeoning the victim with the ashtray or stabbing him with a pen, the accused employed her *shoe!*"

Defence counsel then undertook a theatrical demonstration to equal the prosecution, which included a passable imitation of Harold Lloyd, as Mr. Sweet stood on one foot, reached down, pulled off his own shoe and nearly fell down doing it; then, still on one foot, he lifted the shoe above his head as though to strike someone with the heel—and nearly fell to the floor once again.

Titters and a scattering of applause among the spectators prompted a reprimand from Judge Reid: "I advise counsel for the defence that this is a courtroom and not a vaudeville stage."

Replied Mr. Sweet: "I apologize for the undignified display, My Lord, but surely we must not forget that Mr. Tucker was an amateur rugby player of some note, and that these items were within *his* reach as well, ready to be used as a weapon against, supposedly, a slip of a girl standing on one foot with a shoe, one without.

"I challenge the court to look at the evidence, look at my client, and conclude that there is reasonable doubt that this girl overpowered a two-hundred-pound man and beat him to death with her *shoe*. Moreover, you have seen the coroner's report—while not conclusive, the forensic evidence suggests that the shoe may not have been the murder weapon at all.

"My Lord, my client has already lost her job, her freedom, her good name and her happiness, on the basis of what is turning out to have been a hare-brained charge, inspired more by sensational press reports than by the facts of the case.

"I remind the court that Miss Decker is not without support. Her landlady, the owner of Miss Mildred Wickstram's Residence for Professional Women, has offered to put up bail of any reasonable amount."

On this note, Mr. Sweet returned to his seat and Judge Reid retired to his chambers, while spectators unleashed a hum of excited chatter—then fell silent minutes later upon the re-entrance of Judge Reid, who rendered his interim decision: "The Vancouver Police Department has in my view been less than comprehensive in its investigation. I order them to undertake a closer examination of the circumstances, including a renewed effort on the part of forensic science to determine what exactly killed Mr. Tucker.

"As for Miss Decker, I order that she be released on her own recognizance, under the care of the aforesaid Miss Mildred Wickstram."

MILDRED CATCHES UP with defence counsel on the first landing of the courthouse steps, beside an indifferent stone lion.

"You were brilliant, Mr. Sweet."

"It was embarrassingly easy. I have no idea what the police were using for brains."

She takes Tristan's arm and they proceed down the marble steps to the lawn.

"The police are not paid to think, darling, you know that. Still, embarrassed though you may be, the aforesaid Miss Wickstram owes you a favour."

"You never seem to call unless you want one."

"Touchy. It must seem that way, I know. Things have been hectic lately."

"And how. But I had to learn about all this from the papers, don't you know. It rather hurts a chap's feelings."

"Oh dear, I've accrued more debts! However should I settle my account?"

"Our two sides haven't taken fixed positions. Should we go into arbitration?"

"If we do, we must settle quickly. I'm to be at the lock-up at five to fetch Dora."

"Conveniently, I happen to have booked a room just across the street," he says, referring to the Italianate palace that covers the entire block between Georgia and Robson.

"My goodness, that *is* convenient."

With her arm in his, they proceed into the Hotel Vancouver, observed from above by a row of terracotta moose and buffalo.

189

CHAOS IN THE COURTROOM
Aquarian Hearing Shaken by "Occult Power"
Dallas MacElwee
The Victoria Colonist

The initial hearing into accusations of fraud against Edward Peter Collins, known by his followers as Brother Osiris, took a bizarre turn on Monday.

Collins stands accused of stealing a donation of twenty-five thousand dollars from Ida Arrowsmith and using it for his own purposes.

The accused is a slight, delicate man with iron-grey hair brushed back pompadour-style, a short, clipped beard, penetrating eyes and a warm smile. Behind the defence table he appeared serene, and showed neither concern nor surprise at the events that followed.

As the hearing began, nothing seemed unusual at first. Judge C.E. Drummond-Hay called the court to order, and following a brief conference with the two lawyers, T.P. Morton and Nathan Rimmer, the testimonial phase began.

Sydney M. Backstone was sworn in, a florid man who once edited esoteric magazines and one of the signatories of the so-called "Aquarian Manifesto"—a document denouncing the defendant and his assistant, Muriel Riffle (who calls herself Madame Zura) in no uncertain terms for having succumbed to temptation and joined the dark forces surrounding the community, which have thus far been kept at bay by something called the auric egg.

Mr. Backstone's purpose was to provide a general overview of the colony's structure and daily regimen. However, upon taking the stand, without uttering a word, the witness opened his mouth, groaned and crumpled onto the floor of the witness box.

The courtroom erupted as Backstone's wife Celia rushed to his aid, and Dr. Earl Hall administered smelling salts.

Mr. Backstone, having been rendered unable to continue his testimony, was assisted out of the building by the court officer.

After Judge Drummond-Hay managed to restore order, lawyer T.P. Morton stood to begin his opening argument.

Morton had barely begun his speech when he stopped in mid-sentence and gazed about in a confused manner, while the court looked on in shocked silence.

After what seemed like an interminable pause, Morton said, "This is ridiculous, but I've entirely forgotten what I was going to say!" He then shuffled back to his seat and buried his head in his hands.

A moment later, spectators gaped in disbelief as, whether from the same cause or from simple shock, several Aquarians slumped in their seats and keeled over onto the floor.

Events took an even stranger turn in the next few moments when Judge Drummond-Hay opened his mouth to declare a recess, coughed several times, then began to bark like a dog.

At this point a grave silence had fallen like a shroud over the courtroom; to this reporter's ear, it was the same silence that attended a public announcement listing the latest soldiers to die at the Somme.

When Judge Drummond-Hay finally found his voice, he could only manage to croak, weakly, "This court is adjourned."

Outside the courthouse, a crowd of spectators and curious onlookers gathered, telling and retelling the story with embellishments at every utterance. An even more heated gathering assembled to one side, exchanging impassioned views on who or what was responsible for this mystical donnybrook.

Many attributed the disruption to the power of Brother Osiris—who, they claimed, could injure enemies through the power of his thoughts.

Others referred to something or someone they called a Dark Adept, the theory being that the chaos in the courtroom was a result of an evil spirit's macabre sense of humour.

Much is left to discover, but interested observers will need to wait until the hearing resumes, following an adjournment of one week.

CHAPTER 36

IN HIS NAÏVETÉ, Inspector Hook walked into Blatchford's office in a positive frame of mind, and with a list of available officers who might make up his team.

The chief, who felt offended by the judge's remarks and by the defence attorney's flippant characterization of events, responded that, as per the court order in hand, the VPD would devote no further resources until Mr. Tucker's cause of death could be positively determined.

"But sir, Miss Decker has been effectively released! Surely you can see that the case against her is falling apart."

"Inspector, you've been getting on my nerves with your whining requests for additional resources on a settled case. By no means am I prepared to assign you a man, much less a team, to track down a short yard-goods salesman with an odd walk and a sad face, who may or may not talk with a lisp."

"But under the circumstances, given that the individual qualifies as a person of interest, surely due diligence—"

"Mr. Hook, don't lecture me about due diligence. In this instance, due diligence means you will have to produce concrete evidence if you want to convince me your so-called person of interest isn't a figment of your imagination. So far, you have only succeeded in making a pest of yourself. I wonder what possessed Barfoot that he would promote you. *Twice!*"

As usual, Hook left the office in a state of utter humiliation except for the feeling in the back of his neck that the chief was ragging the puck for reasons of his own. What might *he* have to do with Tucker, Palmer and Pine?

He has seen this sort of thing before with army brass in civilian life—their resistance to anything that might complicate a situation beyond their mental capacity.

Or maybe the chief just doesn't like him.

Whatever the case, Hook is snookered, with nobody to investigate who isn't either dead or seemingly fallen off the face of the earth.

Except for a short guy with a funny walk.

CHAPTER 37

AT PRESENT, MCCURDY has become fed up with Mr. Good-Evening's routine, though Mr. Good-Evening doesn't seem to mind.

Normally, he sees work not as a virtue but as a means of supporting one's vices. And one might think his elevated situation would allow him an elevated range of vices; but this doesn't sit well with Mr. Good-Evening, whose quarter hour determines the other twenty-three.

For Mr. Good-Evening (and McCurdy to some extent), the hours following one broadcast are defined by the prospect of having to perform the next one: reciting ninety seemingly random items as though they belong in the same discussion, despite creating an overall picture as jarring and incomprehensible as radical Dada. He must read this infernal nonsense with diction that can penetrate the overlay of speaker hiss and be understood by listeners with an imperfect command of English.

And he must perform his circus act in fifteen minutes, seven times a week.

It would be unwise to attempt such a feat when sozzled, muggled or in a state of fatigue—especially with Mrs. Dixon's sadistic eye for a tongue twister and her eagerness to record every mispronunciation and report it upstairs.

Which means that, in order to accommodate Mr. Good-Evening, McCurdy must arrange his affairs so that nine p.m. is the middle of his day—allowing time to recover, to sleep if possible, then time to achieve the correct balance of stimulants and depressants to face the microphone once more.

At this moment it's seven a.m., hours too early for a knock on his door to fully register—until a stab of panic jolts him awake: memories of previous early-morning knocks, coppers with calloused knuckles and hobnailed boots and a rolled-up telephone book...

Where are my glasses?

Spectacles in place, eyes open, with a groan he rolls his sodden log of a body so that the legs will drop over the side, and uses the resulting leverage to pull his torso to an upright condition.

Leaning forward, he massages his back until it will bend, and after heaving his body to standing, waddles to the door.

With a well-earned instinct for caution he turns the knob and pulls it slowly and gingerly until the door is slightly ajar, prepared to slam it shut should the party on the other side happen to be a policeman, a political fanatic or a moviegoer who resents Janet Gaynor winning the Academy Award.

Paris. In his checked evening suit, which looks much the worse for wear; and the concierge's skin tone can't disguise the bruising around his left eye. For the first time McCurdy can remember, Paris seems rattled.

"Terribly sorry to disturb you, Mr. McCurdy, sir, but I wonder if I might come in for a quick word."

McCurdy opens the door wide—and quickly—to admit his visitor, whose presence on an upper floor is a violation of Quadra Club rules.

"Come in at once, Paris. But while you're here, the name is Ed."

Paris steps over the threshold onto the waxed hardwood and looks the place over as though it's the first time he has entered a member's quarters (which it probably is), inspecting the Empire bed, the Hamadan rug, the fireplace tiles and coloured glass, the mahogany mantel and the oval mirror.

"Swanky crib, sir."

"It's Ed, Paris, I beg you. Remember, you kept my face from getting smashed."

"For which you provided a generous gratuity, sir."

"Even so, it's Ed or get the hell out of here."

"Okay, I dig." At a window, Paris looks down at the railway tracks, then from side to side, as though to see what life looks like up here.

McCurdy directs the concierge to one of two club chairs beside the fireplace. "You look like you could use a drink, and as far as I'm concerned it's the middle of the night."

"It isn't, but I surely could, sir."

"Ed."

"Ed, I'm George."

McCurdy shuffles to the side table and produces two glasses with a modest two fingers each.

They lift their drinks. "To better days, George."

"Got that right," says Paris, putting away his whisky in one gulp.

It takes time, and two more whiskies, to get to the reason behind Paris's visit. With acquaintances of different races, McCurdy figures, knowledge comes in droplets, over time.

At some point, McCurdy did a search on Paris at the paper— mostly in the Sports archives, as it turned out; of his progress from Truro, Nova Scotia, to Montreal, then to Vancouver—by which time he was known as the "coloured wonder" who had set a record for the hundred-yard dash and become Western Canada's heavyweight boxing champ, both at the same time.

When Jack Johnson came to the city for the Victor McLaglen fight and the world champion couldn't find a hotel, Paris put him up (he had played drums at Johnson's Chicago club), then went on to act as his personal trainer during Johnson's tour of Europe.

After his return, Paris coached the city's lacrosse club, until some louts in the stands pelted eggs and he produced a pistol. The fans nearly lynched him and he was promptly fired.

The Quadra Club is what Paris calls his "interim day gig."

Rather than question the battered concierge in his silk pajamas, McCurdy goes to the closet and puts on his dressing gown and slippers, then pours two more drinks.

"Tell me about the shiner, George."

With refill in hand, the concierge begins to relax enough to drop the Jeeves act and speak normally.

"You know 'bout my gig at the Lincoln?"

"Near Hogan's Alley. I plan to go there myself if they'll let me in."

"Well, last night the band is cookin' with Oscar in the pocket and Gatemouth wailin', the joint was jumpin', folks all muggled from tossin' shots of scrap iron, when these two tall honkies push their way through. At first I can't make out their faces through the smoke but they comin' closer an' I see one of them and he's the same mothafocka in swanky threads who came at us that night outside. Then I think I'm seein' double because damned if I'm not lookin' at twins! Like two cufflinks! Can't tell one from the other!"

McCurdy braces for what's coming. Paris takes a sip of whisky, then another, and continues.

"So I sees them gogglin' at me, hands in the pockets of them long coats, and one nods to the other, and I'm thinkin' these ain't just any mug men, we got a couple torpedoes gonna pull out heaters and shoot the place up—but no, they bring out they fists, so we cut the riff and everyone in the joint goes quiet, then these two start barkin' at me shit I never heard before—What's a Quashie?—but I knows the gist of what they're sayin' and I get hot and we get it on right there.

"Ed, the Limeys fight with heads and boots. You saw them big boots yourself, belt buckles filed sharp, pullin' 'em out and swingin' 'em around like whips, look at this shit they did here." Paris stands up and turns around so that McCurdy can see the razor slit down one side of his trousers, exposing his bare leg from hip to knee with a trickle of dried blood down to his sock. "Then he starts aimin' at the neck, like he's gonna give me the Harlem Sunset.

"So I played slugger, dropped one ape with a short left hook and overhand right, then a feint and a straight right put the otha mutha on his back. They be down permanent if I had my heater, after what they called me, I go to diddy-wah-diddy to get 'em good."

"Then it sounds like it was probably for the best that you weren't armed."

"Maybe so, maybe not, 'cause they say they're comin' to my crib, so I might need my gat after all."

A splinter of guilt lodges in McCurdy's stomach. In some way, he feels responsible for putting the man's life in danger.

"A gun in the home is one thing, George, but you don't want to be seen a second time waving one around."

"Got that right. Helen works as in-house kitchen mechanic for the Bentalls. She don't wanna lose that gig 'cause her man's in the caboose."

"George, maybe this isn't the best time to tell you that the twins are named Norton and they're what you'd term badass. They throw jurors out windows and they murder men for no reason."

Paris absorbs this, then frowns. "That 'splains the little alligator in the front row."

"You might as well continue, because I have no idea what you're talking about."

"A Mr. Charlie, a white jazz fan been coming in lately. Usually, we get the white folks at the late sets, rat-assed from the bars, but this short little bird digs the first set every night, same table, leaves right after, just a peewee with a funny walk.

"Well, soon as that rumble starts, Peewee whirls around with a shiv, like he's a bruno hisself."

"You mean he pulls out a knife?"

"Not a knife—it was a friggin' ice pick, man! Now what's some five-foot honky doin' carrying around an ice pick?"

"When he left, do you have any idea where he went?"

"Someone said he's at the Belvedere, but after this I 'spect he's at the station boardin' the first thing smokin'."

CHAPTER 38

FOR THREE DAYS, DI Hook has hunted his diminutive quarry without result, haunting the lobbies of hotels down the ladder of gentility, from the Blue Guide listings to the shabby fleabags full of veterans on inadequate pensions.

The procedure hasn't been without risk. Sooner or later, his inspections are bound to lead him into a Joe Celona creep joint—either owned by him or under his protection. Hook hopes it won't come to that. Getting up Celona's nose is an excellent way to get hammered down to a pulp by higher-ups.

At worst, his devotion to the case could put him in the intersection of Granville and Hastings, directing traffic for the rest of his life—having upset the delicate entente cordiale between Vancouver's city fathers and the so-called underworld, by annoying Joe Celona.

Not to mention the prospect of Celona's hefty squad of apes and goons, whose job it is to deal with people who are bad for business.

This investigation could cost him not only his job, but his knees.

A couple of years ago at an in-camera city council meeting, council reached a majority consensus to the effect that, since the Joe Celona organization was the best of a bad lot, his use in eliminating rivals and freelancers outweighed his moral cost to the city.

Understandably, city fathers preferred not to make a public announcement of Celona's exemption from the normal rules of civilization, or to acknowledge that Celona did any business at all other than to operate Celona's Tobacco, just across the street from City Hall and always with a stock of the mayor's favourite stogies.

In no way had Hook expected a tip from McCurdy, for whom the word on the street has become as foreign as the latest gossip in Timbuktu. Also surprising that the information came not from Miss Wickstram, but from a drummer with the Oscar Holden Band.

Ed never mentioned he was a jazz fan.

But a tip is a tip, especially when there have *been* no tips. So Hook's one-man inquiry has made its way to a pocket of hotels in name only, whose location in the shadow of the Georgia Viaduct condemned them to a life of slow deterioration until the entire area is rocks, weeds, junk and the detritus of desperate people.

As the longest concrete span on the continent, the viaduct was an engineering marvel and a model that has inspired other North American cities.

Last year, cement began falling off the viaduct in chunks, and people were injured below. This year, a driver hit a water-filled pot-hole, which caused the vehicle to hurtle over the railing, plummet twenty feet, and embed itself in the roof of the Drill Hall.

To mitigate structural deterioration beneath the deck, the concrete spans have been propped up with logs—while a cavalcade of Hudsons, Studebakers, Auburns and Fords roar back and forth, oblivious to what is underneath them, like happy skaters on thin ice.

Looking around him, not for the first time Hook wonders, *Is this why we won the war?*

Just south of the viaduct, he passes a line of idle men leaning against walls, yawning and scratching their arms, and stops at the corner of East Georgia and Main to evaluate the Belvedere Hotel across the street.

At Jeanie's insistence, Hook is carrying his Detective Special, in a shoulder holster that pokes into his armpit.

To go by the state of the windows, the top two floors of the Belvedere are uninhabited, while the second floor has milk bottles on the sills, indicating the presence of renters on a weekly rate.

He crosses Main Street, hopping out of the way of a speeding Packard, and waits for the trolley to roll by—formerly leaf green, now red and white, a safety measure against maimed pedestrians.

The front entrance of the Belvedere is a thick, windowless, unmarked slab of a door—clearly, alcohol is consumed within. (In this part of town, a blank door might as well be a neon sign.)

Pulling the heavy, corroded door is a test of arm strength—but as soon as it swings open a crack, the would-be visitor is hurtled backward by the deafening rumble of many, many men talking at once, in sentences that are unintelligible but emphatic.

A man not far away shouts a coarse expression at someone from a neighbouring table, to be reprimanded by a commanding voice emanating from the bar at the far wall: "Now then! Now then!"

From which Hook concludes that at least *someone* is in charge.

The room looks like every other workman's beer parlour in Vancouver—as plain as a Quaker meeting house but not as clean, designed to serve a congregation of men in wet wool, muddy boots and a variety of headwear, from sweat-stained caps and battered fedoras to trilbies that long ago lost their centre creases.

The air is a composite of cigarette smoke, stale beer, bad teeth and Lysol.

Hook's first item of business is to locate the chap responsible for renting rooms at this so-called hotel. Peering through the haze and over the heads of drinkers, he spots a rotund chap behind the bar, the apparent owner of that stentorian voice, furiously decanting beer from a spigot and up to his elbows in beer foam. Asked where one might book a room, the barman jerks his head in such a way as to indicate a door situated behind the bar and to the left.

Hook knocks briskly, pulls the door open and steps into an office about the size of a walk-in closet.

Seated behind a desk that takes up half the room is a hairy man in a stained collarless shirt with armbands holding up the sleeves, slumped over an adding machine perched on an uneven pile of papers. He gives no indication that he is aware of a visitor as he pokes the keyboard and pulls the crank—*click, click, whir! Click, click, clank, whir!*—so relentlessly that he seems to have become a machine himself—albeit a misshapen, unhealthy machine.

Click, click, crank, whir! Click, click, crank, whir!

Hook hesitates before speaking. To disturb this man at his work could be like derailing a train; the shock could give him a heart attack, so he just stands there and waits.

On the wall behind the desk is a W.H. Grassie calendar depicting a flat, empty country road in an unnaturally thick spruce forest, trailing away to an improbable waterfall.

His molar beats out the time, thumps like the drum in a slave galley.

"Whadya want?" *Click, click, whir!*

And the interview begins. At no time does our man look up. It is as though Hook is talking to a fat robot.

Hook holds up his warrant card, which is ignored. "Good morning, sir. I'm Detective Inspector Hook of the VPD."

Click, click, whir! "So?"

"Are you the man I talk to about a room?"

"A what?"

"A room in your hotel."

"No room. Second floor's full up." *Click, whir!*

"And the guests? Who are the guests?"

"See them? Out there?" With his crank hand he points at the door.

"In the beer parlour?"

"Out there."

Hook opens the door to view a steaming heap of male humanity.

"So they're all loggers, then."

"Shut the door! Can't hear you!"

Hook obeys. "I repeat, are they all loggers? Are there any... businessmen, for instance?"

Click, click, whir! "Don't be daft."

"So the second floor—"

"Is full. We rent rooms on the second floor, and it's fully booked."
Click, click, whir!

"And what about the third floor?"

At last, the bookkeeper decides to take a look at this pest.

"Nobody's on the third floor, that's who. You don't wanna go up there."

"Why?"

"There's nothing up there. It stinks up there. Try the Main Rooms down the street—fifty cents and the fleas are free." He laughs at his own joke. His teeth are worn to stumps like those of a hippopotamus.

Hook sniffs the air in an exaggerated way. "I'd say something stinks down here, as well."

The eyes narrow. "What was that you said?"

"Stinks. You know—pongs. Smells to high heaven. Like your breath."

"What's that s'posed to mean?" The bookkeeper's right hand plucks a cigar stub from the ashtray, while the left hand casually opens a drawer. Hook just as casually opens his coat, exposing the straps and holster; a pause follows, then the hand returns to the desk. (Which is why Hook chose this pain of a harness in the first place.)

Hook's hand comes out of his coat with his warrant card.

"A copper, are you?"

"I already told you that. One of the windows on the third floor is open—about two inches, actually. It was propped up with a shoe— an oxford toecap, to be precise. Who's the roomer?"

A pause, then: "You got a warrant?"

"In my experience, hotel clerks have one or two rackets on the side. Selling rubbers, for example—and recommending places to use them. What's *your* sideline, sir?"

"No warrant? Get the feck out of here, copper, I got work to do."

"This is a murder investigation. Do you have any idea the shit you'll be in if it's the guy I think it is?"

The bookkeeper glowers in his chair, weighing the pros and cons while lighting his cigar stub.

"Okay. Okay. One of the rooms on the third floor might possibly have someone in it. Is there a law against that?"

"It depends on who's getting paid. If it's not the hotel owner, that *would* be against the law, though profitable—an off-the-books rental could command a four-star price, depending on the guest's, er, circumstances. Do you know the penalty for knowingly harbouring a fugitive?"

"Listen, Officer, I don't ask *why* they want a room—why should I?"

"So I take it that your guest is *not* a logger."

"Not a chance. His mitts are too clean."

"Did he have a funny walk?"

"I wasn't laughing."

"Is he tall or short?"

"Damn it, tall, short, how do I know?"

Hook waits while the bookkeeper adds up potential liabilities, whether to inform or hold tight.

"Short. Short! Okay?"

"How short?"

"What's short? I said short! Short! Very short! Up to yer fecking armpit, okay?"

THE CARVED NEWEL post at the foot of the staircase has seen better days, and better clientele; in fact, the Belvedere was a semi-swanky hotel once. Now it's a dump, thanks to the Georgia Viaduct.

That's progress for you.

At the second-floor landing, Hook peers down the dismal hall: mildewed wallpaper, lit by bare bulbs in the ceiling and a greasy window at the far end (and this is the "fully booked" floor).

He continues up the stairs, now more gingerly because the steps aren't as firm and the banister sags where the rungs have sheared off. Accumulated grime has made the treads as slippery as wet moss where the carpet has been stripped off like an adhesive bandage from a wound.

What an idiot: Why bring a pistol and not a flashlight, so you might know what you're aiming at?

Blackness up ahead. He stands at the top of the stairs, waiting for his eyes to adjust. At the far end of the hall he sees a crack of light where the window has been patched—no, entirely covered—with plywood.

He feels for the nearest wall and gropes about until he manages to find a switch.

Nothing. Between Hook and that minuscule crack of light is not a single working bulb.

He snails along the wall and down the hall, feeling his way ahead and counting doors, with the floor creaking under his feet like it did in *The Terror*, until he comes to what he calculates to be the room with the part-open window.

He removes his sidearm from its holster and stretches his back, for the weight made him lopsided. He takes a deep breath, then uses his thumb to switch off the safety, which scares him shitless—and not just because he could kill a man with the twitch of a finger, but also because this plainclothes-issue sidearm, a short-barrelled American thing, is inaccurate beyond about six feet. No match for a war-issue Webley, though the kick of a Webley could sprain your wrist.

He is about to knock on the door, but hesitates. If the occupant yells Who is it?, what does he answer—Room service?

Hook opts for the brute solution favoured by the Dry Squad, gripping the knob and turning it soundlessly, easing the latch out of its socket as far as it will go and softly pushing the door a fraction of an inch, until he is certain the deadbolt isn't set.

He backs up two paces, lowers his left shoulder and lunges forward.

But before his shoulder meets the door, it swings open, suddenly and deliberately, so that by his own forward momentum Hook catapults into the room, flailing his arms to keep upright, then losing his footing completely when his left leg crashes straight through the fir floor down to the knee. Heart pounding, he pushes the floor with his free hand to extricate himself, only to sink farther down as the rotten wood around him crumbles and splits under his hands. Meanwhile, below, his legs are frantically flailing about (as though they might propel him upward), which causes him to sink yet farther, all the way down to his armpits, so far down that he feels his right foot break through the plaster ceiling of the room below.

What must that look like from downstairs?

Now everything is still, except for the pounding of his molar—and the soft creak of receding footsteps outside and down the hall. Even in his current state of shock and mortification, he is certain he can hear a trace of a skip in that step.

After assessing his position, Hook concludes that he has no way to go but down, which he means to do as safely as possible. He feels his way around the ceiling with his right foot (the pioneering foot) until he finds a pipe. Without dropping his now-useless pistol (never drop your weapon—lesson one in training), he leans down with his left arm in order to get a grip on a water pipe, intending either to ease his fall or to swing down like a monkey.

His left hand touches something—not the water pipe but the bracket joining the water pipe to the joist, then the water pipe itself—and he realizes he has overbalanced, so that the bracket comes loose, his grip on the pipe fails, and now he is plummeting straight down, through splinters, rot and gypsum flakes, to land on his arse on a linoleum floor, then to scramble to his feet, blinded by plaster dust.

A figure springs from the bed, and an enormous fist slams into his jaw.

PART III

I need a bath, some chow, then you and me
sit down and we talk about who dies, eh?

—Al Capone

CHAPTER 39

CHURCHILL DELIVERS INSPIRING SPEECH
New Westminster "Tested by Fire"
Max Trotter
Staff Writer
The Vancouver World

In its forty years of existence, the BC Provincial Exhibition has been the venue of choice for many inspirational persons, including much of the royal family.

It may be said that our eminent visitor for 1929 has topped them all: Winston Churchill.

Newly at liberty following the Conservative defeat, ex-chancellor Churchill arrived on Sunday in a private railway car, courtesy of steel magnate Charles Schwab of the CPR.

Winnie was accompanied on his cross-Canada speaking tour by his son Randolph, and by Andrew Rhys-Mogg, the air ace (MC, DSO, DFC), Randolph's second cousin and a fellow Etonian.

Since his arrival in Vancouver, Mr. Churchill has been investing heavily through the Vancouver Stock Exchange, committing two thousand dollars to a Calgary oil and gas venture and a similar amount to Canadian Grain Export Ltd. Such a vote of confidence from the man who reinstated the gold standard is certain to provide a much-needed boost for the brokers of Howe Street.

After Mr. Churchill spent his weekend painting land-scapes on Grouse Mountain, it was New Westminster's turn to host the great man.

Wearing a brown lounge suit, a bow tie, a brown trilby hat, and carrying a brown malacca cane with a silver knob, the great man favoured the Provincial Exhibition with a rousing speech before a crowd of twenty-two thousand.

His stirring words could not have been more wel-come to discouraged citizens after last week's fire turned seven exhibition buildings into ashes, necessitating the use of tents, and casting the entire future of the fair in doubt.

Accompanying the ex-chancellor onstage were Premier Tolmie, Mrs. Tolmie, and New Westminster mayor Wells Gray. Son Randolph and Mr. Rhys-Mogg were said to be resting, having become over-refreshed while dining and dancing on the Hotel Vancouver's scenic Panorama Roof, followed by a nightcap at the Regent Hotel's sumptuous bar.

In his address, Mr. Churchill hailed British Columbians for hosting a fair of such magnitude despite the recent catastrophe: "You are a people tested by fire, and you have come through the fire. I admire the courage and resources of those in charge, which have been such that not even the heavy blow you have sus-tained has been able to mar the success of your noble undertaking.

"You have exhibited a perseverance and a dogged courage that does not brook defeat—a quality that con-stitutes the backbone of the British race."

Thunderous applause followed.

Over the next week, Churchill is scheduled to speak in Vancouver and Victoria, after which the party will travel to Los Angeles, where Churchill will be hosted by William Randolph Hearst, Charlie Chaplin and the actress Mary Pickford.

HOOK WAKES UP sneezing. His eyes blink open with difficulty, for he is lying under a blanket of plaster and bits of lath. He stares up at the huge, ragged maw in the soot-grey ceiling and wonders how he got here.

Looks like he's comin' round now...

Above him, two faces come into view. One is brown; the other fat and sallow, with flat teeth like a hippopotamus. Hook can't quite make out what they are saying because his ears are plugged with gypsum dust, but from their gestures he concludes that an argument is taking place.

I thought you killed him! Jesus, what in the feck happened? And who's gonna pay for this?

Listen mothafocka, fo' twenty-five mothafockin' dollars a week, ain't no mothafocka gon' tell me I'm gon' pay for some mug man drop in from the mothafockin' ceilin' with a gat!

Okay, okay, Al, easy, don't get excited. The problem we got on our hands here is the bird's a copper.

Damn! Jesus! Shit, man, what kind of jive podunk is dis town? No coloured hotel, nothin' but dis pigsty, an' now some bull busts down from the muthafockin'— ·

Stop! Stop that, Al, stop, please, it hurts! ... Okay! Okay, okay, okay, no feckin' rent! Okay? I'll give you back your feckin' rent, now is that fair? C'mon, what more can you ask?

A better room, mothafocka!

While negotiations are taking place above him, Hook looks inward and takes inventory: multiple contusions, stiff neck, cracked or broken jaw...

He sneezes and spits plaster. "Can someone please find my cigarettes?"

THE WARD AT St. Paul's Hospital is a large, boxy room with high windows along one side, the other three walls containing five white enamelled steel beds, occupied, with a spindle-back chair at the foot of each one.

Once he is able to raise his head from the pillow, and after unknotting his neck, Hook takes a look at his fellow patients.

A man with his leg in a plaster cast, held aloft by a sling, rope and pulley, suspended from an overhead water pipe, confers quietly with, presumably, his wife, seated beside his bed. The patient to the gentleman's left, having assumed a half-seated position, one arm wrapped in a cast dangling from a metal gibbet, holds a pencil between his teeth as the forefinger of his good hand scans a betting form from Hastings Racecourse.

Across from Hook, a man with his neck in a leather and metal traction device utters a strained greeting; Hook can only wave in return, because he can't move his jaw. His upper and lower teeth are wired together; the entire lower half of his face won't budge. His jaw aches damnably, now that the freezing has worn off.

Like a half-forgotten dream, he tries to piece together the preceding events: the door, the floor, the hole, the pipe, the rain of plaster and wood fragments—how did this happen? This spurt of memory is followed by a wave of self-criticism: Where did he go wrong? What should he have done, and at what point?

It comes to his mind that the same question might apply to life as a whole: retrospect is patchy and unreliable; there is no way to rewatch that key scene in the movie that you missed because you were distracted by someone coughing behind you, and now you have lost the thread of the plot.

He remembers the time they left Lucille with Jeanie's friend Tilly to see *After the Fog*, and they both dozed off in the first half-hour, and when they woke the lighthouse keeper was attacking his daughter with an axe and they had no idea why.

His mind is wandering. Miscellaneous thoughts and memories swirl about, merging with the present as though everything is a dream. Can one be fast asleep with one's eyes wide open? Is his broken jaw itself a dream?

If so, he'd like to wake up soon.

A red-haired man looms above him, with a freckled face, and glasses with thick, round tortoiseshell frames; he is wearing a spotless lab coat over a three-piece suit with a gold watch across the vest below a mustard stain. He is holding a clipboard in one hand and a pencil in the other.

"Good morning—Officer Hook, am I right, sir?"

So it isn't a dream. And the broken jaw is real. "Jish."

"Good. I'm Dr. Rush."

They are shaking hands. Hook doesn't know how his hand got up there. Like most people lying helpless in a hospital bed, he feels at the mercy of anyone who happens by.

Dr. Rush seems surprisingly comfortable conversing with a man whose jaws are glued shut and who therefore has lost the ability to pronounce vowels.

"Tell me, Inspector Hook, wasn't that Panama Al I just saw outside?

"Woojash?"

"The lightweight who socked you in the jaw."

"Jeshus."

"I saw him fight Al Foreman at the Arena. Panama Al certainly does pack a punch."

"Jish!"

"Now, I want you to take it easy and avoid a lot of talking—it's only cracked, but you have a fair bit of swelling there. Your jaw will remain wired shut for about a week. Don't worry, you'll get used to it, and you'll be able to speak more clearly once the swelling goes down."

Dr. Rush glances over his notes. "Oh—and you've had a concussion, so your thinking might be impaired for a few days. We'll keep you for observation tonight, and when you go home tomorrow, be on the alert for symptoms. You may notice lapses of memory, odd smells, strange thoughts, but be assured, that will pass as well."

"Schings, galtr."

"You're more than welcome, Inspector. By the way, those strained neck muscles will give you trouble when you look to the left. Shall I let Panama Al come in now? He's been waiting to see you for quite a while."

"Jish cheeze."

"I'll do that, then."

While awaiting his visitor, reasonably sure that he won't be punched again, Hook lies back and does further inventory. Trouble looking to the left? No, not just trouble—the neck is a stone column that refuses to budge an inch.

As for concussion, surely a person with a brain injury would *know* if he has a brain injury, the way somewhere in his mind a drunk *knows* he's sozzled—but of course that would depend on just *how* sozzled...

He gingerly probes his mouth with the tip of the tongue and locates two loose molars on the left, and one missing...

The molar. The tooth is gone.

Can it be?

"I can't tell you how sorry I am about this whole thing, sir."

Hook jolts out of a half dream. The visual space formerly occupied by Dr. Rush now contains a compact man with brown skin, shorter and trimmer than Dr. Rush, with a broad nose and hair cropped close to the scalp. Standing beside the bed, he has the look of a puma in a double-breasted suit about to pounce, and he speaks with a faint Spanish accent Hook doesn't remember from their previous encounter.

"Inspector Hook, my name is Alfonso Teofilo Brown. I am known in the profession as Panama Al."

Hook nods, painfully.

"And I sincerely regret what has happened to you from the bottom of my heart."

"Shill veit."

"Thank you for that, sir. I appreciate it."

"Bugen ja."

"So the doctor told me. That means your mouth must have been open when I connected."

Hook will try and remember that tip the next time he is sucker-punched after falling through a ceiling.

"I had a similar fracture fighting Jimmy Russo in '24, and I know how it feels. But that was in the ring, and this was in private life. Officer Hook, I swear on the grave of my mother that you are the first civilian I have punched in my life."

"Shill veit! Yer vus shelkig."

"That is true, I was startled out of a dead sleep. It seemed like the whole ceiling collapsed, and there was a man with a gun in his hand."

Hook refrains from nodding. "It musha bn neshty."

"It was, and at the end of a nasty week. I was waiting two days for management to cough up my winnings, stuck in a town without decent accommodation. You are friendly people, but I cannot say the same about your hotels."

Hook's mind drifts to the argument he overheard in the Belvedere Hotel—the word *motherfucker* comes vividly to mind. Does Panama Al have two ways of speaking, depending on the listener?

Maybe Hook will himself come out of this with a new language, called lockjaw.

He makes note of this Quam-like thought. Dr. Rush may be right about the concussion.

"I can see you need your rest, Officer Hook, so I will not trouble
you any longer."

"Schinks fu kalgn."

"It was the very least I could do. I am catching the next train
to Toronto, so I doubt that we will meet again. I fight in Montreal,
then New York. Then I go to Paris. I have a manager there. His name
is Jean Cocteau..."

It's a concussion, no doubt about it.

HOOK AWAKENS. JEANIE is looking down at him with tears in her
eyes. "Blimey, look at yer clock, ducky, it's like the dog's bollocks!"

"Ee wads a bugzer."

"A what?"

"A bugzer." Hook mimes with his fists.

"Say that again would you, ducky?"

"A bugzer."

"Buzzer? Busker? I'm tryin' me best."

"Bog-eh-zhr!"

"Blimey, are ye sayin' the gadgie ye went up against was a *boxer*?"

"Jish."

"What was that, luv?"

He nods his head, carefully.

"Ye were fighting a boxer? Had ye gone daft?"

"Na. Uza mishtag."

"What?"

"Uza mishtah."

"A mistake, did ye say?"

"Jish!"

"When the station called, it took the heart out of me. I thought
ye'd been shot like poor Constable MacBeath—only twenty-three,
he was."

"Awe, petch, em solly."

"When yer mate Quam said you were at the ozzie, I blarted all the
way here. I thought of Lucille losin' her da."

He waits while she mops her face with her hankie, bless her heart.

"Wezz Lushel naw, phet?"

"Who?"

"Lushel. Ur dosher."

"Where's Lucille, ye said?"

"Jish, phet."

"She's with Tilly Wallwork—didn't I tell ye, ducky? Tilly's one of the Wallworks from Moulton, ten miles from home like. We're bezzies now. She came over when I was near foolish with worry..."

"Dunterry, petch, shillviet new. Ellbefin. And da chooth es gung." She puts away her handkerchief. "Sorry, come again, ducky?"

"Da chooth es gung!" He makes a twisting motion with his wrist next to his chin, then throws the imaginary tooth onto the floor.

Her lovely face takes on a puzzled expression for a split second, then the light goes on. "De ye mean yer bad tooth? Gone? Oh ducky! I'm so chuffed, my back teeth are *achin'*!"

DRAMATIC SURPRISE AT AQUARIAN HEARING
Dallas MacElwee
The Victoria Colonist

The dingy courtroom would have made an admirable setting for a photoplay in which, at the crucial moment of the hero's trial for murder, the heroine, blond and blue-eyed, bursts into the room full of grim-faced lawyers and spectators to prove the innocence of the accused.

The only difference at the resumption of the hearing in Nanaimo was that the heroine was the one who caused charges to be laid in the first place.

Mrs. Ida Arrowsmith, an heiress from North Carolina, has accused Edward Peter Collins, known as Brother Osiris, of using a donation of over twenty-five thousand dollars, not for building a schoolhouse as intended, but for his personal use and that of Miss Muriel Riffle, who goes by the name Madame Zura.

From their knowledge of the case, spectators in the courtroom looked forward to a short session and a speedy verdict. While this proved to indeed be the case, it was not as expected.

After Judge Drummond-Hay called the court to order, the first witness to step into the box and place her hand on the Bible was none other than the key witness—Mrs. Ida Arrowsmith from North Carolina, who made the original accusation.

To the consternation of everyone in the room, Mrs. Arrowsmith proceeded to reverse the statement that initiated this court proceeding, by declaring that she had given Brother Osiris the money as "a personal gift, free and clear."

"I only wish I had contributed more," she said.

The courtroom erupted in astonished muttering, while the opposing lawyers and the judge gaped in disbelief. The only person in the courtroom who seemed unsurprised by this development was the defendant himself, who sat serenely behind the defence table with a half smile on his face.

Drummond-Hay asked, "Madam, do you mean to tell this court that you gave this man twenty-five thousand dollars with no conditions attached whatsoever?"

"It was $25,850," corrected Mrs. Arrowsmith. "The money was to be utilized at Brother Osiris's discretion."

"It has been noted that the cheque was payable to the Aquarian Foundation and not to Edward Peter Collins. What do you have to say to that?"

"That was the Brother's desire. I would have preferred to make it payable to E.P. Collins, but he said no, that it should be made to the Aquarian Foundation."

"Was anything said about how the funds should be dealt with?"

"I told him he had absolute control and could do what he wished, that it was a gift to him."

"Thank you, Mrs. Arrowsmith."

After a pause, defence counsel Nathan Rimmer rose from his seat with a smile that was almost a smirk, saying, "That is all for the defence, My Lord."

"I have no questions for this witness," prosecutor T.P. Morton said, glaring daggers at the elderly woman, who seemed blithely indifferent to the consternation she had brought about.

"Witness may step down."

Nodding briskly to Judge Drummond-Hay, Mrs. Arrowsmith left the stand. Stunned spectators watched as she proceeded down the centre aisle to the exit, with not a sound in the room but the click of her heels on the varnished hardwood floor.

Counsel Rimmer and his client shook hands and traded satisfied whispers, leaving the prosecution to pack his ruined case into his briefcase and go home.

Drummond-Hay then declared a mistrial, followed by a comment about the deleterious effect on the community, having "a gaggle of money-mad Americans" in our midst.

"If this lunacy is not checked," he said, "I fear that British Columbians will be put to the expense of maintaining half of them at Essondale."

INVESTMENT BROKER DIES ON TRAIN
Body Discovered in Radio Car
Max Trotter
Staff Writer
The Vancouver World

J. Walter Addison, the investment counsellor who just days ago accompanied Winston Churchill on his tour of British Columbia, died suddenly while en route to Toronto aboard the Ocean Limited.

Mr. Addison, who once served as minister of militia and advised the war minister, was found lifeless in the radio car. The time of death is undetermined, but he had been listening to the radio.

"The passenger was just sitting there with his eyes closed and his earphones were on his head," said Elmer Maxwell, the steward on duty. "We thought he was asleep."

Mr. Addison's remains were disembarked at the Jasper train depot after Dr. Nelson Barkhouse pronounced him dead, attributing the cause of death to a brain hemorrhage.

As a friend and advisor to defence minister Sir Sam Hughes, J. Walter Addison was a prominent figure throughout the war, having served as honorary colonel of the militia, and as a commission agent for purchases by the War Office, until his dismissal amid charges of war profiteering.

Since the war he has maintained an office in the Hotel Astor in New York, as an agent for the administration of private fortunes, and as an investment counsellor to luminaries such as Winston Churchill, whom he accompanied on the ex-chancellor's trans-Canada tour.

Mr. Addison's body has been shipped back to Vancouver. A forensic analysis is to be conducted by Vancouver coroner F.C.V. Condon.

CHAPTER 40

HERE IS SEYMOUR *exchange. Do I have suite four eighteen, the Quadra Club?*

Here is Ed McCurdy speaking. Who is calling, please?

I have Miss Mildred Wickstram on the line. Will you take the call?

Please put her through.

SWITCH

Millie, you sound like you're inside a sewing machine.

That's because I'm calling from the exchange. If you must know, I'm the replacement operator filling in for Miss Rook.

Do you mean you've come to your senses?

Don't be patronizing. It is a temporary measure. A cash-flow situation.

Why didn't you ask me for a loan?

Because I haven't sunk that low. Now, do you want to hear the reason for this call, or not?

Do you intend to charge for this information?

Of course, darling.

Damn. Oh very well. What's the story, sister?

I canvassed the girls in the exchange about Manchester hoodlums in the city. Lilly Tuborg remembered having connected Feetham, Campbell and Linden. She accidentally overheard a discussion concerning two clients—and I think I found your twins. Now, what is that worth to you?

More money than I can afford, I expect.

Plus there's the finder's fee for Lilly.

I'll mortgage my vocal cords.

Fine. Well, it seems that in Manchester the Nortons were common hoodlums who rose in the ranks in the usual way, by eliciting money from shops for fire protection—from themselves.

Calvin's wife has it that Manchester yobs are a dim lot. Surely they were nicked.

It seems the twins made up for it by working as a team. Nothing was pinned on either, because nobody could tell which one did the deed.

However, they nearly bought it at the Wolf and Howl on Chepstow Street. According to press reports, a Colin Amos of the Gooch gang, seated at the bar, said to the room at large, "Well, look what the cat dragged in." Reggie—the accused rat—took umbrage, and an altercation ensued, which ended abruptly when Dwight produced a carving knife and shoved it into Mr. Amos's lower back. Mr. Amos, naturally, dropped to the floor. But Dwight was not satisfied. Outraged at the insult to his brother, he leapt on Mr. Amos like a panther, stabbing and twisting the knife with each thrust. The number of stabs and twists vary from one paper to another. As you might imagine, scribes with the Daily Mirror *revelled in it: "Cozy Bar Becomes House of Horror" sort of bollocks. Initial charges were laid, then dropped. After a witness fell out of a window, the others couldn't remember a thing.*

So the Norton twins in Vancouver are immigrants, who came to Canada seeking a new life?

Not exactly. It seems they are on the lam—as you would put it— from a host of other charges. Deportation orders have been issued, and are under appeal.

I take it they secured legal advice?

They certainly have. And with Elliot Linden representing them, they'll be old men before they're on a boat home.

CHAPTER 41

UPON ARRIVING HOME from work, Mildred finds a note in the mailbox, hand-delivered.

> *Coming for you, darling.*
> *Yes, I am here.*
> *Though at present we are rather occupied with wining and dining, I shall drop by sharpish—now that I know where you live.*

She needs a drink at once. Andrew always liked suspense, and the payoff was never pleasant.

She slams the door shut and heads straight for the icebox. At the counter she prepares two pink gins, then takes them up the stairs to Stella's room, where she finds her sole boarder already has a drink before her, courtesy of Dora Decker, who is seated at the table nursing a cup of tea.

Someone has made Miss Aspen's bed, complete with hospital corners, and the pillowcase is fresh. The room has been swept and dusted.

"I see you two have become acquainted—and one of you has been busy."

"Dora is making herself useful. I like that in an accused murderess."

Dora frowns. "Miss Wickstram, I'm really not sure I understand Miss Aspen's sense of humour."

"I hear ice clinking, Millie. Was that for *moi?*"

"Yes, but I see Dora's been making herself useful there as well."

"That's because the girl doesn't have a red cent and I'm a good tipper. Bring that over here."

"She's right, Miss Wickstram. And I doubt that I'll be asked back to my old job—it's the *appearance* of the situation, as Mr. Pine would say. And I'd rather go to jail than back to Saskatchewan."

"Just carry on then, Dora, jolly good. Rent is the least of my concerns right now."

"You're very kind, Miss Wickstram. I haven't seen much of that in Vancouver so far. Please take my seat."

Mildred takes Dora's place at the table and watches in fascination while, balancing her half-full cup and saucer in one hand, the girl manages to seat herself on the carpet with her legs tucked under her skirt, then to produce a packet of tobacco and papers—only now does she set down her saucer, not a drop spilled—and proceeds to roll a cigarette.

"Dora, were you ever a dancer?"

"Oh no, Miss Wickstram. We didn't dance."

"Seventh-Day Adventists," Stella adds. "They don't dance, they don't sing, they don't drink and they don't play cards on Sunday. How people live that way is beyond all."

"She's been mum about her background. I'm surprised you were able to worm that much out of her."

"I like to know my onions. By the way, what's that sound?"

"I'm drinking my pink gin. With no ice."

"Sounds more like desperate slurping to me. Here—take this, you'll be needing a second straight away. You can apply the ice to the bags under your eyes while you spill the goods—how's tricks?"

"I'm afraid I've received another love letter from Andrew. Hand-delivered this time."

"So the heel knows where you live."

"He emphasized that in his note," Mildred says, then turns to Dora. "My husband is—"

"Miss Aspen explained your husband, ma'am. He sounds crazy as a rat in a cup."

"As a what?"

"Crazy as a rat in a cup. It's an expression we used at the granary."

Stella lights a cigarette and blows smoke with a hiss. "Rats in the granary, rats in the office, rats for husbands—and they say the city has a rat problem."

CHAPTER 42

HOOK DISCOVERED AN unexpected benefit of his cracked jaw.

When Jeanie bundled Lucille into his arms, he attempted to speak endearments, but all that came out were nonsense syllables and saliva...

At which Lucille smiled. The loveliest smile that ever there was. He seemed to be speaking her language.

Naturally, their moment of mutual understanding was short-lived. As foretold by Dr. Rush, the swelling went down rapidly, and no amount of fake sputtering produced any improvement in Lucille's attitude. At least Hook is now comprehensible to adults, though his wired-together teeth cause him to talk like a lush.

And he has a bone to pick with Jeanie. He's had it on his mind since the hospital.

Like all men, Hook considers himself fully in tune with the times. Although it was certainly not the thing to do in Waldo, he is well-versed in the activities of the fast set now that the back seat of a Ford has replaced the porch swing and the parlour sofa. But even so, it comes as a rude surprise for any man to discover that his mate may be more experienced than he thought—perhaps more experienced than him.

He nudges Jeanie gently and speaks in a whisper, so as not to wake the baby. "Are you ashleep, pet?"

"Only dozing off, ducky. What is it?"

"Something ish preying on my mind. Where did a girl as young as you get da dope on da mug men? I'm talking about your knowledge of the twinsh in Masshester."

"Manchester, did ye say?"

"Mancheshter, yesh."

"I told ye bout the Norton twins 'cause I thought ye'd want to know, is all."

224

"But you shpoke in sush detail. Like you were there yourshelf."

"I read about it in the papers an' heard about it in church. St. Luke's was slaverin'."

"I know, pet, I know, but even sho, the picture you painted... The *feel* of it... Did you spend moosh time in Manshester yourself ash a girl?"

"Goostrey's only thirty minutes by train, luv, what d'ye think?"

"You went to the big city by yourshelf? Were the streets safe for a girl on her own?"

"I went with the other girls, of course. We'd have a wee of a time. Took the train and hid with the luggage 'til it reached Piccadilly, so we didn't have to pay. We saw photoplays at the Rawtenstall. It was grand fun."

"How old were you, pet, when you were out on the razzle?"

Jeanie rises to one elbow, fully awake now. "What are ye getting at, luv? Yer feshed about something."

"It's about the Norton twinsh, the things you've seen, the shtories you tell. For a girl from Gooshtrey. It makes you seem awfully familiar with the, the seamy side of Manchester."

"Oh, ducky, did ye think I was on the farm milkin' cows?"

"Well, not exactly, but shtill—"

She sits up straight. "I'll tell ye everything ye want to know. I have nowt to hide from ye."

A long pause follows. Jeanie waits, her arms folded under her breasts, looking at him with a peculiar expression.

Hook decides not to prod further. He has enough to investigate as it stands. "Ash a matter of fact, pet, I can't think of anything I want to ashk right now. You jush go back to shleep."

CHAPTER 43

See me at once re Famous Flapper —F.C.V. Condon

A WEEK LATER, with a sore but movable jaw, DI Hook is back at the constabulary, leafing through the accumulated mound of directives, requests, complaints and wanted notices, and among them he finds a memo from the coroner.

How long has it been there? *At once?* Does that mean it was urgent? Has he missed out on a key piece of evidence?

Why is he so easily rattled?

Increased confusion or agitation: Did Dr. Rush mention that at some point? Another word escapes him, it starts with a C. In any case, what is he doing sitting here on his arse when something has been labelled urgent?

In a cold sweat, he climbs the four flights of stairs to the forensics lab, two at a time.

While catching his breath at the door, he looks at the reinforced window. Why would someone fire from outside the door if the door wasn't locked?

Hook tries the handle; once again, it's unlocked.

He steps inside and takes a closer look at the little hole in the glass from the other side, a spider web of fascinating little cracks...

He snaps alert. How long has he been standing here staring at a hole?

Concussion. That's the word the doctor used.

"Inspector Crook! Where on earth have you been?"

Condon is standing by the metal table. His lit pipe hangs from of his lower lip, causing it to droop on one side. He is wearing the same suit he had on the last time they met.

"My name is Inspector Hook, shir, but you're getting close."

"Well, whatever you're called, it's about time. You look as though someone hit you over the head."

"Again, shir, you're close. While pursuing a suspect I fell through a ceiling and a boxer broke my jaw."

"A *boxer*?"

"His name is Panama Al."

"And you were hit on the head?"

"I was."

"Ah. That explains it. Well, smarten up and come have a peek— I've made a remarkable discovery."

"Does this have to do with your smelling apparatus, shir?"

"Oh, so you do remember things—that's a good sign. No, I asked you here to discuss your Famous Flapper case."

"Actually, the word is *Fatal*, or at least was. I understand the prosecution has chosen not to proceed—that the case is, for all intents and purposes, closed."

Condon frowns for a moment, then presses on, his enthusiasm seemingly undiminished. "Yes, I might have known that, but in any case, what I have to show you is still damnably interesting."

Hook follows Condon into the lab. The memory of a pig's carcass and an enormous one-toothed cat still troubles him.

And wouldn't you know, there he is—slumped in the corner, on the army cot, leaning against the pillow like a Turk without a hookah.

Condon leans over his desk and paws through his notes. "Please feel free to sit down with Lewis," he says over his shoulder.

Hook would rather share the cot with a wolverine.

Condon locates his notes and continues.

"Do you remember Judge Reid ordering a re-examination? Well, I was only too happy to do so, since it wouldn't come off my budget, which is measly enough as it stands."

"*Measly* would describe every departmental budget in the force, shir—with the exception of administration itself."

"Indeed! Indeed! Well, Inspector, to make a long story short, when we took delivery of Mr. Addison's cadaver, I noticed a small pinkish spot on his collar. I took a peek at the spot through the microscope—and what do you think it turned out to be?"

"Probably blood, I expect."

"It was brain fluid!"

A pause follows while Condon, whose pipe has gone out, tamps it carefully with a long forefinger, re-lights and continues.

"A bit of blood would be no surprise after a vessel in the brain hemorrhaged. But that little trickle of brain fluid"—he illustrates trickling brain fluid by wiggling one forefinger down the side of his neck—"which of course would be covered up by the earphone, told a different story.

"With that in mind, I took another peek inside Mr. Tucker's head—luckily, he was still in the morgue. His wife came for a quick look, but hasn't yet returned for the remains. My impression is that she didn't like him much."

"As far as I can tell, nobody did."

"I find that's often the case with murdered men—usually, there are a number of people who would have *liked* to murder him."

"It does complicate the question of motive."

"In any case, I sawed open the skull and took a good long probe into Mr. Tucker's brain—and what do you know? A sharp object had been inserted deep into the temporal lobe!" Condon illustrates this with the same forefinger. "Someone thrust what might well have been an ice pick straight into Mr. Tucker's ear!"

"Would you excuse me for just one moment, shir?"

"What?"

"I need to visit the facilities."

"Certainly."

Hook slips quickly into the lavatory and is shocked to find himself emptying the contents of his stomach into the toilet. He hasn't chundered like this since he drank a pint of lemon gin at the age of fifteen. Evidently, his distaste for forensic science has gotten worse—maybe a side effect of his concussed brain.

"Something disagreed with you, Inspector?"

"Bit of an upset stomach, shir. Please continue."

"Well now, Mr. Hook, picture this. Our man lifted Mr. Addison's earphone, plunged"—that forefinger again—"an ice pick into his left ear, then replaced the earphone, and Bob's your uncle. No passersby would notice anything unusual—a passenger had simply fallen asleep listening to the radio.

"Then it occurred to me that the same thing may have happened in Mr. Tucker's case, except the assailant covered his tracks by concealing them with other blows to the area. Now, what do you think of that?"

Condon is close to chortling with glee. Hook glances at Lewis, who glares back with an expression of morbid satisfaction.

This whole business is starting to grind on DI Hook. He imagines the forensic analyst describing a shrapnel injury with the same sort of boyish pep.

CHAPTER 44

Dearest,
   I adore the lavender wallpaper, my poppet, but not the beastly linoleum. Really, darling! A tad humdrum, wouldn't you say?

WHEN MILDRED RETURNS from the library, she finds a dead pigeon waiting for her on the veranda. Someone decorated it with red ribbon and a bow and laid it at the top of the steps, claws up.

More of Andrew's work—as was the bouquet of dead flowers last time, with of course another toxic note.

Having served at Whitehall when the Propaganda Agency dropped leaflets over German trenches, Mildred knows a demoralization campaign when she sees one; knowing Andrew, she should have seen this coming.

Andrew is having his fun.

Five minutes later, she climbs the stairs to Stella's room, where she finds Miss Aspen in her usual spot by the window, smoking a cigarette, with an open book to one side of her face to take advantage of what's left of her peripheral vision. Hearing Mildred, she removes a pair of glasses as thick as the ice cubes in her pink gin; she just hates being seen in the things.

"What fresh whammy has happened now, Millie?"

"What do you mean, Stella?"

"You're frightened. Your footsteps on the stairs were like those of a baby goat chased by hyenas."

"My husband is trying to drive me crazy. This time he's left behind a dead pigeon."

Stella emits something like a cackle. "What an imaginative way to send a poison pen letter—by poisoning a carrier pigeon!"

Failing to see the humour in that, Mildred sets fire to a cigarette, swearing under her breath.

"Watch your language, honey, you're not a stevedore."

The door opens and Dora enters with a shopping bag, which she empties onto the table: a carton of two hundred and fifty Chesterfields, a box of Purdys chocolates and a box of Ganong Chicken Bones for Stella, as well as a tin of Swan tobacco and rolling papers for herself. "Miss Wickstram, do you know anything about the dead bird on the veranda?"

"I do indeed, Dora. I couldn't bring myself to touch it, I'm afraid."

"Not to worry, ma'am. I found a shovel and buried her in the back-yard. Or maybe it was a he."

"Trust me, Dora, it was a she."

"It don't matter. One of God's creatures just the same."

"What a sweet way to look at things, darling," Stella says. "Most people see animals as *their* creatures, to be disposed of as they see fit."

"That was Andrew's view of horses, certainly." Mildred looks at the red coal at the end of her cigarette; how she would love to apply it to Andrew's forehead.

"Speaking of animals, Dora, come over here. I want you to look in the side table drawer."

Dora opens the drawer and produces a small silver pistol with a mother-of-pearl grip. "It's a gun."

"Right you are. It's called a Baby Browning. It was a sweet gift from Broncho Billy Anderson, after I dressed him for *The Great Train Robbery*. He gave pistols to the whole crew. Bill was sentimental about guns."

"Does your pistol have bullets?"

"It came fully equipped, yes."

It never occurred to Mildred that one of her tenants might be armed. "Stella, what on earth were you planning to do with a loaded gun?"

"You really wanna know?"

"I do."

"Shoot myself, honey, the self-checkout. Who else do you think I can hit these days?"

"Very funny, ha-ha. Well, just so you know, I'd rather you didn't."

"Ditto—at least for the time being. But you never know, and a girl must maintain her standards. In the meantime, this little fellow could prove useful—I mean, surely there's someone around here with a pair of working peepers."

"I can shoot, Miss Aspen," says Dora. "At the wheat pool they paid us a penny a rat. I used Daddy's air gun. Once I made a whole dollar!"

A long, rueful sigh from Stella. "Millie, I never thought I'd ever say this, but maybe we could also use a Broncho Billy in the house."

CHAPTER 45

A POLICE MOTORCYCLE is a tool for traffic control, for escorting important people and for chasing down speeders and bootleggers. Police inspectors don't ride motorcycles to and from work because they're noisy and undignified, and they stain one's trousers with motor oil.

In addition, Jeanie's taste for the thrill of speed has diminished since Lucille arrived, and she imagines (like any policeman's wife) all the ways her husband could be killed on the machine, leaving his family behind, destitute.

Hook naturally regrets this development; giving up his motorcycle was like losing a leg. At the same time, he isn't willing to blame it all on baby Lucille. In any case, as he explained to Jeanie this evening, there are exceptions to every rule, and on this occasion the safest possible form of transportation to his destination would be on a noisy machine.

Any officer seen at night unobtrusively entering and leaving Joe Celona's house on swanky Angus Drive would immediately acquire a reputation as a copper on the take from Vancouver's public enemy number one.

Put another way, the more noise he makes, the more innocent the visit will seem.

The Celona residence in Shaughnessy is an ultimate bungalow in the Arts and Crafts style, an English cottage made of lumber and proportioned for giants.

Hook allows the motorcycle to idle a few minutes, revving up the motor at intervals to show he isn't trying to be stealthy; he even gives the horn two chipper toots—*Here I am!*—before shutting down.

He dismounts, pauses so that anyone looking out their window gets a good long look at him, then strides down the walk, up the stone steps and into the shadow of the front porch—where he slams into a figure so massive he seems to fill the entire door frame.

Hook is barely able to get a good look at the ape he just bounced off before his shoulder is seized in a giant fist and he is shoved into the vestibule, to be joined by a second gorilla, this one with narrow eyes and cheekbones like fists.

In a triumph of style over nature, both of them are impeccably dressed in silk summer suits, despite the June weather.

These two human battering rams propel him farther inside and down a carpeted hall.

The plaster above the wainscotting along the hall is virtually papered with framed photographs; each one features Celona, looking at the camera with the same half smile and metallic stare, in the company of a political figure, a sports champion, a celebrity, a movie star... Hook feels slightly dizzy, either from his collision with the ape behind him or from his concussion acting up.

His escorts usher him into what could be a Hollywood depiction of a den, with a brass chandelier, built-in bookshelves and cabinets, and a dormer window seat. From the contents of a side table, the man is—unsurprisingly—an avid reader of detective fiction featuring the Lone Wolf and Philip Trent.

Hook seats himself in a leather club chair facing an imitation Chippendale coffee table that contains several copies of *Black Mask* magazine. Opposite is a fireplace with what looks like a whole tree trunk burning in the grate.

Sitting back in the club chair next to him, at leisure, his legs crossed, is Joe Celona.

A moment of silence, while the atmosphere settles and the two men—police officer and career criminal—size each other up.

Celona is a stocky individual with a five o'clock shadow on a surprisingly chiselled face, like a statue atop a lump of clay, and brown hair in a swept-back pompadour. He wears a brown smoking jacket, round glasses and a half smile that looks like it could turn warm or cold, depending on the circumstances.

"Inspector Hook. Welcome. Welcome to my home. Please make yourself comfortable. Would you care for a cigar?"

Celona leans forward and extends an open mahogany humidor displaying a neat stack of Havana Coronas, each one worth more than several packs of Ogden's, even if Celona gets them wholesale. (Jeanie should be glad he hasn't developed a taste for the things.)

The gaping box under his nose breathes an aroma of caramel and brandy and cedar. If he were to smoke one, would that constitute bribery? (Quam would certainly say so, the prig.)

Hook reminds himself that Celona is Italian, and that Italians are a proud people. You never know when something will become a question of honour and someone will produce a dagger.

"Thank you, sir, that's very decent of you."

"Not at all, it's my pleasure." Celona selects two cigars, deftly clips both with a gold cutter, then produces a gold novelty lighter shaped like a derringer.

Hook draws on his cigar and allows the smoke to drift up his nose; comparing the smoke that infuses his senses to the smoke that comes out the butt end of an Ogden's would be like comparing velvet and tin. He must not become accustomed to this level of enjoyment. This is how coppers go bad.

Celona smiles, knowing what a good cigar can do for a chap, then gets straight to the point. "So, Calvin, I take it your visit has something to do with ice picks in ears and two birds clipped the same way. The police think it might not be a coincidence."

Hook nearly chokes. "Jesus Christ, Mr. Celona, that's not public information. How—"

"Easy now, Inspector, relax, no need to take the Lord's name in vain. Many people in my business like to keep tabs on your coroner. Did you know that they call him Canada's Sherlock Holmes? Now, that is high praise."

Hook makes noises of agreement. "Yes, Mr. Celona, F.C.V. Condon is a national figure."

"And not for nothing! These days a yegg can't afford to leave a hair behind, thanks to that snooper. Ya know, Calvin, I hear tell someone tried to blow up his house—with him in it! Can you imagine? Now, who would wanna do a thing like that? I'll tell you who –a spiteful human being, that's who. Spite and hatred, *orrendo*. 'The human being is meant for good, but designed for evil.' Who said that?"

"I have no idea, sir."

"Well, whoever it was, he was goddamn right. Makes you think, don't it?"

Hook nods thoughtfully, or so he hopes. "Yes. Yes sir, indeed it does."

"Now, here we got two birds get bopped with an ice pick—and I guarantee you it was an ice pick. Well, of course they pinned it on this Fatal Flapper chick. That's what she was there for, and boy it cost plenty. The only thing was, our Fatal Flapper flapped away..." Celona pauses to puff his cigar awake, then wipes his nose with his handkerchief. "That was a joke, Calvin. It was s'posed to be funny, why aren't you laughin'?"

"Um, I'm, I was, er, listening carefully, sir."

"Well, listen some more. Speaking to you as a human being, I'm glad she was sprung, bless her heart. But the Combination outta New York don't see it the same way. Them boys are very, very tough and they can be mean, very mean. It was a delicate situation, a question of balance. They needed to control the story so certain people don't get the wrong idea, capisce?"

Hook nods. Celona has lost him, but this isn't the time and place for close questioning.

"With the flapper out of the picture, it's only a matter of time before the papers start yakking about 'organized crime'... Now, Inspector, when you and I say we live in a city where crime is 'organized,' we mean under *control*, as compared to Chicago—am I right? Capisce?" He smiles, though Hook hasn't moved a muscle. "I'm glad you agree.

"So let's you and me take the broader perspective, Calvin. For comparison's sake let's look at Seattle, where you got the Billingsley gang, the Marquette gang—ex-coppers, sad to say—plus you got the Olmstead gang—more coppers, tsk tsk, and of course Puget Sound is absolutely *crawlin'* with freelancers.

"Take that situation an' whadya got? You got shootouts in parking lots and some dead flatfeet, family men who was just walkin' their beat—now, I ask you, is that good? No. It's not good. Shootouts in parking lots, who wants that? Nobody wants that."

A pause, while Celona gazes reflectively at his cigar tip.

Hook experiences a spike of anxiety in his stomach, brought on by either the concussion or the atmosphere. Suddenly, the room feels cooler, despite the still-roaring fire. He becomes aware of the two goons looming above the back of his chair.

Celona smiles in a friendly way, but with eyes like wet stones.

"Calvin, I like you. You're a straight cop, in a city that's going to shit with yeggs, firebugs, roughnecks, street roughs, grifters, dope fiends, shocking vandalism, the youngsters are going to hell—*mannaggia che cazzo*, Inspector. Where would we be without good coppers on the streets?"

Hook nods. Celona is starting to make sense. That too might not be a good sign.

"What I'm trying to say, Calvin, is the world needs rubes like you."

"That's very generous of you, sir."

"You being sarcastic?"

"By no means. It's gratifying to hear you say there are *any* straight coppers in Vancouver."

"Anywhere, Calvin. Try anywhere. At the command level, if they can't be bought then they wouldn't have the job."

Hook has developed a headache now. He would kill for a cigarette, but he's got this lit cigar between his fingers like someone's stiff willy, and if he were to put it aside and get out his pack it could be seen as an insult to Celona's hospitality. So he tries inhaling cigar smoke, and spends the next few moments hacking into his handkerchief.

"What can I do for you, Inspector? Would you like something to drink? Perhaps a sip of whisky. Pour two whiskies would you, Stanley?"

As Hook catches his breath, one of the bodyguards shoves a crystal glass with three fingers of amber liquid into his fist.

Hook accepts, nodding thanks. As expected, the whisky is a grade of Scotch he has never encountered before, sliding like liquid gold down the flat of the tongue with a peaty aftertaste, then around the mouth and up the nose, an infusion of smoke and peat and smoked fish and bacon and pepper and pipe tobacco and toffee... *This is indeed how coppers go bad.*

"Feeling better? Everything copacetic?"

"Very much better, thank you, sir."

"My pleasure. As I said, Calvin, I like you. It'd be a big loss to the force if you got yourself clipped." He takes a puff of his cigar. "And there's your family to consider—by the way, how are Jeanie and the baby? Lucille, isn't it? Nice name."

"If I may ask, sir, what are you getting at? Am I under threat here?"

"No, no, no, nobody is under threat in this house. And the dropper you're looking for is long gone. It's the people he works for that concern me. Not naming names here, but their motto is *Leave no witnesses*. Be a shame to see you become one—capisce?"

"Are you suggesting they might ice every copper on the case?"

"Well, let me put it this way: if jurors are fair game..."

"But if that is so, then the dropper might be seen as a witness too."

Celona ponders the coal on his cigar. "You know, Calvin, I don't think he thought of that."

INSPECTOR HOOK SOLVES THE CASE
Ed McCurdy
Special To
The Evening Star

Thanks to a combination of scientific research and detective skill, two murders that have paralyzed the city with fear are now solved.

VPD inspector Calvin Hook, in tandem with coroner F.C.V. Condon, have proven virtually beyond doubt that Ralph M. Tucker and Walter Addison were both killed by the same man—a professional assassin from New York.

The murder weapon, as determined by modern forensic techniques, was a sharp object that penetrated the brain, causing instant death.

According to Inspector Hook, "It was a matter of putting together witness statements that would seemingly have nothing to do with the perpetrator, but took us to the same destination. Together with the method of killing, it left no doubt that organized crime was involved."

Hook then consulted a professional research librarian (who prefers to remain anonymous)—who, after a search of reports on the Chicago and New York underworld, determined that the killings, along with descriptions of our suspect, pointed to one man.

Abe "the Ghost" Amberg is known to New York police as an "enforcement contractor" for the newly formed National Crime Syndicate, sometimes known as the Combination. Amberg's weapon of choice is said to be the ice pick, which he can thrust into the intended victim's ear, penetrating the brain and causing death, in such a way that the perpetrator makes a clean getaway.

With so little exterior evidence, as in Addison's case, the murder is often mistaken for a stroke or hemorrhage.

In Mr. Tucker's case, the assassin disguised the cause of death by inflicting other wounds besides—hence the state of his office when the body was discovered, and the mistaken conclusion that led to charges against Miss Decker, as the so-called Fatal Flapper.

One respected jurist, who requested anonymity, declared the case to be "a triumph of policing. This is what happens when minds and skills come together to bear down on a case."

Credit is also due to VPD chief Morris Blatchford.

Since replacing the unloved Lionel Barfoot, Blatchford has gained a perhaps unjust reputation as an inflexible bureaucrat and something of an arriviste.

An observer remarked that the outcome of the case could cause his critics to think again.

It was Chief Blatchford who suggested that Inspector Hook team up with "Canada's Sherlock Holmes," Coroner F.C.V. Condon, demonstrating considerable administrative acumen, and leading detractors to concede that the VPD's push for "departmental modernization" might bear fruit after all.

CHAPTER 46

See me immediately —Chief Blatchford

NORMALLY, HOOK WOULD rather put a sharp stick in his eye than endure another meeting with the chief. If he weren't a family man he'd have already packed up the motorcycle and headed back to Waldo to find work on the railroad.

But this time he's rather looking forward to it.

As usual, he is standing in front of Blatchford's desk, staring at the jar of sharpened pencils beside the blotter, while Blatchford pretends to finish up some paperwork before addressing the nonentity before him.

"You've been having a swell time of it, haven't you Inspector?" Blatchford says without looking up. "Rubbing elbows with public enemy number one." Now he lifts his eyes for what he thinks is a flinty stare. "Are you thinking of switching careers, Inspector Hook?"

The inspector pretends to think about this (two can play at that game), then says, "I'm afraid I don't quite understand your question, sir. Could you rephrase it, please?"

"Hook, you were seen by a neighbour on Angus Drive, entering and exiting Joe Celona's house. The homeowner called to complain about a motorcycle revving its engine and honking its horn. There are at least two more witnesses to this disruption, as well. Now, from the evidence, one might conclude that you're either the most flagrantly bent copper in the force, or a ding-dong who doesn't know his ass from his elbow. Which one are you?"

A pause follows. Blatchford practises his steely glare some more.

"It was an off-the-books briefing, sir. A fact-finding interview, to provide background for my final report on the Tucker case. Mr. Celona was most helpful."

"Oh, he was, was he? So that's how you manage to come off as such a smartass, by sucking up to mobsters. Well, Inspector, now we know that the perpetrator has flown the coop. You've made a remarkable career out of producing nothing and getting promoted."

"Sir, with respect, I didn't promote myself."

"Exactly. How did you manage it? And now this." Blatchford picks up the folded newspaper on his desk. "Look at this." He presents the headline—*Inspector Hook Solves the Case*—and the icy stare becomes the stink eye.

"We don't need grandstanders, Hook. Especially, we don't need grandstanders on the pad. I'm going to the super, and if I have anything to say about it, in a week you'll be walking the night beat in Hogan's Alley."

Hook takes his time, for this is the moment he has been waiting for since the day Blatchford took office.

"Forgive me, sir, but have you actually *read* the news report?"

The chief lifts one eyebrow. "Something you wish to add, Inspector? Does the headline not tell the story?"

Hook forms an expression combining innocence with misgiving. "No, sir. No, I have nothing to add—or rather, I have a confession to make. There's a statement about you in the body of the piece, a statement attributed to me, that may well be false. You'll find it in the last paragraph."

Hook watches, savouring every second, while the chief rummages in a drawer and produces a pair of small, round reading glasses, winds the stems around his ears, bends over his desk and reads. His reading speed is slow.

A period of silence follows.

Blatchford takes off his glasses, folds them carefully, tucks them back into the drawer, plucks a partially smoked stogie from his ashtray (its end chomped to a disgusting mush), and lights it with a kitchen match, fouling the air with the pong of burning rubber.

Hook continues: "My report to the super said the same thing, sir. Surely you remember warning me to avoid going on—I think you called it a wild goose chase. I took that advice to heart, sir, and went straight to an informed source. What you just read was what I said— but as you know, I recently suffered a concussion. Was what I said not correct, sir?"

Hook worked out that speech last night during the usual wakeful hours, and tried it out on Jeanie this morning, together with the innocent look. Jeanie said he should have been an actor on the stage.

At length, the chief sighs, in the way of a father who regrets having lost his temper with a spirited but beloved child.

"No, Inspector. Not wrong, no. Overzealous perhaps, but not wrong. My reprimand may have been a bit overemphatic. Let's put the issue behind us, shall we? Cooler heads must always prevail. We pick up our socks, and we carry on."

The chief reaches down, a drawer slides open, and he produces a file, which he hands to the inspector with an air of finality. "It seems a gentleman from Nanaimo withdrew a great deal of money from the bank, then was seen boarding the *Princess Elaine* to Vancouver. His luggage arrived, but he didn't. One of the suitcases was empty.

"Inspector Hook, I am dispatching you to Nanaimo."

"But sir, what about the Tucker case?"

"Hook, you yourself admit you're getting nowhere on that file—just as you got nowhere with the Doukhobor murder. And since you worked so well as a team, take along Sergeant Quam in the fraud department, who is getting nowhere as well.

"Dismissed."

DEFENDANT SKIPS BAIL YET JURY ACQUITS
Cult Leader Slams "Gross Miscarriage of Justice"
Dallas MacElwee
The Victoria Colonist

Monday's grand jury trial of Robert Nettles began with a bang and ended with a whimper.

Robert Nettles, the former secretary-treasurer of the Aquarian Foundation, having unsuccessfully sued Edward Peter Collins, known to followers as Brother Osiris, became himself the subject of an action, to be tried before a grand jury under Chief Justice Aubrey Morrison.

The day after Judge C.E. Drummond-Hay stayed all charges against the cult leader, after what Drummond-Hay called "the most chaotic hearing in BC history," Collins proceeded to lay a charge of embezzlement that could put his former first mate in prison for several years.

When the doors to the courtroom opened, Collins

was among the first to enter, carrying a walking stick and impeccably dressed in what looked to be a new tailor-made suit, with his beard neatly trimmed. Choosing a front-row seat from which to view the proceedings, Collins wore a hint of a smile, suggesting that in his mind the tables had turned.

Within five minutes, the courtroom was packed to the walls. In Nanaimo, the internal battle between Aquarians has become the talk of the town. Nothing this exciting has happened since the Wanderers won the National Challenge Cup.

The air was literally buzzing with anticipation by the time Chief Justice Morrison called the court to order and swore in members of the grand jury. Morrison then took note of the empty defendant's chair.

Crown counsel Victor Harrison leapt to his feet, obviously embarrassed. "My Lord, I regret to say that the defendant, Robert Nettles, currently out on bail, has failed to appear."

"Has he absconded?" asked Chief Justice Morrison.

"I do not know, My Lord. The police are looking for him as we speak."

The courtroom began to rumble with discussion, much of it over Nettles's evident betrayal of his bondsman—a lawyer and fellow Aquarian named Elliot Linden, who pledged his house on De Courcy Island in order to post bond.

To everyone with any knowledge of the case, Nettles's absence was a prima facie admission of guilt.

Chief Justice Morrison ordered the trial postponed until the following day, at which point Robert Nettles would be tried *in absentia*.

Next morning, and no Robert Nettles.

Before proceedings began, however, Elliot Linden, the defendant's bondsman, stood up and announced that he had material evidence for the grand jury.

Overruling an objection from the prosecution, Chief Justice Morrison acceded to an in-camera meeting, and the grand jury filed out of the courtroom.

When the jury returned and the foreman announced a verdict of "no bill"—that "the charges alleged have not been sufficiently supported by the evidence to warrant a criminal prosecution"—Collins's smile disappeared and he became livid, loudly denouncing the jury, defence and justice.

Chief Justice Morrison coolly replied that, having seen Mr. Linden's submission, he had advised the jury on the verdict, having determined that the charges between Brother Osiris and the secretary-treasurer amounted to a "slanging match between members of the Aquarian Foundation over who should control the assets."

"There are other courts in the province to settle such disputes," the chief justice asserted.

Collins promptly left the building, after pausing to issue a general malediction to all present: "This entire trial is part of a cunning, satanic plot to destroy my work, led by traitors in this room! It is a gross miscarriage of justice and an offence against God, and I curse you and damn you all to hell!"

CHAPTER 47

HOW INCONVENIENT.

Seated at his usual table, McCurdy notes that the Stranger's Lounge is currently being monopolized by a party of six members and two attractively dressed female companions, who are in the process of raising their glasses for a rendition of "For He's a Jolly Good Fellow" in honour of a pink, nervous gentleman with a white carnation in his lapel.

—*which nobody can deny!*

As they bray out the last note, one of the ladies kisses the pink man on the cheek, which causes him to redden further. Paris discreetly replaces their empty glasses with another round, then glides back to the corner bar to pour McCurdy's usual.

Accepting his drink, McCurdy waits for the revellers to stop bellowing and light their cigarettes—and a Toro Grande cigar for the pink gentleman.

"Thank you, Paris. I see you have your hands full tonight."

"A bachelor party, sir. The room will quiet down soon. They'll be off dancing at the Lester, I expect—the Originals are playing tonight."

While they wait for the room to recover its dignity, McCurdy consults *As a Man Thinketh*: *A man only begins to be a man when he ceases to whine and revile, and commences to search for the hidden justice which regulates his life...*

Hidden justice. In the course of his career, McCurdy has found justice to be more often hidden than not, if it can be found at all.

At last, the celebrants have paid their bill, exited the building, and are staggering down Hastings Street to the tune of the "The Whiffenpoof Song":

We're poor little lambs who have lost our way,
Baa, baa, baa,
We're little black sheep who have gone astray,

Baa, baa, baa...

As their voices fade into the night, McCurdy gets up from his table with his empty glass, joins Paris at the corner bar, takes a stool and accepts another three fingers.

"George, I'll get right down to it. Our adventure with the Bobbsey Twins has created a rummy situation for us both."

"Man, you ain't flappin' your gums there, Ed. At home my frau is damn near to giffin' me the bum's rush."

"As I understand it from last we spoke, the concern is that the Norton twins might show up at your crib with heaters, and even if you're not snuffed, your frau will be out of a gig."

"True dat, if the Bentalls find out Helen's old man got a bad rep."

"My suggestion is this: I have been asked to take temporary lodgings elsewhere, which means you could move into my, er, my crib."

A pause follows while Paris gives him a long *What planet did you come down from?* stare, then lets out a guffaw of amused wonderment.

"Man, you gone goofy, or is them cheaters blind to colour? That morning someone saw me look into your crib, all the livelong day Mr. Charlie was nailin' me with the stink eye. I dig that you want me play like I'm the house peeper, suss out who is this cat messin' with you, but messin' in white folks bidness is a white job, know what I'm sayin'?"

"So what do you propose we do, George, get police protection?"

The question occasions more laughter. "I dunno, but one thing sure, in Vancouver the coloured folks don't move into the white neighbourhoods—now, you surely noticed that."

"Except that I have Mr. Good-Evening as leverage. I tell the management that Mr. Good-Evening is under threat, he's gonna hire a minder or else call in the coppers. I'll say you're my temporary butler or something. You answer the telephone, say 'Mr. McCurdy's residence,' stuff like that. Ever seen *What the Butler Saw*? Play that butler."

"Is he Black?"

"That's not the point."

"If he ain't Black, how do I act like him?"

"Ever see *Othello*?"

"That's the play, right?"

"That's the one."

"You sayin' it has a Black butler?"

"This is getting us nowhere, George. I recommend you move in and we take a wait-and-see attitude. 'Self-control is strength. Right thought is mastery. Calmness is power.'"

"Jesus, Ed. Who talks shit like that?"

CHAPTER 48

FOLLOWING HER EXPLOSIVE testimony in Nanaimo, Mrs. Arrowsmith's intention was to return to North Carolina as soon as possible, but when she ventured to De Courcy Island to pay her respects (and another ten thousand dollars) to Brother Osiris, he greeted her so warmly, and told her that she had a "special place in the Work," and invited her to Centre House, the colony's communal dining hall and socializing area.

There they talked for three hours, during which he imparted a message from her departed son, whose sudden death of pneumonia at twenty-five opened a wound that would never heal. She had never mentioned it to Brother Osiris before this. He just *knew*.

By early evening, Mrs. Arrowsmith knew she had found her life's work—supporting the Ark of Refuge by every means at her disposal. She made up her mind to settle on the island, take part in the Work and rescue the human race from the dark forces that dominate the world.

She was installed in a comfortable house, though it was a bit rustic for Mrs. Arrowsmith's taste, whose fifty-room mansion in Asheville, North Carolina, contains fifteen bathrooms.

Over the following days, the aging dowager has had the privilege of meeting privately with the Brother several times, to speak about her previous incarnation: Saint Hildegard of Bingen.

"Ida, you have Hildegard's musical voice, and as you settle in as part of our family I have no doubt you will experience visions as well, and know the secret mysteries of the universe."

In all her years, Mrs. Arrowsmith has never felt so... special. Her life on De Courcy is proving to be a magical time and it is certain to do wonders for her spiritual and physical well-being.

Her days are spent painting landscapes and taking short walks around the colony (avoiding the primal forest and rough terrain);

often she takes lunch with other disciples in the common dining room, where she mingles with these hardy, deeply committed souls, who eat so sparingly, yet are able to maintain a seemingly inexhaustible appetite for hard work—like the Negro servants back in Ashville, with their sturdy bodies and cheerful disposition.

Of course, Mrs. Arrowsmith is well aware that manual labour is essential to the Aquarian cause—both for the community's sustenance and as an ongoing test of a devotee's commitment to the Work. As Brother Osiris said to her in that Delphic way of his: All work is for the Work.

One afternoon she happens to be collecting pretty little stones on South Beach (she plans to make decorative vases out of jars by sticking the stones on with putty) when, purely by chance, she runs into one of the disciples—a Mr. Elliot Linden, who says he is on his way to the potato field.

Mr. Linden invites her to take his arm and venture into an undeveloped part of the island, to view some of the work being done that will transform the community into a self-sufficient whole, and a model for the world to come in the Age of Aquarius.

While making their way down the path to the garden currently in progress, Mrs. Arrowsmith and Mr. Linden discuss the meaning of Aleister Crowley's Ante-Primal Triad of Not-God (*Nothing is. Nothing becomes. Nothing is not.*), until they reach a rocky rise above Pirate's Cove, from which they can watch men and women clearing the land by hand, using picks, shovels, hoes and mattocks, and carrying the stones to the shore in baskets.

The scene would be like one of Millet's peasant paintings if it weren't for the athletic red-haired woman in black, currently standing over two men as they struggle with a particularly huge boulder, shrieking at them for their lack of effort. She is waving a riding crop, kicking one disciple in the behind and threatening to have the other thrown into the water.

Observing her shocked expression, Mr. Linden assures Mrs. Arrowsmith that everything here must be seen in the context of a test—a test to determine one's spiritual commitment.

"Oh Mrs. Arrowsmith, you can be sure that Brother Osiris runs a tight ship when it comes to sluggards who do not realize the urgency of the Work. Standards of devotion are high, as you might expect, when we're talking about the fate of humanity."

"But who is that woman and why is she screaming at those men?"

"Ah. Madame Zura has the unpleasant task of administering the tests. Believe me, it's a huge responsibility. Those who fail can be banished, sent off the island with no money and only the clothes on their backs, destitute in a foreign country. To condemn an individual to such a fate isn't an easy decision.

"Therefore, punishment is inflicted not with rancour but in sorrow. When Edith Puckett was invited to drown herself so that her spirit could come back and report on the afterlife, it was a test—like the test the Almighty set out for Abraham over his willingness to sacrifice his first-born..."

As Mrs. Arrowsmith listens carefully, she remembers something Brother Osiris said to her yesterday afternoon, that *Every day is a gift—and a test.*

Clearly, he foresaw the reservations that would come to her mind, and answered them beforehand!

As Linden conducts Mrs. Arrowsmith back to her house, they continue their discussion of Crowley—specifically, that *Every man and every woman is a star. A star is an individual identity; it radiates energy, it is a point of view. Its object is to become the whole by establishing relations...*

But while outwardly discussing *The Aquarian Gospel*, Mrs. Arrowsmith can't repress the disturbing memory of what she just saw, particularly of Madame Zura's use of the riding crop; it reminds her of the plantation when she was a child, terrible stories about men having been whipped until their backbone showed. But of course that was during slavery...

"Mr. Linden, what does *The Aquarian Gospel* say about the infliction of pain on others?"

"I don't think it is mentioned, Mrs. Arrowsmith. Why do you ask?"

"It's just that Brother Osiris radiates such spiritual power—was the abuse I saw really necessary?" She pauses, for she can barely form the words. "I suppose I am asking if it is possible Brother Osiris has a cruel side as well?"

Linden visibly bridles at the suggestion. "Oh Mrs. Arrowsmith, cruelty for the greater good can hardly be termed *abuse*—and I assure you, if pain is inflicted, it's an important part of the Work."

But she took pleasure in it... As the memory comes to mind, the magic of the Ark of Refuge begins to dim—or rather, change colour—like the spark in the Brother's eyes, illuminated by the match with which he lit his pipe, when his eyes grew so pale that the irises seemed to fade into the whites. This occurred in Centre House over tea, and again yesterday.

Of course, she doesn't breathe a word of this to Mr. Linden. It would upset him terribly.

FOR HIS PART, Elliot Linden is in a brown study over Bob Nettles, who hasn't been heard from since he jumped bail.

Linden's evidence as an Aquarian secured the Nettles verdict—by producing an application to the Supreme Court for an injunction to restrain Edward Collins from dealing with Aquarian Foundation funds, signed by the governors of the foundation. It was this evidence that resulted in the "slanging match" verdict.

Fine—but Bob Nettles didn't know that would be the outcome. Was he such a heel that he was willing to let Linden lose his house in order to make a getaway?

Or has something more sinister happened?

A community infected by malevolence and distrust is a natural hive of speculation and rumour; word has already circulated among devotees that the former secretary-treasurer somehow came to grief.

For the first time since he graduated from Osgoode Hall, Elliot Linden feels a craving for justice.

CHAPTER 49

FROM TIME TO time in June, there comes a welcome break from the rain, usually around suppertime, when the clouds part to allow for a sliver of blue sky and a trickle of sun to appear, which affords the Hook family just enough time for a stroll down Commercial Drive before the stores close.

Passing by the Grandview Theatre, they stop to look at the lobby cards for *Son of the Gods*, coming soon; then they visit Manitoba Hardware, where Hook and Lucille wait for Jeanie to buy rat poison.

Lucille is in reasonably good form as long as he jiggles the carriage. No telling whether it's the motion she likes, or the sound of squeaking springs.

Hook has been getting noticeably more sleep of late; any bouts of sleeplessness were generated by his boiling brain.

In the street, a nipper rides by on a bicycle too big for him, and with a cigarette pack attached next to the spokes with clothespins to make the sound of a motor.

Jeanie comes out of the store with a can of Rough on Rats, drops it into her string shopping bag, and the three continue to the Florida Market, where she buys eggs for Chester pudding, which is to follow Hindle Wakes and mushy peas. (Hook chooses not to parse the ingredients of northern cookery.)

Then they buy lemon sodas from a vendor working out of a tricycle cart. As they continue down the street, Jeanie slips her arm through Hook's; she has exchanged her house dress for a day dress— *Still a cuddlesome girl*, he thinks—and stylish as well, in her cloche hat and the summer dress she bought from Spencer's at half price.

He is about to broach the subject on his mind, but Jeanie is ahead of him. "How did ye fare with the chief this time round, ducky? Did he snape at ye again? Did he threap ye down? Blimey, every time I hear ye've got a meeting I get feshed over whether ye got the sack."

"Well, pet, this time it was mixed nuts, but a winner overall—up to a point. Homicide and fraud are now permitted to confer on a case."

"Cor, ducky, that was what ye wanted in the first place!"

"Correct, luv. But this is a different case—though remarkably similar, in its way. It involves fraud and possible murder among cult members, but in this case a suspect has been identified, and in fact it looks open and shut."

"That's what we heard about the Fatal Flapper—but then came along the short gadgie with the funny walk."

"I tell you, pet, I nearly had him dead to rights before it all went pear-shaped."

"Along the road he could 'ave put yer light out for good, ducky."

He pushes the carriage through a cloud of steam emanating from the partly open window of Mock Sing's Laundry. Sing has become a neighbourhood celebrity after an attempted robbery, during which the thief threatened him with a pistol made of wood and shoe polish. Sing responded with a hot flatiron that inflicted a glaring facial burn, resulting in the arrest of Mr. Walter Smith, who had robbed three other Chinese laundries the previous week.

"The gunman was a worry, pet, I know. He finally buggered off back east on the Ocean Limited—and clipped another victim in the process."

"So yer sayin' he's not in the nick?"

"Afraid not, luv. He's in New York by now. But for this new case it will be different, because Sergeant Quam will be with me to assist."

"That's no comfort, ducky. Sergeant Quam is a quilt."

"Quam can surprise you when he's not talking gibberish. Just so you know, this time our suspect is a con man named Edward Collins, who calls himself Brother Osiris."

"D'ye mean the bigamist who runs that Aquarian bunch of rich American nutters outside Nanaimo?"

"Pipe down, pet, the lady in the doorway is giving you the eye."

"Oh, that's Hilda Carruthers, she's as blind as the back of yer neck."

They pass the Gallo d'Oro Restaurant, its door open to tempt pedestrians with the aroma of basil, oregano and hot olive oil.

"Luv, about this Brother Osiris—how'd you get so... *informed*?"

"Ye asked me that question before, ducky."

"I know. But I had a concussion at the time."

"Aye, an' I'm Mae West. Well, here it wasn't the papers, it was Tilly Wallwork's radio—all about the merlock who got charged for stealin' money from a granny and won the court case with black magic. Then the bird who brought charges against him disappeared on a ferry with a suitcase full of money. A row between horkers, sounded like to me."

"Except that it appears the suitcases reached the dock without him. One contained shirts and drawers and some such, while the other suitcase was empty."

"Ye think he fell overboard?"

"Or jumped, or was tossed over the side. Either way, the money surely didn't drown with him."

"Some will say he was bewitched by black magic like at the trial, an' if that's so, there's nae tellin' what went on."

"You're right, pet, but the possibilities narrow down a bit. Our man was the secretary-treasurer of the Aquarians—and wouldn't you know, the Aquarians had an account with Tucker, Palmer and Pine."

Jeanie barely resists clapping her hands with glee. "Oh ducky, how bloomin' interesting!"

"Maybe, luv, but the fact is, I want to back out of the case."

"Why? Yer an ace, ducky, anyone else is sure to make a bollocks of it."

"Except for one other thing—the case is in Nanaimo, you know, the mining town."

"Aye. In the Lancashire collieries they call it the miner's graveyard."

"But mines aren't involved here."

"Unless they threw 'im down one—an' put a double on the ferry in his place."

"Oh dear. Never thought of that, pet. I suppose it's possible."

"More possible than black magic, I reckon."

"What has me—What's your word? *Feshed*?—is to be leaving you alone with Lucille."

"Try to remember, during the war it was the normal way of things."

"Except there's no war on now."

"But when ye think about it, there's always a war on somewhere, somehow."

That sounded like something Quam might say. But a war between what and what? Rather than quibble, he nods thoughtfully. (He's still having trouble grasping some concepts, but there's no point in worrying Jeanie further.)

"I know ye have yer duty to do, ducky, and besides, I have a notion. Ye remember just now I mentioned Tilly Wallwork from Moulton?"

"Of course I know Tilly. She's your best mate."

"Aye, well ye mustn't breathe a word of this to a soul—especially not her husband, Ernie."

"I've never met Ernie Wallwork."

"Well ye might, so knit yer gob, fer ye can never ken what Ernie will do."

"Pet, believe me, any secret is safe with me."

"Well, since her Ernie left—he's with a gang mendin' the flume over in Capilano—their landlord's been pokin' through her drawers when she's out an' makin' smutty remarks when she's in. Last week, Mr. DuBois cornered her in the back porch and she had to knee him in the goonies. Tilly could do with a place to kip 'til Ernie comes home. Ernie's a hotspur, ye know. He weighs near eighteen stone."

NEW CHARGES LAID AGAINST CULT LEADER
Dallas MacElwee
The Victoria Colonist

The conflict between Edward Peter Collins, known by his followers as Brother Osiris, and a group of disgruntled Aquarians entered a new phase yesterday, when Elliot Linden, a disciple and a lawyer, filed a claim in which he charges the cult leader with fraudulently obtaining contributions in the amount of $12,340.

Following Linden's lead, another disciple, Ida Arrowsmith, in a complete about-face from her previous testimony on behalf of Brother Osiris, has filed a claim for forty-two thousand dollars, plus ten thousand in personal damages, naming Collins and his associate, Muriel Riffle, also known as Madame Zura, as defendants.

Mr. Collins has filed a defence in which he denies the allegations against him, claiming that all contributions were given voluntarily and that his teachings are anything but fraudulent, being based on the overwhelming inspiration of unseen spiritual forces, and therefore intended only "for those whose consciousness of the spiritual realm has taken them to an appropriate level of understanding."

Mr. Linden takes issue with this claim, saying, "This so-called defence is another way of saying *Buyer beware*. Any swindler would make the same argument—that only the gullible need apply."

CHAPTER 50

See Me Re Nettles Case —F.C.V. Condon

WITH A DEEP sense of unease, Hook drags himself upstairs to the fourth-floor lab, pulling on the railing with one hand to compensate for the unwillingness of his legs.

A veteran never knows when a war experience will enter the picture.

Non-veterans think the experience of war hardens a man, which may well be true of men who have served on the front lines—in the infantry, hardness is a survival tool that results in numbness, as some kind of scar tissue.

But not in Hook's case—as a veteran who served behind the lines, who heard the gory details of warfare straight from the horse's mouth, and observed what it did to the horse.

When it comes to memories of the war, vicarious experience can be as haunting as the real thing.

Of all the terrible stories he heard at Rugeley Camp, none of them described man shoving an ice pick into another man's brain, in a railway car, while he is listening to the radio. It makes the war seem almost quaint in comparison.

He pulls open the now-familiar door with the curious bullet hole in the window, and there before him on the angled steel table he sees a sodden shoe, stuffed with a congealed yellow substance, on a medical tray.

What fresh carnage is this?

At a distance from the shoe, framed by the scale's overhead dial, sits Condon's behemoth of a cat, looming over the medical tray as though about to dine.

"Lewis, get out of that!" Emerging from his lab, Condon gestures with his unlit pipe. "Now, be a good boy and stay away from the evidence."

Lewis glares at Hook, bares his fang, lumbers down the angled table to the far end, turns toward him and sneers.

No. He doesn't sneer. He's a cat.

The concussion, acting up again.

Condon points his pipe stem at the shoe, or what's left of the shoe, sitting on the table. "Well, Mr. Cook, what do you suppose we have here?"

"I would say that it's a shoe, sir."

"Indeed, but what *sort* of shoe?"

Eyeing the shoe's yellow-and-white stuffing, Hook refrains from taking a closer look. "I'm afraid I don't know much about shoes, sir."

"Just bit of the Socratic method, Inspector, thought you'd be interested. But be that as it may, what we have here is a shoe, found washed ashore in Semiahmoo Bay by a cannery worker on his way to work. What caught his attention was that it contained a human foot."

"Ah. And inside the shoe is—"

"What I just told you, Mr. Cook. A foot. You see, that's bone and cartilage at the joint where the foot became separated from the remains."

"Came apart at the ankle? Surely the process would have taken months."

"Not necessarily. Salt in the ocean acts as sandpaper, while the leather bubbles up in no time. As for the foot itself, had he drowned in the middle of the Georgia Strait, the body would have survived relatively intact; but in shallower water, rich in oxygen, shrimp and crabs would be munching on the body within a matter of hours. A pack of dogfish would take care of the larger muscles in an afternoon, and in a fortnight he could be pretty well picked clean."

Here we go, Hook thinks, glad to have skipped lunch.

"The foot separated from the ankle but was protected by the shoe, don't you see, so the breaking down was much slower.

"Now look at the sole of the shoe—it's rubber, and rubber floats—especially in salt water. So when the body came apart, the foot rose to the surface, to be carried along by ocean currents. Now, assuming our man drowned in the Georgia Strait, the current would have carried the foot south—to approximately where the shoe was found.

"Now I am given to understand that a check of missing persons produced the name Robert Nettles, who disappeared while on the ferry from Nanaimo to Vancouver."

Hook looks down at the half-smoked Ogden's between his fingers and wonders how it got there. "Yes, we're now aware of Mr. Nettles. The fraud department was looking into his dealings on Howe Street. As it turns out, there's only one Nettles in Nanaimo—he handled finances for a cult called the Aquarian Foundation."

"Inspector, your job is beginning to look like a game of blind man's bluff."

"In which everyone is blindfolded."

The coroner laughs appreciatively. "Haw! Indeed! Indeed! In any case, I called the bank, and the manager referred me to a teller named Alfred Hazel—and yes, indeed, Mr. Nettles did wear rubber-soled shoes; in fact, tellers frequently remarked on how loudly they squeaked on the marble floor."

"So this, this *thing* before us is what remains of Mr. Nettles."

"May what remains rest in peace," Condon says, ushering the inspector back into the examination room, where the two men pause in front of the open door.

"I'm to take the investigation to Nanaimo, sir. The plan is to search for the last person to see Nettles alive."

"If it's a case of murder, I doubt that Nettles was simply thrown off the boat, where he could just swim around until he was rescued. He would surely have been unconscious when he hit the drink. And I expect it would all have to be done quietly—it was sunny that afternoon, and people would have been out on deck."

"An ice pick would have done the trick."

"Haw! Indeed! Indeed! Now, that would be a coincidence!"

As Hook opens the door to leave, again the bullet hole catches his eye.

"By the way sir, I was wondering about this bullet hole here. The inside is a neat hole, while the outside has little cracks spread in a sort of web."

"Yes, that's the common pattern—especially with reinforced glass."

"Except that, sir, to make those cracks, the round must have come from *inside* the room."

A pause follows, then Condon sighs, as though embarrassed. "Oh dear. Well, I suppose someone was bound to catch that sooner or later. Well done, Mr. Hook." He strikes a flame with a kitchen match and lights his pipe, taking his time.

"Do you see that machine over there? As you know, it's for mounting pistols for examination. Well, I was doing a test, and I turned my back for one moment, and wouldn't you know, that little imp over there—"

With his pipe stem Condon indicates the massive animal crouched at the other end of the table.

"Bad Lewis. Bad, bad Lewis."

Lewis couldn't care less.

CHAPTER 51

QUAM TEMPORARILY SHOVES his plate aside, leaving a half-eaten piece of coconut cream pie; for the first time that Hook has witnessed, he seems to have lost his appetite. "*Nanaimo*, sir? Was our experience on the Verigin case not miserable enough?"

The inspector can understand how the memory of the Verigin case—or to be more specific, the Stirling Hotel—might continue to nag the sergeant. More than the cold, it was the smell. It's always the smell. For the inspector, what lingers unpleasantly in the mind is the smell of talcum powder and fermented fruit.

Which provokes the question, What must Hook himself smell like, to Quam? As he fires up an Ogden's, the inspector reminds himself that the sergeant doesn't smoke.

"Sergeant, I'll admit that the Verigin case was not pleasant."

"Are you indulging in sarcasm, sir?"

"Not at all, Mr. Quam. It was understatement. If there's no acceptable hotel, perhaps we can pitch tents somewhere."

"Good thinking, sir, there are some quite comfortable surplus tents at the Army and Navy."

"Thanks for the tip, Sergeant. I shall take it under advisement. Shall we carry on?"

"Of course."

"To sum things up in a nutshell, our suspect is a cult leader, an ex–postal worker named Edward Peter Collins, who calls himself Brother Osiris. Who seems to have had a falling-out with one of his henchmen. They press charges back and forth, in court, out of court—and then the henchman disappears, having last been seen boarding the *Princess Elaine* to Vancouver."

"His luggage arrived without him. We have forensic evidence to suggest that he was dumped in the drink."

"What evidence was that, sir?"

"What's left of a shoe and a bit of bone and gristle."

"Oh." Quam reaches for his pie, then thinks better of it. "Of course, it might have been an accident, kids climbing on the railings, people leaning too far over to see—"

"No, Quam. Nor was it a case of suicide—because if so, who took the money?"

"Maybe he threw it away. If he was about to commit suicide, he wouldn't need it."

"You can't take it with you, that sort of thing?"

"Well, that's another point."

Hook fumbles for his bottle of Aspirin—something about the sergeant always gives him a headache. "No. No, it is not *another point*. Sergeant Quam, I can see that you're not quite ready to accept this assignment. But you're going to have to come to grips with it, because it's a direct order."

Quam puts his plate in front of him, forks half a sliver into his mouth and chews, pleased for a moment. Then a frown creases his normally placid forehead.

"Wait, sir! Isn't that what the provincial police do? And what about the Mounties?"

"Recruitment was a fiasco, Mr. Quam. The provincial police is a pack of oafs who contaminate more evidence than they find. And the Mounties on Vancouver Island are worse; they're from back east and they don't know their arse from their elbow on the West Coast."

"Sir, if I may say so, you paint a gloomy picture of the men who tamed the West."

"My point is that these chaps don't know the territory, when it comes to kooks and fanatics. The Doukhobors are one thing, but go north up the coast from Vancouver and you've got your Finns, Norwegians, Danes, the Catholics, the Mormons and God knows how many freelance missionaries out there, preaching away."

"Back home, black hats and buggies was about the size of it. And the oblates, of course."

"My point exactly."

"Ah, but the Lord loves them all, sir."

"Do you really think so, Mr. Quam?"

"I don't believe everything I think."

"What do you mean?"

"I'm not sure."

Hook sucks back cigarette smoke and pulls it down to the base of his spine.

"Still and all, sir, with Mr. Nettles dead, why involve the fraud department?

The inspector's headache is getting worse. "Mr. Quam, fraud comes into it because it was the most likely motive for the murder. A group of disciples have got wise and charged Collins with fraud. This is more or less the same charge our victim—Mr. Nettles—made a little over a week ago. And as you know, Nettles had dealings with Tucker, Palmer and Pine."

Sergeant Quam thinks about this. "Sir, what about Chief Blatchford—interdepartmental meddling, and so forth?"

"The chief is issuing a revised memorandum."

Quam is cornered. "Oh. Oh dear. Well, in that case... Will there be snow in Nanaimo?"

Hook isn't sure the sergeant knows where Nanaimo is. "Not in June, Sergeant, just constant rain—more or less the same as here. The trial starts on Monday, so we'll leave Sunday—"

"After church, of course."

"Of course. Look on the bright side, Mr. Quam. If we can find a witness, it'll all be duck soup."

"Eating soup can be messy, sir."

"I'll be sure to bring a napkin."

CHAPTER 52

THE BOTTOM FLOOR of the blockhouse is near completion, with a door and window frames and a cement floor. A trap door has been installed in the corner, made of steel and secured with a heavy lock.

A ladder through a hatch leads to the larger second floor, which has walls now, and windows that provide firing positions in all four directions.

Seen from the outside, the blockhouse appears top-heavy, pressing down as if to crush the room below, and the three men inside.

"Our workers seem to have picked up the pace," observes Roger Flagler—although, when he donated ninety thousand dollars to the Work, what he had in mind was something other than preparing for war. If he wanted to go to war, he would have joined up in '16.

"The Brother has taken on two more men, and also some fellows he calls his protectors," Backstone says.

"Who are they protecting him from?" Linden asks.

"I don't think they're protecting him at all," Backstone replies. "One of those men is Krause—that's the fellow Brother Osiris was with when he made Barney Sullivan's head swell like a balloon. I spoke to Barney, he said that Krause would follow the Brother to hell and back."

"I never liked Krause," Flagler says. "But I never expected him capable of black magic."

"Roger, we are now reasonably sure that Brother Osiris has been taken over by a Dark Adept. If that is so, it means that Dark Adepts have already penetrated the auric egg."

"Now that you mention it, Sydney, I can feel the malevolent presence, I felt it in the air when I left the house this morning."

"Which is why we must take steps," Backstone says. "*Urgent* steps."

Linden is immediately on his guard. "And what steps might those be, Sydney?"

"I am acquainted with a noted psychic in Blaine, just over the border in Washington State. I can vouch for her, as she was a regular contributor to *Dees Magazine* while I was editor."

"An astrologer is she? Past-life regression? Converse with the dead?"

"No need for condescension, Elliot. For *Dees Magazine*, she writes an advice column under the name Helena Horos. I knew her as Madame Feglerska when she spoke at the retreat at Indralaya on Orcas Island. Altogether a brilliant woman, with a deeply learned mind. Madame Feglerska is able to draw from her occult knowledge and experience to address personal problems as sent in by the readership."

"She is indeed a remarkable woman," Flagler agrees. "Born among Moldovan peasants—yet, in a trance, she speaks perfect Latin. And she has a substantial following in the US."

Backstone nods enthusiastically. "And with a remarkably down-to-earth personality. A plain-spoken woman who refuses to speak in pious platitudes."

Feeling a pang of unspecific dread, Linden fires up a fresh cigarette with the end of its predecessor. "You haven't enlisted her help, have you, Sydney?"

"I certainly have, Elliot. I sent a telegram to *Dees* requesting her mailing address in Seattle. Before the reply had even arrived, I received a psychic response from her, followed by a letter a few days later. She said that she has already been in contact with our Dark Adept, she knows who he is and she is willing to facilitate communication through Ed McCurdy as the Dark Adept's Spirit Host. She learned through clairvoyance that the Dark Adept goes under the name Mr. Good-Evening."

Linden is grateful for the dim light, because his companions can't see him lift his gaze to heaven and mutter a swear word. To him, the discussion just crossed the line between spiritualism and derangement.

Linden is about to announce his departure from the conversation, and from De Courcy Island as well, when Flagler unexpectedly erupts.

"Oh! I see it now! Of course! It wasn't the Brother who abducted my wife, it was the Dark Adept!"

"Yes, Roger," replies Backstone. "Once the auric egg has been pierced, they will do what they want. If they are not stopped, the island will be infested with them. Surely you can see that, Elliot."

But Linden has already left the building.

CHAPTER 53

"JESUS, HONEY, WAS that the best you could do—a frickin' *poet*?"

"A failed poet, actually."

Mildred lights a cigarette. She is not ready to discuss her long-term relations with McCurdy. It's all too complicated for her mind to deal with. The truth is that she lacks an alternative. Tristan has valentines for eyes and would be drooling over her day and night, and she has enough on her plate right now.

McCurdy is the best she can do. Plus, he owes her a research fee for Abe the Ghost.

"And am I to understand he's nearly as blind as me?"

"Yes. I've recruited John Milton."

"Who's John Milton?" Dora asks, seated at the foot of the bed, rolling a cigarette, legs crossed.

"A dead poet," Mildred replies. "A real bluenose, you wouldn't like him."

"So instead of Broncho Billy for protection we get a blind poet dressed like a maître d'."

"He's a broadcaster. It's the uniform."

"Broadcaster? What's he going to do when the ex shows up—*read* to him?"

McCurdy fidgets in his dinner jacket, standing in the doorway, feeling as if he's trapped at a ladies' tea party; except that one lady is rolling a cigarette, one is a stroppy blind hag and the other is in war-surplus khaki coveralls (like a boiler suit with a waist).

Unwilling to just stand there as an object of female ridicule, he bows and tips his hat. "It's been delightful making your acquaintance, ladies. Now, Miss Wickstram, if you would just show me to my room—"

"Do you play baseball?" Dora asks.

Mildred ushers the new guest downstairs to a room just off the front hall.

"Why did you bring a baseball bat, Eddie?"

"It was the only thing I could think of. A policeman told me a baseball bat is a highly effective weapon at close quarters—especially with unionists and Wobblies."

"I suppose it doesn't require much of an aim."

"There's that as well, yes." McCurdy wipes his glasses for a better look at Mildred's boiler suit.

"Millie, you look like a Munitionette."

"Has my skin turned canary yellow?"

"No, it's your outfit. It's protective. It suits you. Maybe you should run a women's petrol station."

"For female motorists—there may be five of them. In any case, I hope you find the room comfortable. You're used to something more posh, I'm sure."

He pushes down on the mattress, which is developing a sag in the middle, then perches on the edge of the bed, which squeaks briefly, then calms down. "It is an excellent room, Millie..."

He looks up upward—at the swell of Mildred's bosom above the cinched waist of her boiler suit; she reminds him of a French actress whose name he forgets.

A long pause follows, while they both search for something to say.

DEATH OF A HIT MAN
Rolin S. Cobb
The New York Illustrated Daily News

The proverb "Who lives by the sword dies by the sword" was never more apt than in the case of Abe "the Ghost" Amberg.

One of the most notorious New York killers, said to be responsible for up to seventy murders, Amberg met his maker in Brooklyn last Thursday evening amid a hail of bullets from a tommy gun.

Though just five foot two in height, Amberg was once described by a judge as "more violent than Dillinger," before he was acquitted of murder on a procedural issue.

Amberg has beaten every charge since then—hence his chilling moniker.

Ever loyal to the Mob, Amberg was once heard to say, "You agree to kill for money, so when you kill, it becomes a duty."

If so, nothing could be more fitting than when four assassins did their duty in Brooklyn on Thursday last, ending a life that seemed charmed by the devil himself.

The following was disclosed to this reporter by an official from within the NYPD, who must remain anonymous.

Amberg had just arrived that afternoon by train from Montreal. After leaving Union Station in his new Lincoln coupe, he proceeded along Utrecht Avenue. When he stopped at an intersection, a black Hudson sedan carrying an unknown number of armed mobsters pulled up in the adjacent lane.

Realizing his peril, Amberg sped away even before the light changed, with the sedan in hot pursuit.

At Forty-Fourth Street, Brooklyn, shots from the Hudson shattered the Lincoln's rear window, forcing Amberg to swerve from lane to lane in an effort to escape, until the two cars came abreast between Ninth and Tenth Avenues near Sunset Park.

Leaning out of one passenger window, one gunmen had begun firing into the driver's-side window of the Lincoln with a pistol, when from the back seat a volley of submachine gun bullets sliced through the hit man's brain, so that the now out-of-control Lincoln crashed into the stoop of a brownstone at 923 Forty-Fourth Street.

Amberg died immediately.

In Chicago, Al Capone was asked who might have been responsible for the murder. His reply: "I wouldn't know, but I'm sure it wasn't personal."

CHAPTER 54

GOOD EVENING. HERE is the CNR news service, brought to you by the Vancouver Evening Star.

The US economy continues to soar, and Yale economist Irving Fisher assures the public that if a correction comes, it will be brief and harmless...

In the Soviet Union, General Secretary Joseph Stalin has expelled rival Leon Trotsky to Kazakhstan, while riots have broken out between Palestinians and Jews over control of the Western Wall. Great Britain has suppressed the Iraqi uprising in Mesopotamia with the deployment of RAF bombers, while in Samoa, New Zealand colonial police killed eleven unarmed demonstrators, and in Rome, with the creation of a Vatican city-state Pope Pius XI emerged from the Vatican after sixty years of papal self-imprisonment...

In the US, federal agents have arrested gangster Al Capone for contempt of court following his testimony before the federal grand jury. Capone posted a five-thousand-dollar bond and was released. In London, the Judicial Committee of the Privy Council has ruled Canadian women to be legal persons eligible to become members of the Senate. Meanwhile, in Canada, Prime Minister MacKenzie King declared himself completely convinced of the reality of the spiritual world after contacting dead family members through a medium...

This ends the newscast. From the news desk of the Evening Star we wish all our listeners, on the farms, the lumber camps and of course on the trains, a restful good evening.

ANOTHER ONE DOWN—another confused jumble of factlets, strewn across the length and breadth of the land.

As he has since the Norton twins came into his life, McCurdy scurries out of the building, hunched under the drizzle, down the cement steps and across the sidewalk, where he ducks into the waiting taxi.

"Keefer Street, Dennis," he says, pulling the door shut and brushing off the rain on his hat. "Five twenty-nine."

The taxi propels forward, fast enough to shove his back against the coarse velvet seat. "It's not an emergency, Dennis, no need for the lead foot."

He removes his silk scarf. He has been wearing it as protection against a cold in this unseasonably dank month. He caught a cold last February; naturally, so did Mr. Good-Evening, who was inundated with remedies by mail—bottles of Friars' Balsam, preventative enema powder, medical cigarettes...

"So Dennis, tell me, you think the Tigers will say with the league or not? If they do, someone's going to kill, what's his name, that umpire—" McCurdy stops speaking, having become aware that this is not his usual driver, and that the auto, a Buick Master Six—not a car for the common man, much less a taxi.

He turns his attention to the back of the driver's head. No, it isn't Dennis.

Self-control is strength. Right thought is mastery. Calmness is power...

He speaks in a calm voice above the surrounding traffic. "Driver?" He raises his voice. "*Driver?*"

Not a peep from the front seat, so McCurdy decides to trot out Mr. Good-Evening, the voice of God, the voice he uses fifteen minutes a day: "Driver!" As though in reply, the man behind the wheel slams the pedal to the floor and the Buick surges forward, sharply enough that McCurdy has to clutch the looped passenger strap with both hands.

Momentarily, he wonders if he is a prisoner, or hostage, with no possibility of escape—Buick rear doors are rear-hinged, which means that McCurdy would be snatched outside and flung onto the road the instant he pulled the handle, then skip along the pavement, filleting his skin with every skip, and traffic roaring both ways, and trolley tracks—

Stop. His imagination is running away with him.

Self-control is strength...

He braces himself as the Buick lurches to a halt, abruptly enough to bounce him off his seat.

Now kneeling in the footwell, he turns sideways just in time to see the door flung open. The shadow of a man's arm reaches inside, a pair of farmer's hands grip his coat and he is hauled straight over the running board onto the sidewalk, where he is frog-marched up the steps to the Empire Building and thrust into a metal lift the size of a coffin.

As the lift creaks and clanks its way upward, his captor blind-folds him with a handkerchief and binds his wrists with a line of hemp using one hand, while the other maintains a grip like a carpenter's vice.

"Terribly sorry for the inconvenience, Mr. McCurdy," says a voice in his ear. "I see you're dressed for dinner."

"They're work clothes, actually."

"You're a waiter?"

"Of a sort, yes."

His captor seems surprisingly middle-aged, considering his physical strength; nor does the posh Boston accent go with those thick, calloused hands. The fellow is either a gentleman farmer or severely down on his luck.

Again, McCurdy trots out the voice of authority: "See here, Mac, you do realize that kidnapping is a capital crime, punishable by—"

"Ah, that sounds like Mr. Good-Evening speaking. Don't worry, Mr. McCurdy, you'll soon be rid of his clutches."

Rid of Mr. Good-Evening?

He is about to ask for an explanation when the lift moans to a stop, the scissor-like metal door squeals open and a rough palm claps the flat of his back and firmly thrusts him out of the lift.

"Sir, you still have time to avoid getting yourself in terrible trouble. We can forget this all—"

McCurdy is dragged out of the elevator onto what smells like a waxed linoleum floor. Twelve paces down a hall they stop while his companion delivers five measured knocks, and at almost the same moment a door squeals open.

Apparently, they are expected.

Another pair of hands joins the first and he is bundled into what could be either a wasps' nest or an electric generator.

Aummmmmmmm...

Aummmmmmmm...

McCurdy identifies the sound as human voices, humming tune-lessly. The amount of echo in the room suggests that they are in a generous empty space, with a high ceiling and a hardwood floor. It might be a ballet studio but for the stench of smoke, incense and perspiration. (Already he can feel his asthma acting up.)

He is propelled forward until his shins run into the seat of a chair, then turned around and seated—in a dining chair, he thinks, with a cane back and an oval frame.

Immediately—and alarmingly—a hemp rope is looped over his head; the weight on the back of his neck suggests that it's a noose.

Self-control is strength...

"Do not be frightened, Mr. McCurdy, you will not be harmed," whispers a woman's voice, a not-unfamiliar voice, but with a foreign accent he can't place; he notes her perfume, a mixture of flowers and smoke that suggests something vaguely pagan. "The purpose of the procedure is to make the demon uncomfortable in the body of the possessed. It lays the ground for the ritual itself."

"Madam, this noose has certainly made *me* uncomfortable—and did you say *demon*?"

McCurdy knows nothing about demons, other than from what he heard back in Sunday school about the Sabbatic Goat and the Whore of Babylon. Is it the Whore of Babylon speaking to him right now?

Whoever she is, she seems to have left his side, leaving him alone in his chair, in a room of wasps.

Aummmmmmm...

Aummmmmmm...

The humming seems to close in around him as it grows louder, then becomes suddenly soft when he hears a female voice—it's the same woman who spoke to him before, now speaking with a sonorous resonance reminding him of Aimee Semple McPherson, curing cancer over the radio.

In the name of Ishvara the Source of All Things, I call on Narasimha to grant your servant the strength to contain and expel evil, and Ed McCurdy the strength to withstand the agony of redemption and union with the Infinite.

Aummmmmmm...

Aummmmmmm...

If McCurdy betrays this communion, may his throat be cut across, his tongue torn out, his body buried in the sands of the sea at low tide...

Restrained, blindfolded, with a noose around his neck and facing the prospect of having his throat slit, McCurdy cries out in alarm when he is sprinkled with a sand-like substance with an evil, chemical smell—

Ye huts, ye prets, ye daemons, with these three primigenial elements, salt, sulphur and mercury, I summon the Dark Adept whom ye know as Seth, who drowned Osiris in the Nile, whose telluric, temporal name is Mr. Good-Evening—

The humming all around him swells to triple forte as a second chair is placed with its back next to his. Now someone is seated behind him; he can feel the heat of the speaker's body through the cane chair back and can smell that smoky perfume.

Aummmmm...

Aummmmm...

GRAW! A guttural voice roars, an inordinately disturbing voice that could not possibly be from the same woman—and yet it is definitely coming from the person behind him, he can feel the slats against his back vibrate with each roar.

GRAW!

Then from across the room he hears a sound he recognizes from previous police encounters—of a splintering door in the process of being kicked in.

Ello ello, ello, what's all this then?

The humming stops cold. Amid the incense and smoke, silence.

We're wi' the force an' yer all to remain in this room—ye'll be read out yer charges presently, dinna pretend ye donna why we're 'ere!

Release that man at once! yells a second voice identical to the first.

Someone removes the noose and blindfold and unties his wrists. While his eyes accustom themselves to the light, all he can see is a smoky haze. "Could someone return my spectacles, please?" This is spoken not with the voice of God but with the voice of a tired man who wants out of here as quickly as possible.

"Here are your spectacles, Mr. McCurdy," says the gentleman who accompanied him in the lift—tall, about sixty, wearing what looks like a blue choir gown, with an embroidered symbol on the chest consisting of interlocked triangles surrounded by a serpent eating its own tail, and topped by a swastika like the crest of the Fernie women's hockey team.

McCurdy rises unsteadily to his feet and scans the congregation— also in blue robes, and hoods that shadow the top parts of their faces—who clear a path for him to join the two tall plainclothes policemen standing beside the smashed door.

It's the Norton twins, horse-faced and long-toothed as ever, carrying police batons instead of shillelaghs. One of these intimidating creatures is holding up a card—presumably his warrant card, but nobody is about to take a closer look.

The other Norton twin assumes his own version of the voice of authority, which comes out sounding like some sort of town crier: "Mr. McCurdy, sor, come with us now! The rest of ye remain while I summon a paddy wagon!"

Adds the second: "We've been keeping the lot of ye on obbo for some time, ye and the nutter ye follow, an' now yer bloody well nicked!"

McCurdy takes a parting glance around the room, at the hushed figures standing against the walls beneath a series of images painted on what look to be scrolls, the largest of which depicts a lion's head with a human torso, angel's wings and two clawed hands tearing the entrails from a horned demon lying on its lap.

At the far wall he spots the turbaned, robed woman who intoned spells from the chair behind him, sidling her way quickly toward an open window, the aquiline nose, swarthy complexion, the enormous hoops for earrings—the last time he saw Madame Feglerska, she was conducting a seance in a Masonic hall, pulling ectoplasm from her stomach.

Already she has one foot on the fire escape.

The Norton twins practically carry McCurdy, sandwiched between them, down three flights of stairs and out the front door, drag him down the steps, and deposit him into the open door of an auto, parked by the curb with its engine running—not a gangster's flivver like the Buick, but a Dodge Deluxe, a sedan favoured by high-income professionals.

"Get in, ye git, 'fore they smell a rat!" One of the Nortons slams the door shut and the two scurry down the street.

Waiting for him in the back seat is man in a business suit, smoking a cigarette. (As soon as the door slams behind him McCurdy feels his asthma acting up.) The bird is wearing spats over his shoes, which alone is a reason for suspicion.

"Mr. McCurdy, hello. My name is Elliot Linden. I expect you're glad to get out of there."

"Frankly, Mr. Linden, I'm not sure yet. Anyone who employs the Norton twins—"

"Oh, Reggie and Dwight—we have a solid arrangement, and they do what they're told."

"Really? Why?"

"Because in Manchester they're up on charges of robbery, assault and manslaughter. My firm is all that stands between them and extradition, and they owe me thousands in legal fees."

"Sounds like a form of indentured service."

"Ha! By Gad sir, you are a character!"

The auto pulls away from the curb. McCurdy notes that the driver in front is wearing a chauffeur's hat. Through the rear window, he sees the Norton twins scuttling toward an alley.

"You've had a long day, Mr. McCurdy, you look spent. I imagine you'll want to be heading to the Quadra Club."

"I would appreciate that, sir—but you can understand my interest in knowing what the fuck is going on."

His companion shakes his head, wearily. "I know, Mr. McCurdy, I know, the whole thing is a complete fiasco. I'm sure we'll all laugh about it someday."

"I look forward to collapsing with mirth. In the meantime, I'd be grateful for a broad summary."

"What about a whisky?"

"Yes, that too."

Linden opens a mahogany cabinet built into the seat in front of him, pours whisky into two crystal glasses and hands one to McCurdy, who drinks eagerly. (Where on earth did he purchase a bottle of Chivas?)

"In a nutshell, it began with a case of what we might call mistaken identity. McCurdy, are you at all familiar with a man who calls himself Brother Osiris?"

"My understanding is that he's a shyster who bamboozles gullible rich Americans. Of course, that may be an unfair assessment of the man."

"No, I don't think it is."

"It makes you wonder what his followers are using for brains."

"Yes, it does. My wife and I will be asking ourselves that question for quite some time."

A pause follows.

"The problem as I see it," Linden says, "is that wealth deprives people of their sense of the absurd."

"Or maybe that's why they became wealthy in the first place— they're the guys who didn't get the joke."

The Dodge pulls up in front of the Quadra Club and McCurdy opens his door. "By the way, is this the horseshit behind the poison pen notes and the curses I kept finding on my pillow?"

"What curses? I have no idea what you're talking about."

"Never mind, Mr. Linden. Thanks for the lift."

Linden hands over his business card. "Goodnight, Mr. McCurdy. Call me when—not if—you next need a lawyer."

STANDING OUTSIDE THE door to his room, it occurs to McCurdy that he has no key—and at this hour Paris's band will be well into their second set. Nevertheless, he knocks, just in case.

No answer, as expected. He turns and heads back toward the stairs, when the door opens behind him and Paris steps into the hall in McCurdy's bathrobe, looking like a middleweight boxer about to shake hands with his opponent.

"Mr. McCurdy," he whispers. "Please come in quickly."

McCurdy obeys, knowing Paris's sensitivity to the club rules on race. Stepping inside, he can see that his rooms have been kept precisely as he left them, though with less clutter.

"I'm surprised you're not at your gig, George."

"The Lincoln gig cacked. Oscar wants to take the band to Seattle— the speakeasies there pay top cabbage. Helen snapped her cap at the idea, so I join Bricktop Smith at the Patricia next week."

"You'll be pleased to hear the Norton twins are no longer a threat to human life."

"Cool. Then you'll want your crib back."

"No hurry. I'm here for a change of clothes."

"Yeah, you look kind of messed up."

McCurdy pulls a Gladstone bag out of the closet and piles clothes on the bed. "Any action so far?"

"Yesterday I open the door, this biddy—"

"What do you mean, biddy?"

"Biddy. A dame of a certain age. A mature woman with a broom."

"Okay, a cleaning lady, so what?"

"Man, she take a gander at me an' she scream like a steamer hotfoot down the hall, goddamn do I shut the door fast afore the neighbours come out."

"What did she look like?"

"A cleaning lady. A dame with a broom."

"Anyone can get a broom, George. Is there anything you can tell me other than that she's a biddy and she was afraid of you? Because that could describe every cleaning lady in the building."

"Okay, cool, a *white* cleaning lady. You honkies all look alike to me."

"Very funny. Except that, at the Quadra, there is no such thing as a white cleaning lady."

SOMETIMES THE TELEPHONE rings late in the evening, and somehow you just know who's on the other end of the line.

Andrew.

It keeps ringing—eight times, nine times—so now Mildred is certain. She picks up the receiver, slams it back into the cradle, then heads for the kitchen and opens the icebox door—and it starts ringing again. Knowing Andrew, this could go on all night.

All right, Andrew, what the hell do you want?

Goodness, dearest! Not a pleasant start to our joyous reunion.

What did you expect, for God's sake? You've been harassing me for a week!

Did you misinterpret my love notes?

A dead bird? Dead flowers? Lovely Andrew, very touching.

At this moment the front door opens and McCurdy enters with a brown Gladstone bag.

She hands the earpiece over to McCurdy. Her hand is trembling more obviously than she would prefer. "It's for you."

McCurdy, who has experienced quite enough adventure for one evening, looks at the earpiece as though it might explode. "It's *him*? What should I say?"

"Tell him to go fuck himself." She retires quickly to her room and closes the door before she begins to blubber, mortified that Andrew can still have this effect on her composure, six years on.

McCurdy holds the earpiece in his hand like an ice cream cone and speaks into the mouthpiece.

Good evening. You've reached the Wickstram residence.

Ah. So you're the one.

Which one do you mean, sir?

Taking the piss are we? Cheeky bugger, obviously you don't know with whom you're dealing.

Oh, I think I do. You're the mean, drunken wife beater who's flying low. The RAF *produced a good number of those, I understand.*

Ah—from injury to insult. First you shag my wife, then you demean my dead friends. Tell me, old chap, did you serve?

A pause follows.

Thought not. You're a tosser and a bounder and I demand satisfaction.

The line goes dead.

On the way to his room, McCurdy opens Mildred's door a crack. "We just had a frank discussion. I think it went rather well."

No answer. He closes her door softly and goes back to his room, and to bed.

WHAT TIME IS it? Where are my glasses?

It's always disorienting to wake up in a dark room stuffed with unfamiliar air.

As he gropes blindly for his glasses, McCurdy discovers another person in the bed.

Mildred.

What can it mean?

He takes a moment to weigh the situation and decides to avoid it entirely by pretending to go back to sleep. (He wonders whether he should snore for effect.)

"You're a faker, Eddie," she whispers. "You're not asleep, stop pretending."

He opens his eyes. A thin band of light from the street slides through the gap between the roller blind and the windowsill so that he can see her outline, in a dressing gown, lying on top of the bedspread.

Though thoroughly unnerved, he decides to take a lighthearted approach. "To what do I owe this unexpected honour, madam?"

After a long pause, a small voice says, "Eddie, I'm scared."

He can't remember the last time he heard Mildred speak without irony. He therefore decides this is not the time to be witty.

"Your husband—"

"*Ex*-husband, really. The Andrew I married died in combat."

"Very well, your *ex*-husband who was threatening you is now threatening me as well. We're talking about a sozzled nutter who's killed people before."

"I don't mean to defend him, but there was a war on."

"No matter. After the first one, it gets easier—at least that's what Earle Leonard Nelson said."

"You're comparing Andrew to the Gorilla Killer? Is that supposed to be reassuring?"

"I'm trying to say that you have good reason to be frightened."

"I appreciate that, Eddie. Put your arm around me, would you?"

He slides his left arm under her shoulders and holds her in a sideways hug. As they lie there together in silence, she relaxes somewhat, huddles against him and appears to fall into a doze.

Her knee inadvertently covers his, and as the bed warms up, so does McCurdy, and before long he experiences the inevitable swelling down the way. Thankfully, the light is too dim for her to behold the small tent just beside her left knee.

"You're squirming, Eddie."

"Sorry." He wills himself to relax, without success.

"Eddie?"

"Yes?"

"We're not going to do it... are we?"

He isn't sure whether her question calls for a double or single negative, but it doesn't matter, the answer is the same.

"I think not, Millie, no."

"Aren't you even curious?" He hears a grin in her voice, suggesting she might have cheered up a bit.

"Um, well, for one thing I have no... no protection on hand."

"That's bullshit, isn't it, Eddie?"

"Actually, yes."

"So?"

"It's because afterward we'd both be different people, and we don't know who that will be. It's a risk I'd prefer to avoid."

"I think I know what you mean. The situation can change quickly."

"Yes. Suddenly, you're in bed with a relative."

"It sounds incestuous..."

"Which is against the law, you know..."

The discussion is becoming silly. Rather than continue, they drop off to sleep.

In his dream, Mr. Good-Evening is before the microphone, reciting his well-worn introduction—only, when he looks down at the items to be read, they are in one of those foreign languages with multiple consonants and strange-looking accents above the letters, and when he opens his mouth to speak, gibberish flows out.

At some point, Mildred slides under the bedclothes for warmth.

THE DOOR BURSTS open as though it was kicked.

"*I knew it*! Turn on the light, Randy, we have them in flagrante."

"Wait 'til I find the switch, would you, old boy? It's as dark as your hat in here."

The two men loom over the bed, silhouetted against the window. From the sound of their voices, both are drunk.

Mildred's eyes flash wide open and she rises to her elbows, simultaneously. "Andrew! Bloody hell, have you completely lost the plot? What do you think you're doing? What do you want?"

The other intruder turns on the light with one hand; in his other hand is a folding camera. Mildred sits up with her back against the headboard; though still in her nightgown, she pulls the spread up to her neck.

While he decides on his next move, McCurdy pretends to be asleep.

"Get them now, Randy, while they're in bed together."

Andrew's companion aims the camera and shoots. "I'm not sure about the light, mate."

"As long as it's visible." Rhys-Mogg turns and addresses Mildred. "It's for the divorce, dearest. I plan to be the petitioner. It will be in all the newspapers."

"Andrew, do you actually think I want your money?"

"Not my money, princess. My honour."

"Your *what*?"

As often happens when this sort of a man gets thoroughly sloshed, Andrew Rhys-Mogg abruptly flies into a rage, barking in slurred tones a tirade that can surely be heard from outdoors. "Mildred, do you know what you did? Do you have any idea how you made me feel? The humiliation I suffered in front of, in front of... Dammit, you *snootered* me!"

Andrew takes out a silk handkerchief and wipes his face, then turns to the other chap for support. "Randolph here saw what I suffered—did you not, Randolph?"

"You were absolutely gutted, old man. I saw it with my own eyes."

"You are bloody right, and I'll be dashed if I'll put up with this impudent tosser getting into her knickers! Do you know, Randy? The blighter didn't serve!"

"He's a bounder, that is certain," Randolph replies, and takes another photograph.

Aware that the invective is now aimed in his direction, McCurdy reaches for his glasses, which have toppled off the side table; nothing to be done without them, so he slides off the bed onto his hands and knees and gropes about the floor.

"Wait! Randolph, do you see the shirker over there? Do you see him scurry away like a rat?" Andrew crosses the room and picks up the baseball bat McCurdy left in the corner. "Of all the blasted nerve! By Jove, Randy, I think I shall give him a jolly good thrashing!"

Looking up from the floor, McCurdy winds the temples of his glasses around his ears in time to behold not a decorated air ace, but a puffy young man with pomade hair, a cleft chin and a soiled tuxedo, obviously drunk, standing over him with the baseball bat he brought here for Mildred's protection.

Well done, McCurdy. Top drawer.

Mildred scrambles over the bed, clutching her dressing gown to remain decent. "Andrew, you're tight as an owl and you're making a beastly mistake. Stop it at once!"

Both Mildred and Randolph recognize the alarming look Andy can take on when he's illuminated with drink—it's a look that can clear a room in seconds.

"I say, old bean, it's hardly the thing to bash a man about when he's on the floor."

"Don't be a git, Randy, he's been shagging my wife!"

"Even so, old boy, you can't hit him with the flat of the bat, don't you see? It's not a cricket bat. You could do real damage there."

Andrew brings the bat up to his face and turns it around. "Oh. So I see. Well then, so much the better!" He lifts the bat over his head and prepares to strike—and is spun to his left as a loud crack echoes throughout the room.

For a second everyone freezes as they watch a red wetness seep down the arm of Andrew Rhys-Mogg's tuxedo, just below the shoulder pad.

"By Jove, Andy, you've been shot!"

"By Jove, I have!"

Scrambling out of harm's way, McCurdy encounters Stella Aspen standing just inside the door in a silk kimono and holding a small silver pistol, with Dora Decker standing behind her in neck-to-toe flannel.

"Stella! Jesus Christ!"

"I came down to complain about the noise. I'm glad I did. It's much quieter now."

Andrew presses his handkerchief against the wound in a failed attempt to staunch the blood. "Dash it, Mildred, that daft cow shot me!"

"Andrew, you're ossified, and were about to beat a man to death with a baseball bat."

"He was shagging you!"

"No, Andrew, he was here to protect me. In his feckless way, he was being a gentleman."

"That's very decent of you, Millie," McCurdy says, then turns to the door. "Miss Aspen, are you aware that you just shot a man?"

"Did I really? I must have aimed low!"

"You hit his shoulder, Miss Aspen, you didn't aim low—"

Now they hear the doorbell, followed by the front door opening and closing, then leather soles climbing the stairs.

"Excuse me, ladies," says a voice from the hall. "Would you be so kind as to allow me to pass through? I wish to have a word with my son."

Stella turns her head in the direction of the voice. "Just who are you anyway, buster?"

"Regrettably, madam, I am the ex-chancellor of the exchequer."

"A champion, did you say?"

Dora puts her hand on Stella's shoulder. "You're thinking of the board game, ma'am. I don't think it's that."

The occupants of the room stare speechless as a barrel-chested, middle-aged gentleman steps into the room, in a homburg hat and evening dress, a bow tie, a wide face with jowls, and a mouth that droops slightly to one side. He is smoking a cigar.

"Randolph, what is the meaning of this?"

"Father! I say sir, Andrew has been shot."

"Shot where?"

"I think she winged him around the armpit."

The visitor turns to the bleeding man standing beside the bed. "Does that seem reasonable to you, Andrew?"

"Feels like it, sir, yes. There's a beastly amount of blood—"

"You've made a complete cock-up of the evening, son. What the devil brought you two plonkers here in the first place?"

"Andrew became very upset about his wife—his *estranged* wife, I should say," Randolph replies. "The loss of face, don't you see. He left the gathering in an excited state. I felt it only my duty to—"

"What utter rot! While your cousin was working himself up into a murderous lather, you shook another pitcher of martinis and flirted with the niece of the minister of lands."

Randolph produces his camera. "Not so, father. I broke off with Miss Patullo and came with him fully ready to assist. Our purpose was to produce evidence. For the divorce, if you want to know—"

"I most certainly do *not* want to know." Holding his cigar in front of his chest, the speaker turns and addresses the room. "Ladies, I apologize on behalf of my son, who owes his expulsion from Eton to his cousin over there. Andrew could drink a bottle of ink and then pick a fight with the desk."

"Father, I protest your unfair characterization of my chum—"

"Shut up, Randolph. You're only adding to my considerable disappointment. And as for you, Andrew, yes, you are as usual absolutely tanked. Pie-eyed. Despite your gongs, you are a pogey, and I despise a man who cannot hold his liquor."

"Sir, I think I'm losing blood rather quickly."

The older gentleman inspects Andrew's sleeve, now sopping wet. "Poppycock, it is barely a flesh wound. We in the Sixth Battalion called it a *caress*."

He turns to Mildred, who is sitting on the edge of the bed lighting a cigarette. "Mrs. Rhys-Mogg, I do apologize for my wastrel of a nephew and my pusillanimous son. I salute your initiative in seeking out your destiny."

"Sir, I must object to that. My wife deserted me in my time of—"

"Keep quiet, Andrew, that neanderthal club in your fist says all that needs to be said about your state of mind. Consider yourself fortunate that this fine woman over here is a frightful shot."

"Couldn't hit the broad side of a barn," Miss Aspen agrees.

"Assuredly." Then, turning to Dora: "Unless it was a rather decent shot—what do *you* think, miss?"

"I wouldn't know, sir, I've never held a pistol in my life."

"Quite. May I see the instrument, madam?"

"Certainly." Stella extends the weapon, grip first, in the general direction of the voice.

Gripping his cigar between his teeth, he examines the weapon rather expertly. "Ah yes, the VP—*Vest Pocket*, don't you know. Came out back in 1908, hasn't improved since. Belgian—and like the Belgians themselves, lacking in striking power. Shoot a man from over a yard and his waistcoat would protect him from serious harm—"

He stops himself. "Pardon me again, ladies, firearms are an enthusiasm of mine."

He extends the weapon to Stella, handle first; Dora accepts it on her behalf. "I'll hold it for her. Miss Aspen is very tired."

Churchill, however, has turned his attention back to his son. "Randolph, tootle along outside with your friend and ask our driver for the first aid kit. And know that upon our return to London I may very well take away your Bentley.

"And I apologize to—might I call you Mr. Good-Evening?"

"Actually, sir, I'd rather you didn't."

"Fair dinkum, as the Aussies would say. Well everyone, difficulties mastered are opportunities won, and there is ample reason to consider the evening a measured success, and to put this entire incident behind us. I am sure that Mrs. Rhys-Mogg will agree that, in these perilous times, none of us needs another scandal in the newspapers. Remember that the price of greatness is responsibility. I shall leave you on that note. As that gentleman over there would say, a restful good evening to you all."

With a quick nod he turns and exits the room in a cloud of cigar smoke.

A few moments go by before Stella breaks the silence. "Who was that, anyway?"

"His name is Churchill," Mildred replies.
"Whoever he is, he's damned wordy."

SHOCKING DISCOVERY AT UNDERWORLD BURIAL
Rolin S. Cobb
The New York Illustrated Daily News

The interment of Abe "the Ghost" Amberg, the infamous underworld assassin who died last Thursday in a blizzard of gunfire while driving to his home in Bensonhurst, took a grotesque turn while the casket was in transit from the hearse to Mount Carmel Cemetery, Queens.

The funeral at the F.G. Guido Funeral Home on Clinton Street had been a low-key affair, attended chiefly by the immediate family. Likely due to the notoriety of the deceased, prominent crime families chose not to attend, though tributes of flowers worth thousands of dollars lined the chapel, including a six-foot Star of David made of scarlet carnations.

Accompanying Amberg's widow, Maisie, was Harry "Gyp the Blood" Horowitz, a suspect in the murder of Herman "Squeezy" Rosenthal.

Amberg's fifteen-hundred-dollar casket is said to have been paid for by Al "Scarface" Capone.

The grisly discovery occurred just after the cortège reached the cemetery and the copper and steel casket was lifted from the back of the Studebaker hearse.

To observers it appeared as though one of the six muscular enforcers who served as pallbearers lost his footing in the pebbles, causing their heavy burden to dip momentarily to one side.

As a mourner, who asked not to be identified, observed, "The remains must have rolled sideways. But still, it seemed odd that the pallbearers were having so much trouble. Abe weighed maybe 165, tops."

The apparent imbalance caused the casket to topple farther sideways, so that the lid fell open and its contents tumbled onto the lawn—revealing not one cadaver, but two.

It was immediately evident to all that a false bottom had been installed to provide room for a second corpse—a device for disposing of murder victims that is as well-known as cement shoes.

Later it was ascertained that the casket had been purchased from a branch of the National Casket Company, a legitimate business owned by Giuseppe "Joe" Profaci that allows him to report his occupation as "undertaker" in tax documents.

A search was undertaken of National Casket Company files in an effort to identify the second corpse through burial records. The only name for which no grave could be identified was a Canadian investment dealer, Alvin Pine, who died seemingly of a brain hemorrhage in a suite at the Hotel Astor—where, sources say, he was staying as a guest of Mr. J. Walter Addison, a prominent Canadian investment advisor and alleged war profiteer.

Anyone with further information is urged to come forward by contacting the Seventy-Eighth Precinct, Brooklyn.

GOOD EVENING. THIS is the nightly news service of the Canadian National Railway, brought to you by the Vancouver Evening Star.

Valencia, Spain, has declared martial law, while in Berlin, Germany, thirty-two people were killed in clashes between communists and police, and in Nuremberg a parade of sixty thousand Nazis opened the Fourth Party Congress. In Afghanistan Saqqawist tribesmen have captured the city of Kabul, where rebels are said to be committing acts of rape and looting, while in Yugoslavia King Alexander has suspended the constitution, and in Chicago gangster Al Capone is set to testify before a federal grand jury about his alleged illegal activities...

In New York stocks suffered a sharp downturn as interest rates soared to twenty per cent, and last year's influenza is estimated to have caused two hundred thousand deaths worldwide, while in Canada polio has struck Vancouver and Alberta as well as Manitoba and Ontario, bringing the total to four thousand cases. In British Columbia, the ruling Conservatives have declared their commitment to, quote, apply business principles to the business of government, unquote...

You have been listening to the radio voice of the Vancouver Evening Star. As we end our broadcast, we wish all our listeners—on the trains, on the Prairies, on the seas, on the docks and in the parlour—a restful good evening.

CHAPTER 55

WE'RE OFF THE line, Mr. McCurdy.

"Thank you, Elwood, that went smoothly."

When a man enters the world of public performance, he is at the mercy of technicians—staff who can make him sound like a canary or duck, thereby wielding the power of life and death with the turn of a knob.

For smooth relations with the man behind the glass, as with the unseen audience, it behooves an announcer to mount a pretense of affability.

The situation demands symbolic expressions of departmental teamwork when, as far as the technician is concerned, the reader is vastly overpaid for work that anyone short of a deaf mute could perform.

"So Elwood—what are the Monarchs' chances against the Midgets next season?"

Not a hope in hell, Mr. McCurdy. With Kendall and Wheat we're unbeatable.

"I thought you'd be a fan—you're from Rossland, right?"

Grew up there. Why?

"Is Elwood a common name in Rossland?"

It's a family name. It means "noble wood" in the old country.

"Something you name the eldest son type of thing."

That's the tradition, I'm told. Means nothing to me.

"Still, it's something in common with King George."

What?

"King George the Fifth. You might be Elwood the Tenth, for all we know."

Mr. McCurdy, what are you getting at?

"I know of a proofreader from Rossland who works on the paper, name of Dixon—but his first name is Earl, not Elwood."

That's my stepfather. My dad was Elwood Mertle. He died a while back.

"My condolences, Elwood. Now I think I need a private conversation with your mother."

"MRS. DIXON, MAY I have a word?" The telegraphist-editor is in her cubicle making notes—no doubt critical of his enunciation this evening.

"On what topic, Mr. McCurdy?"

"I wish to speak about the unfortunate accident."

"Most unfortunate," Mrs. Dixon replies, as though thinking about something else.

"I agree fully. In fact, I think it brings into question the technical expertise of our man Elwood."

She finally looks up from her work, nostrils flared. "Elwood applied for the position at my urging. His record has never been less than impeccable. What are you insinuating?"

"My concern is about Elwood's ability to work with electricity. I wonder where he received his training—or if he was indeed trained at all."

Mrs. Dixon's cheeks redden as well. "Elwood served his apprenticeship with his father, an electrical engineer—a DSO, if you don't mind."

"I stand corrected. Most impressive. So I take it that Earl Dixon is your second husband."

"I'm not a bigamist, Mr. McCurdy. Mr. Mertle died six years ago."

"Ah. So it's a case of *mortui vivos docent.*"

"I assure you, my husband was very much alive at the time. But in any case, I really don't care to have a personal discussion with you about family matters."

"I apologize. It's just heartening to see a family working as a team. *Manus manum lavat,* and all that. Oh—and one more thing, Mrs. Dixon: I should have thanked you when you offered to clean my suite. Terribly sorry you were frightened by my valet."

"You're talking gibberish, Mr. McCurdy. I fear you've had a brain injury. I shall have to report that."

"Do as you like, Mrs. Dixon. But your husband will still have a lisp."

CHAPTER 56

HAVING BEEN IN service less than a year, the *Princess Elaine* to Nanaimo looks as though it belongs on a hobbyist's mantelpiece with its fresh paint and gleaming glass; no rust, no trace of soot on the three smokestacks. For the passenger, it's like being aboard a model ship.

Quam isn't charmed by this. A native of Moose Jaw, where the largest body of water is a prairie pothole, he insists on spending the entire two-hour trip, if not inside the lounge (where sea sickness is inevitable), then standing beside the lifeboats (remembering that there weren't enough of them on the *Titanic*).

"Sir, I wish there were some other way to get to Nanaimo."

"What way might that be, Sergeant? Should we swim?"

"I can't swim, sir. I don't even like wading."

Despite the fresh air, Quam becomes nauseous the moment the ferry passes Brockton Point, and the sight of a pod of dolphins and a humpback whale is lost to him as he feeds the seagulls with the contents of his stomach, so that by the time the *Princess Elaine* rounds Duke Point he looks as though *pallor mortis* has set in.

That is why, once the vessel has landed, noting that Quam is still unsteady on his feet, Hook opts for the Malaspina Hotel, a seven-storey edifice steps away from the wharf; with a barbershop, a cigar store and reading rooms for men and women, it's an improvement on the Stirling in Nelson.

"Welcome to the Jewel of Nanaimo," chirps the desk clerk.

"We'd like a room please," Hook says.

"Certainly, gentlemen. That will be ten dollars."

Hook hears the sucked intake of breath behind him.

"What is it, Mr. Quam?"

"That's double the allowance, sir. We must find another hotel."

Although the investigation was ultimately a success, that was not good enough for the press—who, always hostile to the police, leapt at the opportunity to turn a woman named Dora Decker into an innocent lamb led to the slaughter, thanks to a rush to judgment on the part of investigators.

The facts speak otherwise.

Far from an innocent lamb, Dora Decker was a secretary in name only, who dressed in a suggestive manner for the purpose of luring investment clients to put their money into a firm that was under investigation for fraud. As well, confidential evidence suggested a history of inappropriate relations with her former bosses, including her married, murdered employer, Ralph M. Tucker.

Dora Decker was far from the angel depicted by some members of the press. Rather, this individual was a smooth operator in the cynical world of investment dealing. The question to be addressed was whether or not she had committed this crime, or any other crime.

The investigation lost its way when the fraud department refused to co-operate with the homicide department; meanwhile, for its part, the homicide department balked at participating in what was called "a case of interdepartmental meddling."

A direct order was issued by myself, to the effect that homicide, fraud and forensics would henceforth pull together as a team.

The message was heard and, as a result, the crime was solved.

At the end of the day, the outcome was a demonstration of an ongoing need for the process of departmental modernization to continue.

This remains the key to better performance of the VPD's core mission—which is, and has always been, to uphold the law and to protect the public.

CHAPTER 57

LYING IN BED with a gulletful of Linden's Chivas Regal, DI Hook places the ashtray on his stomach and fires up an Ogden's, while across the room Quam is mumbling prayers in his sleep. The inspector reflects on recent events with a certain sense of wonder—that they might find themselves in this ten-dollar room in this temperance hotel, having spent the evening in what must surely be the bridal suite with what seems to have been the last man to see Robert Nettles alive—who proceeded to recount a remarkable tale about Dark Adepts, Brothers of the Shadow, a woman with a whip and the end of the world; and all revolving around a flim-flam man and his strange hold over some rich Americans.

Hook had never heard such a pile of bollocks in his life.

Moreover, as Mr. Linden would have it, he is quite possibly the only person sane enough to give a reliable witness account.

Sometimes when Jeanie makes him go to church, Hook finds himself wondering if life isn't just a series of random coincidences, one after the other. (Something about Reverend Sutherland's call to prayer sends his mind in a contrary direction.) But in this case, rather than put it to pure chance or the will of our Lord and Saviour, Inspector Hook chooses to believe that Linden *followed* them here—Linden, who brings Chivas along with him, who can afford ritzier lodgings.

Elliot Linden will bear watching; then again, he is a lawyer, and don't they all?

In any case, the most probable outlook at present is that the Nettles case, like the Doukhobor assignment of two years ago, will end up a yellowing file in a drawer marked *Inconclusive*.

But unlike the Verigin case, there will be no accolades for Hook and Quam, and certainly no promotions. Based on Hook's recent experience with the chief, the opposite is more likely—a demotion back to sergeant on some pretext, with lower pay and three mouths to feed, including his own.

A thankless business.

With an effort Hook pushes aside these daunting thoughts and settles under the covers. Across the darkened room, Quam has stopped mumbling in his sleep; instead, from the way he smacks his lips, he seems to be *eating* in his sleep.

Hook notes that while the sergeant no longer smells of fruit, now he gives off a whiff of condensed milk.

CHAPTER 58

*After their spiritual decay is complete, Dark
Adepts develop supernatural abilities with
which to seize upon and control a Host.*

*An Adept can invade the Host's muscles, bones and brains
during possession, and can probe the Host's memories.
It can mimic the voice of the Host, so that their closest
friend might only detect a shift of opinion and attitude.*

*The Dark Adept has an enhanced sense of smell, to
a degree where it can smell the Host's soul.*

*Dark Adepts are unable to fly, other
than in their smoke forms.*

—The Aquarian Gospel

BY NINE A.M., a crowd has already formed on the plaza in front of
the Nanaimo Courthouse, an impressive stone edifice with round
arches and pyramid-topped towers, designed to counter the town's
reputation as a camp full of itinerant miners.

To one side of the steps, a clutch of haggard people huddles
together—clothes muddy and ragged, women's hands red and rough,
men unshaven—surrounding a dishevelled older woman in torn
stockings and a once-expensive tweed skirt.

Conspicuous among the group is Elliot Linden, wearing a herring-
bone suit, homburg hat and spats. Fresh from a sound sleep in his
relatively luxurious suite, he interrupts his conversation with a
wretchedly thin chap and waves a greeting to the two official visitors.

"Good morning, officers! Please allow me to introduce you to my fellow plaintiffs—those who have remained in the community. As a reward for our loyalty, we've all been banished from the island."

A fellow with a terrible rash covering his face and hands joins the conversation. "His men piled us into the *Khaba* and dumped us on Valdes Island, which is nothing but brush."

"The *Khaba* is a boat," Linden explains.

"Does he have a fleet?" Quam asks.

"A fleet of two. There's also a Brixham trawler called the *Lady Royal*."

"The Brother sailed it across the Atlantic single-handedly," the man with the rash adds.

"Or so he claims," Linden says. "At this point, I'm not prepared to believe anything he says."

Already the presence of plainclothes police officers has attracted other disciples, along with general onlookers—and a few representatives of other cults in the region, attracted to the prospect of a supernatural event.

The sergeant wearily extracts his notebook and pencil, having had a bad night thanks to Hook's disgusting cigarette smoke, whose stale odour has permeated every stitch of clothing he brought with him. "How do you spell *Khaba*?" he asks.

Linden introduces them to the lead plaintiff, an older woman who is suing Edward Peter Collins for over twenty-five thousand dollars, and who tells them in a Southern accent that her name is Ida Arrowsmith.

Hook displays his warrant card. "Good morning, madam. I am Inspector Hook, and this is Sergeant Quam. Tell us—what happened to you folks?"

The question (coming from a police officer) seems to open a valve, releasing an effusion of injury and outrage all around, beginning with Mrs. Arrowsmith. "We were marooned on an island over yonder, like outcasts! We were made to sleep in tiny tents on the bare ground!"

"You were camping, then?" Sergeant Quam asks.

"Mrs. Arrowsmith once had fifteen bathrooms!" retorts a man named Jim Barley.

"Does anyone know how *Khaba* is spelled?" Quam asks.

"Never mind that, Sergeant," Hook says.

"It means 'the soul appears' in Egyptian," Jim Barley says. "A pharaoh who built a lot of tombs."

Hook reaches into his side pocket for cigarettes—and Aspirin, for already these people are giving him a headache. "Please continue, Mrs. Arrowsmith."

"I declare I was punished as a traitor! And all I did was to question Madame Zura's treating of a fellow disciple like chattel."

"She's a slave-driver!" someone behind shouts.

"Madame Zura does his dirty work for him!" a tall, long-faced woman announces, having plowed her way to the front of the group with the sheer force of her grievance. "The woman is a Dark Adept herself!"

"Could everyone please not speak at once?" Quam has already broken one pencil trying to keep up.

"The look he gave me when I questioned Madame Zura's behaviour chilled me to the bone!" Mrs. Arrowsmith says. "I was afeared of what might be waiting for me in my house, so I stayed with Mr. Barley here—"

"But the Brother tracked her down mentally with his special powers."

"I spent the night enveloped in a disgusting black cloud."

"It was a dreadful night for all concerned," Jim Barley says. "My back went into spasms and it's still not better."

"The next day, Madame Zura forced me to scrub floors until my knees bled!"

Quam, whose second finger is acquiring a blister, wonders, *Couldn't they just go to church?*

"Could we back up a bit, please?" Hook says, finally. "First, what is the *Khaba*, besides being an Egyptian king?"

Linden holds up one hand. "To clarify, Inspector, they're talking about an ocean tugboat bought with Aquarian funds, along with the *Lady Royal*, a Brixham trawler of twenty-five tons—"

"The *Lady Royal* was a gift from his followers in England," says the woman behind him. "They loved him so much."

"Oh, he's been doing all right for himself, you can be sure! The money still pours in every week from the *Chalice*." This from an Ethyl Squires, her eyes glittering like an enraged bird.

"He converts the money to gold coins," adds the man with the rash, "because the economy is about to collapse."

"That's a bad rash you have there, Curtis," says a voice behind Quam's back.

The man with the rash scratches his neck. "It's the Brother's curse. It's the 'affliction of doubt.'"

"No, Curtis," the unseen voice replies, "it's the hogweed. Valdes is rife with the stuff."

"He has a fortune locked in a cellar under the blockhouse," the long-faced woman says. "Alvin Wheeler helped him buy gold from miners in Rupert."

Jim Barley nods agreement. "The Brother has Alvin convinced he's the reincarnation of John the Baptist."

"He told us we were on Valdes for our own safety," Mrs. Arrowsmith says. "He said he was working on an extremely powerful spiritual force—the Sixth Ray, he called it."

"It's also called the Red Ray," Jim Barley adds.

"But it's not the Brothers of the Light he's summoning, now that the auric egg has been broken," Ethyl Squires says. "That's a certainty."

"Dark Adepts are everywhere," adds the man with the rash, who says his name is Curtis Barlow. "You can see them lurking about in the corner of your eye."

"And we're supposed to be the lucky ones," says Mrs. Arrowsmith, bitterly. "The rest have been banished altogether, left down the coast with the clothes on their backs, and told to make their way home as best they could."

"He said they were unfit to pass through the Gateway of Truth," Curtis Barlow adds, helpfully.

"The Brother has turned from a saint into a demon," the long-faced woman says.

"And Madame Zura is happy to assist him," adds a voice behind Hook's back.

"As I told you, she does his dirty work," says the long-faced woman.

"We carried firewood until we fell down from exhaustion."

"We worked from morning to midnight."

"On rations of brown bread with a teaspoon of jam."

"And one teaspoon of tea to twenty gallons of water!"

"I've broken my last pencil," Sergeant Quam says.

Hook has run out of patience. "Could everyone calm down enough to tell me why you put up with such treatment? Who forced you to stay, and how did they do it?"

He has lit up another Ogden's without thinking. Already there are four butts dug into the grass by his feet.

Mrs. Arrowsmith answers immediately. "He could control our bodies, of course."

Adds Mrs. Squires, "He mentally controlled every mind and every soul that came near him."

A pink-faced man with a salt-and-pepper beard pushes past Jim Barley and introduces himself as Sydney M. Backstone and his wife as Celia. (The two of them together could be porcelain ornaments in Kew Gardens.) "As one with experience in these matters, I can attest that he used black magic to strike me unconscious during the previous trial."

Hook has become as confused as Quam, whether from the concussion or the situation is an open question. In an attempt to get things back on track, he turns to Mrs. Squires. "You say he controlled you, Mrs. Squires. How did he manage to do that?"

"Through fear! He could murder people at will. Everyone knew he could sever their ethereal body from their physical body!"

"He put an awful powerful curse on Attorney General Pooley," says a voice from behind.

"If he's not dead yet, he will be," says another.

"In ritual terms he performs the execution by intoning a curse and slashing the air in the shape of a cross," Backstone says, lighting his pipe. "It's an Incan ritual."

"My Sydney knows all about ancient rituals," Celia Backstone chimes in. "And as Mrs. Squires told you, the Brother has joined the Brothers of the Shadow."

Mrs. Arrowsmith again: "Do you think I would have given the evidence I did at the first trial if I weren't bewitched?"

"With my own eyes I saw a Dark Adept standing at the foot of our bed," Celia Backstone says. "His eyes were hollow, as though they'd been plucked out. His skin was reptilian."

"Believe you me, officers, all signs point to the auric egg having been broken," Sydney Backstone says, which seems to bring the subject to a close.

"What are you people talking about?" Quam asks.

"Never mind, Sergeant. Here's another pencil, just take notes as best you can." Rather than inquire as to what an auric egg consists of, Hook decides to steer the subject to the events that have brought them here from Vancouver.

"We've been assigned to look into the disappearance of a man named Robert Nettles. Mr. Linden suggested that someone might have witnessed something. Can anyone help us with that?" Hook looks about for Linden, who is nowhere to be seen.

The first to answer is Earl Coffin, whose wife, Josephine, has a curious squint.

"Bob Nettles was cursed by the Brother. I expect a Dark Adept threw him into the ocean."

"More likely he induced Bob to jump himself," suggests Josephine.

"Or it could have been the same Adept who infected Henney Krause," Curtis Barlow says, scratching his neck. "Someone, I forget who, said they saw Bob taken off the island by Krause and Jack Hirst."

Adds Cora Fisher, "At around the same time, Alexandra Gibb swears she saw the Brother standing on his front steps smoking his pipe, with a smug look on his face."

At this moment the front doors of the courthouse open. The sergeant-at-arms steps outside and holds up both hands to achieve silence.

"Ladies and gentlemen, the session has been delayed one hour."

"Why? What's wrong?" someone cries out.

"I am not at liberty to say." Ignoring the volley of questions from the disciples, he backs into the building and shuts the doors.

As the crowd begins to disperse with annoyed mutterings, Linden appears at Hook's side. "I spoke to the clerk on the q.t. The defendant has failed to show up, just like Bob."

"The Brother is still on De Courcy Island, then," Earl Coffin says.

"Along with the truly deluded," adds Linden.

"Of course, with the auric egg broken, their souls might all be under the command of Dark Adepts," Sydney Backstone says.

"What is an auric egg?" Hook asks Linden.

"You don't want to know," Linden replies.

"I saw one of the creatures," Mrs. Backstone says. "At the foot of the bed—"

"You already told them about that, Celia."

"Did I, Sydney?"

"Yes, you did."

Quam draws the inspector aside. "Sir, do you think he absconded? He is our only suspect at present."

"I don't know, Sergeant, but I take your point. Mr. Linden, how do you get to De Courcy Island?"

"Arvid Pedersen ferried supplies every week. He'll take us on his tender for thirty cents if he's not busy. Come with me."

CHAPTER 59

THE *FREYJA* IS a thirty-two-foot wooden tender barge with a small cabin and a prow, moored to Tarbet Pier. As they board, Hook fires up an Ogden's to ward off the stink of creosote, diesel fuel, grease, wood rot and dead fish.

For his part, Sergeant Quam finds the slight motion under his feet already has him flailing for something to grasp hold of. The motor clatters to life, fills the air with toxic blue smoke and accelerates into Departure Bay.

Keeping his grip on the gunwale, Quam hears the water hiss as the boat plows its way through the waves, a sound he finds most alarming.

Standing at the helm, Captain Pedersen addresses the sergeant. "Yaw heard about the sea serpents?"

"What? What did you say, sir?"

"The sea serpents."

"Are there sea serpents in these waters?"

"Naw, but they's wolf eels a yard long. I seen one put his spike teeth clear through a man's arm." As illustration, Pedersen extends his right arm and makes a claw with the hand. "Yaw see, here's they jaws an', an' here's yor arm, don't yaw see..." He moves his other hand in a spiral from below until it grapples onto the left. "Like that—except the teeth go straight through, don't yaw see."

Quam moves inboard and sits with his back against the cabin, waiting for this to be over.

"Just keep yor arms away from the gunwale an' yul be fine."

"I think the sergeant has heard enough, Arvid," Linden says.

"Yaw, I see that." Pedersen laughs softly, cutting himself a wad of chaw with a penknife.

"A cruel joke, if I may say so."

"Well, yaw can't resist." He sticks the bladeful of chaw into his mouth, withdraws the knife, wipes it on his trousers, then pushes the throttle and heads the *Freyja* toward the channel separating two islands, Mudge and Gabriola.

"If I may butt in here, my name is Inspector Hook of the Vancouver police, and I have a few questions."

Hook's first question is interrupted by a loud blast somewhere up ahead, then another.

"Was that a rifle?" Linden asks.

"No," Hook replies. "It was a boom, not a crack or a shriek."

Another explosion sounds in the distance, as though to confirm Hook's opinion.

"Oi'd say dynamite, moiself."

"Or mortars," Hook replies. "Am I right that you ferried supplies from Nanaimo for the Aquarian—" He turns to Linden. "What's the proper word—colony?"

"*Cult* is about right," Linden replies.

Pedersen thinks, scratching his right cheek. Chewing tobacco has turned his teeth the colour of walnuts.

"Supplies? Yaw, we took stuff over every week."

"What sort of stuff, in general?"

Pedersen works on a scab under his left cheekbone. "Oh, there'd be flour, sugar, coffee, tea, feed—"

"Stockpiles for Armageddon," Linden says.

"And rifles, ammo, feed—"

"Against the breakdown of civilization."

"But not all of it, mind. There were other stuff."

"What other stuff was that, sir?"

Pedersen spits tobacco juice over the gunwale. "Oh, there were prime beef, French wine, whisky, chocolates, Jell-O..."

"Jell-O?"

"Yaw. Raspberry, it were." Pedersen uses a stained rag to wipe a trickle of blood running down his cheek.

"Sir!"

"Yes, Sergeant?"

"I see smoke!"

"Where is that smoke coming from, Mr. Pedersen?"

"It's where we're headin', oi'd say."

Pedersen blows his nose with the rag, shoves it in his pocket and pushes the throttle, creating more blue smoke in the air, with a louder hiss coming off the prow.

As the barge slides into Pirate's Cove, they see the results of at least some of the explosions—the Brixham trawler on its side like the carcass of a humpback whale. Just aft of the words *Lady Royal*, enormous holes have been blown out of her hull by explosives or grenades.

"I don't see the *Khaba*," Hook says.

Quam asks, "The what, sir?"

"The boat, Sergeant, not the Egyptian pharaoh."

"I don't appreciate the sarcasm, sir."

The smoke that Quam noted earlier is billowing from just up the hill, clinging to the treetops like cotton swabs and drifting to shore.

Hook lights another Ogden's to blend with the smell of burning wood and turns to Pedersen. "Do you think someone set a forest fire, sir?"

"Naw. She's wood smoke but not trees—more like a house fire."

"Well, gentlemen," Linden says, "shall we take a look?"

"Oi'll stay back here with *Freyja*," Pedersen says, leaning on the gunwale. "Oi have no stomach for dead bodies." As though for punctuation, he discharges a remarkable stream of brown spittle onto the pebbles.

THE THREE MEN trudge up a narrow dirt road; Quam, whose lungs are in better shape, has taken the lead.

Pausing for breath, Linden says, "I must warn you, Inspector, that there are enough weapons on the island to fill an armoury."

"If someone was going to shoot at us, Mr. Linden, wouldn't they have shot at us already?"

"True, that's a thought."

When they stop to catch their breath again, Hook is surprised to see Quam reach into his coat, pull his service weapon from its holster, spin the cylinder and check the chambers, with remarkable dexterity for a man who fears and hates pistols.

"I see you've had some weapons practice, Sergeant."

"In my spare time, sir. A firearm is a toy when you're off duty."

"What is that supposed to mean?" Linden asks, and receives no reply.

Hook is unarmed, and embarrassed about it. Rather than endure that holster gouging into his armpit all day, he stored the weapon in the hotel safe and forgot about it.

At the top of the hill, the road passes through what was once the Ark of Refuge, the pride of the Aquarian movement, a collection of small frame houses, and what appear to be a dormitory, a meeting hall, a dining hall, barns for horses, cows and chickens (of which there are none), as well as various structures for storage and shelter—a basic, utilitarian set-up not unlike Rugeley Camp.

It looks as though a cyclone hit.

Everything that could be wrecked in a short time has been hacked to pieces: windows have been smashed out, doors ripped away. The ground glitters with shattered glass.

Someone attempted to burn down the meeting hall, leaving the walls scorched black. Next to the dining hall, apple trees lie uprooted on the grass.

Someone even chopped down a spruce tree, which crushed the roof of the house next to it.

"That's my house," Linden says to Quam.

"Do you think you were targeted, sir?"

"Targeted or random, what difference does it make?"

All along the central roadway, furniture has been chopped to pieces, stacked into piles and set alight with petrol, using torn books and artwork as kindling.

Someone had gone at a piano with an axe and now the metal frame is lying on the ground. Someone shot holes in the water tanks with a shotgun.

It is as though a small-scale Armageddon has taken place.

With their eyes streaming from the smoke, their faces red from the singeing heat of blazing bonfires on both sides, the men walk farther up the road.

For Inspector Hook, it is as though they were transported into a ruined French village—Ripont perhaps, or Courtecon.

He once heard a soldier describe walking through one after a shelling as "a walk through a burning tunnel." It's like that, except that a French village would have burnt less fiercely, the buildings being made of stone and not wood.

Another difference is the absence of the sight and smell of corpses—both equine and human.

"I'm afraid I can't join you, officers. I can't feel my legs. I can't explain it. Don't ask me to."

"Best you stay down anyway, sir," Hook says. "There may be someone up there who is armed and dangerous."

"This is not a place for civilians," Quam adds.

Linden looks up at him. "I couldn't agree more, Inspector. I only wish I had a choice."

Leaving Linden glowering in the low bushes, Hook sprints across the clearing after Quam, who has already reached the bottom of the stairway.

"Seen anyone?"

"Who might that be, sir?"

"Never mind. As you were."

Following Quam's considerable bottom upward one step at a time, Hook looks down at Linden seated in the brush with legs splayed, trying to massage some feeling into them.

Upon reaching the top stair, Quam, having witnessed many such scenes in serials, braces his foot against the edge of the landing, grasps the door handle and propels his body inside, like King Baggot did in *The Hawk's Trail*.

Eager to have a look, Hook climbs as quickly as his lungs will allow, steps onto the top landing—

And now he is dangling in mid-air, surrounded by wood, with only his grip on the door's threshold keeping him from plummeting a good thirty feet—meaning a broken leg, or possibly a lost leg by the time he reaches the hospital and gangrene has set in.

"Mr. Quam!"

And his response is the same—legs flailing uncontrollably, feet scraping at slippery bark.

Like a cat that has fallen out of a window, his legs windmill frantically, scraping at the spruce's slippery trunk for the stub of a branch, maybe, but instead they find nothing but air—helplessly flailing in mid-air, and a part of his mind knows he has fallen into a state of panic...

"Mr. Quam!"

"Here, sir!" Two meaty fists grip Hook's wrists.

Thank God for Sergeant Quam.

Together they manage to wrestle Hook's body over the threshold as far as his armpits, and now he is back in the Belvedere Hotel, and his legs are thrashing through the ceiling into Panama Al's room a floor below...

By leaning backward, Sergeant Quam is able to attain enough leverage to heave his superior farther inside, across the threshold as far as his waist, then to haul the inspector along the rough cedar flooring like a sack of grain, before he himself collapses onto his bottom.

Hook remains still for a long moment, thoroughly unnerved, then says, "Well done, Sergeant."

"Call of duty, sir."

Quam rises to his feet and begins an inspection of the premises, with no further thought about what has just occurred.

Hook takes a seated position, legs dangling over the threshold, and scans the ground below, looking for his hat; then looks across the clearing at Linden, still seated in the brush like a lawn ornament.

Meanwhile, Quam has paused at the far wall (if it can be called that in an eight-by-ten shack) to read what seems to be a poem, mounted and framed.

Let the Light within the Mind of God
Stream into the minds of men.
Let the Light illuminate this Earth.
From where the Will of God is known
Let purpose guide the wills of men
Let Heaven heal the race of men
Let Love and Light pour from the sky
And seal the door where evil dwells.

"That's not at all bad, sir. Though I couldn't say what it's about, it has depth."

Hook isn't interested in poetry at the moment, having turned his attention to the Philco radio on the side table. He switches on the machine, and they listen to the Hart House String Quartet playing Beethoven through a curtain of electronic hiss.

"Maybe he liked to listen to classical music, sir."

"More likely it was Mr. Good-Evening. He wanted the news before anyone else on the island."

"There are too many know-it-alls about, sir."

"Quite so."

Hook goes to the door and waves to Linden, who doesn't respond. He hollers his name several times, with the same result.

"Mr. Linden doesn't seem to be awake," Hook says.

"Someone at the courthouse said Collins could mentally paralyze people."

"Do you believe that, Sergeant Quam?"

"It doesn't accord with the Gospels, I will say that."

Hook notes that the two supporting beams beneath the top landing have been partially sawn through, a simple booby trap for the first man to stand on the deck with his full weight.

He crosses to a side window, through which he can see through a gap in the trees and past a stone-lined dugout he recognizes as a gun emplacement, down as far as Pirate's Cove and the hulk of the *Lady Royal*.

From this vantage point he can see far enough to just make out a boat in the distance, chugging its way out to sea as it starts to disappear over the horizon.

"Mr. Quam, what do you see out there? I think I'm starting to need glasses."

"It looks like a tugboat, sir. I think it's the—what was it? The *Khaba*."

THE TWO POLICEMEN manage to skirt the top landing and climb down to the ground, where a quick search locates Hook's hat; then they cross to the edge of the clearing, where Linden looks up at them from his seated position. "Well, officers, how did it go?"

"You didn't notice?"

"Notice what?"

"Oh, nothing much. Essentially, there's nothing to report. Collins has flown the coop."

"And Madame Zura is with him, I'm sure."

Linden rises nimbly to his feet.

"Are your legs any better, sir?" Quam asks.

"It was two charley horses at once," Linden replies. "Very painful."

"I thought you said they were numb."

"I don't think the condition of Mr. Linden's legs is relevant at this time, Sergeant."

"You're probably right, sir. Please forget I asked, Mr. Linden."

They make their way down the path, through the clearing, past the Tree of Knowledge, then through what has now diminished into a gauntlet of bonfires, and down to the *Freyja*, where Pedersen perches on the gunwale, smoking a pipe and scratching his cheek.

"What did yaw see up there?"

"A war zone without bodies," Hook says.

"Arvid, if you keep scratching that you'll get an infection," Linden says.

"Or bleed to death," Quam adds. "Once it starts, you never know."

Inspector Hook is in a gloomy mood over the state of the investigation. Once again they will return to the precinct empty-handed, having wasted resources on what the chief will term, predictably, "another wild goose chase." And this time there will be no fortuitous ending, their lack of accomplishment will not be celebrated, their future will not be assured.

Inspector Hook pulls on yet another Ogden's, driving another nail in his coffin.

BACK AT THE Malaspina Hotel, Elliot Linden takes his leave of the two policemen, shaking hands and presenting each officer with his card. "Officers, with all the new laws governing police procedure, you might find yourself in need of representation yourselves."

"We will take that under consideration, sir," Hook replies, sliding the card into his wallet.

The two policemen return to their room to fetch their kit (and Hook's service weapon) and then settle their bill, including a penalty for late checkout, inflicted by the desk clerk without a break in his smile.

What matters is that they just have time to catch the evening ferry back to Vancouver and their own beds, and let unconsciousness declare an end to this miserable business.

CHAPTER 60

Outlaws killed outlaws, and the community
is better off without them.

—Al Capone

THE *PRINCESS ELAINE* docks at Pier B, and while the dockworkers are still securing mooring lines to the bollards, the two officers stride down the ramp and cross the rain-slick pier to the terminal.

"I can give you a lift on the motorcycle," Hook says—reluctantly, for with Quam it's like having a Frigidaire strapped to your back, but it's the least he can do for a man who saved him from serious injury.

Quam stops abruptly halfway across the pier, and turns to Hook, his lozenge-shaped head at an unusual angle, as though perceiving the faint sound of a bird.

Instead of replying, he says, "Sir, with your permission I should like to pay a visit to Unclaimed Luggage."

"The victim's luggage is at the station, Mr. Quam. Other than the fact that Nettles failed to pick it up, what is there to know?"

"Something has come to mind, sir."

"What?"

"A thought, sir. A suspicion."

"Quam, as you said yourself, one doesn't have to believe what one thinks."

"Sir, if it's not too much trouble I'll just carry on."

"Oh very well then, yes, carry on with your hunch. It can't make things worse." (Although Hook knows from experience how things can indeed get worse.)

A stevedore directs them to the freight shed, where a man on a tractor points to the far wall and an open ticket window, a sort of Dutch door manned by someone in a CPR porter's uniform.

The two policemen approach the window, and Quam extends his warrant card to the gentleman inside.

From the worn uniform to the watchful cast of his eyes, the luggage attendant puts Hook in mind of desk clerks he has known.

The sergeant may have smelled something.

Hook opts to step back and allow Sergeant Quam to follow whatever he has in mind.

"What can I do for you, officers?" The man really shouldn't be smiling with those teeth.

"Sir, we're here about the lost luggage of a man named Robert Nettles, who was on the *Princess Elaine*. We're aware that you were on duty at the time."

This is the first Hook has heard of it. He didn't think Quam capable of such trickery—it was part of his charm.

Backed into an imaginary corner, the attendant co-operates. "Yes. In fact the police were here about that weeks ago, is there a problem?"

"Never mind that, sir. Where exactly was the luggage stored?"

"What do you mean?"

"Is there another meaning?"

"What does it matter?"

Sergeant Quam leans over the sill so that the attendant has a clear view of the expression in his eyes and the smell of his breath. "Just answer the question, sir, if you don't mind."

"Very well then, I'll show you if you like." The attendant shrugs, and all but rolls his eyes, as he unlatches and opens the bottom part of the Dutch door to allow them entrance.

"Please come in and take a look. Not that there's anything to see." The sergeant nods. His eyes have become watery.

"Appreciate your co-operation, sir."

Hook follows the two of them into a small, windowless room, nearly empty at present; ferries produce a quick turnover of lost and found items, and unclaimed baggage is almost nonexistent.

The wide shelves that line two walls are empty, except for a rotting duffle bag, a sagging cardboard suitcase and a disintegrating